WITHOUT
A
COUNTRY

ALSO BY AYŞE KULIN

Last Train to Istanbul

Love in Exile

Aylin

Rose of Sarajevo

Without a Country

Ayşe Kulin

Translated by Kenneth Dakan

Previously published as *Kanadı Kırık Kuşlar* by Everest Yayınları in Turkey in 2016. Translated from Turkish by Kenneth Dakan. First published in English by AmazonCrossing in 2018.

Published by AmazonCrossing, Seattle

www.apub.com

Amazon, the Amazon logo, and AmazonCrossing are trademarks of Amazon.com, Inc., or its affiliates.

ISBN-13: 9781503900974 (hardcover)
ISBN-10: 1503900975 (hardcover)
ISBN-13: 9781503901001 (paperback)
ISBN-10: 1503901009 (paperback)

Cover design by David Drummond

Printed in the United States of America

First edition

WITHOUT
A
COUNTRY

Author's Note

As a Turk, I owe an eternal debt of gratitude to the scientists, some of whom appear by name in the pages of this novel, who helped to modernize Turkish universities and educate a golden generation of my fellow countrymen.

Hitler expelled these men and women from German universities in the 1930s simply for being Jewish, leftists, or critics of Nazism.

I would like to dedicate this novel to Professor Philipp Schwartz, the neuropathologist who inspired my character Gerhard Schliemann, along with:

Curt Kosswig, who was instrumental in the founding of the Bird Paradise nature reserve in Manyas and the city zoos in Istanbul and Ankara that I fondly remember visiting as a child;

Dr. Eckstein, who treated me for typhoid when I was seven years old;

Professor Ernst Hirsch and Professor Dr. F. Neumark, whose memoirs I read while researching this novel;

Professor Carl Elbert, the art director of the Ankara Opera;

Professor Kantorowicz, a pioneer of modern dentistry;

and all the others who played leading roles in the advancement of art and science, some of whom are now resting in cemeteries in Ankara and Istanbul.

January 25, 2016
10:17 p.m.

Dear Esra, beloved granddaughter,

You were upset with me when we parted, the first time that's ever happened. As you were flying back to İzmir, no doubt a bit shocked by my reaction, I was thinking I shouldn't have brought up that unpleasant subject right when you were leaving. There is a lot we need to talk over, more than I can possibly put in an e-mail.

Esra, my dear, I was insisting you move to England because I have your best interests at heart. Surely, you can't think that I wouldn't prefer you here with me in my final years? I know how much you love your homeland and that you adore Istanbul. But it is our fate to move from place to place. My father and mother, too, loved their homeland and their city. But the day came when they had to leave that home behind without so much as washing the cups from which they'd drunk their morning coffee. Father and Mother began a new life in a new country, and they suppressed all those painful memories. They wanted to raise their children free of old hatreds. Your own mother did not know the real reason we moved to this country until many years later. She thought your grandfather was offered a position at the university hospital and then just fell in love with Istanbul and decided to stay. All of that is true, if incomplete. He did remain here for many years because of his love for this country and its people.

Back then, foreigners were treated well. People didn't dwell on religious differences. In Istanbul, particularly, where Greeks, Armenians, and Jews had lived with Muslim Turks for centuries, all faiths were respected. Muslims would light candles in churches. Christians and Jews would make sacrificial vows at Muslim shrines and distribute meat to the needy if their wishes were granted. As you know, my dear girl, all that has changed. The country that centuries ago welcomed the Jews fleeing Spain and then embraced our family in the 1930s is no more. Those wonderful days are gone forever. Unfortunately, politics has contaminated religion, which should be a conduit for love.

It's too late, much too late in life, for me to emigrate. You're still young, though, and you deserve to live in peace. You were right to say that Turkey is your country, but the hatred and violence are too much. Many years ago, I criticized my brother for starting a new life in America, but as it turned out, he must have sensed what was coming. Now it's your turn to fly! Go now, before it's too late, unless, like my parents, you're prepared to flee with only as much of your home as you can squeeze into a handbag. If a certain so-called intellectual had not begun digging into which of us carry Jewish blood in our veins, I would never have told you any of this. You're right—bombs can explode and injustices are committed everywhere, but here, in a place where hate crimes go unpunished, you are no longer safe. These anti-Semites are filled with hate. At the very least, they will break your heart. And a broken heart aches forever.

If you complete your specialized training in England, you could get the opportunity to work there or even become a citizen. I will help you any way I can, provided you agree to leave Turkey.

God willing, we will have time alone together soon, and I will be able to tell you more. Come to Istanbul for the Bairam holiday, and let's talk then.

May God watch over you, my dear.

Your loving grandmother,

Su

Part One

Our Land of the Star and Crescent

Again, We Yearn for Home

March 1933
Frankfurt

Elsa stood in the doorway, fighting back tears. Permitted to take nothing more than a handbag on her journey, she was agonizing over what to bring. If only she could record every single silly object in her memory for eternity. The Gobelin cushion her grandmother made was resting on the sofa. Intermingled with the porcelain menagerie she had been collecting since childhood, family photographs perched in front of the books lining the shelves. The grandest frame enclosed the wedding photo in which, seated sideways on a taboret, the train of her gown artfully arranged at her feet, Elsa beamed at the camera. Gerhard was standing close behind, his hand on her shoulder as if to say, "Trust me. You will be safe from now on." But, now, that same man was giving Elsa only minutes to flee her home.

Were they doing the right thing?

If only they had waited a little longer. They could have talked it over, come to a decision.

Elsa walked into the dining room and opened the door of the sideboard. Sinking to her knees, she reached to the back of the bottom shelf and caressed the stack of Meissen dinner plates. It was a wedding gift from Tita and was the most precious item in her aunt's trousseau. Aunt Tita, with no children of her own, had been like a mother to Elsa—one far more understanding and loving than her real mother was. Elsa's leather knapsack from her days as a high school Girl Guide was deep. Surely, she could squeeze in a plate or two as a memento? She could almost hear Gerhard's voice: "Are you out of your mind? We're trying to escape with our lives, and you're fussing over some old plates!"

Okay, but maybe some family photographs. Could she fit an entire album? And what about her hatbox full of precious letters? The ones written by school friends were bound with blue ribbon; the postcards from Father and the instructive epistles from Mother were in a large beige envelope; Gerhard's awkward professions of love and amateurish poems lay knotted inside a length of lace-edged cloth.

At the end of that first summer apart, Elsa had commended his decision to study science, joking that he showed no promise as a poet. Gerhard vowed never to write her another love letter, then composed dozens more. The memory of his ingenuous lines had always put a smile on her face, but at this moment, tears welled up in her eyes as she tried to remember the shortest one. Was it: *Your eyes of coal / Your hair of silk / The princess of my soul / In my heart forevermore . . .* ? Should she take that poem with her to read aloud one distant day to her grandchildren? It gave her a moment of pleasure, this image of herself as a grandmother whose beauty had once inspired flowery tributes, but there was no time now to riffle through old letters. If she wanted grandchildren one day, she would have to hurry.

Elsa caught sight of her pale face in the sideboard mirror. Her left eye was twitching, that recurring sign of deep distress. Then the tears came. "Thieves!" she screamed between choked sobs. "Those wicked thieves!" Her identity was being stolen. Her history, her memories, her letters, her friends, her house, her street, her city. A madman whose greed had eclipsed his reason was stealing her life, and her husband was powerless to stop him.

She knew Gerhard was blameless. It was she who had urged her husband to apply to the Universität Frankfurt am Main. A romantic fancy had drawn her here: the writer she most admired was the city's most famous son. She had believed that, in a city where Goethe's writing table, his inkpot, and even the cake tins from his kitchen were still preserved, she would be surrounded by art, would breathe it in every moment of every day. If the city's fathers so cherished Goethe, she was certain they would value ordinary citizens as well, especially those who happened to be scientists.

Elsa, whose heart still raced every time she walked past Goethe's house and who knew the great man's poems by heart, was now forced to concede her naïveté.

She brushed away the tear sliding down her cheek and picked up the letter on the table.

> *Elsa,*
> *The clerk bringing you this note thinks that I have forgotten my exam questions at home. Get the beige envelope in the right-hand drawer of the bookcase, put my passport in it, and give it to him. Then, go immediately to Peter's school and pull him out of class. Tell the teacher your mother has fallen ill (don't worry; she's fine) and that you need to visit her at once. Take nothing but your passports, all your jewelry, and whatever cash is in the safe. Do not draw attention to yourself! Board the first train to Zurich. We will meet at the end of the day at your parents' house. We must hurry. You understand, don't you?*
> *G.*

"All my jewelry?" she grumbled on her way to the bedroom. The only jewelry she owned was the wedding ring on her finger. Oh, and the ruby brooch from Tita. She got the hatbox down from the top shelf, retrieved the key hidden inside, knelt in front of the wardrobe, and opened the safe. Ah, she'd forgotten Gerhard's gold pocket watch, a wedding gift from her father. There was some costume jewelry on the dresser, but they'd never get anything for it. Oh, the fancy face cream she had bought only last week! But it wouldn't fit in the bag.

Idiotic to dwell on such nonsense; there was no time for self-pity. She knotted the ring, watch, and brooch into a handkerchief. She clutched at the gold chain around her neck . . . its dangling pendant . . . good heavens! With trembling hands, she removed the symbol and stuffed it into an envelope, along with the banknotes from the safe. She went to the kitchen. Some coins left over from her daily shopping, the total of her personal savings, were squirreled away in the breadbox. She carefully slipped them into the knapsack and, on a whim, rushed back to the bedroom to grab a small compact and a tube of lipstick. Done.

It had been nearly half an hour since Helmut the clerk had gone off with Gerhard's passport, and here she was, still running in circles. Elsa sighed and reluctantly entered the room where her baby daughter was sleeping.

***

Gerhard was picking his way across the lawn, mindful of the wildflowers, when he saw a squirrel hop down from a tree, sit upright, and begin sniffing at something between its paws. A smile spread across his face for the first time in days. He and his wife were lucky. At least they didn't live in Northeim, like his mother and elder sister. The letter from his sister a few weeks earlier had concerned him deeply:

As if the gray days and bone-chilling damp weren't bad enough, being surrounded by these gloomy old buildings feels like being buried alive. But nothing's been worse than the lack of jobs. You remember our neighbor Rudy, about your age? Anyway, he was out of work for nearly two years before he finally found something—and it was thanks to the Nazis! Life had been so hopeless here, and all of a sudden (you won't believe I'm writing this) the Nazis, those despicable Nazis, showed up to organize festivals, concerts, and parades. Even Mother and I have joined in the fun. And they've clamped down hard on disorderly conduct, so there's no more drunken brawls. They're helping the needy. They even sent a college student to Gisele's house—she lives on our corner—to tutor her blockhead son in math. Then, when some other parents asked for tutors too, the Nazis started a special class at the town hall. They keep track of deaths and funerals and send money to the families. Of course, they still don't like Jews. But so far, they don't seem to want to bother us, and life here is so much better. I suppose we'll just have to wait and see what happens.

Yes, they were lucky to be in Frankfurt, far from those miserable towns where the Nazis held sway.

He and Elsa had married young and had two healthy, adorable children. Eager to please his future father-in-law, Gerhard had pursued a master of science degree, a decision he'd had no cause to regret. He not only enjoyed his job but also found it deeply rewarding. Furthermore, he and his family were tenants in a so-called zigzag house in one of the new settlements designed by progressive architect Ernst May. The rent was reasonable, even though they lived in a neighborhood of intellectuals just a short walk from the university hospital where he worked. Life was good, but Gerhard couldn't help feeling anxious about the increasingly harsh rhetoric from Berlin. He could see that all was not well in his homeland—or in the rest of Europe. In the wake of the Great War, the continent was struggling with border disputes, unrest, mass internal migration . . . Gerhard felt blessed to be able to devote himself to his research and his students. He'd always assumed that if he kept a safe distance from politics, he would be left in peace. Now he wasn't so sure.

For all his determined optimism, the raid a few nights earlier had left him shaken. He and his wife had just settled into bed when they heard cars, the furious barking of the neighbor's dog, and heavy boots in the stairwell. They'd leapt out of bed and rushed to the window, seeing several police vehicles parked out front. Ears pressed to the front door, they'd tried to understand what was happening and prayed their children wouldn't wake up. Loud knocking. Bellowed questions. Doors opening and closing. A short time later, the squeal of tires announced that the police were leaving. The apartment building became deathly quiet. When Gerhard reached for the doorknob, Elsa seized his wrist. Her left eye was twitching.

"I need to find out what's happening. I'll ask the Hansels and be right back," Gerhard said. He went down to the floor below and tapped on the door.

"Who is it?"

"It's Gerhard Schliemann, your neighbor. You don't have to open the door, Mr. Hansel. I was wondering if you could tell me why the police came."

"They were searching for a gun. Supposedly, they'd been tipped off. What would I be doing with a gun? What they really wanted was to intimidate me."

"You have my sympathies. Are you all right? Do you need anything? I can bring you a sedative."

"I don't want a sedative. But can you bring me some peace of mind? I need the strongest dose you've got," the elderly man said.

"Peace of mind is in short supply these days. We'll have to try the black market. Good night, neighbor."

Elsa, who was waiting for him at the front door, ran into his arms. "The next time, it'll be us. Mark my words. They'll find some excuse. My God! You haven't brought your father's rifle home, have you?"

"No, of course not. What business would I have with a rifle? I gave it back after I went hunting in the village."

"I'm scared, Gerhard."

Her left eye was still twitching.

"Don't worry, dear. Nothing will happen to us."

His words rang hollow, even to himself. Not so very long ago, he hadn't hesitated to sound off at the bar after his third beer, had thought nothing of sitting in the university cafeteria with a colleague reading an opposition newspaper, and hadn't been afraid to warn a National Socialist student to check his politics at the laboratory door. But now he was scared. As scared as a rabbit being chased by wild dogs. Was this what life would be like from now on?

"It's all my fault," Elsa had said. "I wanted to move here."

He put his arm around her shoulder and led her to the bedroom.

"Don't be silly. We'll forget all about it by tomorrow."

But the fear continued to gnaw at him. He kept bracing himself for a knock on the door, suffered restless nights punctuated by vivid nightmares, and woke up each morning exhausted and anxious. And yet, a normal, happy sight, like that squirrel nibbling at an apple core on the green lawn, could still lift his spirits.

Spring was on its way. Trees would be in flower before the week was out, transforming the university gardens into a paradise. He should think about good things, and then good things would come. Any day now, he would be named chair of the pathology department. The current head, Herman, had already tendered his resignation and would be leaving at the end of the month for a new life in America. Everyone knew Gerhard had been recommended as his replacement, so he should be thinking about—

"Oh!" he exclaimed at the touch of a hand on his arm.

"Gerhard, did I scare you?"

"Ah, Rudolf, it's you. No, I was just thinking," he said to his colleague. "It's a lovely day, isn't it?"

"I'm not so sure about that. Come with me for a moment."

Slipping his arm through Gerhard's, Rudolf led him under a chestnut tree, cast a quick glance around, and whispered in his ear. "Gerhard, get out of here. Right now. I found something out at dinner last night. My brother-in-law's a policeman. You know him. We've played tennis together. Anyway, he'd had a few drinks when he let it slip that they're planning detentions at the university today. If I were you, I'd get my wife and kids and go to another city, or even abroad, if you possibly can."

"What are you talking about? Are you sure?"

"Remember that department meeting Herbert called, the one about organizing against the suspension of constitutional protections?"

"Yes."

"Did you sign the petition?"

"Yes, of course I signed it. Most of us did."

"I missed that meeting, so I never signed. Everyone who did is about to . . ."

"About to what?"

"They're all getting rounded up today."

"Did your brother-in-law name names?"

"No, he didn't. But when I ran a few by him, he just glared at me. Don't lose any time, my friend. This is serious. You need to get out of here as fast as you can. And I need to hurry and warn some of our other colleagues."

Gerhard stood stock-still for a moment, watching as Rudolf rushed off. He broke into a sweat. Then he clutched at the nearest branch and bent over, the boiled egg he'd had for breakfast coming back up. Pulling himself together, he ran to his office. The first thing he did was reach for the telephone to inquire about trains to Switzerland, but he jerked his hand back as though from a flame. What if someone was listening in? He pulled a sheet of paper out of his drawer, scribbled a quick note, sealed it in an envelope, and called for a clerk. He handed the envelope to the man, along with a small tip.

"I've just realized that I forgot a file at home this morning, the one with my exam questions. You know the address, Helmut. Could you hop on your bicycle and fetch it before Frau Schliemann goes out to the market? Take this note telling her where to find the file. Be quick about it, please. I need those questions before my class starts."

As the clerk hurried away, Gerhard shouted out after him, "If I'm not in my office when you get back, leave it on my desk."

Gerhard turned to the papers on his desk, selected his most recent research notes, placed them in his briefcase, and left the building. Walking briskly in the opposite direction to the one Helmut had taken, he reached the street and hailed a cab. Once he was settled with his briefcase on the seat next to him, he gave the driver the address of a bank. If he withdrew everything in his account, would it attract attention? It would be prudent to withdraw only enough for the journey. Not that he had much in his account to begin with.

He told the bank teller that his mother-in-law had fallen ill, so he had decided to send his wife for a visit, and, depending on hospital costs, he might be back in a few days to withdraw more. He noticed the teller seemed a bit taken aback by this unsolicited chatter, and he shut his mouth.

When Gerhard came out of the bank, a streetcar had just pulled up. He jumped on it, questions swirling in his head all the way back to campus. Could this be an elaborate ruse hatched by someone who coveted the chairmanship of the pathology department? No, that was ludicrous. But what if Rudolf was mistaken, and it was just a baseless rumor? If Gerhard rushed off in a panic only to slink back a few days later, he would become a laughingstock. How could he be certain? But better a laughingstock than to endanger his family. The prudent course was to leave at once, knowing he could always return if no arrests were made. Elsa would get to visit her parents, and they would be delighted to see their grandchildren. Yes, there was no harm in claiming that his mother-in-law had suddenly taken ill.

The envelope containing his passport was on the desk when he got back to his office. He slipped it into his inner jacket pocket. He gathered up more of his research and, briefcase in hand, went to get his coat from the hook behind the door. But his coat wasn't there. Could someone have taken it? His hands turned clammy, and he wiped sweat from his brow. He was searching desperately when he came face-to-face with his reflection in the glass door. He was wearing the coat. Gerhard left his office, made certain the door was closed behind him, took the stairs two and three at a time, and scurried toward the main gate. Eyes on the ground and without glancing at the guard in the sentry hut, he dashed out into the street and hailed the cab rounding the corner.

"The train station," he told the driver, and collapsed into the back-seat. His heart still racing, he closed his eyes and tried to remember the prayer his mother had made him say at bedtime every night.

"May the angel who redeems from all harm bless the children . . ." He couldn't remember the rest. Would God protect those who prayed only in times of need?

A traffic cop stopped the cab to let a squad of SA troopers pass. Gerhard thought he heard the driver mutter an expletive. He would have liked to join in, but restrained himself.

The train station was crawling with police. Gerhard stalled for a few moments, slowly counting out coins to pay his cab fare. But he had to go through that entrance sooner or later. Looking straight ahead, he non-chalantly strolled past the policemen, even pausing to reach into his coat pocket, pull out his cigarette case, and stick a cigarette between his lips. He considered asking for a light, but decided not to push his luck. Once he was safely inside the yawning space of the hall, he lit a match. His hands were trembling, and he shook his head in disbelief. Here he was, quaking in fear, just seconds after imagining himself audaciously asking a policeman for a light. It reminded him of how, when he was young, he would nearly wet himself in fear while on the high branches of the trees in his grandfather's garden, but he'd nonetheless keep climbing to the top.

After a few soothing drags on his cigarette, he glanced around the neoclassical hall as though seeing it for the first time. So many details were missed in the bustle of daily life. In all his previous visits to the station, he'd been either rushing to catch a train or completely preoccupied with the children and his family's suitcases.

Today, the cigarette dangling from his lips, he looked up at the iron-and-glass ceiling and down at the gleaming floor. There were long lines in front of the ticket counters. When it was his turn, he calmly asked for a seat on the next train to Zurich.

"There's a nonstop departing in an hour," the clerk said, "and then another one in the evening, but that one has a connection."

"The next one, like I said. The one leaving in an hour."

"Would that be first class, sir?"

Gerhard hesitated, but this was no time to fritter away money on luxuries.

"Second class," he said. "One way."

Putting his ticket in his pocket, he quickly walked over to his platform. The train hadn't pulled in yet, and there were only a few people waiting. Could that woman with a child in her arms be Elsa? No, Elsa didn't own a green coat. A little boy was running toward him, his hair a shock of corn silk, but it wasn't Peter. He walked along the platform and entered the waiting area. The only person there was an old woman hunched over her knitting. He paced the length of the platform, back and forth, dozens of times. Every so often, he'd walk over to check at the main entrance and the ticket counters. The platform grew increasingly crowded, but there was still no sign of his wife and children. The minutes grew shorter, and he seemed to feel each tick and tock of the enormous clock suspended from the middle of the vaulted ceiling.

Calm down, he told himself. *You'll be on the train soon. Calm down. You'll be safe.*

But what was taking Elsa so long? What if they missed the train? They should have been here by now. Then came the horrifyingly familiar sound of heavy boots. He instinctively headed for the shelter of the waiting area. The old woman was gone, replaced by a rowdy group of students. After a moment, Gerhard peered outside. Swarming the platform in their hobnail boots, lederhosen, and feathered alpine hats was a contingent of Bavarian tourists. He'd been spooked over nothing.

He went over and gazed up at the train bulletin again, even though he had long since memorized that day's two scheduled departures for Zurich. He went back to the platform.

Why wasn't his train here yet?

At that very moment, the ghostly, cool wind rushed against his face, heralding the approach of a train. He grabbed his ticket, and, as he was rechecking his carriage number, the train rounded the bend, belched a puff of coal smoke, and shuddered to a screeching halt. The platform started bustling. Gerhard anxiously waited for all the passengers to disembark. He had barely clambered into his carriage when someone called out from below.

"Excuse me, sir. Hey, you!"

He had a split second to decide. Should he pretend not to hear, continue into the carriage, and hide in the restroom?

He turned and looked.

An elderly man was holding up a boy of about three or four. Gerhard took the boy, set him down, and offered a hand to the man.

"These steps are so high," the man said with a bashful smile as Gerhard hoisted him aboard.

The pair headed down the aisle in search of their seats, and Gerhard was grateful when the boisterous child ducked into a different compartment. In his, a young man and a middle-aged woman had already taken their seats. Gerhard placed his briefcase and coat on the luggage rack, then began roaming the train in search of his wife and children.

They were nowhere to be found in second class.

He got off the train and ran to the first-class carriage. The conductor stopped him and asked for his ticket. Gerhard's stammered explanation was rejected. Giving up, he walked along the platform, scanning the windows on both sides. They weren't in first class either.

Defeated, he reclaimed his seat and pressed his face against the glass, doing some rough calculations in his head. Unlike him, Elsa wouldn't have been able to head straight for the station. Only after waking their baby, changing her diaper, dressing her, and feeding her would Elsa have been able to go pull Peter out of school. Then she would be held up by a dozen inquisitive teachers and administrators. What scared him most was the thought of his wife packing her bag. She'd agonize over what to take. When they'd moved to Frankfurt, she'd insisted on bringing a bulky hatbox of old letters. What if she'd refused to leave it behind again? He moaned in frustration, provoking a startled stare from the lady next to him. He knew his wife. She'd arrive late, dragging that hatbox and God knows what other sentimental nonsense.

The steam whistle sounded. He stood up, opened the window, and leaned out for one last look at the platform.

"Please close the window," someone said. "It's windy."

Gerhard shut the window and sat down. He didn't recognize any of the stragglers hustling past his window. His wife and children were not on this train. He was sure of it.

What if the police, having failed to find him, had taken Elsa to headquarters?

What if they turned her back at the border?

What if he never saw his wife and children again?

His plan had seemed so reasonable that morning, but now he wondered how he could have ever left them behind. He imagined the worst: Elsa's interrogation.

What would she do if they said, "Confess! You were one of the agitators behind the arson, weren't you?" She wouldn't know what they were talking about. Her left eye would twitch; her hands would tremble. "Agitators?" she'd say. "Arson?"

That ominous fire had been a turning point. Gerhard had heard so many accounts and seen so many photos that he felt like he'd been there.

It had happened less than a month ago. Not long after nine in the evening, a passerby heard breaking glass. Shortly afterward, flames shot up inside the Reichstag. The German parliament building was left in smoking ruins.

When Hitler had arrived at the scene, Goebbels, his minister of propaganda and the man who purportedly said, "If you tell a lie big enough and keep repeating it, people will eventually come to believe it," was watching the blaze.

The Nazis now had the lie they needed to crush the Communist Party and consolidate power. Civil liberties were suspended, and the reign of terror began. Hitler seemed unstoppable.

Gerhard sighed. Days earlier, he had listened to Hitler's speech on the radio. That voice shaking with rage was still ringing in his ears:

The honor of the nation, the honor of our army, and the ideal of freedom—all must once more become sacred to the German Volk! The German Volk wishes to live in peace with the world.

He pressed his hands against his ears and flushed in shame as he remembered his reaction when poet and playwright Bertolt Brecht fled with his family to Denmark shortly after Hitler took power. He'd criticized Brecht for abandoning his country and scolded Elsa for overreacting to the Nazis' thirst for power, warning her to hold her tongue before it got them into trouble. Yet here he was, fearful and jittery, on a train bound for Switzerland, with no idea where his wife and children were.

Gerhard was furious with himself. How could he have deluded himself into thinking things would be okay? The Nazis had just opened a camp to hold all their political prisoners, and surely things wouldn't stop there.

How foolish and how human, he thought, *to believe that trouble will never come calling, right up until it knocks on your own door.*

Farewell, Homeland

After crossing the Swiss border without incident, Gerhard leaned back, closed his eyes, and surrendered to the gentle rocking of the train. But whenever he managed to nod off, he was jolted awake by nightmares or by the train's frequent stops.

As the train finally approached Zurich sometime after midnight, Gerhard suddenly realized that Elsa's parents had no idea they were coming. He decided he'd better call from the station. The doorbell might not rouse them, but a ringing telephone should.

Once he was off the train, he realized that he had neither a phone token nor the Swiss currency to purchase one. None of the exchange bureaus were open this late, either. He dashed back to the platform and found a conductor. Explaining that he needed to make a call, Gerhard opened his wallet to demonstrate the currency problem.

"You're in luck," the conductor said, reaching in to snatch a couple of bills with one hand as he produced a single token with the other. "I always keep a few in my pocket for this very reason. Nothing wrong with making a bit of a profit as we help others out, now is there? Our wages don't go very far these days, you know."

Gerhard smiled his thanks while inwardly cursing the man's greed. He ran to a phone booth, pulled a small notebook out of his bag, and found his in-laws' number. After the fourth ring, his father-in-law picked up, his voice going from confused to alarmed when he realized who was calling. Gerhard spoke in reassuring tones.

"I'm in a phone booth at the train station here in Zurich. I'm sorry I woke you up. I left Frankfurt in such a hurry that I didn't have a chance to call . . . Yes, that's right. I'm in Zurich . . . Don't worry, they're fine. They're coming on the next train . . . I'll explain everything when I get there . . . I only have one token, and it's about to run out. See you soon."

He ran out to the taxi stand. At least there wasn't a line at this hour. As the cab sped through the empty streets, he wondered how to explain why he had left Elsa and the children behind.

There was nothing to do but tell the truth.

He'd feared for his life.

Anyway, Elsa would be on the next train. There was no reason to panic. The fascists were coming after men; they didn't bother with women who didn't hold an important position of some kind. Ever since Peter was born, Elsa had devoted herself to domestic duties. Nobody could claim she was competing for work with Aryan women. And as for Susy and Peter, they were children. Not even Nazis could take issue with children.

Less than half an hour later, Gerhard was sitting in the Hindbergs' kitchen, munching away on a slice of apricot jam–slathered toast to quiet his grumbling belly.

"I still don't understand how you left Elsa and the children behind," his mother-in-law was saying. "I wish you'd all come together."

"I thought they'd catch the train I was on."

"When they didn't, you should have waited."

"It's me they're after. They won't arrest women and children."

"That's what you think!"

"Gertrude, please!" Gerhard's father-in-law admonished.

She shot him a look, then stormed out of the kitchen.

When the men were alone, Paul, Gerhard's father-in-law, said, "You've been traveling all day, so I suppose you don't know what's happened."

"Something happened?"

"The German parliament has passed that constitutional amendment they've been drafting since the Reichstag fire."

"Oh no!"

"Yes. The Law to Remedy the Distress of People and Reich is in force. As of today, Hitler has the power to make laws without passing them through Parliament. March 24 will go down in history as the day German democracy died."

"But how could that happen? Didn't anyone oppose it?"

"They changed the rules of procedure. And there was intimidation. The Communists were all either in jail or in hiding. Opponents were prevented from taking the floor."

"But even after the latest elections, the Nazi party still doesn't have a majority. Doesn't it take two-thirds of Parliament to pass a measure like that?"

"You're right. But the Social Democrats were the only party to vote against the act."

"What!" Gerhard nearly choked on his coffee, splattering it on his shirt. "That makes no sense. Why would the other parties go along with it?"

"Because of that Reichstag Fire Decree. You know Hitler's been using it to imprison his enemies, unleash his storm troopers, suspend civil liberties. He's beaten the other parties into submission. And today they gave up, the cowards."

"I don't know why I'm so surprised," Gerhard said. "Two weeks ago, they forced the mayor of Frankfurt to resign. Just like that, after ten years. Landmann completely transformed Frankfurt. To see a progressive like him, the first Jew ever to hold that office, replaced by a filthy Nazi!"

Gerhard's stomach churned, the toast threatening to come back, just as his breakfast had.

"Son, are you all right?"

"I'm fine," he lied. He'd left his wife and children behind, in a fascist country with a sham parliament at the mercy of a dictator. Paul handed him a napkin, and he dabbed at the stain on his shirt.

"If you've had enough coffee, let's go to the sitting room."

Gertrude had pulled her armchair over to the window and was peering out at the street. "Go to bed," she said to Gerhard. "We'll wake you when they come."

"I'll wait up with you."

Gerhard huddled on the edge of the sofa, his chin in his hands. The images that had tormented him on the train began running through his mind again, more vivid than before. Elsa being interrogated about her husband's whereabouts. An officer holding a pistol to Peter's head. Elsa, defiant and in tears, as another officer dangled their baby girl from the window.

"NO!"

Was that his voice? Had he really shouted like that? His in-laws were staring in horror.

"If only . . . oh, how I wish I hadn't . . ."

Too proud to gratify his mother-in-law with a show of remorse, he stopped himself from saying more. If only that train would arrive! The journey normally took ten hours, but with the connection, the endless starting and stopping, and the repeated checking of papers, it would probably be much longer than that.

"Paul, I'm going to our room," Gertrude announced.

"Okay, dear. Try to get some sleep," her husband said. "I'll wake you up when they get here."

"Sleep! At a time like this?"

She can't bear to look at me, Gerhard thought. *And I don't blame her.* The morning's fear of arrest was nothing compared to these pangs of conscience. But it was too late. He'd allowed cowardice to get the best of him and jumped on the first train, abandoning his family. What if they were still at home? Perhaps he should call the apartment?

He crossed to the phone. No, he mustn't. A neighbor might hear it ringing and realize they'd fled. For the hundredth time, he told himself to remain calm. By panicking, he might endanger his family. They must be on the train right now. Otherwise, Elsa would have called to ask if her husband had arrived. He sprang to his feet and began pacing the room.

"Gerhard, you're making me dizzy," Paul said.

Gerhard sat back down on the sofa.

"How are you getting on with your research? I took a look at those articles you sent. I've got a few questions for you."

"Fire away," Gerhard said.

Two hours later, the men were so engrossed in genetics, blood types, and miracle cures that they failed to notice Gertrude standing over them with two steaming cups of linden tea.

"What are you talking about? Politics?"

"No. Something far more consequential!" Paul said. "The latest advances in our field of medicine."

"Ah, I see. I hope you haven't talked our son-in-law's ears off."

Gerhard was deeply grateful that his father-in-law had distracted him with a subject for which they shared a common passion.

"Were you able to get some sleep?" Paul asked his wife.

"Certainly not. I've been in the kitchen baking a cake for the children. They'll enjoy it when they finally get here."

"If it's ready, we wouldn't mind a slice," Paul said.

"I'm making it for them, not you. And anyway, it's still in the oven." Gertrude set the cups of tea on the coffee table. "What on earth is taking that train so long?"

Gerhard was muttering something about delays and connections when his father-in-law silenced him with a wave of his hand.

"We'll wait. Calmly and patiently."

The two men sipped their tea in silence as the room filled with the vanilla scent of rising cake. Gertrude's arrival had broken the conversational thread, and neither man had the energy to retrieve it. Gerhard rested his weary head against the back of the sofa, but fought to stay awake, afraid of his in-laws' judgment. He closed his eyes for a moment to soothe their burning.

In his dream, he was wriggling like a fish deep in a dark-blue sea, unable to decide which shore to swim toward. He struck out to his left and then to his right. Then, a fish with shimmering scales floated into view. It had the face of his baby girl, her mouth coming closer to kiss his cheek. He closed his eyes tight to make the dream last. Then he heard Elsa's voice. She sounded so close.

"Aren't you going to welcome us, Gerhard?"

His eyes flew open.

He jumped to his feet, nearly dropping Susy, who'd climbed on his lap to kiss him. He threw his arms around his wife and his son, kissing them again and again. Then he sank back onto the sofa, buried his face in his hands, and allowed himself to sob like a little boy. Susy grabbed at his knee to pull herself up to standing. She tried to take a step, but fell.

"Oh, Elsa! Did you see that?"

"She's been pulling herself up on the crib bars for months but managed to stand up all the way only about two weeks ago."

Gerhard picked up his daughter, feeling sheepish to have missed such a big milestone.

"Come to the kitchen, everyone," Gertrude called. "Breakfast is ready."

Stumbling to the kitchen with Susy in his arms, Gerhard felt, for the first time in his life, that the reins had completely slipped from his hands. He didn't know where he would find work, how he would live, or what tomorrow would hold. All he knew was that the simple, ordered existence that had been his until yesterday was gone forever.

Poised to begin a new life whose course he couldn't begin to envision, he felt like a baby taking its first steps: timid and anxious, but full of excitement.

Time in Zurich

Over the next few weeks, Gerhard and his family settled into life in Zurich. Elsa, who kept busy with housework and the children, didn't seem to mind being a refugee in her parents' home. Peter, who was enrolled in a primary school two blocks away, also seemed perfectly content. As for little Susy, she was happy to bask in her grandparents' endless adoration. Everyone adapted quickly, except Gerhard.

Although he hadn't expected to find a position at one of Zurich's university hospitals this close to the end of the academic year, he'd been confident that one of the city's many hospitals and laboratories would want him. When nothing came through, he had applied to employers throughout Switzerland, and even to medical colleges elsewhere in Europe and in America. Those who deigned to respond sent tersely worded letters stating in no uncertain terms that, alas, there were no positions available for an eminent pathologist such as himself.

Gerhard cursed his lack of foresight. He'd grown so accustomed to professional acclaim that he'd foolishly imagined himself to be untouchable, despite knowing full well that discrimination against Jews was increasing daily. He should have brought his family to Zurich long ago. Now, he was competing with thousands of other German émigrés.

The latest letter from his sister described the Nazi-led boycott of Jewish businesses launched soon after his family's flight from Frankfurt. The newspapers, too, were full of reports of Brownshirts harassing any customers who dared patronize Jewish-owned shops.

Even worse was the Aryan paragraph passed in mid-April. Doctors, teachers, lawyers, and other professionals with a Jewish parent or grandparent were barred from civil service across Germany.

The stuff of nightmares was becoming reality.

Since Gerhard couldn't camp out in his in-laws' home forever, he would have to take whatever he could find. He could work as a sales-clerk, a remedial tutor for medical students, even a taxi driver . . . there was nothing dishonorable about honest work. But for this to have happened just as he was about to be named department chair! Desperate, he spent his days scouring the help wanted ads in the local papers. One day, his father-in-law interrupted this demoralizing search with a proposal.

"Gerhard, what would you think of helping me out while you're waiting for a reply to your job applications?"

"Of course. What do you need?"

"I've decided to set up an office."

"An office?"

"An employment agency, but with a twist. I'm going to compile a list of the names and specializations of Jewish scientists and academics who've lost their jobs in Germany, and try to place them elsewhere in Europe."

You might find me a job first, old man, Gerhard thought as he calmly asked, "Are you planning to rent space somewhere?"

"I'm going to use the downstairs bedroom."

Gerhard stared at him in bafflement, thinking of how crowded the house already was since his family's arrival.

"And what would you like me to do in this office of yours?"

"You can assist me with the filing."

"What about expenses? I mean, you'll need a phone, supplies . . ."

"I'll request a small fee from our applicants, just enough to cover operating costs."

Gerhard was silent for a long moment. "Are you trying to create work for me, sir?"

"No, Gerhard, it's not about you. I have academic contacts all over Europe, and by God, I'm going to use them to help people. I get done lecturing by four in the afternoon, and I intend to spend the rest of my day on this. Seeing as you have some free time at the moment, I would appreciate your help. That's all!"

"I understand, sir. I wonder if you would mind adding my name to your list of job-seekers?"

"You're at the top of the list. Now, shall we go downstairs and start organizing our new office? Then you can begin creating files by professional grouping, and we'll review our applicants."

"How will people find out about your agency?"

"I've prepared an ad to put in the newspaper. But whatever you do, don't tell Gertrude. We were saving up for a new oven, but I've already spent it all on the ad."

Gerhard's mother-in-law might not have noticed the inconspicuous ad that appeared a week later in the inner pages of the *Neue Zürcher Zeitung*, but purged academics of all backgrounds learned that the Association to Assist German Scientists Abroad was now operating out of Zurich. Applications began pouring in. Gerhard filed each, including his own, by career group. He arranged rows of binders on the office shelves and then stood back to survey his work. His heart sank. Those hundreds of scientists—some of them Jewish, some of them Communist, all of them unfairly dismissed—seemed to be staring back at him with pleading eyes.

Would they really be able to find employment for them all?

In the following days, Paul and Gerhard rarely discussed Hitler's regime. Even when several heinous decrees were passed in a single day, Gerhard and his father-in-law would avoid mentioning it, almost as though they had entered an unspoken pact. Perhaps it was simply more than they could bear, or perhaps they hoped morning would soon come and bring an end to this night of torment.

But one morning in late April, Paul waved a newspaper in his son-in-law's face and finally let loose.

"Have you seen this? They've essentially outlawed kosher ritual slaughter!"

"Let's hope this mania for harassing Jews doesn't spread to Switzerland," Gerhard said, not letting on that he himself had never been particularly observant.

"Switzerland is a neutral country! They would never allow Hitler to mess with the world's safety deposit box."

Gerhard sighed and hoped the old man was right.

Just a few days later, they read that the Law Against the Overcrowding of German Schools and Universities would limit Jewish enrollment to 1.5 percent of the total student body, including at the university level.

A raft of discriminatory acts followed, one after another: Jewish doctors were no longer allowed in German hospitals, Jewish pharmacists couldn't operate drugstores, Jews were banned from taking the bar exam, and Jews couldn't participate in sports.

At the dinner table, Paul remarked to Gerhard, "It's a good thing you came here when you did. Not only would you be unemployed, you wouldn't be getting any exercise, either."

"Father, I'm afraid I fail to see the humor in it," Elsa said. "They've taken over everything."

"They're even going after the police now. Göring has founded a special Nazi force—they call it the Gestapo," Gerhard added.

And in fact, that same week, the newspapers reported that Frankfurt's chief of police, a full-blooded Aryan, had been fired simply for speaking in defense of union leaders, Social Democrats, and professors arrested on trumped-up charges.

Meanwhile, the Action against the Un-German Spirit campaign led by the German Student Union began organizing mass book burnings. On the tenth day of May, bonfires were lit in eighteen different university towns. Rudolf wrote to Gerhard the following day:

> *I am so relieved that you heeded my warning and were not there to witness, as I was, the shameful events of last night.*
>
> *An enthusiastic crowd gathered at nine o'clock in Römerberg Square, the site of the Fountain of Justice in Goethe's* Poetry and Truth. *They built an enormous pyre out of brushwood and scraps of lumber. A metal container of gasoline was produced, and the pyre burst into flames. There are no words to describe the vile and disgraceful scene. A villager's cart had been rented for the occasion. A pair of oxen drew the rickety vehicle, which was heaped with books, up to the pyre. Marching behind the cart were students, professors, deans . . . It mortifies me to write this, Gerhard, but you would have recognized many of them—men and women who, like me, live in fear of losing their jobs. And then, who do I see but Father Otto, the very man who baptized my children, clambering into the oxcart to deliver a speech. And it was he who threw the first book into the flames. Can you imagine? Even the clergy has crossed over to the other side!*

Paul, too, received a letter, his from Professor Hammen, a colleague in Berlin. He read a section of it aloud to his son-in-law:

> *Certain events defy description, but I will do my best. Thousands flocked to Opera Square last night. Books*

*plundered from the nearby university library were con-
veyed to the square in wheelbarrows. Many hundreds
of books were also brought from the far ends of the city
in delivery vans. Those very same university students to
whom we have dedicated our lives, the ones whose moral
characters we seek to elevate and whose intellectual horizons we strive to broaden, began tossing books, one by
one, onto the bonfire. Many of them wore the brown
shirts favored by members of the SA and SS.*

*I watched through binoculars from a nearby build-
ing. It was an unbearable sight, but I, as a scientist, considered it my duty to witness and record each detail of the
depravity unfolding below, that moment humanity lost
its collective mind.*

*Dr. Goebbels addressed the crowd in a speech that
was also broadcast live on the radio. "No to decadence
and moral corruption!" he told the students, exhorting
them to rid Germany of "the intellectual garbage of the
past." The students continued to cast those works deemed
"un-German" into the flames, chanting, "Against class
warfare and materialism, for the community of the people and an idealistic way of life! I deliver to the flames
the writings of Marx and Kautsky!" and "Against decadence and moral degeneracy, for decency and customs in
family and government, I deliver to the flames the works
of Heinrich Mann, Ernst Glaeser, and Erich Kästner!"*

*One after another, on it went. Sigmund Freud,
Albert Einstein, Emile Zola, Maxim Gorky, Marcel
Proust, Jack London, Ernest Hemingway, and our own
Nobel Laureate, Thomas Mann . . . all were consigned
to the flames. Thousands of books reduced to ashes be-
cause their authors are Jews, or Communist, or nihilists,*

*but in truth because the power of ideas poses a threat to
Hitler. The bonfire rose to the skies, and the students we
are educating—ah, Paul! The students we have failed to
educate—chanted and danced. That sea of fire shooting
sparks and spewing ash . . . my heart, too, was reduced
to cinders that night. Do you remember what Heinrich
Heine wrote a century ago in that scene where Christians
burn the Koran? One of Heine's characters, a Moor, says,
"This is but the prologue. Where books are burnt, people
in the end are burnt, too." How prescient! I shall save my
tears, for I fear the worst is yet to come.*

*Paul, I wish I hadn't needed to write you this let-
ter, but let me offer my deepest apologies on behalf of
Germans everywhere, for*

Paul peered at Gerhard over the frames of his spectacles. "The rest is
private. Hammen and I have been friends since childhood."

Gerhard waited for his father-in-law to finish the letter before saying, "What this proves is that an entire nation can go insane."

"It is also an indication of the depravity to which a despot can
drive his countrymen, Gerhard. I don't know when it will happen, but
Hitler will be gone one day, and only then will sociologists be able to
analyze what has happened, and why. What I mean to say, son, is that
evil, too, can be instructive."

"That may be, but Hitler's not going anywhere soon. Just yesterday, civil servants were instructed to turn in the names of any colleagues who've dared to criticize the government."

"And, most likely, anyone against whom they bear a grudge. Soon,
people will be ratting out their neighbors to prove their own purity.
Germany has been transformed into a den of spies and traitors."

The two letters were far more chilling to Gerhard than the daily reports on the radio and in the papers. Those eyewitness accounts

wormed their way into his dreams, visions of black and curling pages giving way to scattered human limbs and dashed brains. For the first time, he submitted when Gertrude offered him one of her calming herbal teas before bedtime.

As Gerhard's homeland continued to deteriorate, he stopped feeling sorry for himself and came to realize how blessed he and his family were to have left when they did. He threw himself into his work, which he had dubbed "Paul's special project." The old man would join him in the office until midnight, writing letters to every academic he knew and pleading with them to find positions for the names on his growing list. So far, they had been able to place someone in Denmark and another two in France—just three out of hundreds. Still, for those three people and their families, it meant everything in the world.

About two weeks later, Paul arrived home with a delighted smile. "I'm going to Geneva this week. Gerhard, would you like to come with me?"

"I wouldn't mind a walk along the lake."

"We won't have much time for walks, but we will be visiting a friend of mine who lives right on the shore. If what I learned today is true, we will be meeting with the one person in the world who can solve our problem."

"Which problem, sir? We have so many."

"How to help our applicants. This could be the light at the end of the tunnel."

"Who is your friend? What does he do?"

"He's a professor of pedagogy and the former president of the University of Geneva. He's been advising the Turks on how to found a modern university. I must be getting old, Gerhard. I should have thought of him immediately. I thought it best to speak in person, so we're paying him a visit."

"What's your friend's name?"

"Malche. Albert Malche."

But the morning they had planned to set out for Geneva, Gerhard found Paul sitting at the breakfast table with a long face.

"Malche called early this morning," Paul explained. "He's going to Istanbul."

"Oh! Didn't he know about our appointment?"

"Yes, but he was awaiting news from Turkey."

"What kind of news?"

"Last year, at the request of the Turkish president, Malche submitted a report on educational reform to that country's minister of education. He didn't expect to be taken seriously by the Turks, who often interpret science through the lens of religion. Imagine his astonishment when he learned that his report had been well received. They even offered him a consulting position—he'll be helping to found their new university. He leaves for Istanbul today."

"Well, we can always meet with him when he gets back."

"That's what I'm upset about. He expects to be there for six months."

"We'll write to him, then."

"That looks like our only option. Let's get straight to work, Gerhard. I know it's a Sunday, but we need to work on this until dinnertime. We can't let another day pass," Paul said. He quickly finished his egg, gulped down his coffee, and got up from the table.

Gerhard was caught with his mouth full. He couldn't understand why there was such a rush. Even so, he left his half-full cup of coffee behind and followed his father-in-law to the office.

They decided to start by recommending only three people to Malche. A list of dozens might frighten him off. By noon, they had finalized a carefully worded letter asking if it would be possible to send a representative to Turkey to discuss employment prospects. It was signed by Professor Paul Hindberg on behalf of the Association to Assist German Scientists Abroad.

A short note arrived from Malche the following week:

> *I will forward your request to the authorities in Ankara and be in touch.*

To Gerhard, it felt as if a door had opened and through the crack streamed a thin ray of light. Happily, he didn't have to wait long for more news, this time in the form of a telegram:

Expecting representative stop Malche

"Congratulations! And to think you'll get to see Istanbul!"

"Son, you know I'm giving final exams this week. You're our representative."

"Me?"

"You'll do exactly what I would. Present our list of candidates to the authorities and negotiate terms if it comes to that."

"I'm not sure I can. And Malche is your friend, not mine."

"If you'd been able to stay in Germany, you'd be chairing a department right now. And chairs have to negotiate. We have our three candidates. If you meet resistance, don't insist on professorships for all three. One is better than none. I know you can do this."

A City with a Sea Running Through It

On a hot July day, Gerhard boarded the Orient Express and settled in for the long journey to Istanbul.

Once, in college, he and some friends had set out in a third-class carriage from Berlin, getting as far as Venice by washing glasses and peeling potatoes to pay their way. It was the most fun he'd ever had. When he later told Elsa of this adventure, he left out the bit about washing dishes.

Settled now in a comfortable seat by the window, Gerhard gazed out at the familiar thick forests, red rooftops, and charming villages of Central Europe—scenery marred, on occasion, by the blight of industry. When he wasn't looking out the window, he read books or drifted into an uneasy sleep. He had stopped allowing himself to hope for a better future. His new motto was "whatever happens, happens." He was on his way to the East, and he would embrace the famed fatalism of the Levant.

On the third day of the journey, Gerhard caught sight of the ancient ramparts of Yedikule and the blue expanse that was the Sea of Marmara. Just ahead, he could see hundreds of pointed minarets straining toward the low-hanging white clouds.

Hugging the walls of Topkapı Palace, the train rounded the Sarayburnu promontory.

Had he been transported to a land of make-believe? Was he dreaming?

It was nothing like the cities he'd seen in Central Europe or on the Mediterranean, but it didn't match his idea of the Middle East, either. He hadn't spotted a single camel.

The train chugged into Sirkeci Station.

A small suitcase in hand, Gerhard stepped onto a platform that smelled of coal and the sea. The gentleman who approached with a smile and an outstretched hand turned out to be Erim, a professor fluent in German, a language whose intricacies he had mastered while earning a doctorate in mathematics at Nuremburg University. Gerhard was surprised. He'd never met a Turk who had been educated in Germany.

"Good morning! I'm taking you directly to Darülfünun, the university. You can rest at a hotel after the meeting or join me for a tour of the city, whichever you prefer."

"Will Professor Malche be at the meeting?" Gerhard asked.

"No, but you'll see him tomorrow. We'll have an early dinner this evening, and then I'll take you to your train. We've booked a sleeping compartment. You see, Professor Malche isn't in Istanbul—he's expecting you in Ankara tomorrow morning."

"Is the university we're going to now the one being reformed?"

"Yes. As you'll see for yourself, it's terribly behind the times. The building itself, the professors, the system . . . everything is hopelessly outdated. It needs renewing, top to bottom. The state has been providing our brightest students with scholarships for advanced studies abroad. Our resources are limited, however, so we are founding a university adhering to European standards right here in Turkey. This was our founder's idea, and the only way to keep up with the times. Herr Schliemann, our shared ideal is to propel our country to its rightful place among the most advanced countries of the world. We will do whatever it takes to achieve this."

Gerhard smiled broadly. "Good for you, my friend," he said, certain now that he had come to the right place. He had only just arrived in this strange land, but the young professor's idealism and enthusiasm were infectious.

Present at the meeting were twelve faculty members, several of them German speakers and the rest fluent in French. They briefed Gerhard on their plans for the university, and he recommended several mathematicians and physicists.

Afterward, Gerhard accompanied Professor Erim and three other Turkish professors to a restaurant. Gerhard expected kebab, but the plate placed in front of him contained a meat stew of some sort nestled on a delicious mound of smoky eggplant mash. And there was a crisp salad composed of diced tomatoes, cucumbers, and red onions. He tried and failed to pronounce the Turkish for this "shepherd's salad," or *çoban salatası*. Next on the menu was a cloying dessert, half of which he got down, and a tiny cup of coffee. He thought it more polite to push away the cup of black sludge than to grimace openly with the attempt to take a second swallow of it.

Now, his belly full, his eyelids were growing heavy. He would have loved to tour the city, but he badly needed a nap. Promising to return at seven that evening, Erim dropped him off at the hotel, where he collapsed on the white coverlet.

When Gerhard awoke, the sun was low on the horizon. He struggled out of bed and splashed water on his face. Unaccustomed to napping, he felt confused and muddleheaded. And his trousers were badly wrinkled. He had a second pair in his suitcase, but wanted to save them for his meeting with Malche. Resorting to an old trick, he removed his trousers, spread them out under the coverlet, and smoothed them with his hand. The tub filled as he shaved. By the time Erim arrived, he was a new man.

"We're going to take a ferry to Asia," Erim explained as they climbed into a taxi. "It's just a twenty-minute ride on the Bosphorus; we'll cross over from Europe. Let's be sure to find seats facing west. Nothing is as magical as an Istanbul sunset."

They got out of the taxi at the quay and walked through the crowd toward the approaching ferry. Gerhard stared at the elegantly attired men and women disembarking from the boat, at the sturdy, heads-carved women clutching string shopping bags, at the scrawny steve-dores bent double under their loads, at the vendors hawking grape juice and sesame rolls, at the stray dogs and the napping cats and the squawking seagulls. Side by side teemed the rich and the poor, the styl-ish and the ragged. The ancient buildings and monuments were majes-tic and proud, timeworn and shabby: everything a study in opposites. He was jolted out of his reverie by an ear-splitting howl.

"That's the ferry," Erim said.

That raucous whistle, which Gerhard would one day learn to love, sounded again as a thick black cloud surged out of the smokestack. He instinctively clasped his hand over his nose, but a breeze arose out of nowhere and dissipated the smoke. The clouds still hung in the sky like fluffs of wool and now were tinged lilac.

Gerhard and Erim climbed the stairs to the upper deck and found seats facing the European shore. Seagulls were wheeling and diving, dipping their wings in the sea foam and scrapping for bits of bread that passengers threw from behind the railing. Directly in front of him, countless domes and minarets were etched against a scarlet sun and an ever-changing, multihued sky. Gerhard got goose bumps. He wasn't a particularly religious man, but the vision before him, this ancient city seemingly sinking into the sea along with the setting sun, was surely a masterpiece of that great artist known to some as God.

Erim was asking him something. He wanted to know what Gerhard thought of Istanbul so far.

"Magnificent," he said without hesitation.

This city, which so little resembled the land where he had been born and bred, somehow seemed worthy of every superlative.

When they drew up to the opposite shore, he watched as the mooring lines were secured, waited as the creaking ferry met the groaning dock, and surged with the crowd over the gangplanks and up the stairs to the station.

Gerhard turned around for another glimpse of the deep-blue sea.

"We're quite early for the train, Herr Schliemann, but there's a *meyhane* nearby. Allow me to treat you to a glass of wine," Erim said.

Gerhard couldn't think of a more welcome proposal. A short walk took them to a rustic seaside establishment, where they sat at a wobbly wooden table.

The waiter brought little plates of salty white cheese, pale-green melon, wrinkled olives, and bread. A bottle of wine was soon produced, and Gerhard's glass was filled.

He forced himself to finish the first swallow and smiled graciously, but his companion was not fooled.

"Perhaps our wineries need reforming, too. I should never have served white wine to a German."

"No, no . . . it's most refreshing."

"Would you like to try our national drink? I'd be happy to join you."

"Yes, please." *It couldn't be worse than the wine.*

The waiter placed two tall, slender glasses in front of each man. He filled one of Gerhard's with water and poured two fingers' worth of a colorless liquid into the second. When water was added to the liquid, it turned a milky white. Gerhard's initial alarm was overcome by the fragrant scent of anise. The waiter added two cubes of ice to the mysterious concoction.

"I advise you to eat something first." Erim had speared some cheese and was holding it out.

A bit of bread, an olive, a sip of *rakı*, a chunk of melon, another sip of ice-cold rakı. The men clinked glasses and smiled at each other.

"Be sure to have a sip of water after each sip of rakı. There's a reason we say, 'Rakı won't sit in you the way it sits in the bottle.'"

"How true. No alcoholic beverage does."

Erim raised his glass. "To your honor."

"To the success of the university reforms."

They were deep in conversation when Erim cried out, "Oh! I must ask for the bill at once, or you'll miss your train."

Gerhard leapt unsteadily from his chair. He couldn't miss the train! What if he disgraced himself in the eyes of his father-in-law and of Malche?

Erim paid, then slipped his arm through Gerhard's and practically carried his woozy guest all the way to the train station.

"If the train's already left, what will I do?"

"We'll catch it. And once you're onboard, have them make up your bed at once and try to get a good night's sleep, Gerhard Bey."

"Erim Bey, your wish is my command!" Gerhard grinned. "How strange. I feel so at home here, and so relaxed."

"That's the miracle of rakı. One floats up above the clouds without a care in the world."

Professor Erim accompanied Gerhard to his compartment, placed his suitcase up on the rack, and instructed the conductor to ensure that the German's bed was made up and that he was awakened half an hour before the train arrived in Ankara.

Gerhard thanked his new friend from his heart, and they bid each other farewell. His bed was ready, so he hung his jacket on a hook, then lay down, still fully dressed. *Has the rakı gone to my head? Or is it Istanbul?* was his last thought before falling fast asleep.

A City Created
out of Nothing

An insistent knocking roused Gerhard from a deep sleep. He sat up and listened. A man outside the door was speaking in a strange tongue. His watch, where was it? In his pocket? Last night, that nice fellow, Errem—no, Emren?—had told the conductor to wake him up. He could still taste that white drink smelling of anise. He'd drunk too much and barely made it to the train in time. What was odd, though, was that he could remember everything. His head wasn't even throbbing, though several glasses of wine always left him with a splitting headache. Now, where were his shoes? He must have kicked them off in the middle of the night. And his pants, too? Gerhard spotted them lying in a wrinkled heap in the corner, shoes under the table. He got up and opened his suitcase, laying everything out on the bed. Once dressed, he stepped out of his compartment in search of the toilet, then proceeded to the dining car. The moment he sat down at one of the white-clothed tables, a waiter brought over jam, butter, a variety of cheeses, and olives. Olives for breakfast? Were there no sausages? He asked the waiter in French. No! "Ooph, ooph," the waiter offered. Ah, *oeuf*, eggs. Yes, a hard-boiled egg would work. But the waiter brought him a cheese omelet. Gerhard shook his head. Did Turks have cheese and olives with every meal? But he was hungry, and the omelet was tasty. Before long, he'd polished off everything on the table. Gerhard ordered a coffee. No, not that little cup of engine fuel again! Tea would have to do.

An elderly couple was waiting for his table, so Gerhard nodded, stood up, and returned to his compartment. He brushed his teeth, combed his hair, and reorganized his suitcase, placing the file he would be presenting to the minister on top. Just then, he felt the train begin to slow as it pulled into the station. Gerhard lowered the window and peered out. That man in a straw boater holding himself ramrod straight like a true Prussian must be Malche. He looked roughly the same age as Gerhard's father-in-law.

Gerhard disembarked and went to introduce himself.

"Welcome, Herr Schliemann. Did you have a pleasant journey?" asked Malche.

"It was wonderful. And I had a most productive meeting with a group of professors in Istanbul yesterday. I am so pleased to have been briefed before today's meeting."

"We'll be assembling at the ministry of education at two this afternoon. First, we'll have lunch at Karpiç, a fine restaurant run by an ethnic Georgian who fled to Turkey with the White Russians some fifteen years ago. He serves the best food in Ankara. While we're eating, we can prepare for the meeting."

"If you don't mind, I'd like to stop by the hotel first and drop off my suitcase. Perhaps you could give me the address of the restaurant so I can get out and see some of the city, then meet you later?"

"I'll pick you up at the hotel at noon. This city is nothing like Istanbul. There's not much to see beyond that boulevard over there. It runs from the train station all the way to the presidential mansion in Çankaya. This is a new city—it's still being built."

"I gathered as much from the train window. I didn't have the opportunity to do any sightseeing in Istanbul, but I'll never forget that sunset on the Bosphorus."

"Herr Schliemann, a renowned Turkish poet was once asked what he most enjoyed about Ankara. 'Returning to Istanbul,' he replied!"

Despite Malche's remarks, Gerhard was determined to stroll through the streets of the new capital city. From the second he set foot in the hotel, everyone he met, from the receptionist to the bellboy, asked him in broken German, French, or English how he found their city. It was still under construction, but its inhabitants were already proud, and eager to have its praises sung by visitors. Truth be told, this settlement rising from the dusty steppe didn't even deserve to be called a city, not yet. But that didn't stop Gerhard from walking the length of a wide boulevard lined on both sides and down the middle with rows of saplings. One day, it would be a stately, green boulevard. Many of the buildings he saw in various stages of completion were in the modernist neoclassical style popular in Italy and Germany. Gerhard wondered if the architects were among the many students who'd trained abroad. He didn't yet know that some of his own countrymen, led by the urban planner and architect Hermann Jansen, were working on the master plan for Ankara. After walking for no more than fifteen minutes, he stepped into what appeared to be an Anatolian town of ramshackle shops and rough dwellings. Were those sun-dried bricks made from dung and straw? His eyes were drawn to a ruined castle perched high on a hill, but he sighed and turned around. Malche would be expecting him at twelve sharp.

As he made his way back to the hotel, he felt as though he was walking out of the Middle Ages and into a promise of modernity. Gardeners

in waistcoats and flat caps hard at work with their shovels and pick-
axes; sunburnt masons raising the walls of monumental structures; a few
more rows of mud-brick hovels all huddled together for support; towns-
women with gray-and-black checked shawls draped from the crowns of
their heads to below their waists; gentlemen sauntering along in fedoras
and sharp suits; beautifully coifed ladies in high heels and calf-length
sundresses; a Ford automobile honking at a donkey-drawn cart—the
juxtaposition of it all was mind-boggling.

Gerhard was in for another surprise when he accompanied Malche to
lunch. Housed on the ground floor of a former Ottoman inn was what
Malche described as the first modern restaurant in Ankara. The starched
tablecloths and fashionable crowd made Gerhard feel as though he
were back in Zurich. And not only was the chicken Kiev the best he'd
ever had, it was also brought to the table by the proprietor himself, a
bald man in a spotless white coat known to all as Papa Karpiç.

"Did you rest?" Malche asked.

"I opted for a stroll. This place is like a giant construction site.
Everywhere I went, half-finished buildings and streets—"

"There's a popular Turkish song that goes 'Ankara, Ankara, beautiful Ankara. First city created out of nothing.'" He added, "The Turks
really are creating a city from the ground up. And they couldn't be
prouder."

"I can tell. But why build a new capital when you already have a
city like Istanbul?"

"Istanbul is beautiful, but it isn't laid out well. When Ankara is
complete, it will be both beautiful and organized. That is, as long as
the master plan is properly executed. From what I've heard, there have
been disputes between the landowners and the chief planner. I fear that
greed may win the day."

"By taking a position in this unfinished provincial city, you've certainly demonstrated that you're a man of resolve and courage," Gerhard said. "You have my admiration and respect, Professor."

"I'm inspired by this nation's single-minded will to modernize, Herr Schliemann. The recent events in Germany had left me dispirited, both generally and professionally. But here, in a country whose founder is so passionate about science, I am delighted to be of service. I have been working night and day for the past year, with an enthusiasm I hadn't mustered in years."

"How did it begin? Did you approach them, or did they approach you?"

"One of my best students at Geneva Medical College was a Turk. Years later, he showed up at my door. He had not only gone on to become a respected physician, but was also held in such high regard that he'd been named a presidential advisor. I was as proud as any teacher could be. This young man, whose fluency in French has always astounded me and whose name I have never been able to pronounce well—Akil Muhtar—had personally recommended me to the founder of the Republic of Turkey, Gazi Mustafa Kemal."

"You must be a wonderful teacher to inspire such loyalty."

"I'd like to believe so. Anyway, just as I was preparing to settle into a forced retirement, Akil showed up with a letter of invitation from the Turkish ministry of education. Life is certainly full of surprises."

"That it is," Gerhard said. "Your friendship with my father-in-law has been another happy coincidence, both for us and for the Turks."

"Herr Schliemann, a progressive, modern society is arising, here, in the heart of Anatolia, through the efforts of a small band of true believers. With hope, with zeal, for the people, with the people, and—when necessary—despite the people, they're trying to transform this place through mass education. Who wouldn't wish to serve such a noble cause?"

Tears welled up in the elderly professor's eyes, and Gerhard didn't dare interrupt.

"Akil told me that although their resources are limited, their determination to succeed knows no bounds. I warned him that without discipline, a proper education is impossible to achieve. 'Professor,' he said, 'we Muslims are instilled with a culture of obedience.' But I objected immediately. 'Herr Akil,' I said, 'obedience and discipline are not the same. Obedience is unquestioning submission to authority; discipline requires adherence to certain essential rules and duties, yes, but one is permitted—nay, encouraged—to question those very rules and duties.' Akil then told me that I would be acting as an advisor to a man who had spent most of his life in the military. 'Don't worry,' he assured me, 'the Gazi will understand you. He is an idealist determined to elevate our country by training our people in the sciences.' Herr Schliemann, I was so moved. I asked Akil if he would be willing to translate my report himself, but there was no need. The Gazi is proficient in French and able to both write and read in the Latin script."

Professor Malche fell silent, remembering all that had followed.

Just two weeks after receiving that letter, he had arrived in Ankara, where he met with officials from the ministry of education and a group of academics. Filled with fervor for the new republic, he returned to Istanbul, rolled up his sleeves, and set to work. Over the next five months, he solicited the views of politicians, professors, state administrators, students, and even clerks. He inspected Darülfünun's lecture halls, laboratories, and libraries. He monitored lessons and exams. He conducted exhaustive written surveys to assess the abilities of the faculty members.

"Can I get you anything else, sir?"

The elderly professor was jolted from his thoughts by the waiter. "No," he said brusquely, and turned his attention back to Gerhard.

Gerhard, who had long since cleaned his plate, smiled gamely to hide his flagging interest.

"It took me six months to complete my report. I held nothing back, Herr Schliemann. There was very little coordination among departments. The libraries were a disgrace. The students lacked sufficient skills in foreign languages. The courses were overly burdensome and yet oddly unfocused. The same lesson plans had been in use for fifty years. No serious research of any kind was being conducted. Even worse, the relationships among faculty members were actively antagonistic. I reported it all. After all, I had nothing to lose."

"And you submitted this report to the Gazi?"

"Yes. I recommended extensive reform measures. I did not expect them to be warmly received. But I was wrong."

"How remarkable."

"The Gazi studied my report for days, adding his own notes in the margins. The conclusion he reached was this: The future leaders of this republic must be educated in accordance with the latest scientific and pedagogical methods, regardless of gender. This will create a generation that is intellectually disciplined, capable of critical thinking, and skilled in problem solving."

"Amazing. I would never have expected it from a soldier."

"Yes. The Gazi had observed firsthand that poorly educated military leaders led to bureaucratic inefficiency and defeats on the battlefield, and he will not allow that to happen to his republic. The Gazi has entrusted me with this massive enlightenment project, and he insists that I spare no expense in bringing leading professors from Europe and America to Ankara."

Malche had finally finished his lunch. He motioned for the waiter to bring coffee and, too tired to refuse, Gerhard drank the potent sludge without complaint. Malche insisted on picking up the check.

On the way to the ministry, they passed a group of primary school students, the boys and girls alike dressed in peculiar black smocks with drooping white collars. Leading the way was their teacher, a young lady in a matching gray jacket and skirt. The children skipped along, some of them holding hands. Gerhard felt a rush of tenderness for these innocent citizens of tomorrow and silently wished them and their brave new country the best of luck.

Miracle at the Ministry

Along both sides of a long table sat the reform commission members, department representatives, and stenographers. At the head was Minister of Education Reşit Galip, flanked by Malche to his left and Gerhard to his right. The meeting opened with a question posed to Gerhard in French: "Is there a professor of applied economics you could recommend?"

Gerhard immediately named three candidates and read their résumés from the dossier lying in front of him. He then added his personal assessment of each candidate and recommended that a final choice from among the three be made at a later time.

Variations of that first question were repeated, one after another, for positions in Istanbul.

"Could you recommend a microbiology specialist?"

"Got any qualified chemistry professors?"

Gerhard was ready each time. He consulted the index cards prepared by his father-in-law and replied to each query with the names and qualifications of several candidates. The minister and the officials were clearly impressed. Malche, too, nodded his approval and settled back in his chair, content to let Gerhard handle the proceedings. The hours passed as the Turks continued to ask questions and take notes.

A recess was called at last, allowing Gerhard to stretch his cramped legs and relieve his bladder. On the way back to the conference room, he glanced out the tall windows at this city in the making, this rising capital of an ambitious young country untainted by Western hubris and unshackled from its own imperial past. How wonderful to have come to this land of promise!

Twenty minutes later, at eight o'clock in the evening, the meeting was reconvened. After the minutes were read aloud and approved by those present, the minister rose to his feet and made a heartfelt speech.

"Gentlemen," he said, "when the Turks conquered Istanbul some five hundred years ago, they were powerless to prevent the exodus of Byzantine scientists to Italy, where the Renaissance then took root and flowered. But this time, due to the efforts of the men gathered in this room, some of the most brilliant minds in the world will be migrating from west to east, from Germany to Istanbul, where they will contribute to the advancement of our nation. May these men and women of science convey their knowledge and their methods to our youth, and may we shine among the nations of the modern world."

The minister received a standing ovation. It was now time for the signing ceremony. The first signature affixed to the official report was the education minister's; the second was Gerhard's. The minister told Gerhard that he expected the recruited professors to report for duty at once—even those under internment. He would contact the German authorities and insist that they be given special permission to travel to Turkey, where they would be taken under the protection of their adopted state.

Gerhard promised to compile the candidates' responses and send acceptances within three weeks at the latest.

The meeting was over.

"Herr Schliemann, are you leaving Ankara tomorrow?" the minister asked.

"Yes. I'm in a hurry to get back to Zurich and contact our professors with the good news."

"The minister of health wishes to meet with you," Reşit Galip said. "Preparations are under way to open a medical school in Ankara. The building is nearly complete. And we also need professors for the new hygiene institute. Would you object to being of assistance to them as well?"

Gerhard couldn't believe his luck. At this rate, positions would be found for nearly all the doctors on his list.

"I would be delighted."

"In that case, I'll schedule an appointment bright and early. Rest assured, you'll still make your train. Please wait here for a moment." The minister strode off. He was back in a few minutes with the news.

"Minister of Health Refik Saydam is expecting you for breakfast in his office at a quarter to seven tomorrow."

Malche and Gerhard left the ministry building together. As they walked to their hotel, Malche turned and said, "Even in my wildest dreams, I could never have imagined that so many professors would be offered positions. I'm thunderstruck. It was a miracle that the Turks won their war of independence against the West. The reform of their educational system, if all goes to plan, will be a second miracle. Gerhard Schliemann, history will remember your contribution!"

After the meeting the following morning, Gerhard stopped by the post office near the train station. He walked up to the telegraph window, handed the clerk the slip of paper containing his message, and smiled as he imagined his father-in-law's reaction. Written in bold capital letters in German was a single sentence:

POSITIONS AGREED FOR THIRTY NOT THREE
STOP

Fifteen Million Strong in Fifteen Years

On the evening of October 29, 1933, Professor Ernst Hirsch and Gerhard Schliemann ran into one another at the main gate to Dolmabahçe Palace, former home of sultans. Having exchanged greetings, they proceeded together through the flower-filled grounds. Gerhard, who had visited Hirsch in person with an offer to teach commercial law at Istanbul University, wondered how the professor was finding his new life.

"Are you happy living on the Asian shore?" he asked. "Isn't commuting by ferry every day a bit of a pain?"

"It's a real nuisance on foggy days or when a southwester is blowing, but the views make it all worthwhile," Hirsch replied. "Why, as I was crossing over just now I saw the most amazing pyrotechnics. Thousands of rockets bursting above the Bosphorus and the Golden Horn, the patterns of color showering down on the city. The ships' whistles tooting, the drumbeats rising from both shores, the military fleet saluting from the harbor with volleys of cannon fire. The bridge, minarets, and squares festooned with strings of colored bulbs. What a sight it was!"

The trees and gardens of the palace, too, were adorned with colored lights, and the waterfront had been specially illuminated for Republic Day.

"Have you settled in yet?" Hirsh asked. "Are you content in Pera?"

"I've landed on my feet, friend. A wonderful apartment, fully furnished, in a nice building in Grenadier Street just down from the main boulevard. I've already gone out and found blankets, sheets, cutlery, dishes, pots, and pans. Everything's ready for when my wife and children arrive this weekend. The only thing left for Elsa to do is pick out curtains."

"I wish you many happy days in your new home," Hirsch said. "What about school for your children?"

"My girl's too young for school. As for Peter, we considered leaving him in Zurich with his grandparents so he could get a proper education, but then we found out there was a German school here in Istanbul. We're so relieved not to split up the family."

"You would have regretted it. I have a little girl, too. She stayed in Germany with her mother. I miss her terribly."

Somehow, Gerhard hadn't pegged Hirsch for a father. Assuming the marriage had ended in divorce, he didn't ask any more questions as the two friends joined the men in dinner jackets and the women in evening gowns streaming up the palace staircase. They both gazed for a moment at the dozens of marble columns, at the gilded ceilings, at the massive chandelier with 750 lamps hanging from the central dome, at the opulence amassed by the mighty empire that had ruled from this city for some five hundred years. Then they plunged inside.

Hirsch paused in front of one of the tall windows and gazed at the illuminated waterfront. The fireworks were still under way.

Gerhard placed a hand on Hirsch's shoulder. "Professor, are you okay?" he asked.

"Am I okay? Me?" Hirsch's voice trembled with emotion. "I—a man dismissed from his professorship and forced to leave behind his work, his home, and his homeland, despised for being a Jew, called inferior—am standing here now in a splendid palace on the edge of Europe, where I have been invited as a distinguished guest. Yes, I'm okay. In fact, I've been reborn."

Gerhard swallowed hard. Tears of gratitude swam in his eyes, too, as he watched the colored lights playing on the dark sea. Life had presented him with a mysterious wrapped box, and out of that box had emerged a country called Turkey. From the moment he had set foot in this land, it seemed as though all he touched would turn to gold.

Not only had he been treated with the utmost respect and consideration, but every scientist and academic he had approached in Europe had accepted, with minimal negotiations, the positions on offer. The only person who had needed time to consider was the one standing here now, counting his blessings. Hirsch was torn between a position in Amsterdam and the offer from Istanbul, and he had been the last to decide. But he had opted for Istanbul and, within a mere three weeks, Gerhard had fulfilled his promise to the Turks of recruiting candidates for every single position. In doing so, he had distinguished himself in his father-in-law's eyes, made his wife proud, and been gratified to overhear his mother-in-law singing his praises to her friends over homemade ginger cake and tea.

Gerhard's personal business, too, had gone off without a hitch. During his second visit to Turkey to have the contracts signed for the doctors recruited by the Ministry of Health, he had managed to rent an apartment as well.

Having braced for a life in which he fed his family by tutoring students in their homes, he was instead given a position teaching pathology at Istanbul University Medical School. The salary was sufficient for a rental within walking distance of St. George's, the school his son would attend.

His new landlady, who wanted time to get the apartment freshly painted and cleaned, had asked when he expected the ship bringing his furniture to arrive. Gerhard hadn't wanted to say he'd left everything behind.

"I'll get everything we need here."

"You'll have to get started at once. You won't find ready-made furniture in Istanbul. And craftsmen take time."

"We'll do it as soon as my wife gets here. We can always sleep on mattresses on the floor at first."

"You can't live like that! I'd suggest staying at a hotel, but there are four of you. It would be a terrible inconvenience, especially with a baby." The landlady, an elderly Armenian he addressed as "Madame," the title Turks used for non-Muslim women, was muttering to herself and barely audible.

"Don't worry, Madame Saryan. We'll manage."

"Forgive me for poking my nose in where it doesn't belong, but my tenant on the ground floor, Monsieur Sarfati, passed away a couple of months ago. His only child, a daughter, moved to America ten years ago. When he died, I wrote and asked her what to do with Monsieur Sarfati's possessions. In her reply, which I received just last week, she instructed me to distribute to charity whatever her relatives here didn't want. Two days ago, the relatives took away the last of the silver, the paintings, and the bibelots. They left all the furniture, though. The truly poor would have no space for those enormous dining and sitting room sets, and the bed is huge as well. They're all still there, downstairs. You're welcome to take whatever you like."

Scavenging through the furniture of a dead stranger! It was a distasteful idea. Still, Gerhard knew his landlady meant well.

"I'll have a look," he said, mainly so he wouldn't appear ungrateful.

54

They descended two flights of stairs and entered a stuffy, dark apartment. Swatting at the dust particles whirling in the shafts of light that snuck through red velvet curtains, Gerhard walked through the sitting room, the kitchen, and the bedroom. The antique furniture was exquisite. The relatives must not have appreciated its value. The worn sofa and armchairs could be reupholstered. The oak table and chairs could be polished. The finely crafted nightstands and wardrobe would need only a good dusting.

He felt like throwing his arms around Madame Saryan's neck. How lucky could a fellow be?

Gerhard's thoughts were interrupted by Hirsch, whom he could barely hear above the orchestra and the murmur of hundreds of guests.

"Pardon?" Gerhard said.

"I might seem a little overwrought, but to have suffered so much and to have ended up here, of all places—"

"I know how you feel. Only half a year has passed since I fled Frankfurt. Yet here we are in a new country, charged with a sacred mission. As the minister of education told me at our first meeting, we, the scientists of Europe, are expected to convey our knowledge and our methods to the youth of this country. We are expected to play an instrumental role in shaping the young minds of an entire generation of future leaders. It's as daunting a task as it is inspiring."

"It certainly is," Hirsch said. "Ah, look who's over there! Let's go say hello."

On the evening of October 29, 1933, it was with great optimism that Ernst Hirsch and Gerhard Schliemann made their way to greet Professors Neumark, Löwe, and Kosswig. The five compatriots toasted their good fortune and their new lives, none of them aware of just how rocky the road ahead would be.

A Tangle

February 24, 1934
Istanbul

Dear Mother,
It snowed again this morning. Through the window, I can see the lovely sight of a city muffled in white. If only it weren't so difficult to heat our home.

In my previous letters, I wrote all about how beautiful Istanbul is and how friendly and helpful the Turks have been. Sadly, but perhaps inevitably, there is a less pleasant side to life here, one I've slowly begun to see. You'll remember the red velvet curtains belonging to the deceased tenant downstairs and how I decided that getting them cleaned would be more bothersome than simply ordering new ones? Well, the curtain maker failed to deliver on the agreed day. The children's rooms face east, and the sunlight wakes them up early every morning, so I hung sheets in their windows. It was still too bright. I was forced to go out and buy blue roller blinds and install *them myself. Then, the very next morning, the curtains I'd ordered arrived! This was my first lesson in avoiding needless expense. In this country, deliveries are never made on the promised date, but they do arrive eventually.*

Furthermore, I was rejoicing in the sunny weather, which extended well into November, when winter struck out of nowhere. In the gloom and chill, everything seems much less pleasant. It's impossible to find anything in this city. I wanted to knit sweaters for the children, but the wool is stiff as a board. The thread is poor quality and keeps snapping. The soap doesn't lather. The bread is soft and white, with little nutritional value, and Peter won't eat my homemade brown bread. I have to carry our washing through several neighborhoods to get to the nearest laundry. This is a miserably poor country. But I mustn't complain, for if nothing else, we needn't fear for our lives here. We must be thankful for our blessings!

I've even grown accustomed to a different day of rest, but Peter still hasn't adjusted to school. He misses his old teachers and his old friends. Because he is a native German speaker, he was placed in an advanced class and finds the lessons difficult. We help him with his homework and try to be understanding. The poor boy is also struggling with Turkish, which is as perplexing a language as any on earth. Luckily, several boys his age live on our street. On the weekends, they all play ball together in a nearby vacant lot or, now that the weather is so bad, visit one another's homes. Thanks to them, his Turkish is improving.

Young Hanna is becoming more irresponsible with each passing day, and I wish you hadn't insisted we bring her with us. I won't deny that I enjoyed her amusing company on the long train ride. She was also a great help with the housework during our first weeks in Istanbul. Then, something came over her. She won't listen to me. When she should be cleaning or cooking, she sticks Susy in a stroller, clambers up the steep hill to the main street, and goes window-shopping for hours on end. Gerhard has stopped scowling over my having brought Hanna without consulting him, but I don't dare complain to him about her. I'll have to handle the situation myself. When we come visit Zurich over the summer holidays, I intend to leave her there. If she weren't so useless, there would have been no need for me to hire a local woman to clean four days a week. This woman, Fatma, also makes delicious pastries and local dishes. Mother, I know you're frowning at the extravagance of my having two domestic helpers, but wages are so low here, and Fatma is also helping me to improve my Turkish.

I told you all about our neighbors in my first letter. The lack of a shared language has made it impossible to do much socializing, much as I like the Atalay family upstairs. However, there is a Jewish family and an Armenian woman in the building who speak passable French. For now, they are my closest friends. Have no fears about your grandchildren's religious upbringing. Our Jewish neighbors observe all the holy days, even if I sometimes miss one. Two days ago, Peter was invited to a Bar Mitzvah. Here in Turkey, the holy days of all faiths are celebrated with great enthusiasm. Prayers and religious ceremonies are a major part of everyday life. On Christmas, which the Armenians celebrate in January, Madame invited all the children in the building to her apartment and had a present for each one under a fir tree set up in her sitting room. When our Muslim neighbors sacrificed a sheep for their holiday, they sent us a heaping plate of raw meat. We decided halal butchering wasn't all that different from kosher, and Gerhard and Peter were happy to devour it. Of course, the happiest member of our family is Susy. She eats, drinks, sleeps, and is spoilt terribly by the neighbors. Turks adore children. The butcher shop, corner grocery, and patisserie where I do my shopping always give her little treats, and she's grown quite plump.

But as I mentioned at the beginning of this letter, not everything is going well. Gerhard, who was so full of hope when he started at the university, seems quite distressed these days. I gather that some of the Turkish professors have not taken kindly to their new colleagues. And the Turks who lost their jobs when the old university was closed are openly hostile. They're determined to make the Germans' lives a living hell, and have gone so far as to spread false rumors to incite the students. They criticize the Germans for not knowing Turkish and claim they are unqualified, the accusation that wounds Gerhard the most. As you know, Gerhard helped to recruit the leading candidates in each field. It isn't as though the Turks hired them out of pity! Gerhard warned me not to talk about this with anyone.

Another complication is that, right around the time I arrived in Istanbul, a new medical school opened in Ankara. But this time, the German government insisted on approving all the Germans hired to work there. At first, we assumed that the Gazi (that's the title Muslims give to a great military leader, like this country's founder, Mustafa Kemal) was trying not to antagonize the German government. Gerhard later learned that Hitler was furious when he found out that so many of the Jewish academics fired in Germany had been given positions here. He pressured the Turkish government to fire them all. When the Turks refused, Hitler announced that, from now on, only Aryan professors will be permitted to go to Turkey. That's why Aryans have been hired at the new medical school in Ankara and at some other institutions. There are even a few of them at Istanbul University.

So, the faculty of Istanbul University now includes Islamist Turks from the old university who cling to the old ways, the Jews Gerhard helped to place, and the Aryans approved by Hitler, not to mention non-Jewish Germans who fled Hitler's regime for political reasons!

As you can imagine, our social life has become complicated to say the least. When we attend official functions, we do all we can to avoid Hitler's men, but we can still feel them glaring at us. It's a tangled mess!

I try to look on the bright side. The variety and flavor of the fruits and vegetables here is astonishing. My Turkish neighbors have taught me to cook vegetable and bean dishes with olive oil. I'll make some for you when we visit this summer.

I was thinking, Mother, why don't

There was a loud banging on the front door, and Elsa ran to open it. A forlorn-looking Peter stepped inside, took off his coat, and threw it on the floor.

"Peter! What are you doing? We don't throw our things on the floor. And you haven't taken off your cap." She followed Peter and tried to remove his woolen cap. He held on tight with both hands. When she finally got it off, she screamed.

"What happened to your hair?"

Peter, whose thick shock of blond hair had been clipped nearly to the scalp, was on the verge of tears.

"Who did this to you? Son, tell me this minute!"

"The barber."

"Which barber? Why? Have you been punished for something?"

"Because of bugs."

So that was it. Lice. Even so, how could they cut her son's hair without her permission? In the morning, she would march over there and demand an explanation. She'd brought special shampoo from Zurich. There was no need to shave the boy's head.

"How many children are infested?" she asked Peter.

"I don't know. The barber came to the school and shaved everyone's hair off."

"What about the girls?"

"Them, too."

"Don't be upset, sweetheart. It'll grow back thicker than ever," she said. "In two months, nobody will be able to tell the difference. Now go wash your hands, change your clothes, and come to the kitchen."

Elsa walked back to the little writing desk in her room and resumed the letter.

> *you and Father visit us here this summer? The sun would do you both good.*
>
> *As I was writing this, Peter got home from school. He's had all his hair cut off because of a lice infestation. The poor boy. He looks like a pumpkin.*

Elsa stopped and read the last few lines. Deciding it was better not to mention the lice, she scratched out what she'd written and hastily concluded the letter so she could make Peter something to eat.

> *Peter got home from school, and Susy will be waking up from her nap soon. Duty calls. I will write to you again at the first opportunity. Take care of yourselves. You and Father are constantly in my thoughts.*
>
> *Your loving daughter,*
> *Elsa*

Setbacks

With a fanfare of enthusiasm, goodwill, and optimism, Istanbul University had been officially inaugurated on Saturday, November 18.

As it turned out, however, the German-style discipline required to transform Turkish aspirations into daily reality was in short supply. The necessary departmental coordination and curriculum planning were incomplete. The German professors were unable to have their lesson plans translated in time. Chaos soon reigned over this new university of 3,500 students.

Nobody had had the patience to implement Professor Malche's painstakingly prepared master plan, and the resulting disarray was particularly pronounced in the medical school. The school's buildings were dilapidated, its laboratories undersupplied, and its equipment and supplies unusable. Horrified by the sight of the school's thirty microscopes, Gerhard had shouted, "Send them all to a museum! Their value as antiques will be appreciated there."

The new morphology institute had been completed, but the electrical sockets weren't wired. Neither the deans' nor the chancellor's offices responded to the complaints and petitions the German professors submitted.

The hospitals run by the Ministry of Health were operating under what Gerhard considered wartime conditions, with two and even three patients to a bed.

Some of the shortcomings were understandable. After all, Turkey was a poor country recovering from years of war and upheaval. But something else was upsetting the German hospital administrators and professors: Turks resented them. Surely, the émigrés told themselves, the Gazi has no idea this is happening. It was he who had invited them to Turkey and he who had allocated scarce resources to offer them professorships and implement their reforms. Now, with the Gazi focused on running the country, the chancellor and the deans were expected to run the universities on their own. In truth, the chancellor, who was also the Gazi's physician, was an ineffective presence, a figurehead rather than a hands-on administrator. As for the deans, they showed up to work every day, but did very little. For them, the only measure of success was the number of budgetary pennies pinched.

Compounding the Germans' hostile reception on campus was the campaign some newspapers had launched to sway public opinion against them. There were days when Gerhard found himself at the end of his rope.

It was on one such day that Gerhard met up with Hirsch at Koço's Meyhane, one of their favorite haunts. Hirsch had taken his first sip of rakı and was contemplating the shimmer of late-evening sun on the still waters of Moda Bay when Gerhard stomped in, waved a rolled-up copy of *Cumhuriyet* under his nose, and said, "Will this backbiting never end? If only they devoted more time to science and less to mischief-making. Your Turkish is better than mine. Tell me what they're saying today."

Hirsch glanced at the headline and laid the newspaper on the table with a sigh.

"Why isn't Elsa here?" he asked.

"We couldn't find anyone to stay with the children."

"What about Hanna?"

"Hanna! It's a long story. I'll tell you later. Now tell me what this says."

"I can't promise my Turkish is up to the task," Hirsch said. Anxious not to upset his friend further, he tried to soften the journalist's malicious tone. Foreign professors were accused of violating their contracts, of not having authored scholarly papers and books, and, in what was presented as the greatest failing of all, of not having learned sufficient Turkish to wean themselves from classroom translators.

"The nerve!" Gerhard said.

"This is all because our salaries are much higher than those of our Turkish colleagues. They feel like they're being treated unfairly."

"It's true, our salaries are higher. But our contracts forbid us from any outside work. The Turks all have their own private clinics and offices. They end up earning far more than we do."

"Come on, Gerhard. Whenever anyone falls ill in this city, they insist on being treated by a German doctor. They seem to think we can work magic. It's only natural that Turkish doctors would resent us."

"Do you know what they wrote in this same newspaper last week? Basically, the ministry of education was accused of having snapped up Jewish academics on the cheap, as though we were sold in bulk to the highest bidder. The byline said . . . hang on, I'll remember. Ah, Yunus Nadi! Anyway, at the end, this Nadi character demanded that our contracts be terminated. Have you heard about this?"

"Of course I have. But did you know that *Tan* published a response dismissing Nadi's complaints as gossipmongering and describing us as a glittering constellation of scholars? It was a long article. I'll find it for you if you like."

"Don't trouble yourself. It annoys me just as much when they pile on the flattery."

"Listen, my friend," Hirsch said. "I was trained as a legal theorist. We need to be analytical and identify their real motives. We're not the target; we're just an easy mark. It's the Gazi and his reforms that they want to attack, but they don't dare do it openly, so they set their sights on us. Can't you see that?"

Gerhard gulped a mouthful of rakı from the glass his friend had filled. The national drink, once so strange to him, went down smooth as water these days.

"I need some ice."

Hirsch waved to the waiter and gestured to Gerhard's glass.

"I left that first meeting so impressed by their determination to modernize. What happened to all that enthusiasm? Why are these reactionaries being tolerated?"

"People resist change. The Turks have been resisting change for centuries."

"You, me, all of the professors I recruited . . . we find ourselves between the reformists and the old guard—right in the line of fire. Had I known it would turn out like this, I might never have come."

The waiter arrived with an ice bucket and placed two cubes in Gerhard's glass with a pair of silver tongs.

"The waiters here are smarter than the scientists. All it took was a flick of your finger for him to understand that I wanted ice. In Germany, the waiter would have come over to the table and asked what you wanted," Gerhard said.

"We won't be in Germany again for a long time. You've learned to communicate with this country's waiters, my friend. I suggest you learn to get along with its professors, as well."

"But how? They oppose new research, oppose their students reading scholarly literature, oppose original thinking, oppose questions, oppose new ideas. What they really want is for time to stand still. And they call themselves scientists!"

"Perhaps some of the fault lies with the Republicans. They expect the public to swallow the medicine of modernity in one great gulp. And what happens? The patient vomits it right back up."

"You're a legal scholar. You have the luxury of dissecting thorny questions one step at a time. I'm a doctor. If I were to remove a tumor one piece at a time—a bit today, a little next week, some more next year—the patient would die. To be effective, treatment must be immediate, swift, and thorough!"

"Yes, but we're not talking about an individual here. We're talking about an entire society composed of millions of people with all kinds of different problems . . ." Hirsch's sentence petered out as his eyes were drawn to the full moon, which had just emerged from behind a silvery veil of cloud. He popped a few roasted chickpeas in his mouth and took a sip of rakı, followed by a sip of water. "Never mind all this, my friend! Let's enjoy the moonlight. We can't allow a few reactionary professors to get us down. Now, what were you saying about Hanna? She hasn't left you, has she?"

"Actually, that's exactly what she's done. She found a lover and ran off."

"You're kidding! A German?"

"No, a local."

"But how do they communicate?"

"Love has its own language, they say."

"How did they meet?"

"In a shopping arcade in Beyoğlu, just up the hill from our home. The one full of drapers and haberdashers. Hanna was forever running off to the shops for a bit of thread or a button. As it turns out, she was flirting with the son of a shopkeeper. His family paid us a visit and asked for her hand. Elsa stalled, saying she couldn't consent to an engagement without getting permission from the girl's real family first. So, two days ago, Hanna left a note saying she had eloped, just like that!

"How old is she?"

"Twenty-two. She's of age, but Elsa's the one who brought her to Istanbul, and she feels responsible for her."

"How unfortunate," Hirsch said.

"It was my mother-in-law's doing. She expected Hanna to help Elsa with the housework and the baby. Nobody even bothered to tell me. Imagine my astonishment when Elsa got off the train with this strange young woman in tow."

"When I saw Hanna in your house, I assumed she was a relative."

"Not at all. She managed to get out of Germany and ended up at her aunt's in Zurich. The aunt is an acquaintance of my mother-in-law, who then took it upon herself to arrange a position for her friend's niece. And that's how we ended up with Hanna."

"What about the man Hanna eloped with? Do you know much about him?"

"He's from a family of Sephardic Jews. They own several shops in the arcade, so they must be reasonably well-off. Anyway, Peter's the only one who's actually sad she left."

"Your little boy has good taste. Hanna was a beautiful girl."

"That beauty has brought nothing but trouble. We had to notify both the Turkish authorities and the German consulate that she was no longer residing with us. She might be of age, but we could still be held responsible for any trouble she causes."

"You have my sympathies." Hirsch raised his glass and said, "May it all work out for the best. Prosit!"

"*Şerefe*," Gerhard replied. "That's the first Turkish word I mastered." He finished off his rakı and stopped the waiter from refilling his glass. "I'd better slow down, or I'll end up missing the last ferry. I have enough problems at work. The last thing I need is another problem at home."

"Bring the tray of meze, please," Hirsch told the waiter in his heavily accented Turkish. Then he looked Gerhard directly in the eye. "Don't make too much of these setbacks at the university. We can't allow a handful of disgruntled professors to make us forget our gratitude to this country."

"That's precisely what has me so upset! I've been working day and night to help my students succeed, but all this mudslinging makes me want to give up. I can't help it."

"Don't let them get you down, my friend. We've come so far. You even learned Turkish."

"Well, I've picked up a bit from Fatma, our cleaning lady, and from shopkeepers. My Turkish will never be as sophisticated as yours."

Hirsch, who had taken private lessons since his first day in Turkey, was already competent in legal terminology. He contemplated the tray of small plates the waiter was holding and selected a few in what Gerhard took to be flawless Turkish.

"Leave on the table melon, cheese, salted mackerel, and that stuffed vegetable, waiter, sir."

The waiter smiled. "Your wish is my command."

"So, then, Hirsch," Gerhard asked, "how much longer will it be until you escape your solitary existence? When will I have the honor of meeting your wife?"

"Very soon. I'm expecting Holde to arrive by the end of this month."

"Elsa will be so pleased," Gerhard said. "She needs friends who share her background and speak German. The few she's met live quite far from us. I wish you'd move closer by."

"I'm afraid that's a promise I can't make! I've become terribly attached to having morning tea on the ferry as we glide across the Sea of Marmara."

A close friendship had developed between the pathologist and the legal scholar. Once a week, they would meet either at the meyhane in Moda or at a Russian restaurant in Pera. Their approaches to the challenges of their new lives may have differed, but on one subject they were fully agreed: Istanbul was a paradise. Even the least promising alley of worn cobblestones and ramshackle wooden houses could open onto the most breathtaking vistas. This was a city of surprises and unexpected beauty, a city that made one grateful to be alive.

That night in the meyhane, as the full moon peeped through the clouds, the rakı flowed as freely as the conversation. Gerhard, indeed, nearly missed his ferry. Panting after a mad dash to the quay, he took a seat on the side of the boat that would afford the best views of Seraglio Point, rested his chin on his chest, and promptly fell asleep.

A ticket collector was tugging at Gerhard's arm when he opened his eyes. Blinking and confused, he asked, in German, what the man wanted.

"Off, off. Ferry finished. Kaput!"

Gerhard gazed around the empty deck. He was the last passenger. He must have nodded off. He stood up, straightened his collar, thanked the man, and walked to the exit. The rush of cool air sent his head spinning for a moment, but he steadied himself. He trotted across the gangplank and onto dry land, only to find that he was still on the Asian shore, in Kadıköy! How could that be? He turned around, but the gangplank was gone and the ferry's lights were off. Was he dreaming? No. What had happened, of course, was that he, a total idiot, had fallen into a drunken slumber, failed to disembark, and been carried back to Asia on the return trip. The man who'd woken him was smoking a cigarette a little farther along the quay. Gerhard went over and tried to ask what time the next ferry would leave.

"No boat," the man said. "Kaput. In the morning." He held up six fingers. Then he tossed his cigarette into the sea and walked off.

It was getting cold. Gerhard turned up his collar so it covered his ears, but he was still shivering. He had enough money for a cab, but the car ferry wouldn't be running at this hour, either. It was complicated to live in a city on two continents. He stood at the end of the quay for a long while, the wind pelting his face with salt spray, and felt as helpless and alone as at any time in his life.

He considered going to Hirsch's house. But his friend was probably asleep and might not even hear the doorbell. No, it would be better to find a hotel near the quay. He spotted a building that resembled an apartment block more than a hotel, but the sign clearly read "Özlem Oteli." He stepped inside. The man at reception understood that he wanted a room, but kept repeating a word—*Peşin! Peşin!*—Gerhard didn't understand. Why hadn't he thought to bring his pocket dictionary with him?

When he'd first arrived at the university, he'd been provided with a German-speaking assistant for work and a first-year student to help with tasks like getting electricity and gas connected to his apartment. He'd appreciated the help but wondered now if he shouldn't have taken private lessons like Hirsch. It was only when the receptionist started rubbing his thumb against his fingertips that Gerhard understood: "*Peşin*" must mean "advance payment." He pulled out some cash, accepted his room key, and scribbled *5:30* on a slip of paper.

"Wake me up. Wake me up," he said in Turkish, simultaneously miming the action. In his room one floor up, he removed all his clothing but his shirt and threw himself onto one of the twin beds. Exhausted and still a little tipsy, he fell asleep at once, without a thought for his worried wife.

A knock on the door awakened him at the appointed time. He put on the jacket and trousers he'd spread out on the other bed, slipped on his shoes, and grabbed his coat.

Downstairs, he politely refused the glass of tea awaiting him. Better to grab tea on the ferry. But when he stepped into the street, he was enveloped by a thick gray mist. The ferries wouldn't be running in this fog! Unable to see more than a few feet in front of him, he nonetheless made his way to the quay among the lonely cries of foghorns. The small crowd that had gathered there was starting to thin. They must have lost hope. He wanted to ask someone when the fog was expected to lift, but was his Turkish up to it? Ordinary commuters were unlikely to know French or German. Chilled and defeated, he hesitated for a moment before setting off for Hirsch's house in Moda.

Hirsch did a double take when he saw his friend at the door. He couldn't help laughing when Gerhard explained what had happened.

"Have you eaten?"

"I was going to get tea and *simit* on the ferry."

"The fog will lift in a couple of hours. Come on in."

Hirsch set a jar of jam and some butter on the kitchen counter. "Have you contacted Elsa?"

"How could I? We don't have a phone, and I didn't want to wake up our landlady. It's still too early."

"You're in trouble," Hirsch said.

"Am I ever! What's worse, I'll have to go straight to the university without stopping at home. I have class at nine."

"Listen, my friend. As someone who's been married far longer than you, I advise you to skip your class and get home before Elsa calls the police."

"My students—"

"I'll stop by the medical school and inform your assistant. He can handle today's lectures," Hirsch said. "You just worry about your wife."

Elsa, who sometimes joined her husband for dinner with Hirsch, knew when the last ferry departed and that it took twenty minutes to reach the European shore. A rough sea might add another ten minutes, at most. Perhaps her husband had chosen to walk home from the European quay or had been unable to find a cab. That would add an extra thirty minutes. But now it was going on two in the morning, and there was still no sign of her husband. Had a thief mistaken him for a rich man and stabbed him or hit him over the head? Poor Gerhard

might be lying in a puddle of blood in a back alley. She was desperate
to talk to someone, even Fatma, who knew not a word of German. But
Fatma had finished her work and left at five, as always. The children
were asleep. If only troublesome Hanna hadn't disappeared! Hirsch
didn't have a phone and was too reserved to use his neighbors' phone.
In an emergency, phone messages were left at the corner shop and delivered to Hirsch by the errand boy in exchange for a tip. But the shop
wouldn't be open at this hour. Even so, Elsa found the number, threw
on a robe, and walked down two flights of stairs to Madame Saryan's
apartment. They could call the police as well. Once she was at the door,
though, she thought better of it and trudged back up. She stretched out
in bed and tried to sleep. But an hour later, she was back at Madame's
door, reaching for the bell, pulling her hand back, reaching for the
bell . . . No, she couldn't do it. Back upstairs, she ate an apple, stared
at a book, wrote a letter to her mother, tore up the letter. Then she
marched downstairs again and rang the bell before she could change
her mind.

In next to no time, Madame had her reading glasses perched on
her nose and was dialing the number Elsa had given her. As expected,
nobody answered at the grocer's. Next, Madame called to find out what
time the last ferry had arrived in Europe. Then she called the police
station and asked if there had been any reports of an accident or crimi-
nal incident. There were none. And no sign of Gerhard at the local
hospitals. Elsa heaved a sigh of relief, thanked Madame, and went back
upstairs.

Madame appeared at Elsa's door a few minutes later with a pot of
tea and Elsa's favorite pastry. Conversing in limited French, a smatter-
ing of Turkish, and an abundance of body language, the women passed
the better part of an hour chatting and nibbling on the nut-filled,
crescent-shaped buns Madame had baked just that afternoon. When
Madame left, Elsa climbed into bed again and, exhausted as she was,
prayed for her husband's safe return. She felt utterly helpless. Perhaps

Gerhard was with another woman? But he wasn't that kind of man, and even if he were, he wouldn't stay out all night. Then again, that's what her cousin had thought until her husband suddenly announced that he had fallen in love with another woman and wanted a divorce. Elsa decided that, after she sent Peter to school in the morning, she'd take Susy and go to find her husband at the university. Surely, he'd be there. He would apologize, she told herself, say he'd missed the ferry and spent the night at Hirsch's.

But what if she couldn't find him at the university?

She told herself to stop worrying and might even have fallen asleep.

Susy woke up at six. Elsa changed her diaper, fed her, and left her in bed with some toys. Around seven, Peter came into the kitchen and asked where his father was. Elsa told him that Gerhard had left early for a meeting. Once her son was fed, dressed, and on his way to his nearby school, she watched from the window, as always, until he had rounded the corner. Normally, Gerhard walked Peter to school, and they turned to wave to Elsa before disappearing. Today, Peter was too busy joking around with his friends to remember to wave to his mother.

"That's how it goes," she said aloud. It was just as her mother had told her. A daughter will always be yours, but a son is only yours for the first few years. After that, he'll belong to his friends, then to his girlfriends, and finally, to his wife.

But did Gerhard still belong to her?

Elsa sat down in front of the window and took up her knitting. Ignoring her daughter's fussing, she kept her eyes on the street, her nervous hands stitching row after row.

Fatma arrived at five past nine. Before she'd even had a chance to take off her coat, Elsa asked her to take Susy out for a long walk. She tried to explain that her daughter hadn't slept well last night. Fatma was none too pleased at the prospect of pushing a stroller up and down the steep cobbled streets, particularly in winter, but she was seldom called on to help with the children. Her employer must have her reasons. Muttering to herself, she bundled Susy up and left.

It was past ten when Gerhard stepped into view at the end of the street. Elsa picked up his briefcase and, just as he was nearing the building's front door, hurled it out the window. The briefcase hit his back with a thud and fell to the ground.

"Take your briefcase and go back to wherever you spent the night," Elsa yelled.

Gerhard picked up his briefcase, walked through the door, and stepped into the hallway, where he came face-to-face with Madame Saryan.

"Welcome, Monsieur. Your wife has been expecting you since last night." As always, Madame spoke to Gerhard in French.

"I nodded off on the ferry."

"Make excuses to your wife, not me." Much as a sudden drop in temperature signals that rain is on the way, the frigidity of her tone warned that a storm was brewing upstairs.

Gerhard smiled, slipped past her bulky frame, and pretended not to hear the parting words she addressed to the back of his head: "Turkish, Armenian, or German, you men are all the same."

Upstairs, Gerhard found that he couldn't get his key to work. There must already be one in the lock on the other side. He rang the doorbell. No response. He held the button down with his finger.

"What do you want?"

He kept his voice low and measured. "Please open the door. Let's not cause a scene in front of the neighbors. I'll tell you what happened when I get inside."

"You can tell me from out there. Then I'll decide whether to open the door."

"Elsa, stop being so childish. Please."

"I'm listening!"

"Madame is listening, too," he hissed. "Do you want her to hear everything?"

"Why shouldn't she? After all, she's the one who waited up with me all night. She's the one who called the police and checked the hospitals."

And that's when Gerhard finally got it. Elsa had been worried sick, terrified that something had happened to him. He'd expected his wife to simply assume he had missed the last boat, but that wasn't fair.

"Darling, I'm so sorry. Open the door, please. You'll laugh when I tell you what happened."

"I'm listening."

"Let me in and I'll tell you."

"Like I said, tell me first. Then I'll decide whether to let you in."

Gerhard squirmed impatiently. Yes, he'd been an idiot, but that didn't mean he deserved to be locked out of his own home. Was he really expected to explain himself through a closed door? What if a neighbor came down the stairs and saw him pleading with his wife, like a philanderer begging for forgiveness?

"Elsa, I'm asking for the last time. Will you open the door?"

"Not until you explain yourself."

"All right, then. Suit yourself!"

Briefcase in hand, Gerhard marched down the stairs, shot through the door and along the street to avoid any falling objects, and didn't slow down until well after he had rounded the corner.

When Elsa heard his footsteps in the stairwell, she rushed over to the window in time to see her husband disappear.

Had she been too stubborn? What if he didn't come home again tonight? What would she tell Peter? She sank onto the chair by the window, then sprang back to her feet with a scream. That damn knitting needle! She started crying, but were they tears of pain, regret, fatigue, or loneliness? It was the loneliness that was getting to her, she decided with a sniff. Ever since they'd moved to Turkey, her only close companion and confidant had been her husband, and the threat of losing that was more than she could bear. The Turks had been friendly and helpful, had graciously invited Gerhard and Elsa to their homes, and fussed over Susy and Peter. But the lack of a shared language was a huge barrier to true intimacy. Virtually none of the local women spoke German, and Elsa's Turkish was still limited to the superficial and mundane. She was most comfortable with Germans, but the émigré families were scattered in far-flung neighborhoods. The Hirsches lived on the Asian shore, while the Reuters and the von Hippels lived miles away, in Bebek. Now that Peter was settled into school in Pera, the family couldn't move to Bebek, much as Elsa wanted to. Cabs were expensive, and she was afraid of getting lost if she took a bus.

And so, Elsa was largely confined to the company of Madame, the Jewish family upstairs, and the two Germans who lived within walking distance, Hans Reichenbach and Maria Moll. Sadly, neither Elsa nor Gerhard were particularly fond of Reichenbach. By all accounts a brilliant and creative philosopher, Reichenbach was also a terrible snob and would drone on and on in a high-pitched voice about the Turks' lack of intellectual rigor and the futility of efforts to elevate the local culture. Every time he threatened to leave Turkey, which was something he did loudly and often, Elsa would roll her eyes and say to herself, "What's stopping you?" Gerhard ignored Reichenbach, but she remembered a dinner party where the delightful Erich Franck had taken his colleague to task.

"When I, a chief physician and the recipient of research prizes, was expelled from my professorship and my homeland, Turkey was the only country to embrace me," Franck said. "This is my country now, and I won't let you impugn it."

Then he stalked off. The awkward silence around the table was finally broken by the gynecologist, Dr. Wilhelm Gustav Liepmann.

"Erich is right," he said. "Our careers were doomed in Germany. Turkey has given us all the opportunity to make a fresh start and to continue our research. How can you be so ungrateful?"

"My views are my own, and you're not required to share them," Reichenbach countered. "You're welcome to stay forever in your beloved land of the star and crescent. But my abilities are being squandered here."

With more than forty German professors in Istanbul, Elsa asked herself, *why, oh why, did Reichenbach have to live closest?*

In her darker moments, Elsa cursed the luck that had forced her from her homeland, even wrestling with her faith and questioning what it meant to be a Jew. She was proud of her roots, and she wanted to walk in God's ways, but would her people never know peace? Her ancestors had fled pogroms in Bohemia. Her husband's ancestors, too, had moved to Germany in fear for their lives. And then there was Rifka, her upstairs neighbor, the wife of a pharmacist. In curiously accented and halting French, Rifka had told Elsa she was Sephardim, the descendant of Jews expelled from Spain in the fifteenth century. They'd sailed in leaky, decrepit ships to the shores of the Adriatic, then traveled to Istanbul.

Now, centuries later, having fled Frankfurt and ended up in Istanbul just because she was Jewish, Elsa had a neighbor with whom she shared a common faith but no common language. If only there were someone she could talk to!

"Ah, Gerhard," she said aloud. "Life is lonely enough as it is. Don't you leave me, too."

Elsa brushed away a tear with one hand and with the other one kept rubbing the spot the knitting needle had jabbed.

Then she leapt to her feet and ran to Madame Saryan's. At the sight of Elsa's wan face and red-rimmed eyes, Madame held out her arms. Elsa rested her cheek against Madame's capacious bosom and let the tears flow. Wrapped in the arms of this woman so many years her senior, a relative stranger whose language she couldn't even speak, she cried her heart out.

When Elsa was ready to dry her tears, Madame made her a cup of Turkish coffee.

"I'm not sure I can drink that—it's too strong for me."

"Please! I'll tell your fortune."

Elsa didn't know what Madame meant, but she meekly accepted the tiny cup and saucer. She was taking her first sip when she remembered, in a flash, that they were invited to the von Hippels' that evening. A physicist and a Christian, Arthur von Hippel had been fired for having a Jewish wife. The von Hippels lived in faraway Bebek, but she had attended several tea parties there and had grown fond of Mrs. von Hippel. Elsa would be horribly disgraced if Gerhard didn't come home tonight.

The thick, bitter coffee was sticking to her throat, and the tears she thought she'd cried out began welling up in her eyes. A glass of water helped her get the coffee down. Elsa stared as Madame took her cup and flipped it over on the saucer. She was composing a question in her mind in French when the phone rang. Madame went to the foyer to answer it. Elsa could hear her saying, "There's no need. Elsa is here with me." Madame appeared, beckoning her.

"Hello?" she said.

"Elsa, it's me, Hirsch. At the risk of disturbing your neighbor, I wanted to tell you myself what happened last night. It was all my fault. I kept insisting we have another round, and Gerhard was too polite to refuse. Then, as you know, he fell asleep on the ferry."

Elsa listened as Hirsch told the entire story from start to finish. At one point, she even found herself wanting to laugh. But she suppressed it.

"Neither of us realized how worried you would be. We were terribly thoughtless. Elsa, let me apologize. It won't happen again."

These were the very words she had hoped to hear from her husband.

"How did you get this number?" she asked. "Did Gerhard give it to you? Did he put you up to this?"

"Gerhard gave me your landlady's number a long time ago, in case of emergency. He has no idea I'm calling you, Elsa. I simply wanted to explain and to apologize for my role in this."

Elsa thanked him, hung up, and went back to the sitting room. Madame was peering into her coffee cup, studying the streaks and smears left by the grounds.

"Tonight, you make peace. No more fighting. No other woman. But there's a man, and he's sad . . . you'll see this man soon."

"Is it Gerhard?"

"No, not Gerhard. Another man. He will get very unhappy, not now, but soon."

Elsa didn't have the energy to worry about some supposed mystery man. She had more important things on her mind, chief among them Gerhard's whereabouts and tonight's dinner. Perhaps she should tell the von Hippels that one of the children had come down with a fever?

At the sound of Susy's voice in the stairwell, Elsa hastily thanked Madame for the coffee and rushed out to help Fatma carry the stroller.

When Gerhard stepped into the apartment building at the usual hour that evening, he was carrying his briefcase and a bouquet of flowers. He crept up the stairs, careful not to alert Madame, and knocked on the door of his home. Peter always greeted him first, but today it was Elsa standing in the doorway, Susy in her arms. Gerhard lowered the bouquet from in front of his face and handed it to Elsa. She took it without a word, set Susy on the floor, and went to the kitchen to get a vase. Gerhard picked up his daughter and followed his wife.

"Elsa, you didn't forget to tell Fatma about tonight, did you? The dinner at the von Hippels'? Someone has to stay with the children."

It was Elsa's opening to call her husband a drunk, a thoughtless and selfish cad. But she controlled the volume and tone of her voice as she said, "If we're still going, Madame will look after the children."

"You've grown quite attached to Madame. I wouldn't have thought she was the most suitable of companions for you."

"I accept friendship where I find it."

Gerhard put Susy down and went up behind his wife, who was arranging flowers in the vase. He lifted her hair and kissed the back of her neck. Sensing no resistance, he rested his hands on her hips. If Peter hadn't walked into the kitchen at that moment, Elsa would have turned and thrown her arms around her husband. Her face lit up with a self-conscious smile. Her family was happy and together again, and that was all that mattered.

Is There a Spy Among Us?

As always, Elsa and Gerhard set off for Bebek on foot, walking as far as Taksim Square, where they boarded a bus. She found a seat, but he had to stand. It was only after most of the passengers got off in Beşiktaş that they could sit together.

"In a year or two, we might have our own automobile," Gerhard said. "The trip to Bebek will be easy then."

"I don't mind the bus on the way there," Elsa said. "It's trying not to fall asleep on the long ride home that I dread. Let's take a cab back. And that way, the von Hippels won't see us waiting at the bus stop."

"Why would that matter?"

"Oh, I don't know. He's from such an aristocratic family. And she—I'll bet you didn't know this—is the daughter of James Franck, the Nobel Prize–winning physicist. That's what Holde told me."

"Are you serious? James Franck is Dagmar's father?"

"He certainly is."

"Good heavens! We'd better turn around at once and go straight home. They're sure to slam the door in the faces of lowly bus riders like us."

Gerhard was gratified to see that he could still make his wife laugh. She'd been all smiles ever since they'd made peace in the kitchen that evening.

"I know a secret about the von Hippels, too," he said. "One of Arthur's uncles fought in the Great War as an Ottoman officer, and his remains are still in the German military cemetery up in Tarabya. Why the face? Don't you believe me?"

"Such important people. Perhaps I should have worn my ruby brooch," Elsa said. "Then again, Dagmar doesn't seem the showy type."

Elsa's instincts had served her well. The von Hippels, both husband and wife, were as unpretentious as they were gracious. Dagmar had prepared a casual dinner of German-style meatballs, potato salad, and apple cake, just a few of the much-missed flavors of home. Elsa enjoyed every bite.

After dinner, the men took their coffees to the sitting room while the women cleared the table together.

"You have such a lovely home," Elsa said, admiring the view of the Bosphorus, visible even from the kitchen. "If it weren't for Peter's school, I'd like to live in Bebek, too."

"My little ones are still too young for school. Perhaps we could swap homes when they get older, Elsa."

"It sounds like you and Arthur expect to stay here for many years, then. I'm happy to hear that. There are some who would bolt at the first opportunity."

"Oh, we're here for the duration, despite everything—"

"Is something wrong?"

"No. Not for me, anyway. It's Arthur's work. The problem isn't the university; it's his teaching assistant."

"Is his assistant a bad interpreter?"

"Well, Arthur has two assistants. One of them is from a poor family, but has succeeded through his own efforts and intelligence. Arthur thinks the world of him. The other is the son of a well-off merchant. I'm sure you've noticed the way some wealthy Turks dote on their sons. They're brought up to believe that money can solve any problem. Anyway, this spoilt young man, who is neither bright nor hardworking, has been a constant thorn in Arthur's side. Most recently, he kicked up a fuss over a lab coat, of all things. Arthur had given one of his old lab coats to the other assistant to spare him the expense of buying a new one. The spoilt assistant found out and demanded one, too. Then, the chancellor of the university summoned Arthur to his office and warned him not to play favorites. He alluded to the many donations made to the school by the wealthy father and the special treatment he expects. Arthur protested, but the chancellor wasn't having it. It's been weighing on Arthur. Honestly, I'm so happy you could join us for dinner tonight. It's done Arthur a world of good."

"How awful. Gerhard would feel the same way Arthur does."

"Please don't repeat any of this to Gerhard. Arthur would be furious with me for telling you."

"I won't say a word."

"Is that a promise?"

"Yes, I promise," Elsa said.

Elsa considered telling her about Gerhard's disappearance the night before. It would be so nice to open up to a woman her own age who spoke her language. But the moment passed.

Scraping the last table scraps into the garbage, Dagmar said, "Come on, Elsa. Let's go join our husbands."

The men were deep in conversation in the sitting room.

"A Trojan horse, I'm sure of it," von Hippel was saying. "I'll be shocked if he doesn't turn out to be Hitler's spy."

"A spy? Who's a spy?" Dagmar asked.

"It's just a figure of speech, dear. We weren't talking about another Mata Hari."

"Arthur, why do you keep things from me?"

"I share everything with you, Dagmar. I've even shared my fantasy about Atatürk."

"Arthur, do tell us, too, please," Gerhard said.

"Okay, but don't laugh at me. As I was sailing from Italy to Istanbul, I imagined myself becoming great friends with Atatürk and galloping across the countryside with him, mounted on our white horses. I don't know why. It was a fantasy. I'd heard he was not just a great military strategist, but a brilliant visionary. Imagine galloping across the steppe alongside one of the great geniuses of our day, debating the great questions of our times."

"And on a white steed, no less," Dagmar said.

The four of them burst out laughing.

"I'm afraid that Atatürk—am I pronouncing it correctly? I can't get my tongue around his new surname. Well, if anyone deserves the moniker 'the father of Turks,' it's him."

"You're saying it right," Gerhard said. "But I doubt he has time for horses these days. Not to mention, he's been ill. Perhaps you could ride with the minister of education or Prime Minister İnönü instead. They're both skilled equestrians."

"The Gazi's ill, you say?" Arthur asked, reverting to Atatürk's old title, which he found easier to pronounce.

"Two of my medical colleagues were summoned to Ankara for a consultation. But that's all I know."

There was a brief moment of concerned silence before the conversation turned to less weighty matters. They were trading their funniest horse stories when Elsa heard the clock strike eleven. She'd forgotten all about Madame and the children!

On the way home, Elsa turned to her husband.

"What's all this about a spy?"

"The German government is sending an official to the university to investigate all of the émigrés."

"Investigate? Investigate what, exactly?"

"Arthur was about to tell me when you came in. Either he doesn't want to worry Dagmar or he thinks it's too sensitive to discuss openly."

"All I ask is that we don't have to move again."

"Elsa, please don't invent something new to worry over."

Elsa bit her tongue. She gazed out the window and left Gerhard alone with his thoughts. In Beşiktaş, they got off the tram and hailed a cab to take them the rest of the way home.

After they had thanked Madame for waiting up, and softly closed the door behind her, Gerhard turned to Elsa and said, "We won't be going anywhere, darling. Not for a long time. Our children are going to grow up here, in Turkey."

"Thank you, Gerhard. I don't want to nag. I just hate not being treated as an equal."

"If Arthur tells me anything more about this spying business, I promise to pass it all on to you, word for word," Gerhard said.

A week later, the chancellor's office distributed questionnaires in German to all the émigré professors. The German consulate, which had sent the forms, demanded that they be completed in full. Professors were expected to provide their full names, their religions and lineage, and the religions and lineages of their parents, spouses, and in-laws. They were asked to list the regions, cities, and universities in Germany where they had lived and worked; their academic titles and degrees; their areas of expertise and fieldwork; and finally and most importantly, the professors were required to classify themselves as "Aryan" or "non-Aryan."

As soon as Gerhard finished reading the form, he went straight to the chancellor's office.

"What is the purpose of these questionnaires?" he asked.

"The university is not responsible for them. The German government is having a report prepared on German professors working abroad. The consulate asked us to distribute the forms, and we have complied. You can decide for yourselves whether or not to fill them out."

"Something is rotten about this. I bet what they really want is to replace us with their own, hand-picked fascist professors."

"Their wishes are not ours, Professor. We signed five-year contracts, and we will honor them. If both sides are satisfied, the contracts will be extended. As far as we are concerned, these forms change nothing."

Gerhard believed the chancellor, but he knew the German regime would stop at nothing, and that included sowing poisonous seeds of Nazi ideology in the minds of Turkish youth.

Ankara, Ankara... Cure for All Ills

Elsa had just completed the final stitch of the sweater she was knitting for Susy when Madame Saryan came upstairs and informed her that she had a phone call. Gerhard never called her on Madame's phone. Feeling a little anxious, she ran down with Susy in her arms and snatched up the mouthpiece dangling from a long cord. It was Peter's school. They wanted her to come immediately and pick up her son, who had vomited in the classroom.

Elsa found herself in a quandary. It was Fatma's day off, so she couldn't leave Susy at home. And just two days earlier, while she and Madame were chatting in the kitchen, Susy had found a tube of Madame's lipstick and drawn on her sitting room wall. How could she ask her neighbor to look after Susy so soon after that? Elsa took a deep breath, smiled, and looked at Madame guiltily.

"Okay, okay. She can stay," Madame said.

"Wanna go with you, Mama," Susy said.

"You can't come with me, dear. I have to get your brother and take him to the doctor. Stay here with Madame and wait for us. And be a good girl."

"No. Wanna go with you."

"Do you want the doctor to poke you with a needle, too?"

"Enough, Susy. You're staying here with me," Madame said in Turkish.

"No!" Susy said in perfect Turkish. "I don't like you now, Madame."

"Why not?"

"You won't let me wear makeup."

"Today I'll let you. But only for today."

"Lips *and* fingernails?"

"Okay."

"Thank you so much, Madame," Elsa said. "You're so kind to us."

"Off you go! Your son needs you."

Elsa dashed upstairs, changed her clothes, grabbed her handbag, and ran down to the street. She climbed the hill to the main avenue and, when there were no cabs in sight, walked the rest of the way. She would take Peter to the university clinic. Her husband would know what to do. What if her son had typhoid? Gerhard had been talking at dinner about a recent outbreak. He'd told them not to drink any water without boiling it first. Could Fatma have given Peter unboiled water when she wasn't looking? No, Peter had probably eaten unwashed fruit from a street vendor.

She arrived at the school out of breath and in a mild panic. Poor Peter had been quarantined in a room all alone. When he saw Elsa, he jumped up and flung his arms around her. He was a bit pale and smelled of vomit, but he looked well enough.

"We're going to hop into a cab and go and see your father. We need to have some tests done."

"Is it typhoid?"

"We'll know after the tests."

"Mom, will I die if it's typhoid?"

"Of course not! Peter, how could you even say such a thing?"

"Then why are you crying?"

"I'm not crying."

"Your eyes are wet."

"I must have a bit of dust in my eye."

Elsa took Peter's hand and led him to the principal's office, where she called the university and asked to speak to her husband. Only when she insisted that it was an emergency did they agree to get him for her.

"Bring Peter straight here," Gerhard said. "It doesn't matter if he vomited on his school blazer. I'll be waiting in my office."

"Frau Schliemann, Peter won't be allowed to attend class again unless you bring a report confirming he doesn't have typhoid," the principal called out as they were leaving his office.

During the cab ride, Peter felt nauseous, and they had to pull over twice. Although he heaved on the side of the street, nothing came up. The driver clucked under his breath, but at least he didn't throw them out of his cab, as Elsa had feared.

Gerhard was waiting at the main entrance of the university. "Go to my office and have a seat," he said to Elsa. "I'll bring Peter there when the tests are done."

Sitting at Gerhard's desk, Elsa listened to the tick-tock of the clock, which was telling her she'd been waiting for a mere twenty minutes. Gradually, the question drumming in her mind drowned out the clock and even the beat of her own heart: What would she do if Peter had typhoid?

She reached over and picked up the phone.

"Yes?" a woman's voice said.

She gave the operator Madame's phone number.

"Hello?"

"Madame, it's me, Elsa. You are good?" she asked in halting Turkish.

"I should be asking you that. Is everything okay?"

"They are doing tests. If Peter has typhoid, what will I do?"

"You'll take care of him until he's better. He might not even have typhoid."

"Is Susy upsetting you?"

"I'm managing. Don't worry about us."

"Madame, how can I repay you?"

"With a tube of lipstick and a bottle of nail polish," Madame said.

When Gerhard's assistant, Necmi, stepped into the room, Elsa ended the call.

"Hello, Mrs. Schliemann," Necmi said. "There's only one test left. We're waiting for a fecal specimen."

"A what?"

"You know—a stool sample."

"A stool?"

"Forgive my language, Mrs. Schliemann. They need your son to shit."

"Ah, I see. Mr. Necmi, what will happen if Peter has typhoid?"

"He'll be put on a liquid diet for a while to protect his intestines. He'll lose some weight, but he'll recover over time. You'll need to separate his dishes and utensils from the rest of the family's. Oh, and disinfect your house every day."

"Could he die?" Elsa's voice was trembling.

"Die? No! Professors and their families don't die from typhoid. That only happens to patients whose families are too ignorant to know how to care for them. Elsa Hanım, are you crying? Believe me, there's nothing to worry about. And I have some good news to take your mind off this. Atatürk's just invited Carl Erbert, the famous director, to come to Turkey and open a theater department. It won't be long before you Germans outnumber us Turks."

"But Peter's typhoid—"

"Your son hasn't even been diagnosed with typhoid. There's no need to be so worried. What about the Olympics this summer? Are you going to go to Berlin?"

"The Olympics? Mr. Necmi, if my family went to Germany, they'd—"

"Oh, I'm so sorry. I completely forgot. Please forgive me."

Elsa was rescued from the well-meaning assistant by Gerhard and Peter.

"Is it typhoid?" she cried.

"I doubt it," her husband said. "But we'll have to wait until tomorrow for the analysis of the stool sample. The blood test results will be ready in about an hour."

"If it's not typhoid, what is it?"

"Your son has confessed to getting *macun*—you know, that Turkish toffee on a stick—from the street vendor in front of his school. Even worse, on a dare from his friends, he ate five of them. To act like such an idiot at his age . . . I wonder who the boy takes after?"

"You've always been the genius in the family, so I suppose you must mean me," Elsa said.

Gerhard gaped at his wife. When had she become so sensitive? Had he been neglecting her? It's true that he and the other émigrés worked long hours. But they were dedicated scientists determined to give back to their host country. He didn't think he deserved to be snapped at.

The blood test was negative, but they still needed the stool sample results for confirmation. Peter stretched out his legs and slumped in his chair. Elsa rested her hand on his forehead. At least he didn't have a fever.

"Why don't you go home now?" Gerhard said. "Peter can spend the night at the hospital here. He'll be well taken care of. It's probably a good idea to keep him and Susy apart right now, anyway."

"I'm not leaving him."

"Don't be ridiculous. What about Susy?"

"Madame can look after her."

"Elsa, please be reasonable. I'll stay here with Peter. You don't even have a change of clothes with you. And there are no extra beds or private toilets in the patients' rooms, either. Please."

"I'm his mother!"

"And I'm his father—or at least I assume I am."

Elsa glared at him. He went to her and put his hands on her shoulders.

"Don't worry, my dear. I'll bring Peter home tomorrow as soon as we know the results. If it is typhoid, though, we'll have to take precautions. I might even suggest that you take Susy to the von Hippels' for a few days. I'm sure she won't mind. Nothing would make her happier than playing with their little Arnt all day."

"Arnt's so much younger than she is."

"Yes, but they play so nicely."

Elsa finally relented. She knew she shouldn't inconvenience Madame for much longer, and she wondered how Susy was doing. Gerhard promised to call the second the test results came back. Before she left, she softly kissed Peter, who'd fallen asleep, on the forehead.

When she rang Madame's doorbell, it was nearly six o'clock. The door swung open, and Elsa took a step back in horror. Beaming at her in delight was Susy, dressed in a velvet turban and skirt that, even pulled up to her neck, still trailed across the floor. Her eyelids were painted green, her eyebrows penciled black, her lips and nails a vivid red. Elsa groaned at the thought of how long it would take to restore her daughter's face to its cherubic innocence. She thanked Madame, and together they stripped the protesting Susy of her turban and skirt. By roughly tugging the girl's arm every few steps, Elsa was able to get her home and seated at the dressing table. Nearly half an hour and a quarter tub of Pertev Cream later, her work was done. Elsa decided to send Susy to bed a little early.

"But I'm not tired, Mutti."

"I don't care. It's your bedtime."

Susy dragged a chair over to the dresser, climbed up, got the Art Deco clock, and carried it over to her mother in both hands. "Look, Mutti! When the long needle is here and the short needle is here, it's bedtime."

When had her little girl learned to tell the time? She was only three years old!

Gerhard was sitting on a hard chair next to Peter's bed, thinking over what his wife had said. Something about him being the family genius, which would make her the idiot. And recently she'd said something about wanting to be treated as an equal. What had he done or failed to do? He thought himself a considerate man, but if he'd somehow hurt the feelings of his own wife, perhaps he was doing something wrong?

Maybe Elsa wasn't happy in Istanbul. She never complained, but, truth be told, he realized now that he hadn't made any serious efforts to discover her true feelings. He'd been focused on his success at the hospital and the medical school to the exclusion of all else, even his family. He, too, was a stranger in this country, and he was determined to earn the respect and appreciation he had once known in Germany. His patients, their families, and his students—with a few rare exceptions— were not the problem. It was the chancellor and the deans.

Together with Professors Nissen, Liepmann, and Igersheimer, Gerhard had been working miracles at the hospital. Thousands of patients passed through their clinics every day. Most were too poor to pay, but wealthier Turks, too, had stopped seeking treatment abroad and instead came from across Turkey to be cared for by the German doctors everyone was talking about.

Their fame had long since spread beyond the walls of the university. When Professor Nissen gave a public lecture, the hall filled with doctors from Istanbul's private hospitals, as well as academics and thousands of students from outside of the medical field.

And along with doctors, hundreds of women had attended a similar lecture given by Professor Liepmann, the chair of gynecology.

Professor Igersheimer had received a standing ovation when he told his students, "If you continue to study this diligently, you will make some major discoveries within a few years. In the field of medicine, the sun will rise once again in the East."

But even as the professor spoke, a Turkish doctor had leaned over and whispered into Gerhard's ear: "We're kidding ourselves. The Turks could never produce an Einstein."

At the time, Gerhard was outraged. But now, as he looked around his son's hospital room, at the peeling, shabby walls and the rusty bed frame with its sagging mattress, he had to admit he knew what the doctor meant.

The deficiencies at the clinics and laboratories still hadn't been addressed. The administrators resisted appeals for things as basic as a fresh coat of paint. On the other hand, Gerhard knew that Turkey was still feeling the effects of the 1929–1933 financial crisis. Foreign trade had fallen and tax revenues were down. Resources were scarce. Even so, Turkey was a proud and unbowed country, and Gerhard was glad to have come here. He had to admit to himself, though, that his work was beginning to wear him down.

The test results arrived in the morning. Peter didn't have typhoid. Instead of rejoicing, Gerhard started worrying. What was wrong with his son, then? Too many sweets could cause nausea, but the severe stomach cramps and uncontrolled vomiting suggested something more serious. He went into Peter's room and looked at his son, who was still asleep. Against the white sheets, the poor boy looked as fragile as a slender, dry branch. Gerhard didn't have the heart to wake him up. He walked to the head surgeon's office instead. Before he called Elsa, he wanted to consult with Eckstein, a pediatrician based in Ankara.

It was Gerhard who, at that meeting in Ankara nearly three years earlier, had recommended Albert Eckstein as head of the pediatric department in the teaching hospital then being built in the capital city. Eckstein had accepted immediately and had since become something of a legend. In addition to reorganizing the pediatrician clinic, Eckstein had personally treated the children and grandchildren of everyone from Ambassador von Papen to civil servants of all levels and wealthy provincial landholders. He and his wife, a fellow doctor, had traveled to the remotest villages of west and central Anatolia to conduct a demographic and statistical survey of childhood disease.

When Gerhard was put through to Eckstein's office in a mere fifteen minutes, he couldn't help wondering if his friend was also responsible for the health of the switchboard operators' children. Having successfully made an appointment for Peter, Gerhard asked the chief surgeon's secretary to reserve a sleeping car on the train to Ankara.

Rubbing his hands together, he smiled. A trip to Ankara would be good for the whole family. And he would be able to spend time with Elsa.

Turk! Be Proud, Work Hard, Trust ... and Scheme

At eight o'clock in the morning, the Schliemanns got off the train and into a cab that took them straight to Eckstein's consultancy. After a thorough examination, Eckstein concluded that Peter had suffered a particularly ugly bout of food poisoning, probably compounded by some kind of food-related allergy or intolerance. Gerhard blamed the dyes in the Turkish taffy, but he and Elsa agreed to write down everything Peter ate and note any reactions to certain foods over the coming weeks.

Eckstein's assurances had lifted everyone's spirits, and there was nothing to stop the family from enjoying the sights of Ankara for the rest of the day. Their first stop was the manmade lake in Youth Park, where they rowed in circles in a pair of rented boats. Next, they strolled toward the main square, Kızılay. Gerhard was stunned by the progress that had been made in just a short time. The saplings were taller than him now, and the sycamores were high enough to cast a shadow. Not a single vacant lot remained on the main boulevard. Reaching the square, they sat down on one of the benches encircling the ornamental fountain and sampled the famous mineral water sold at a nearby stand. Spotting a monumental granite wall across the street, they ambled over for a closer look at the freestanding figures in the front and at the bas-relief of Atatürk flanked by four naked youths on the back. The children clambered up onto the pedestal, which was emblazoned with the words: "Turk, be proud, work hard, and trust."

Next, they took a cab to the Atatürk Forest Farm, where they had lunch and wandered through the arboretum. Along with the tens of thousands of trees from around the world, Atatürk had imported seeds to test farming techniques in the barren lands of central Anatolia, where onions and potatoes had been the only crops grown.

The children quickly grew tired of urban agriculture, so after a while, Gerhard took his family to Karpiç for an early dinner before their train. The restaurant had relocated to the main boulevard, but Gerhard was relieved to find that the menu was unchanged. He ordered the chicken Kiev in memory of that long-ago lunch with Malche. Elsa wanted to try the borsch, whose fame had spread as far as Istanbul. Susy stuck with the familiar Turkish meatballs, and Peter, after some debate, was permitted the schnitzel. The boy couldn't be expected to go hungry, whatever the doctor might say. At his wife's mention of the doctor, Gerhard asked if the children wanted to hear a funny story about Eckstein.

"Tell us, Daddy," Susy begged.

"When Dr. Eckstein came to Turkey, he brought a top-notch camera with him, and he's been taking photographs of all the places he visits. He even put on an exhibit of his best work from the Anatolian countryside. One of those pictures showed a village girl among bunches of grapes. It was so good that the treasury asked Eckstein if they could use the image on a new banknote. Eckstein agreed, of course, but nobody thought to ask the girl or her family for permission. One day, the girl's older brother arrived out of nowhere and accused the doctor of disgracing his sister."

"They should have paid the family."

"Elsa, the issue was the family's honor. The brother couldn't bear the thought of millions of men handling money with his sister's picture on it. But it was too late. The bills were already in circulation. If Turkish bureaucrats hadn't intervened, Eckstein's innocent hobby could have resulted in a bloody nose or worse. The very concept of a hobby was so foreign—"

"It still is," Elsa said.

"Well, one day, the Turks will have hobbies, too," Gerhard said. "Right now, the only thing they have time for is work. You saw what was written on that memorial: 'Work hard!' Work hard and catch up with the times!"

Back in Istanbul the following morning, the family took the ferry from Haydarpaşa station, on the Asian shore, to Karaköy, just down the hill from their apartment. Having helped his wife and children into a cab, Gerhard got on the tram that would take him to the university.

Madame intercepted Elsa and the children in the stairwell. She asked after Peter's health, then said that a Mrs. von Hippel had called. Elsa was taken aback. She was sure she hadn't given Madame's number to Dagmar. It must be important. Before even going upstairs, she went into Madame's apartment and dialed the number Dagmar had left.

She answered on the first ring.

"Dagmar? It's Elsa. Is everything all right?"

"Not really. Arthur's in trouble. He needs to talk to Gerhard. Would you be able to come by this evening?"

"Well, we only just arrived from Ankara. I'd have to find a babysitter for the children. I'll tell you what—why don't you and Arthur come here this evening? I'll rustle up something for dinner."

"Don't go to any trouble, Elsa. We need your friendship right now, not a fancy meal."

When Gerhard stepped through the front door that evening, the dining room table was laid for guests, and an appetizing smell was coming from the kitchen. Elsa called to him and told him that the von Hippels were coming over for dinner. His first thought was: *I'll never understand my wife.* He was finally home after a long day at work and a night on the train, and Elsa had suddenly decided to invite company over. Not to mention that it was Fatma's day off.

He went into the kitchen and looked at the dried tomato and yoghurt soup bubbling next to a pot of potatoes. Sausages were roasting in the oven.

"Elsa, I wish you'd picked a different evening. We could have left the children with Fatma and treated the von Hippels to Russian food at Rejans."

"Dagmar said that Arthur needed to talk to you at once. Something's happened."

"What is it?"

"She didn't tell me. Can you get Susy ready for bed?"

When the von Hippels arrived a short time later, Gerhard steered his colleague to the study and shut the door behind them.

"What's happened, Arthur?" he asked.

"I've already told you about my assistant, the one who resents me? That it should come to this . . ."

"Start at the beginning."

"I was giving a lecture on electrical applications. There were about twenty students. I was explaining, in French, how large power generators work. The interpreter was an economist, not an engineer.

For that reason, I was avoiding complicated terminology and keeping it very simple. My assistant, the rich one, raised his hand and asked why Turkey didn't produce these advanced generators. Without thinking, I said that there was no need, that Turkey could always import a couple of generators. The lecture ended and I went home. Well, the next day, I was greeted by a protest, a near riot in the lecture hall. They were demanding a boycott of my classes! The chancellor was furious with me. None of it made any sense. Then I found out that the newspapers were all accusing me of 'insulting Turkishness.' I'd supposedly told my students that Turks were incapable of producing advanced machinery. Can you imagine, Gerhard? My Turkish wasn't good enough for me to defend myself. I called you, but they said you were in Ankara."

Gerhard felt physically ill.

"I don't understand. Arthur, I'm so sorry."

"From what I learned later, it was the interpreter's fault. He'd twisted my words. A deliberate act of malice. He told the class that I said they were too stupid to understand terminology, that it was enough for them to know Turkey could sell oranges and potatoes to Europe and get generators in return. Now everyone's saying that I've trampled on the dignity of the Turkish nation. I know who's behind this, but there's nothing I can do. I'm afraid it's too late."

"I thought this kind of thing only happened at the medical school," Gerhard said. "Listen, Arthur. I'll speak to the chancellor tomorrow. We can't allow this. The chancellor would never throw you to the wolves on the word of a few hotheaded students."

"It's the assistant who has been riling up the other students. I didn't trust him, but I never imagined he'd stoop this low. Be careful, Gerhard. I wouldn't want you to draw fire to yourself."

"I was the one who recruited you. And I won't rest until I've done everything I can to make things right."

While Arthur was talking with Gerhard in the study, Dagmar was keeping Elsa company in the kitchen. Having told Dagmar all about Peter's illness and the sights of Ankara, Elsa had moved on to the difficulties of not having any friends living nearby. It was so nice to spend time with a friend in her own kitchen and to speak German.

"But didn't you tell me that Hanna lives in Beyoğlu?" Dagmar said.

"Hanna didn't leave us on good terms. I'd offered to write and ask for her aunt's blessing for the wedding, but she walked out on us. I've run into her twice. The first time, I crossed the street to avoid her. The second time, she did. Then, by chance, Frau Liepmann stepped into the husband's shop in search of a button. Hanna, who was working there, apparently regrets her behavior. She said she plans to visit us one day soon to apologize."

"Would you forgive her?"

"I wouldn't slam the door in her face. And I'll admit that it was nice having Hanna to babysit Susy. Fatma's husband insists she get home in time to make his dinner, and I'd rather not impose on Madame all the time."

"That foolish girl," Dagmar said. "She lost the only friends she has."

"She's young and still has a lot to learn. I hope she's not unhappy."

"Elsa, it just occurred to me. The Belgian family in our building is leaving Turkey at the beginning of the summer. Would you and Gerhard consider taking over their apartment? I know you like Peter's school, but you could enroll him at Robert College, the American boarding school. I think we'd all enjoy each other's company."

In her excitement, Elsa nearly cut her finger with the knife she was using to slice potatoes.

"I'll ask Gerhard tonight."

With Peter and Susy in bed, the grown-ups sat down to dinner. It was a joyless meal, with the men glumly sipping their soup. After a brief and forced conversation about the trip to Ankara, the von Hippels thanked their hosts and rose from the table.

Once the guests were gone, Gerhard summarized for Elsa what had happened at the university. He was too heartsick to talk it over at length. Elsa, for her part, sensed that it wasn't a good time to introduce the idea of moving to Bebek. That night, as Gerhard lay next to his sleeping wife, alone in the dark with his conscience, he wondered if he'd made a terrible mistake. Not only had he moved his own family to Turkey, but he had helped arrange for dozens of other families to do the same. The anguish on Arthur's face haunted him.

The following morning, Gerhard went to the chancellor's office and made the first available appointment.

At three o'clock, he returned, and ten minutes later, the chancellor called him in. Gerhard began by talking about how much Arthur von Hippel admired Turkey, the Turkish people, and Atatürk. It was inconceivable that he would insult Turkishness. Furthermore, von Hippel was a man who had arranged, at his own expense, for eighteen crates of laboratory equipment to be shipped from Germany for the Turkish youth to use.

Gerhard talked until his mouth was dry, then fell silent.

The chancellor heard Gerhard out without interruption and without the slightest twitch or change of expression. When he spoke, it was in a monotone.

"Professor Schliemann, I understand. I do not believe that von Hippel insulted Turks. However, the arrow has left the bow. The press has reported otherwise. Nationalist sentiments have been inflamed. If I don't terminate von Hippel's contract, there will be a revolt in his department. Some have been lying in wait for an opportunity like this. Please try to understand."

"Are you telling me that you are prepared to sacrifice an esteemed professor over a disgruntled student?"

"No. However, I have no choice but to sacrifice a professor for the good of the university."

Gerhard shook his head and stared in disbelief.

"This couldn't have happened at a worse time," the chancellor said. "You've heard about Dersim, haven't you? Nationalist fervor is at boiling point. My hands are tied. Please try to understand."

"Dersim? What is Dersim?"

The chancellor looked as though he wanted to bite his tongue. The stone face had cracked.

"There's been an uprising in an eastern province, Dersim. For the public good, press and radio reports have been banned. It's a tribal rebellion, soon to be quashed."

"Are you telling me that von Hippel is being let go because of a Kurdish uprising way out east?"

"Herr Schliemann, the situation is grave. The Kurds overran a military barracks and slaughtered every soldier. They've set government buildings on fire. They've cut all the telephone wires. This has been going on for months. Nationalists are capitalizing on the many rumors—"

"But why? How did it start?"

"The Ottomans were never able to completely stamp out Kurdish rebellions, so they eventually allowed them a certain degree of autonomy. Now, some of the Kurds are demanding complete independence from the Republic of Turkey. They're burning down schools and torching road-building equipment. A modern state cannot tolerate this, can it?"

Gerhard shook his head, thought of his homeland, and held his tongue. Now he understood. A victim would be sacrificed to the gods to satisfy the wrath of the masses. And the victim would be the honest and honorable man who happened to be his close friend. There was nothing he could do. The meeting was over. He felt so weak in the knees that he waited for a moment before rising. He'd seen this before. It was why he'd left Germany. Nationalism, propaganda, rumormongering, bans on freedom of expression—was that where this county was headed, too?

"Professor Schliemann, are you all right?"

"Thank you for your time," Gerhard said faintly as he stood up and walked out.

The chancellor was still saying something. "I wish there was something I could do. I don't know who fed those lies to the press, but . . ."

Gerhard stumbled down the hallway, dreading his next meeting with Arthur. What would he say? What could he say? *Thank goodness,* he thought, *I've never met that lying bastard of an assistant. If I knew where he was right now, I'd go punch him in the face.*

Gerhard opened the door to the physics laboratory. Alone inside, busy at work, was von Hippel.

"Arthur, will you have a late lunch with me today?" Gerhard asked.

"Come in. I have something to say."

Arthur knew. Gerhard could tell from the look on his face.

"I received a letter this morning. My five-year contract has been reduced to one year. I'll start applying to other universities at once. Forgive me, but I think I'll skip lunch?"

Gerhard went up to him. "I'll do everything I can to ensure you get a good letter of recommendation," Gerhard said, overcome with shame.

Arthur von Hippel's departure would be a loss for everyone, even the assistant who had sabotaged him. He and Elsa would lose friends, as would their children. Istanbul University would lose one of its finest minds.

A refrain was running through Gerhard's mind, and he sincerely hoped this would be both the first and the last time: *Those stupid Turks! Those stupid Turks!*

When he got home that evening and told his wife, she was as upset as he was.

"What are they going to do now?" she asked.

"They'll apply to universities all over the world. I'm sure Arthur will find something."

Elsa left Gerhard with the children and went running downstairs to consult Madame. She came back about twenty minutes later, smiling.

"Why did you suddenly need to visit Madame?"

"I wanted a cup of her Turkish coffee. Don't worry, dear. Something tells me that Arthur and Dagmar will be fine."

Farewell to the Father

Elsa had learned it was easier to walk down Grenadier Street to Tophane and catch the tram to Bebek than to take the bus. She sat up front with Susy on her knee, eager to see her friends and for Susy to get to speak German with kids her age.

Susy's Turkish had gotten far more fluent than her German. She spoke Turkish in the street, in the park, at her ballet lessons, with Fatma, and now with Peter. Even when asked a question in German by her parents, she had begun answering in Turkish.

The ground floor apartment that was once home to the von Hippels was now being jointly rented by the five German professors and their families who lived on the other floors of that same building. One of the three bedrooms was left vacant for visiting friends and relatives, and the other two were used by the building's domestic help. The large sitting room had been converted to a playroom for the children who were still too young to go to school.

Elsa had decided to take Susy there at least once a week for language practice. Now, as she sat on the tram and looked out at the Bosphorus, she prayed silently that Susy would get along with this new group of children.

The tram screeched to a halt in front of Dolmabahçe Palace, even though there wasn't a stop there. Elsa craned her neck and watched as the ticket collector jumped down and ran into the sentry hut in front of the palace. A short time later, he climbed back onto the tram and made an announcement.

"Our Atatürk's fever has broken, and his blood pressure is normal. But he is still unconscious."

The passengers held their breath as he spoke and exchanged worried glances and whispers as the tram started moving again.

"What on earth is going on?" Elsa murmured.

"Mutti, Atatürk is sick," Susy said.

"How do you know?"

"Everybody knows. He's our father, and he's very sick."

"He's the father of Turks. You're German."

"I'm a Turk, Mutti."

Elsa was reluctant to discuss this with her daughter in public, even in German. She would have to sit her daughter down and have a talk that night.

"And I do my prayers, too. Fatma taught me how."

Elsa sighed. That talk was long overdue. She pictured her little girl kneeling on a prayer rug, facing Mecca. Perhaps they should let Fatma go?

At least the visit with the German children went well. Susy played all morning with two boys and three girls, and didn't even get upset when Elsa went upstairs to visit the other mothers. When she came back to collect Susy, secretly hoping her daughter would insist on staying longer, the child obediently trotted up and took her mother's hand. It would be much easier to persuade Gerhard to move to Bebek if Susy grew attached to the other children. Like many fathers, Gerhard couldn't say no to his little girl.

"Did you have a good time today?" Elsa asked on the way home.

"Yes, but those kids speak bad Turkish. I helped them. Then they got mad at me."

"They're German. They don't need to speak such good Turkish. And neither do you!"

"That's not true! I'm a Turk."

"Living in Istanbul doesn't make you Turkish, Susy."

"Mother, I'm Atatürk's daughter," Susy said in Turkish.

"All right, then, we'll change your last name to Atatürk."

"We can't do that! There's only one Atatürk. Only one!"

"That's true," Elsa said.

While the people of Turkey fervently prayed for their sick leader, Elsa was preoccupied with her daughter and her questions of identity. The girl was only five years old. Was it too late or too early to have a serious talk? Who was putting ideas in her head? Elsa was certain that Fatma had taught Susy Islamic prayers, but this notion of being Atatürk's daughter couldn't have come from her. Susy hadn't even started school yet. What would happen when she grew up and got more independent?

When Elsa brought the subject up with Gerhard that evening, he dismissed her concerns. The prayer mat was a passing fancy. It was endearing of the girl to imagine she was a daughter of Atatürk. And the ticket collector's health update was simply an indication of the people's reverence for the president. He'd be fine. Elsa should stop blowing things out of proportion.

One morning a week later, Madame came running upstairs. Atatürk had passed away. Front doors opened and closed throughout the apartment building. Neighbors visited each other to exchange condolences. Everyone, regardless of race or religion, was grief-stricken. Women and men sobbed openly. Elsa gathered around the radio with her neighbors in the Atalays' apartment. The body of Atatürk, who had taken his final breath at five minutes past nine in the morning, would be laid in the Ethnography Museum in Ankara while his final resting place was readied. The people of Istanbul were invited to pay their last respects in Dolmabahçe Palace, where the Father would lie in repose until he was conveyed to the capital city.

Elsa dressed the self-proclaimed daughter of Atatürk in her nicest outfit and sent her to the palace with a bouquet of flowers in her hand and her father at her side. Susy, who had hoped to place the bouquet on Atatürk's chest, returned home terribly disappointed. After waiting for over an hour to get inside, she had been taken home without so much as a glimpse of Atatürk's face. The flowers had been placed on his sealed coffin.

On the morning of November 19, 1938, nine days after his death, Atatürk's casket was sent off from Istanbul on the battleship *Yavuz* with a hundred-gun salute. A funeral train then carried the body from İzmit to Ankara. Susy and the other children in the building spent most of the day listening to live radio broadcasts of the formalities.

Atatürk, who had always been greeted with cheers when he arrived at the station in Ankara, was met this time by tears and funeral marches. His casket, wrapped in the Turkish flag, was placed on a catafalque in front of the Grand National Assembly. It would be guarded by four officers wearing swords. Tens of thousands flocked there, all day and night, to pay their respects.

The following day, Susy, along with a few other children and their mothers and Madame, gathered again in front of the Atalays' radio. The cortege of dignitaries named by the speaker included foreign officers who had battled the Turks not so many years earlier. Yet now, heads bowed, they followed the horse-drawn caisson conveying the Father. Field Marshal Birdwood, the British general who lost a leg in

Gallipoli, raised his baton in respectful salute. Farther back walked students and teachers, workers and peasants, shopkeepers and housewives. The caisson came to a halt and . . .

As the speaker's voice cracked with emotion, Susy rested her head on little Demir Atalay's shoulder and started sobbing.

"What's gotten into her?" Madame asked.

"Not only does she think she's a Turk," Elsa said, "she thinks she's Atatürk's daughter."

The Late-Night Telegram

The sound of a doorbell cut through Gerhard's dreams. He turned over and kept sleeping. They'd been to Büyükada and spent the entire day out on the island enjoying the sun, the sea, and the fresh air. But the shrill sound persisted. Surfacing at last, he switched on the bedside lamp. Elsa was sitting up next to him, rubbing her eyes.

"Someone's here? At this hour?"

They both leapt out of bed and were running toward the door when Elsa went back into the bedroom and grabbed her bathrobe. In the pale light of the stairwell, Gerhard read the telegram.

> Your father had heart attack stop in hospital stop come urgently stop your mother

Elsa ran to Gerhard's side. Her left eye was twitching. "Who died?" she asked.

"Nobody died. Your father is ill, though. He's in the hospital."

Elsa snatched the telegram out of his hand, then sank to her knees. Gerhard crouched down and put his arms around her. There must be something he could say. Why couldn't he find the words? He kept a reassuring arm around her as she cried.

"I have to see my father. I'm leaving for Zurich right away."

"Tomorrow morning, I'll book you a ticket. Come back to bed, dear, and try to get some sleep." Gerhard pulled Elsa to her feet.

"I can't sleep at a time like this!"

"Let's go to the kitchen and have some herbal tea."

"No. I need to pack my bags."

"At this hour?"

"I have to get ready."

Gerhard surrendered. He followed Elsa into the bedroom and pulled her suitcase down from the top of the wardrobe. She started rummaging through the chest of drawers. It was hard to follow what she was saying, but Gerhard patiently listened.

Susy was still young and could come with her, but Peter couldn't miss school. He'd worked so hard to do well and had even taken private lessons over the summer. Fatma would have to be persuaded to live in for twice the pay. Until Elsa returned, she would have to prepare meals, do the ironing . . . Madame, too, could be enlisted when need be.

"I'll be here," Gerhard finally said. "I can take care of Peter."

"I know you can," Elsa said. "But you bring so much work home with you. Papers to grade. Exams to prepare. Fatma will need to spend nights here. You don't have time to do all the cooking and cleaning on top of everything else."

"Come to bed, darling. Rest a little. We'll figure it out."

Elsa was climbing into bed with her husband when Susy came into the room. She looked at the suitcase on the floor and then at her father.

"What are you doing up?" Gerhard asked.

"I had to pee."

"How many times have I told you not to drink so much water before bed?"

Susy shrugged her shoulders.

"Susy, dear, you and I are going to Zurich tomorrow. To see your grandad."

"I don't want to! I'm staying here. I have a recital this weekend. Take Peter."

"Susy!" Gerhard said. "Go back to bed. We'll talk about this tomorrow."

Susy started crying.

"Go cry in your room!" Elsa snapped. Then she got into bed and pulled the duvet over her head. She didn't even see her husband tiptoe out of the room with Susy in his arms, and had fallen asleep by the time he got back.

Gerhard and Elsa got up early the next morning and explained to Peter that he would be staying in Istanbul with his father while his mother and Susy traveled to Zurich for a week.

"A week without Susy! Great!"

"I'll pretend I didn't hear that," Elsa said.

Susy was still fast asleep. Gerhard had sat on the foot of her bed the night before as she kicked, screamed, pleaded, and threatened. Once she had sobbed herself to exhaustion, he'd tucked her in and kissed her on the forehead. She would miss that weekend's ballet recital, for which she had been practicing for months. As young as she was, she knew that her instructor, a White Russian who had jumped ship in the Bosphorus and claimed asylum in Turkey, was likely to throw her out of the troupe. Madame Lydia Arzumanova was of the old school, the sort who left no doubt that the show must go on.

Elsa packed Susy's bag, dreading the tantrum she'd surely throw when she woke up. She went into the kitchen, where Peter had made himself breakfast, and thanked the stars for giving her such a mature son. Anxious to get his wife and daughter tickets to Zurich, Gerhard ate his slice of toast while standing up and then reached for his briefcase. The doorbell rang.

"I wonder who that could be?" Elsa said.

Dreading the arrival of a second telegram, Gerhard hesitated. Peter ran into the sitting room.

"Mutti! Look who it is!" he yelled.

Gerhard and Elsa walked over to the window and looked down at the street. Meekly standing in front of the door, suitcase in hand, was Hanna.

She looked up, and they heard her say, "Aren't you going to ask me in?"

Part Two

Without a Country

From Susy Schliemann to Suzi Şiliman

Susy Esther Miriam Schliemann was only six years old when she became Suzi Şiliman, the name transcribed in Turkish characters on her new national identity card. It was official. She was a Turk. The implications of this momentous change were lost on Suzi, who already thought that living in Turkey made her a Turk. Nor did the new ID card stop her big brother, Peter, from continuing to insist that she and her family were in fact German. As for the boxes denoting "religion" on the children's ID cards, Gerhard had left them blank. Here again, it was Peter who took it upon himself to remind his little sister, repeatedly, that they were Jewish.

The little that Suzi knew about being Jewish she had picked up from her upstairs neighbors in the building on Grenadier Street. It was with the Elliman family that Suzi had experienced her first Passover seder, had feasted until her stomach hurt after the Yom Kippur fast, and had attended Bar Mitzvahs and weddings at the synagogue. Peter had had a Bar Mitzvah, too, but his wasn't the one she would remember for the rest of her life, even if she lived to be a hundred. It was the day of Simon's Bar Mitzvah that Demir had gasped as Suzi stepped into the street, her hair a mass of ringlets magically created with Mutti's curling iron and her dress a beautiful blue, the organza tulle falling several inches below the knee, just as she'd requested of Eleni the seamstress.

"You—you're pretty," Demir had stammered. "You look so different!"

She still had that dress.

It was Madame Saryan who introduced Suzi to another set of beliefs and customs. Making the sign of the cross, they would tiptoe together into a hushed space, domed and dimly lit, the swirling clouds of incense tickling her nose as Madame knelt, her lips silently moving, in front of a stern saint. Sometimes, Madame even let her light a candle and make a wish. In the wintertime, she would help Madame decorate the fir tree, and began counting down the days until she found a present under it. In the springtime, there were eggs dyed dark red, sweet bread, and chocolates wrapped in shiny foil hiding in the oddest places in Madame's sitting room.

Fatma, who had been a presence in Suzi's life for as long as she could remember, followed a different religion still. For the whole month of Ramadan, you couldn't eat or drink while the sun was up. Why? So rich people would understand what it meant to go hungry. You had to get down on your rug and pray all the time. Why? Because you could only get into paradise if you remembered Allah five times every day. And what was paradise? An endless green garden where Muslims went after they died, a place of flowing streams and tree branches heavy with ripe fruit, even in the middle of the winter.

"I want to do prayers, too," Suzi had said.

As soon as Fatma had shown her how to perform *namaz*, Suzi said, "But you don't do your prayers five times a day." And that was when

Fatma explained that honest labor was also a form of prayer. During Ramadan, Suzi would do the so-called child's fast for as many days as Mutti allowed her, rising in the predawn hours for the *sahur* meal before going back to bed, then not eating again until noon. Perhaps the religious instruction she received so early in life helped make Suzi the industrious and empathetic woman she would one day become. While still a little girl, Suzi would recite the mysterious prayers before bed. What drew her to Fatma's religion was the mysticism, the sense that she could talk directly to God without an intermediary, wherever she was. Perhaps it was the product of an overactive imagination, but there were nights when Suzi could swear she heard divine whispers offering her guidance and promises of a happy future. And when she grew older and prayed that the boy she loved would love her in return, she didn't hear the words of the Torah or picture Jesus on the cross, but turned toward Mecca, reciting the same prayers as her beloved.

But it was Demir, the son of the family living on the top floor, who taught her to love Atatürk even before she became a Turkish citizen. And it was Demir who revealed to Suzi her true roots.

Every day after school, Suzi would spend the afternoon out in the street with the neighborhood kids. One day, when the boys had scaled a high wall and jumped into a neighboring garden, Demir had goaded Suzi to do the same.

"I can't jump that far. I'm scared," she'd said from her perch on the wall.

"You're Atatürk's daughter. Be brave! Jump!"

"I'm sick of you pressuring me! And Atatürk's not even alive anymore. Besides, I already have a father. And what's more, Peter says we're German."

"Then why aren't you in Germany?"

"Because my dad teaches at the university here."

"Why doesn't he teach in his own country?"

"How am I supposed to know?"

119

"I'll tell you. When Germany threw you out, Atatürk invited you here. That's why."

"Why'd they throw us out?"

"Because you're Jewish. You know who Hitler is, right? He hates Jews."

"Stop making things up. You always do that," Suzi said, but it was a troubled little girl who waited for her father to come home that evening. When Suzi saw him rounding the corner, she ran to the front door and waited for him to step inside.

"Dad, why do you teach here, not in Germany? Did the Germans throw us out? Who's Hitler? Why does he hate Jews?"

"Suzi! Leave your father alone. Can't you see how tired he is? Go straight to your room," said Hanna, wagging her finger.

"Come along, Suzi," her father said. "Let's have a talk in my study. I'll answer all your questions there."

Suzi stuck her tongue out at Hanna and followed her father.

Gerhard Schliemann believed that an honest question deserved an honest answer, especially when it came from his daughter, who was perceptive beyond her years. It was time to tell her the truth.

He'd hoped to have this talk with his wife at his side, but Elsa had been gone for weeks now, stranded in Zurich as border crossings were closed and train timetables and routes were changed. He wished she'd never gone.

His daughter, who loathed Hanna, spent most of her time out in the street or in the neighbors' apartments. But his teenage son never left Hanna's side. Increasingly resentful of the woman's interference, Fatma had started going home early, and Gerhard was anxious about leaving the children with Hanna instead.

When Hanna had reappeared the morning Elsa was leaving for Zurich, it had seemed like miraculous timing. Elsa, who for the past few years had been crossing the street to avoid the young woman, found herself drawing up a kitchen chair and listening to her tale of woe. Poor Hanna had bridled under a sanctimonious mother-in-law, had pleaded with her husband for a place of their own, and, when he refused and she rebelled, had been smacked in the face.

"I'm leaving you," Hanna had cried.

"Good riddance!" her husband had replied.

Hanna, whose failure to produce an heir had already disgraced her in the eyes of her husband's large, conservative family, had been shown the door. Now, she needed to save up for a ticket to Zurich, so she'd come back to see the Schliemanns, hoping to be introduced to a German family in need of a nanny.

"Actually, Hanna, my father's in the hospital. I'm traveling to Zurich today," Elsa said. "Until I get back, you can stay here and take care of the children and the housework. Then we'll sort something out." She was quick to add, "There won't be much for you to do, though. Fatma is responsible for the cleaning and the cooking during the week. I'd like you to iron Herr Schliemann's shirts, mind the children, do the dinner dishes, and make yourself useful on the weekends, when needed."

Suzi came into the kitchen rubbing her eyes and chanting, "I don't want to go."

Elsa smiled. "I have some good news for you, Suzi. Hanna's back. She's going to stay here until I get home from Zurich. If you promise to listen to her, I won't make you come with me. You'll be able to perform in your recital after all."

"Hooray! Hooray! Hooray!" Suzi leapt into her mother's arms and covered her face with kisses.

That first day, Suzi kept her promise to be obedient, if only because Hanna had saved her from the trip to Zurich. But by the second day, she had started despising Hanna, both for her clumsy attempts to play the role of mother and for the wolfish glances she attracted from Peter. "Hanna the Worm," Suzi called her. Demir thought it was hilarious.

Gerhard sat down behind his desk and motioned for his daughter to sit in the chair across from him. She looked at him expectantly.

"It seems you have some questions. One at a time, please."

"What are we?"

"Humans . . . I didn't say that to make you laugh. I'm serious. Being human is a serious business. We have ID cards because we're human. We used to have German ID cards because that's where we were born. When the German government took away our ID cards, we got new ones from the country where we live."

"So now we're Turkish! Dad, you should tell Peter. He thinks we're German."

"Suzi, even if they took away our ID cards, that doesn't change who we are. We're still German. I mean, I still consider myself to be German."

"Did Hitler take our ID cards?"

"Who told you that?"

"Are we Jews? Is that why our cards got taken away?"

"Yes—you could say that."

"But didn't you say we're German?"

Gerhard took a deep breath. Nationality, ethnicity, culture, religion . . . how to explain the complexity of identity to a six-year-old? The next question came while he was still thinking.

"Did Hitler get mad at us for not fasting on Yom Kippur?"

Gerhard went over, picked up Suzi, and sat back down with his daughter on his lap. "Suzi, most kids your age might not understand the answers to these questions," he said, "but you're not just any kid, and I'll do my best to explain. What does it mean to be a German, a Turk, a Jew, a Christian, a Muslim? Who is Hitler, and what is he doing? Listen carefully and ask questions. But if it's too much, tell me, and I'll stop."

It was way past Suzi's bedtime when she slid off her father's knee. Things were starting to make sense. But as she was leaving the room, she turned and asked her father one last question.

"Dad, can I choose my nationality and my religion?"

"Yes, but there's no hurry."

"Should I wait until I'm eighteen?"

"I'd wait until your twenties, at least. Do you already have an idea?"

"Yes. But I need to think about it some more."

"That's good. Anything else?"

"Yes. Send Hanna away! I can look after things until Mutti comes home."

"You'll need to grow up a bit more first," Gerhard said. When Suzi was gone, he puzzled over her antipathy toward Hanna. The woman never mistreated her. And if anyone did dare to hit headstrong Suzi, they would get as good as they gave.

For Suzi, it seemed as though her mother would never come home. She missed Mutti terribly. Although her father was around in the evenings, he was always in a bad mood. Peter was in love with Hanna, which was gross and meant he no longer played with her or helped her with her homework. Plus, Madame was away on the island of Kınalıada, nursing a cousin who'd had surgery. There was nobody to take Suzi to visit her German friends in Bebek. Fatma used to cheer her up, but now, because of horrible Hanna, Fatma left as soon as her work was done. Suzi's only friend in the world was Demir. She would always have dinner with him and his family when her father was out. One time, after an outbreak of lice at Demir's school, he turned up with a completely bald head. He looked so funny that Suzi had laughed till the tears rolled down her cheeks. But when he held out a matchbox full of lice eggs he'd collected, Suzi thought he was the handsomest boy in the world.

"You're sure my dad will get rid of her?" she asked.

"Even if he doesn't, he'll make her cut all her hair off."

"She'll be really ugly then. Do you think I should put the eggs in her hair while she's sleeping?"

"Nah, what if she wakes up and catches you? Come up behind her when she's sitting in the kitchen and act like you're stroking her hair."

"No way!"

"Well, then, act like you're pulling her hair."

"Okay! And I'll put some eggs on her hairbrush, too."

That's how Demir went from being Suzi's playmate to her partner in crime. They grew so close that when Elsa finally did come home and tried to keep them from seeing quite so much of each other, Suzi lit a candle at Madame's church and prayed for her mother to go away on another trip.

Hanna

When Hanna settled into the Schliemann home for the second time, she found it was a far more agreeable place than before. The family had recently gotten a telephone. With the man of the house at work and the children away at school, Hanna was free to sit for hours on end, chatting with her friends, chiefly Siranus, the salesclerk in her husband's shop. Siranus was one of her two spies in enemy territory. The other was Rebeka, the sister-in-law who shared Hanna's hatred for their mother-in-law.

On this particular morning, Hanna had learned from her first call that Moiz, who was still legally her husband, hadn't yet found another woman. Siranus swore up and down that if he had, she would know about it. Hanna, however, had her doubts. After all, Moiz was a good-looking, charming man, and his drapery shop was swarming with women all day long.

Her second call was to Rebeka, who told her that the Benhayim family planned to use Hanna's infertility as their legal grounds for divorce. Hanna nearly screamed. Why was she still being blamed? She was the one who had visited specialists, midwives, and traditional

Ayşe Kulin

healers. Everything was normal. It was obviously her husband's fault, not hers. There were new tests just for men—that's what the doctor had said. If Moiz had agreed to those tests, they might even have been able to cure him. The man was an idiot.

Her husband prided himself on the vigor with which he performed his marital duties. He'd loved to boast that his extended family had been producing a minimum of five children a year for the last seven generations, at least. The men of his family were all fertility gods, so there was no reason for him to submit to testing. *Or,* Hanna had thought, *you're just terrified of being proven wrong.*

Hanna kept Rebeka on the phone as long as she could, trying to extract every last drop of information. Sadly, the Benhayim family had already made up its collective mind. Hanna would be known to them forevermore as "the barren bride." She was so indignant that, after she placed the receiver back on the hook, she kicked the leg of the sideboard, stubbing her big toe.

She was making a soothing cup of coffee when the phone rang.

"Hello?"

"Good day. This is Ernst. Ernst Hirsch. Is that you, Hanna?"

"Yes, it is, Herr Hirsch. How can I help you?"

"I had arranged to meet Herr Schliemann this evening at our usual haunt, the meyhane in Moda. Unfortunately, my mother-in-law has just been taken to the hospital. No, nothing life-threatening, but it is serious. A heart spasm. Could you please call Gerhard and tell him I won't be able to meet him this evening? I've tried the university several times, but the line is always busy. I'm leaving now for the hospital. Thank you so much, Hanna."

That's all I need right now, Hanna sighed. At her first attempt, the switchboard operator told her that the number was busy. She tried again after she finished making her coffee. Busy. And once again after she'd drunk it. Busy! She was still trying to get through when Suzi emerged from her room and gave Hanna an evil stare. The little girl

126

was the spawn of Satan himself. She was supposedly home with a sore throat, but Hanna decided she was probably just playing hooky so she could be a pest on Fatma's day off.

"I'm trying to get through to your father, but the line is always busy."

"Ask Peter. He'll call for you."

"He's spending the night at a friend's in Bebek. What was that boy's name? Walter?"

"Did he get permission from Father?"

"Of course he did," Hanna said. She wasn't about to fall into the trap of admitting she had allowed it.

"I'm hungry. I want my lunch."

"Go and wash your hands first."

When Hanna turned around, Suzi stuck out her tongue as far as it would go.

"If you keep doing that, one day you won't be able to get it back into your mouth."

Wide-eyed, Suzi took a step back. Did Hanna have eyes in the back of her head? Maybe she was one of those jinn Fatma always talked about.

Suzi obediently went to the bathroom and washed her hands.

"Don't forget to wash your face, too!" Hanna called. "You've been playing with those watercolors again, and you're all grubby. When will you learn to act like a proper little girl?"

"And when will you learn to act like a—" Suzi stopped before she could say "proper lady." Hanna was standing in the doorway.

"I washed my face. Now I want my lunch," Suzi said. She followed Hanna into the kitchen and sat down at the table.

Hanna had been too busy talking on the phone to prepare anything. She began opening cupboard doors and completely forgot about the promised phone call.

When Gerhard reached Koço's Meyhane, he looked around for Hirsch, then asked a familiar waiter about his friend.

"I haven't seen him today."

The waiter showed Gerhard to a table in the back without a view of the sea.

"The usual, sir?" he asked.

"Yes. Thank you."

The waiter came back with rakı, water, ice, cheese, and toasted bread. Gerhard decided to wait for Hirsch before ordering any meze. It wasn't until he had finished his second double rakı that he became truly alarmed. It was going on nine. He asked the waiter if the restaurant had a telephone and was led to a back room, where he was introduced to the proprietor. He dialed Hirsch's number. There was no answer. He asked the proprietor to check that evening's reservations list. Apparently, Hirsch had originally booked a table for three, later changed it to two, and then cancelled altogether earlier that day. How odd! Why hadn't Hirsch let him know? Gerhard called his own number, but there was no answer there, either. He considered walking over to Hirsch's house, but what was the point? If Hirsch wasn't answering his phone, he must not be at home.

Admitting defeat, Gerhard returned to his table. He'd been looking forward to some wise counsel and cheerful camaraderie. Well, having traveled all this way, why not enjoy another glass of rakı? A little tipsy now, his mind began wandering.

Perhaps something terrible had happened to Hirsch? Everyone knew Hitler had stepped up his efforts to intimidate German émigrés. His emissaries and spies were in Turkey to compile files and to advocate for the dismissal of not only Jews, but also suspiciously devout Christians, Marxists, and even liberals and Social Democrats. Had Hirsch somehow become tangled up in this web of intrigue? No, that was unlikely. It was an open secret that Turkish officials were more amused than alarmed by the files forwarded to them by the Nazi government. These clumsy attempts at character assassination had included the so-called exposure of a "radical Marxist activist" whom everyone knew to be an apolitical botanist. Then there had been the Nazi claim that Alexander Rüstow, the chair of economic geography and history, and who had recently coined the term "neoliberalism," no less, was a Communist.

It was all so ludicrous! How could the Nazis misjudge the Turks so badly? Everybody knew that the steady erosion of Ottoman sovereignty had been such a blow to Turkish pride that the founders of the republic had preferred to negotiate away territory rather than accept the slightest encroachment on Turkey's independence. The current Turkish government was not about to allow a German dictator to set hiring policy at its universities.

As Gerhard nibbled on cheese and gulped down rakı, his thoughts turned to Hirsch's personal life. Hirsch and his wife had argued several times in front of Gerhard. Each time, it was Holde who provoked the fight and Holde who refused to be placated. Hirsch had even telephoned Gerhard after their last dinner together to apologize. Everyone could see how unhappy Holde was in Turkey, but of course, she wouldn't be able to return to Germany even if they broke up. Holde was quick-tempered and independent, the kind of woman who would lash out, particularly if she felt trapped. They must have had another fight. Yes, that would explain why the reservation had been changed from three people to two. But why hadn't Hirsch come on his own? Gerhard took another swallow of rakı and decided to order something more substantial to eat.

If only Elsa were here. Nearly three months had gone by. After the long wait for a ticket, the train she was finally able to board was requisitioned for troops and supplies not far from the Swiss border. The passengers had all been sent back to Zurich. Train travel was becoming impossible throughout much of Europe, so an intermediary had arranged a berth on a cargo ship sailing from Italy. Then, days before her scheduled departure, her father had died. Elsa had stayed for the funeral and was now reluctant to leave her mother on her own. Sometimes Gerhard worried that his wife would never return.

His grilled fish and salad arrived, and the waiter refilled his glass. Gerhard was dimly aware that he should stop drinking. But the warm sensation was so pleasant. God bless the man who invented rakı! The invasion of Poland, the death of his father-in-law, the pressures of work, the mysterious disappearance of Hirsch and, worst of all, the absence of his wife . . . if he didn't have cause to drink now, when would he? He smiled at the memory of that long-ago night when he'd had to spend the night at a hotel. Elsa had been so furious with him! Oh, how he wished she were here now. The smile faded, and he whispered, "I miss you, my darling. The loneliness is unbearable. Come back before I start climbing the walls."

When a taxi finally deposited Gerhard on Grenadier Street, it was well after midnight. He stumbled up the stairs to his apartment. The key wouldn't go into the hole. He poked at the lock over and over. The automatic lights went out in the stairwell. He pushed the button and tried the lock again. The lights went out. Again. He'd just gotten the key level with the keyhole when his head started spinning. He leaned forward, hands pressed against the door for support. The door swung open, and he tumbled onto the floor. There was a woman, leaning over him, her long hair tickling his nose. Blond hair, like Elsa's. Elsa? No, she was away. An arm under his head, pulling him up . . . a woman with sweet-smelling hair. Soft hands, like Elsa's, a woman, leaning closer, her breasts near his face, pulling him up, but down she comes, on top of him now, lips against his. *Oh, this is nice . . . Elsa . . .*

As Gerhard rolled onto his side, he gently pulled an arm off his chest. *What! Whose arm?* Elsa was in Zurich. He sat up in bed. She was lying next to him, face turned away, blond hair spilling across the pillow. *Oh no! Not Hanna!* This wasn't a dream. Hanna was in bed with him. He closed his eyes and opened them. He slipped out of bed and realized he was naked. When had he gotten undressed? He couldn't even remember getting home. He scooped his shirt up off the floor and held it in front of him as he ran to the bathroom.

"What have you done?" he hissed at his reflection. He wanted to shout it at the top of his lungs, but knew he mustn't wake the children. The children! He pulled his robe off the hook, wrapped it around himself, and went back to the bedroom. She was still there.

"Good morning."

"Hanna, what are you doing here? Get out of my bed. Get out of my room. Now."

She stretched and yawned. Propping her chin on her hand, she said, "Oh, I get it. You don't remember a thing. Is that it, Gerhard?"

"Get out, Hanna. I don't want you."

"That's not what you said last night."

"We'll talk about last night later," Gerhard said, yanking her by the arm. "Go to your room. Before the children wake up. Get going. Now!"

Looking a little frightened, Hanna retrieved her nightgown from the floor and walked toward the door. Turning around with an injured look on her face, she said, "Peter's not here anyway. He stayed at a friend's last night."

Gerhard sank onto the bed. What had he done? What had he done? At least he wouldn't have to face Peter at breakfast. He had a splitting headache. And his stomach was churning. He stretched out on the bed and tried to remember. He'd been lying on the floor, in front of the door, looking at the ceiling. And then? It all came back to him in fragments. That's where it started. On the floor. He'd never forgive himself. Gerhard sat up in bed, heart racing. It would never happen again. Never.

He got up to go to the bathroom. The door was locked, and he could hear running water. Hanna must be taking a bath. Passing the door to Suzi's room on the way to get a glass of water, he considered looking in on her. No, let her sleep. He needed to bathe, to get clean again, to scrub it all away. *If I were a Catholic, I'd go to confession,* he mused. *I might even feel less guilty. Gerhard, you idiot! You'll live with this for the rest of your life.* He drank a glass of water and put the kettle on.

"I'm done. The bathroom's all yours," Hanna announced from the doorway of the kitchen.

"Both the German and Turkish languages have a formal form of 'you,'" he said. "Please use it. And address me as Herr Schliemann from now on."

"Jawohl, mein Herr!" Hanna said, extending her right arm in the hideously familiar salute.

Gerhard rushed to the bathroom. He stepped into the tub, which still smelled of scented soap, and stood under the cold water, shivering, for a long time. As he was reaching for a towel, he spotted Hanna's underwear on the floor. It was pink. Had she left it there on purpose? He pushed it behind the laundry basket with the tip of his toe.

He'd deal with Hanna later. First, he needed to call Hirsch and find out what had happened the night before. If only his friend had come. If only he hadn't been all alone in the meyhane, drowning his sorrows. Hirsch had better have a good excuse!

Hanna's Ploy

Elsa's journey would be long, with the possibility of delays and unexpected transfers, but she was finally on her way home. Gerhard and the children were counting the days.

Another member of that household was also counting the days.

Gerhard, who had taken to shutting himself in his study and who rarely spoke or looked up from his plate at meals, had just finished having dinner with Peter—who rarely looked at anything but Hanna. Suzi had been invited to Demir's house again.

"Why didn't the Atalays invite you over, too?" Gerhard asked Peter.

"Suzi is Demir's friend, not me."

"That's what I'm asking. Why aren't you friends with Demir?"

"I don't like playing out in the street. And I don't want to play with my little sister, anyway."

"You didn't used to mind. Tell me the truth. Did Demir not invite you, or did you not want to go?"

"I didn't want to, Dad. I need to practice. I have a violin lesson tomorrow. Besides, Suzi and Demir are little kids."

"It would be nice if you spent more time with our neighbors" was all Gerhard said.

"Okay, Dad."

Peter stood up. "Let me help you, Hanna." He took the stack of plates she was carrying. She picked up a jug of water, and they walked to the kitchen together.

"Once you've dropped off those plates, go to your room and start practicing," Gerhard called. "I'll come in a bit and listen to you play." When Hanna emerged from the kitchen, he said, "Don't forget to pick up Suzi in an hour. She needs to be in bed by nine. She's got school tomorrow." Gerhard avoided her eyes as he spoke.

The door to Peter's room clicked shut. Hanna went to the table and stood in front of Gerhard. Clearing her throat, she said, "Herr Schliemann, there's something I need to tell you."

"I'm listening. Make it short. I have some papers to correct."

"I'm pregnant."

For the first time in a long time, Gerhard raised his head and looked directly into Hanna's pale-blue eyes. When he finally spoke, he didn't recognize his own voice. "How does that concern me?"

"You're the father."

"What makes you think that?"

"I've done some calculations. I'm sure of it."

"This soon, after just one time. I don't believe it."

"It couldn't be anyone but you."

"You're forgetting your husband."

"He's infertile."

"Hanna, what do you want? Surely, you can't imagine that I'd divorce my wife for you. I was drunk. I mean, I take responsibility for what happened. But you are not blameless, either. In fact, I wouldn't put it past you to have a lover somewhere. What is it you want? Money?"

"The baby is yours."

"If you are pregnant—and I have my doubts—I can arrange a doctor. I'll cover the costs. Then I'll have to ask you to leave my house forever. I'll pay your travel expenses to wherever it is you wish to go. All I ask is that I never see you again."

"I'm going to have this baby, Herr Schliemann."

A thousand thoughts passed through Gerhard's mind. Should he poison her, push her down the stairs, throw her out the window? If only there was a way to make her disappear. Elsa would be home soon. What could he do? He was guilty, he was cornered, and he felt utterly helpless. He slowly turned his head and gazed out at the lights of Istanbul. The fairytale land beyond the window had turned into a living hell. One muddled moment of passion might lead to the loss of his wife, his children, his career, and his reputation. If he still retained a shred of honor, he should take his own life.

"Whether the child is mine or not, Hanna, I want you to know that I will not be able to help you bring it up. You're on your own."

"You misunderstand me. I don't want to marry you. And I don't need your help."

His eyes still on the minarets rising from the sea, Gerhard repeated his earlier question. "Hanna, what *do* you want?"

"I want my husband back. I was blamed for not giving him a child, even though I know it's not my fault. Now I have proven everyone wrong. He'll be overjoyed when I give him the good news."

"You want to go back to your husband?"

"Yes, and I want you to help me do it. I've counted the days since— since it happened. But I need the advice of a doctor. Is there anything that could make Moiz suspicious? A blood test, for instance?"

Gerhard got up and walked over to the liquor cabinet. He found a bottle of his strongest brandy and filled a glass. What was he feeling? Not relief. Were he to go along with Hanna, he would become complicit in the deception of a husband and an unborn child. Were he to refuse her, he might lose his wife and the will to live. Why was he faced with such a terrible choice? In a moment of weakness, too inebriated to fully understand what he was doing, he had made a terrible mistake. This punishment was all out of proportion to the crime.

"Hanna, please don't carry this baby to term," Gerhard said. "I'll do whatever you want. I'll take you to your husband's house and talk to him myself. You didn't have a dowry. Perhaps it would help if I gave you one now. I know you don't have a family here to help you make peace with your husband and his family. I'll act as your guardian and help you stand up to your in-laws. All I ask is that you end this pregnancy. It's still very early. It would be swift and painless."

"No. The only way Moiz will take me back is if I'm pregnant."

She planned this, Gerhard realized in a flash. She wanted to get pregnant. If he hadn't screwed up so badly, she might even have seduced Peter, a boy. How could he get this monster away from his family? Gerhard slammed his fist down on the table and bellowed like a wounded animal.

Peter came running into the room. "What happened?"

"Your father hurt his hand," Hanna said.

"Hurt his hand? How?"

Gripping his right hand with his left, Gerhard went to the bathroom and locked the door behind him. He'd leave it to Hanna to invent a lie. As he held his hand under the cold water, he watched in the mirror as tears of frustration and regret streamed down his face.

"That's twice now that drinking has gotten me into trouble," he said to his reflection. "Perhaps there's something to be said for Islam's rules against it."

Surprises

Gerhard waved to Elsa as she came down the gangplank. He ran up and pulled her into a tight embrace, released her, and embraced her again. When they were settled in the back of a cab, he took her hand, squeezed it, and didn't let go.

Elsa launched into an account of her return trip to Istanbul, her arrival in Zurich, the bedside vigils in the hospital, the difficulties of caring for her father after he was discharged, the horror of finding him dead, the tears shed at his funeral, and the anguish of being stranded so far from her family as war was declared across Europe. Then she took a deep breath and asked Gerhard how he and the children had been during her long absence.

"Elsa, I have a few surprises," he said. "I've written to you about some of them, but I suspect my letters never arrived."

"Surprises? What surprises?"

"Where do I start? Let's begin with Hanna. She's not staying with us anymore."

"Oh? Who scared her away, Suzi or Fatma?"

"Hanna and her husband have reconciled. She's going back to him, and just in the nick of time, I might add. Peter was developing a terrible crush on her."

"Nonsense, Gerhard. He's just a boy."

"He's going on fifteen and is turning into a young man."

"Who's looking after the children now? Who clears up after dinner and does the ironing? Has Fatma agreed to live in?"

"Well, Peter has dinner at school."

"What's that supposed to mean?"

"Brace yourself. I enrolled Peter at Robert College. He's been boarding there since the winter semester."

"Gerhard! What have you done?"

"Wait—I've saved the best for last. Darling, this is something you've wanted for years. I rented an apartment in Bebek. We move in at the end of the month. Once we're living near Peter's college, we can decide whether he'll board or become a day student."

"But what about Peter's stomach? He can't stay in a dormitory!"

"Do you think I wouldn't take care of that? The school was very understanding. Apparently, he's not the only boy with dietary requirements."

"How did you get Peter to agree?"

"He was dead-set against it at first. One look at the campus was enough to change his mind, though. Those hilltop views of the Bosphorus, the grounds, the gymnasium, the activities, the conservatory . . . ah, and let's not forget the socials organized jointly with the girls' school in Arnavutköy. What more could a boy want?"

"But to have done all this so suddenly, and while I was away!"

"Listen, it was only by chance that I heard about the place in Bebek. I decided to take a look, liked what I saw, and signed the contract immediately. You know how difficult it is to find housing along the Bosphorus. That same day, I had a meeting with the admission officer at Robert College. We agreed that if Peter's courses proved too challenging, he could simply repeat a year. He's younger than his classmates, after all. Once I had registered Peter, I went home and had a talk with Hanna. She was already planning to move back in with her husband when you got home, and Pera is apparently the only neighborhood in the city she'd deign to live in. What I'm trying to say is, I didn't set out to make all these decisions without you. Somehow, one thing followed another."

"What about Suzi? How have you managed?"

"Fatma is there during the day, and Madame has come back from the island. Suzi and I leave at the same time in the morning, and Fatma waits for me to get home. Plus, Suzi has turned into the building's stray cat, with a bowl of food waiting for her everywhere she turns. I find her meowing at Madame's, at the Ellimans', and, most often, at the Atalays'. Once she starts school in Bebek, she'll settle down and have more of a routine."

"Wasn't she upset when Peter went off to boarding school?"

"Those two have been fighting nonstop. Now they'll see how much they miss each other."

"I don't know what to say, Gerhard. It's true I've wanted to move to Bebek. But this is all so sudden."

"Elsa, this is what's best for the family, especially Peter. Once he finishes high school, he'll be able to study engineering at the same college. Hasn't he always said he wants to be an engineer?"

A new home in a new neighborhood, and a new school for Peter. Elsa knew she should be pleased. But these were major life changes, the sorts of things a husband and wife should discuss at length and decide together. That's what they had always done until that day they left Frankfurt. Now Gerhard had moved the family to Bebek and changed Peter's school without having so much as informed her. Couldn't he have waited for her return? Didn't she have the right to see their new home before the contract was signed? There had been a time when the final decision was always hers. She almost felt like she had returned to an unfamiliar marriage and a new Gerhard.

Elsa sighed and patted Gerhard's hand. Whatever he had done, he had done for her and their family. The only thing keeping them in Pera had been the children's schools. He'd sorted that out and found a home in the neighborhood where she'd long wanted to live. He'd wanted to surprise her. What was wrong with that? She was fortunate to be married to a modern, progressive man whose views on marriage were not informed by religious dogma. But to have arrived home after a tiring journey, eager to relax and spend time with her family, only to learn—while still in the cab, no less—that they were moving at the end of the month . . .

"I wish you'd held off on sending Hanna away. She could have helped with the packing. How am I supposed to manage everything with only Fatma there to help?"

Gerhard hesitated. This was the perfect opening. Should he tell her?

"Hanna wouldn't have been of much help to you. She's pregnant. Or so she claims."

"Oh! That's wonderful news. Why didn't you tell me? I'm so happy for her. Now I understand why she decided to forgive her brute of a husband. I'll call and congratulate her as soon as we get home."

"Don't, Elsa! Don't have anything to do with her. I think she lied just to leave us in the lurch again. She made herself disagreeable to Fatma, to Suzi, to everyone in the house—except Peter. And I saw the way she swished her tail at him. Please, let's keep our distance from that deceitful woman."

"Well, if you say so. But how am I going to pack all on my own?"

"I'll arrange something. If we move over the weekend, I can get a couple of office boys from the university to help." Gerhard squeezed Elsa's hand. "The children are growing up, Elsa. We'll all enjoy the peace and quiet in Bebek."

Gerhard was no fool. He knew that his life would never be the same. The secret would be a heavy and constant burden. Perhaps, someday, he would confess to his wife if he felt certain that she would forgive him. But he couldn't risk it now, not so soon. Without Elsa, his life would be over.

Suzi's Life in the New House

Ten days after Elsa's return to Istanbul, the Şiliman family moved to their new home in Bebek, a spacious apartment with views of the Bosphorus from the front rooms and views of a forest from the back bedrooms. Suzi and Peter would have their own rooms, and they'd get to live just down the street from their German friends. But none of that mattered to Suzi. The apartment in Pera had been her home as long as she could remember, and she was heartbroken to leave it behind.

She refused to attend the new school in Bebek, so her parents agreed to let her stay at her old school with her old friends until the summer holidays. Every morning, she would travel by tram with her father to Karaköy and then take the funicular up the hill to Pera. After school, she would wait at Madame's for her father, and they would go home together.

It was inconvenient, but how else could Suzi keep seeing Demir every day?

The following year, despite all her protests, Suzi was taken out of St. George's Primary. Her parents presented her with two options: she could attend either the Turkish primary school in Bebek or the private American school opened for children of the faculty members at the American College for Girls.

Elsa wanted Suzi to learn English, which would allow her to skip the year of language prep normally required before middle school.

"But I'm Turkish," Suzi said, waving her identity card.

"I hope that Turkish ID does you some good one day," Elsa said.

Certain that Demir would approve of her choice, Suzi decided on the Turkish school. Given the language shift, her father insisted she start in the grade below, and she finished her first year as the top student in her class. Gerhard had been right. Once Suzi tasted success, she wanted more. Elsa was proud of both her daughter for making the honor roll and of her husband for his foresight. Would Gerhard ever be proven wrong?

In June of that year, 1941, Ankara and Berlin signed a nonaggression pact. The decision to remain neutral in the war sweeping across Europe was greeted with a sigh of relief by both the citizens and the émigré communities of Turkey. But would the Nazis honor the pact?

Germany had invaded Denmark, Norway, Holland, Belgium, Luxembourg, and France. Much closer to home, Yugoslavia and Greece were under Axis control, and neighboring Bulgaria had just joined the Axis powers.

Fearing the worst, the Turks began preparing for war.

Men under the age of forty had already been reconscripted, and Turkish troops were massed on the Bulgarian border as a precaution. To maintain this army, a special capital tax was levied, one that weighed particularly heavy on the business community in which non-Muslims thrived. Flour, bread, and sugar were rationed. The Turkish government held its breath and waited, trigger finger at the ready.

The German refugees looked on anxiously. A Nazi invasion would spell disaster, deportation, imprisonment, and maybe worse, but the Soviet Union's friendly overtures to the Turkish government were also alarming. Jews had been subjected to centuries of ruthless persecution by the Russians, and after a brief respite in the wake of the revolution, they were finding themselves increasingly in Stalin's crosshairs.

News was beginning to reach them, whispers of just how bad the situation in Germany had become for Jews, leftists, and other "undesirables." Suzi and Peter sometimes eavesdropped on their parents through closed doors, making out words like "extermination" and "camp," and holding hands when their mother cried. They knew that Gerhard hadn't gotten word from his mother and sister in years, and he longed to go look for them. But when the children asked questions later, their parents refused to answer.

Life had become a daily struggle for everyone, whether Aryan or non-Aryan, German or Turk. Inflation was soaring. Food and clothing were in short supply. The impoverished people of Turkey were surrounded by a sea of fire that could engulf their young republic at any moment.

While waiting in line for flour one day, Suzi gleefully pointed to the surname "Şiliman" on her mother's ration card and said, "See! It's good we're Turks now. It means we'll get enough flour for you to make me my favorite cake."

Now that Suzi was going to school in Bebek, she was only able to see "the Pera Gang" on the weekend. She would invite them to Bebek, but her former neighbors, who had watched Suzi grow up, delighted in her visits, and it was much easier to see everyone if she just went to Pera. Madame and all the other "aunties" and "uncles" always complimented Suzi on her perfect Turkish and spoilt her terribly. In the sitting rooms on Grenadier Street, the two subjects on everyone's lips were the shortages in Turkey and the war that had spread all the way from Europe to

Ayşe Kulin

the Pacific Ocean, where Japan and America were bombing each other. Sometimes they cast worried glances at Suzi and lowered their voices. But Suzi didn't care what the grown-ups were talking about. She always felt safe and loved in this building.

When Elsa complained about Suzi's attachment to the old neighborhood, Gerhard defended her. "Bebek's a little boring for them. Children don't care about fresh air and peace and quiet."

It was true. At that time, Bebek was a tiny community of a few eccentric Turks and a handful of foreigners. Any activity along that stretch of the Bosphorus was due to Robert College.

One day, in June of 1944, the Şilimans invited all their old neighbors over to celebrate Suzi's graduation from primary school.

The grown-ups sat at the dining room table with the radio on, as always. The children were eating at the kitchen table when cheers, shouts, and clapping erupted in the other room.

"What happened? Why's everyone yelling?" Demir said.

"The Americans and British have landed in Normandy. They're opening a second front against the Germans. Hitler's days are numbered," Demir's father said. "The war will be over soon."

"They won't get rid of that devil so easily," Madame said. "He'll find a way yet to come out on top."

Two months later, the people of Turkey woke up on the morning of August 2, 1944, to learn that their republic had severed all diplomatic relations and commercial ties with Germany. The approximately six hundred German citizens living in Turkey were to be immediately interned in camps in the rural provinces of Kırşehir, Yozgat, and Çorum.

It was so hot the following morning that Suzi left the house early to sit by the water and wait for her friends. Freddy and his sister, Gerta, were nowhere to be seen. Hans and his brother didn't come to play, either. Where was everybody? She ran over to Freddy's house. A servant opened the door. Inside, others were wrapping things in paper and putting them into cardboard boxes.

Suzi didn't understand what the tearful servants were trying to explain. This time, she ran home. Her mother said that Gerta and Hans and all the other children had gone on vacation to a town in Anatolia. Suzi wasn't buying it. She ran to the corner grocery and called Demir. He always told her the truth.

That afternoon, Suzi went to Bebek Park with Demir, Simon, and his sister, Selin. Suzi couldn't believe her ears. Internment? Freddy, Gerta, and the other kids were friends, not enemies!

"But they're not Turkish," Demir said.

"They were born in Germany, like me. What's wrong with that?"

"You have a Turkish ID card. They don't."

"Why don't they?"

"They didn't want to become Turkish. They probably thought they could go back to Germany one day after Hitler was gone."

"Who wouldn't want to be Turkish?"

"People don't always want the same things, Suzi!" Simon said. "It's time you grew up. Being Turkish isn't always like the songs they teach you in school."

"Demir! Did you hear what Simon said?"

"He's saying that Gerta didn't choose to go on vacation. She had to. They made her."

"Who made her?"

"Turkey. The government."

"Why would the government make people go on vacation?" Suzi said.

But even Demir couldn't satisfy her questions this time. It was a dejected Suzi who came home that evening and sat down with her father.

What her father said didn't make much sense either.

"Turkey tried to stay out of the war, but then decided not to have any relations with Germany. Your friends are German, so they were sent somewhere—where they could be safe, let's say. This kind of thing happens in wartime. The Americans are doing it, too, with the Japanese people who live there. Nobody's perfect, and no country is perfect, either."

Now eleven years old, Suzi had more questions than ever, and none of them seemed to have any good answers.

When Gerta and the others were allowed to come home two months later, they had so much to tell her. They'd been living in an empty school in Çorum with a lot of other Germans. This was the first time Suzi learned about the realities of provincial life far from cosmopolitan Istanbul, and it was a German girl who first taught her about Anatolia.

For some months, Suzi had been taking piano lessons from Uncle Hirsch's mother-in-law, who lived with him and his wife, Holde. Uncle Hirsch had traveled all over Turkey and even stayed for a couple of months in a town somewhere in Anatolia. Suzi decided to ask him about what Gerta had said.

Suzi learned that there were still villages and even towns with no toilets, no running water, and no electricity. She couldn't imagine what that was like. Many of the grown-ups couldn't read and write. Children didn't go to school. Girls were draped from head to foot in black. Why would anyone dress like that?

But Uncle Hirsch also told her that Turkish villagers showed their guests a kind of love and respect found nowhere else in the world. The Turkish phrase for "unexpected guest," he explained, is "guest of God." Suzi sat down on the piano stool prouder than ever to be a Turk.

When the lesson was over and she walked down the hallway to the bathroom, she was surprised to see boxes filled with books and shoes.

"Are you moving?" she asked Auntie Holde's mother.

"Holde and I are staying here. Your Uncle Hirsch is leaving. He has a new job at the law school in Ankara."

Suzi ran into the dining room, where Hirsch was organizing piles of paper on a table in the corner. "Is it true you're going to Ankara?"

"Yes, Suzi."

"But what'll you do all alone in Ankara? You'll get lonely."

"I won't be on my own, Suzi. I'm friends with a couple there. Dr. Praetorius and his wife teach at the conservatory. I'm going to stay in their spare room, and we'll play chamber music every weekend. I'll be surrounded by music. What could be better than that?"

"But your wife's here!" Suzi said.

"Of course I'll miss Holde and my home, but I must go to Ankara," Hirsch lied. He couldn't tell a child that he had applied for a position in Ankara to get away from his wife.

When Suzi returned to her apartment building that day, Peter was passing through the garden on his way home. They teased and jostled each other as Peter unlocked the door. When they heard shouting in their parents' bedroom, they tiptoed over and listened.

"Didn't I tell you never to let her in our house?" Gerhard was shouting.

"Gerhard! Don't be ridiculous. She came by with her little girl. How could I chase her away? And her daughter's just adorable."

"Why would she suddenly show up at our door? What did she want? Money?"

"Well, actually, this wasn't the first time she's visited. It's happened a few times before, but I didn't want to mention it. I still don't understand why you're so angry with her. And after all these years. Just let it go."

"Elsa! You mean you lied to me?"

"I didn't lie. I just didn't tell you."

"How many times has she been here?"

"The first time was right after her baby was born. And there were a few times after that. Why does it matter? Why are you so upset? She makes sure to come when you're not home. She's all alone in Istanbul. She hasn't got any relatives, any of her own people—"

"What do you mean? Isn't her husband Jewish?"

"Sure, but she's from Germany, the same as us."

"Didn't I tell you how she tried to seduce Peter? Do I have to spell it out? She's an unprincipled and loose woman, Elsa!"

Peter leaned over and whispered into Suzi's ear. "Dad's exaggerating."

"No, he's not!" Suzi said. "She kept bending over when she was serving dinner. I saw you looking inside her blouse. Dad's right. She was doing it on purpose."

"She was not. She's pretty, so of course I looked at her."

"She did it to Dad, too. She'd always come out of the bathroom half naked. Wake up!"

"You were just a little kid then. What would you know?"

"Shut up! I know a lot more than you think."

They both pressed their ears to the door again.

"How can you be so vindictive, Gerhard?"

"Elsa, I don't want that woman in my house! And that's final."

When the door swung open, Peter and Suzi scampered away.

"Peter! Suzi! Were you listening to us?"

"We just got home, Dad," Peter said. "We were going to our rooms."

Gerhard stomped out, slamming the front door behind him. Elsa came out of the bedroom.

"Did your father go outside?"

"The older he gets, the weirder he gets," Suzi said.

"Suzi must take after Dad. That's why she's so weird," Peter said. "I've told her a thousand times, but she still thinks she's Turkish, not German."

"Mind your own business, Peter! You're the weirdo. We had to leave Germany, and you still think you're German."

The armistice of May 1945 ushered in the promise of a world where national identity would no longer matter. Hitler's war had killed over sixty million people of all different nationalities. Peter and Suzi were just two of the many children who had been uprooted from their homelands. Little did the children of Europe know that, for the next half century, they would find themselves living in either the Western world or the Soviet bloc.

As the Years Flow By

In August of 1945, Gerhard finally learned the fate of his mother and his sister. They had been killed in a concentration camp. He was sitting at the breakfast table with his children one day, deep in mourning, beating himself up for not having done more to get them out of Germany in time, when the phone rang.

Elsa answered.

"Holde's gone into labor," Elsa yelled as she rushed out of the kitchen. "I've got to hurry." The front door slammed shut behind her.

"Hirsch is going to have a baby!" Peter shouted. "I hope it's a boy."

"Why?" asked Suzi.

"Because girls are impossible."

"She's going to be a girl. They're going to name her Suzi like me, and she's going to marry you one day," Suzi said.

"Don't be ridiculous. I'll be much too old for her."

"Nobody else will want you because you're a know-it-all. And if she takes after her mother, nobody will want to marry her, either. You'll be perfect for each other."

"You and your nonsense," Peter said as he left the kitchen.

The Hirsch baby was a boy.

Hirsch, who had been back in Istanbul during the summer break, was overjoyed. Now as fluent in Turkish as any Turk, and with an impressive command of Ottoman as well, the professor, after careful deliberation, had chosen the name Enver Tandoğan. "Enver" was Ottoman for "enlightened" and "tandoğan" meant "born at dawn" in modern Turkish. His son's name connected the imperial past to the republican present and pointed to a bright future. "Enver Tandoğan Hirsch" was duly recorded in the birth registry in Kadıköy.

Hirsch spent the next two months living with his wife and infant in Istanbul. But then, in October, he returned to Ankara University Law School and the Praetoriuses' spare room as if nothing had changed. Gerhard concluded that Hirsch was still unwilling to devote less time to work and more time to his family, despite the baby. Holde may well have concluded the same.

Worried about the new mother, Elsa began visiting Holde during Suzi's weekly piano lessons. The Schliemanns also invited Holde over for dinner at least once a month. In time, Enver Tandoğan would grow into boyhood and, like so many children born to Germans in Turkey, eventually would start attending the nearest Turkish primary school.

***

Time marched on. One morning, the following year, two letters arrived in the Schliemanns' mailbox. Peter snatched the one addressed to him and ran to his bedroom. Recognizing the handwriting on the other one, Elsa tore it open and started reading aloud to Gerhard at the breakfast table.

> *Elsa and Gerhard, dearest friends,*
> *I am writing this letter with a sense of sorrow I have not experienced since my arrival in Turkey. My colleague, compatriot, fellow musician, bridge partner, and kindred spirit died yesterday morning. It is my sad duty to inform you that, after four days of excruciating abdominal pain, Dr. Ernst Praetorius, the founder of the Ankara University State Conservatory and conductor of the Presidential Symphony Orchestra, passed away in the hospital the morning after an operation. His body was discovered on the floor next to his bed.*

Elsa wiped away a tear. Gerhard reached over, picked up the letter, and began reading where his wife had left off.

> *We have buried our dear friend Ernst in Ankara's Cebeci Cemetery, the final resting place for people of different faiths. As the wind howled and the snow fell, the frozen earth seemed as reluctant to claim him as we were to relinquish him forever. Kate is utterly distraught. She lost her mother only last month. Now, having lost her life partner as well, she wonders how she will go on. I comfort her as best I can. Were my relations with Holde more cordial, I would send Kate to Istanbul to stay in our home for a time. As things stand, however, that would not be possible. You can't imagine how helpless I feel in the face of Kate's suffering.*

Gerhard glanced over at Suzi's furrowed brow and decided not to continue reading aloud.

"Dad, did we know Ernst Praetorius?" she asked.

"You and Peter didn't. He went directly to Ankara from Germany and has lived there ever since. He was a wonderful person. I wish you'd met him."

"The poor man suffered so," Elsa said.

"You all did," said Suzi.

"It was worse for him, sweetie. We were fortunate enough to get a warning, and we got out just in time. Ernst was a Christian, the musical director at the National Theater. Then, one day in 1933, just because his wife was Jewish, he was fired. He applied for work at every single opera house and theater in Germany. He was driving a cab in Berlin when—"

Suzi gasped. "A cab? He couldn't even work with music?"

"No. He and his wife even tried to divorce, but it didn't work. Everyone was still too terrified of the Nazis to hire him. He was unable to feed his family and was on the verge of suicide when Hindemith, a composer well known in Turkey, recommended that Ernst be invited here. They had to sneak Kate out. And that's how he ended up in Ankara."

Gerhard picked up the letter again and continued reading, silently this time.

"Can you imagine, Suzi?" Elsa said. "He arrived in Turkey just two days before the Republic Day celebrations and was expected to direct the orchestra without having rehearsed even once. And he did it! They were so impressed, they extended his contract. Everything was finally going well again for him and Kate—and now this!"

"I feel bad for Hirsch, too," Gerhard said. "He lost his closest friend, and he's still staying in their house."

Gerhard was interrupted by Peter, who came back to the kitchen waving a letter.

"I have some great news!" he said. "This is a letter from the University of California, Berkeley! On the condition that I do well on my finals, I've been accepted!"

"Of course you'll do well," Suzi said. "You're going to America!"

"Oh, son," Elsa said, getting up to hug Peter.

Praetorius' death and his grieving widow were forgotten for a moment as the Schliemanns basked in the good news. Elsa knew she would miss her son, but his stomach had never been good since that childhood trip to the hospital, and she consoled herself with the idea of the healthier diet that would be available to him in America.

After finishing primary school, Suzi had attended the American College for Girls in Arnavutköy. She liked everything about the prep school, a coeducational institution affiliated with what soon would be Peter's alma mater, Robert College. There was just one drawback. All the parties, concerts, theater performances, and other social events were closed to everyone but the Robert College boys. She still saw Demir on the weekends, though. They would go see movies together in Pera and would attend house parties, where they drank tea, ate cake, and listened to the latest songs on a gramophone. Suzi would also visit Madame, who was getting a bit frail, and rather than going home late, she would sleep at Madame's and have breakfast the following morning with her old friends. The Pera Gang had always loved to gather at Madame's, which had the best pastries, but by the end of the '40s, they spent more time at the Ellimans' apartment, the first family in the building to own a record player that didn't need to be wound up with a handle!

When the Democrat Party won the general election in 1950, Suzi and a few other guests were celebrating Madame's birthday in her apartment. The only person paying attention to the radio was Madame, who startled everyone with a whoop of delight. Exchanging bewildered glances, they followed their hostess upstairs to the Ellimans' apartment.

As the news spread through the building, the neighbors emerged to congratulate each other. There were hugs and kisses and tears of joy. Mr. Elliman even did a little jig on his doormat. For the first time in twenty-seven years, and just four years after the first multiparty elections, the Republican People's Party was not in power. Turkey had become a democracy at last!

Suzi and her peers had grown up at a time when fascism and war were tightening their grip on Europe. They weren't quite sure what to expect of democracy, or what it even was, but they were happy to join in the revelry.

"We should throw a party," Demir's father said.

"I'm already having one," Madame said. "It's my birthday today. Come and join us, and if you've got any liqueur on hand, bring it."

"Come on, kids," Simon's mother said. "Help us carry refreshments."

The teenagers fanned out. Apartment doors opened and closed.

"Careful! Don't break that bottle!" someone shouted.

"Does this really mean everything is going to get better?" Suzi asked Madame when they were back in her apartment. The ruling party hadn't yet conceded, and the counting of ballots would continue for a few more days, but the gap between the two parties was huge and growing. Madame confidently opened the door of her china cabinet and started getting out her best crystal.

"Suzi, this is wonderful news. You'll see."

On a September day five years later, it was Madame who would see just how wrong she had been. This was Turkey, after all, the land of shipwrecked hopes.

Suzi's Choice

The year Suzi turned eighteen, she had to decide between being German or Turkish. Germany was restoring the rights of everyone stripped of their citizenship on political, racial, or religious grounds. All she had to do was apply. But if she did, she would lose her Turkish citizenship.

Elsa urged her children to reclaim their citizenship, but Gerhard didn't say anything. His mother and sister had died in a German camp. He would let his children decide for themselves. Peter opted for German citizenship, then applied for American citizenship after he graduated from Berkeley. But Suzi's heart told her she was Turkish. Whenever anyone asked why she had chosen Turkish citizenship, she liked to joke, "It would be such a pain to write out 'Susy Esther Miriam Schliemann' on official forms. From now on, I'm just plain 'Suzi Şiliman.'"

The following year, Suzi graduated from the American College for Girls. The whole Pera Gang and their families were invited to a tea party in the garden behind the Schliemanns' building. There were rows of tables and balloons tied to branches.

After the celebration, Suzi stretched out on her bed and stared at the ceiling, the picture of misery. Everyone who loved her had been there—everyone except Peter and Demir. The first was still in California, while the other was a visiting student in France.

She told herself to be honest, to admit what was really bothering her: there was no future with Demir. She'd assumed that, if she was in love with him, it only followed that he was in love with her. What a fool. What Demir had loved was the attention, the ego boost, the little blond German girl trailing him like a shadow. That's what she'd been doing all her life: chasing after him like a pet poodle. And now—no, not now. Way back then. It should have been obvious to her then, on that day. There was nothing she could do now but stare at the ceiling and feel sorry for herself.

If only there were some way she could change that day, wipe it away. All she wanted was to forget.

It was summer, one year ago. Hot and sunny. Demir had just learned that he'd been accepted by the Grenoble Alps University for a two-year exchange program. The whole Pera Gang was sitting on the top floor of the patisserie in Bebek. They'd pushed two tables together. Peter was home for the summer and, for some reason, he'd deigned to hang out with the younger kids. They were talking about school, graduations, plans . . . The Schliemanns could afford to send only one child abroad to study, and their son, the future engineer, had beat Suzi to it. She would have to attend Istanbul University, and today she was having trouble being happy about it. It wasn't that she envied her brother. It was Demir. He was leaving. And she was staying in Istanbul. Then, for some inexplicable reason, she had turned to Demir, and those stupid words had come out of her mouth.

"So, Demir, I suppose you'll be coming back in a couple of years with a pretty mademoiselle, right?"

Demir stared at her. "Is that what you want?" he asked.

"Sure, why not?" Suzi said, tossing her head. "You're clever and good-looking. The French girls will be falling all over you."

"Fine, then! I will. I'd never let you down, Suzi."

It wasn't what she'd hoped to hear. She raised her tea and said, *"Vive la France!"*

Her friends raised their bottles of soda and glasses of tea. One said, "Let's meet again in three years, right here, and see who's married, who's engaged, and who's going steady."

"I won't be married," Suzi said.

"Why not?"

"My mom says nobody would propose to me. I don't know why."

"I'd marry you," Simon said.

Suzi glanced at Demir out of the corner of her eye, but he was staring out at the Bosphorus.

"That's very kind of you, Simon. But friends don't usually marry each other."

Demir was still looking at the view. She wasn't even sure he'd heard her.

"Whatever. I only said that because I don't want you to end up an old maid."

"Simon, I'll treasure your kind proposal forever, especially when I'm an old maid."

Everyone laughed and the conversation turned to other topics. But Suzi knew her laughter sounded fake.

As she and Peter were walking home together, he said, "Why did you say that to Demir? Why tell the guy you love to go find a girlfriend in France?"

"What's that supposed to mean, 'the guy you love'?"

"Oh, come on. You've been in love with him since you were a kid."

"That's not true! We're just friends. And he's always taken care of me like a brother. Not that you'd understand what that means."

"Yeah, right. Keep telling yourself that."

"Say whatever you want. I don't care. You're just trying to make trouble."

"Suit yourself, then. I was only trying to help. We both saw that Demir couldn't care less about you. And you're graduating from high school next year. Hurry up and find a husband, or it'll be too late."

"You should take your own advice. You're not getting any younger, either, you know."

Miserable as she felt, Suzi couldn't help smiling at the memory of two kids their age accusing each other of getting old. The smile faded. Peter's words had echoed in her heart every day since: *Demir couldn't care less about you.*

She turned her face toward the wall. Maybe no one ever would.

When Suzi became a literature major at Istanbul University, she started attracting plenty of attention.

Mistaking the blonde for a foreigner, young men would circle, move in, find out that she was a Turkish girl, and respectfully retreat. But they'd be back. Unfortunately for her admirers, she also had a knack for repelling unwanted advances.

By the end of her freshman year, she was the only girl in her circle of friends who didn't have a boyfriend. One day, Selin said, "I think your brother was right. You're secretly in love with Demir."

"What makes you say that?"

"You're not interested in anyone else."

Suzi finally decided to let a classmate and fellow bookworm named Hakan hold her hand at the movies. When the lights came up for intermission, he retracted his hand. Suzi wiped hers on her skirt.

"Did your hand get sweaty?" Hakan asked.

"Well—no. I mean, a little bit, yes."

He laughed. "So did mine."

"Did your heart start racing because you were holding my hand?" she asked with a smile.

"I'm not sure. I don't think so."

"My heart didn't race either. We don't have to hold hands during the second half."

"Okay. But I want you to know that I do like you," he said. "You're clever and fun."

"And you're straightforward and funny."

They sat for a moment without speaking.

"I have an idea, Hakan. Let's act like we're dating so everyone leaves us alone."

"All right."

They'd bought tickets at the last minute and been unable to sit with their group. As Pelin and Tahir passed by on the way to the concession stand, they motioned for Suzi and Hakan to join them.

"We're fine on our own," Suzi said with a coy smile.

The news of Suzi's flirtation with Hakan quickly spread all the way to France. That summer, Demir came home with a French girl-friend. The Atalay family couldn't permit an unwed girl to spend the night in their home, so Marie found herself on a cot in Madame's spare room.

Madame and Selin kept telling Suzi that Marie was spending far more time with Simon than with Demir, but she refused to listen. Neither Demir nor Suzi discussed Marie during the French girl's two-week visit. Suzi joined in the sightseeing trips organized for Marie by the Pera Gang and was always courteous to their foreign guest.

Hakan was spending his summer in İzmir, where his family lived. He and Demir never met.

The same week that Marie went back to France, the Schliemanns traveled to Germany. Peter was coming all the way from America to join the rest of the family in Frankfurt.

Nearly a decade had passed since Hitler put a bullet in his head in a Berlin bunker, yet it was only now that Gerhard felt confident his family would be safe. It gave him great pleasure to show his children the countryside of his youth, but he decided against taking them to see Berlin, his favorite city before the war. He'd learned from friends that much of it was either unrecognizable or off limits. Partitioned into four zones by the victorious Allies, Berlin had lost its status as the German capital, and half was now behind the Soviet Iron Curtain.

Even after the devastating war, Germany impressed Suzi with its cleanliness and modernity. Not once, though, did she consider living there. And after his years in America, Peter didn't think highly of anyplace else. But it was no secret that Elsa was pining for her homeland.

The Schliemanns were having dinner together on their last night in Germany, conscious that they might never all live in the same country again.

"Peter," Gerhard said, "if you're able to find work in America and love it as much as you say you do, you could start a life there. Suzi, I know you want to stay in the country where you grew up. You'll get married and settle down there one day. Your mother and I will wait until then. After that, we're going to find a way to spend our winters in Frankfurt and our summers in Istanbul."

"But, Dad, we're a family! We can't split up," Suzi said.

"You'll have a family of your own soon," Elsa replied. "After I married your father, I moved to Frankfurt with him, far from my parents. Life can scatter even the closest family. What's important is that we each find a place where we can be happy."

After Suzi got home from Germany, she avoided Demir and her old friends from Grenadier Street. Invitations came, but she always found an excuse. Demir neither insisted she come nor questioned her reasons for staying away. By the time the universities opened that autumn, their relations were the chilliest ever, and the former best friends rarely met, even though they were now attending the same university. And as for Hakan, he dropped out after his first year, and Suzi never saw him again.

Suzi knew she had no choice but to chart a future that didn't include Demir. Peter had always claimed that Demir was the real reason she'd chosen Turkish citizenship, but she showed how Turkish she had become when she started living by the local proverb "Good things can't be forced."

September Storm

In those days, Suzi wasn't the only person trying to chart a new course.

The people of Turkey were losing faith in the Democrat Party. The widespread exuberance that had greeted the new government was slowly giving way to unease and frustration. That process was accelerated when, in July of 1954, the government passed a law permitting the summary dismissal and forced early retirement of civil servants. The electorate had voted for democracy, not one-party rule and cronyism.

On September 6, 1955, uncontrolled rioting would leave an indelible stain on both Turkey and its government. And, in a quirk of fate, the terrible events of that day would steer Suzi toward the life she had yearned for.

On that sunny September day, Suzi had been out in the garden hanging up a hammock when she heard the phone ringing through an open window. She ignored it. But a minute later, it rang again. Suzi entered the building through the back door and started climbing the stairs. By the time she stepped into the apartment, the phone had gone silent. She was going back down the stairs when it started up again. This time, she answered on the third ring, a little out of breath.

"Hello? Hello?"

"Why didn't you answer the phone?" Demir sounded cross.

"I was in the garden. What's wrong?"

"We took Madame to the hospital. I thought you should know."

"Wait. Don't hang up, Demir. What happened? Is she okay?"

"She fell and hurt herself. They're going to operate. The doctor said—there's no guarantee of success. You should come. She asked for you."

"Which hospital?"

"Balıklı."

"Is that the one in Taksim?"

"No, Yedikule."

"I'm leaving right now. Where are you?"

"Let's meet in Taksim."

"Okay. Wait for me by the monument."

Suzi changed out of her shorts and into a skirt. After grabbing a knapsack, she was out the door in no time. She ran to the spot reserved for shared taxis and jumped into the last available seat, realizing only then that she was still wearing garden clogs. *Whatever,* she thought. All that mattered was getting to the hospital as fast as possible. She regretted having neglected Madame for the past few months. The smell of vanilla and cinnamon buns, the dark church, the endless gifts and comforting hugs . . . Madame was her childhood, her home away from home, her refuge.

Tears rolled down her cheeks as she sat in the backseat of the taxi. She'd been so happy back then. None of the other riders asked why she was crying. Or if they did, she didn't hear them. Suzi had closed her eyes and retreated into her memories. Her lips were moving as she prayed to get to the hospital in time. She became aware of heat, a terrible stuffiness. Why didn't someone open a window?

She realized she didn't even know Madame's first name. Was it Takuhi? Why had they always called her Madame, as though she didn't have a name of her own?

"Don't be scared," a voice said. "The doors are locked. And for goodness' sake, stop crying!"

Suzi opened her eyes and looked out the window. *Oh my God!* What was that crowd doing? There were angry men holding sticks and shouting. The elderly woman sitting in front rolled down the window a crack. *"Allahuekber! Allahuekber!"* came the roar.

"What's going on?" Suzi asked.

"Is it a riot?" asked the man in the gray suit who was squeezed between the driver and the elderly woman.

"I heard rumors of an attack on Atatürk's birthplace in Thessaloniki," the driver said. "That's probably what provoked this."

"What kind of attack?"

"A bomb?" the driver ventured.

"Then why are they angry at us? I don't understand," Suzi said.

"They're mad at the Turkish Greeks, not us."

"How could Greeks in Istanbul have bombed a house in Greece?" Suzi asked. "They're not responsible."

"You're right," said the man sitting next to her.

"Do you know any prayers?" the elderly woman in front asked Suzi as the mob surrounded the taxi. "Open the window a crack and shout out every prayer you know!"

Suzi yelled *"Allahuekber!"* a few times before switching to *"Rabbi yessir velâ tuassir Rabbi temmim bi'l-hayr,"* the lines of the prayer Fatma had taught her all those years ago.

The man next to her leaned closer and whispered, "You'd better not say any more Arabic prayers. But if they ask, tell them you're Turkish. They might believe you—you don't even have an accent."

"That's because I *am* Turkish!"

The man wasn't listening.

The driver rolled down his window, recited a few prayers, and shouted, "Everyone in this vehicle is a Turk. Everyone!"

The men picked up the taxi, got it a few inches off the road, and let it fall. The jolted passengers started panicking. Suzi felt a slight vertigo and closed her eyes. The men found another target, and the taxi started moving again.

"Allah, reunite me with my family. Amen," the elderly woman prayed.

In Beşiktaş, the crowds were even worse. Some of them streamed up past the row houses on Akaretler; others marched toward Taksim. Many of them carried sticks and stones. When the driver turned at the stadium, it became obvious that they would be unable to reach Taksim Square. A mob had filled the streets, the park, the sidewalks. The passengers had no choice but to get out and walk the rest of the way.

Suzi was jostled and elbowed as she fought her way toward the Republic Monument, where Demir was supposed to be waiting. But the crowd was surging down fashionable İstiklal Avenue, and it swept her along, too. Her left clog fell off, and she tried to turn back and get it. Giving up, she pulled off the other one and threw it in her knapsack. Somewhere near Ağa Mosque, a hand roughly grabbed her arm. She turned, and there he was. Demir!

Without thinking, she threw her arms around him. He took her hand, and together they were propelled along the avenue. Along with prayers in Arabic, the swelling throng was chanting, "Cyprus is Turkish; Turkish it shall stay!" A rock smashed a shop window. Then, more and more shattered glass rained onto the street. They were breaking all the windows on both sides of the avenue, all the way from Taksim to Galatasaray. Suzi cried out. She'd stepped on a piece of glass.

"You're barefoot!" Demir said. "Where are your shoes?"

A few shopkeepers were trying to roll down their shutters. Sticks and crowbars clanked against metal as looting broke out.

"Hey! What are you doing?" Suzi shouted at a man scooping up jewelry from a window display.

A stick was raised high above her head. Demir snatched her from behind, by the waist, pulling her away.

"Let me go!" she screamed.

She was half dragged, half carried up some steps and into a dark place, where she was dumped on a stone floor. She sat up in a daze and started rubbing her bruised hip. Demir was trying to bolt an iron door. She limped over to him.

"Were you trying to get yourself killed?" he said. "This is no time for heroics."

Someone started pounding on the door, but Demir had secured the lock. Whoever was out there gave up and left.

As her eyes adjusted to the dimness, she saw that they were in the entry hall of an old commercial building. She closed her eyes and rested her back against the wall, but her legs were giving way. Demir held her up.

"Don't you dare faint on me, Suzi," he said. "Stay strong. We might be here for a while."

His arms encircled her. She opened her eyes and saw, as though through a magnifying glass, his eyes, intense and dark. Demir's eyes. She could see his lips. She could smell him. Then Demir's lips touched hers. She could feel his heart beating against hers. His hands running through her hair. His body pressing close. She forgot all about her aches and pains. All she wanted was to spend the rest of her life in this dark, damp hall, loving Demir and having him love her back.

There was a pounding on the door again. A shouted curse. Silence.

They sat down on the floor, with Suzi's foot in Demir's lap. There wasn't much light, and his fingers were too clumsy to extract the last slivers of glass. Suzi slid over so she was right next to him, their shoulders touching, their backs resting against the wall.

"Why did you do that?" she said.

"Do what?"

"Why did you kiss me?"

"Because I love you."

"Did you bring that French girl to Istanbul because you love me?"

"I did what you said you wanted."

"I only ever wanted you, Demir. Ever since we were kids."

"Then why did you act like you wanted to get rid of me?"

"I wanted you to react, to protest, to ask how I could say such a thing."

"I thought you were letting me know I didn't stand a chance."

"How could you think that?"

"You're the daughter of a German professor. I'm the son of a guy who sells fabric in the back streets of Pera."

"Don't even try it, Demir. Your father owns tons of land in his home province. That's what your mother told my mother."

"I'm comparing their educations, not their incomes."

"What difference does it make? It sounds to me like you were looking for an excuse."

"I have something to say, Suzi. Let's get engaged right away, before we can have another misunderstanding."

"Demir, that's what I wanted you to say that day."

"In front of all those people?"

"We grew up with them."

"Some things should be done in private."

Demir leaned over and kissed her again.

"We need to figure out how to get home," he said.

They got up and went to the door. Demir slid the bolt and pushed the door open a crack. Then he quickly shut it and locked it again.

"It's as bad as before," he said. "We'll have to stay here a while longer."

"Demir, I want to see Madame."

"We'll never find a cab. The buses and trams won't be running, either. I still don't understand what's going on out there."

"How much longer do you think we'll have to wait?"

"As long as it takes. Until things calm down."

"We know every back alley in this neighborhood. Don't you think we could get as far as Grenadier Street?"

"We could try," Demir said, unlocking the door again. "Wait here. You can't go anywhere without shoes." A moment later, he was back with a pair of sandals.

"Winter's coming soon. They wouldn't have found a buyer, anyway."

"How did you know my size?" she asked as she slipped them on.

"I know everything about you, Suzi. Come on, let's go."

The sidewalks were strewn with cloth, shoes, hats, underwear . . . Two women filed past with a wooden pole of some kind hoisted between them. Over it, they had draped dresses, suits, and sweaters. Others were on their knees, picking through the piles of plunder to find bracelets and rings. The reprimands and cluckings of a few ordinary citizens were ignored by the scavengers. There was still no sign of law enforcement.

"Don't let go of my hand," Demir said. "If we get separated somehow, meet me at the apartment building."

Hand in hand, with their free arms held up to shield their heads, Demir and Suzi dashed down the main avenue, past buildings displaying Turkish flags, dodging the broken glass and trying not to trip on bolts of cloth and tangled heaps of garments. They plunged into the first alley. Suzi was limping badly, but they didn't slow down until they had navigated the maze of narrow streets and reached the building on Grenadier. The front door was locked and covered by the national flag. Demir was reaching into his pocket for his key when he noticed something.

"Look! Somebody broke Madame's window."

"Thank goodness she wasn't here. She'd have died of fright."

"And thank goodness my parents are staying at the hot springs in Yalova."

Demir opened the door. Pushing aside the flag, Suzi stepped inside. She got as far as the stairs before she sat down.

"I can't walk another step. It's too painful."

"I'll carry you."

Demir scooped Suzi up into his arms and started climbing the stairs. When they reached the Ellimans' floor, she said, "Let's check on Selin and Simon." Demir gently set her down and rang the doorbell. There was no response. He pressed the button again.

"Simon! Selin!" Suzi called out.

A timid voice asked, "Suzi, is that you, dear?"

"Yes, Auntie Sevim, it's me. You can open the door."

They heard the click of a key, and Sevim Elliman peered out, her face pale, her eyes wide with fright. "Selin and Simon went to the tennis club. I keep calling, but there's no answer." She covered her face with trembling hands and started crying.

"We'll go find them. Don't cry, Auntie Sevim," Suzi said, forgetting all about her foot.

Demir intervened. "Don't be ridiculous, Suzi. How can we get there?"

"The back streets."

"No!" Sevim said. "It's too dangerous. I won't let you. Rafael called and warned me not to leave the apartment. They looted his shop, too. At least he and his workers made it to the London Hotel. He's safe. It's Simon and Selin I'm worried about. If anything happened to them—"

"They'll be safe at the tennis club. The management must have locked the doors," Demir said.

"What is going on? Why are they doing this?"

"I don't know what to say, Auntie Sevim. I heard something about Atatürk's house in Thessaloniki being bombed. It doesn't make any sense."

"What's Thessaloniki got to do with my family? We're Jewish, not Greek. And what difference would it make if we were? Aren't we all Turkish? Do you know what the building superintendent did? He hung a huge flag—I have no idea where he found it—over the front door and told the pack of criminals trying to break Madame's window that only Turkish Muslim families lived here. He swore it on the Koran and said a few prayers. Only then did they back off."

"Good for Raif Efendi!"

"I don't know. Then he grabbed a stick they'd left behind and went over to the corner kiosk—you know, the newspaper place. The next thing I knew, Raif Efendi was smashing their windows. I saw it with my own eyes from my window."

"Our Raif Efendi did this?"

"When he came back, I asked him why. To protect us, he said. He claimed it made him seem more credible."

"Has everyone lost their minds?" Demir said. "Ask us in, Auntie Sevim, and we'll listen to the news together."

The radio was already on, but Sevim turned up the volume, and the three of them huddled in front of it. The reporter claimed that students had been protesting the unfortunate incident in Thessaloniki when certain malevolent elements infiltrated their demonstration in order to cause chaos.

"What do they mean, 'malevolent elements'?" Sevim asked.

"It's probably code for 'Communists.' It's fashionable these days to blame everything on them. Especially now that America has—"

"Did you hurt yourself?" Sevim interrupted. Her wandering eye had landed on Suzi's foot. "Surely you know better than to go out in sandals."

"I ran out of the house so fast when I heard about Madame."

"Ah! Madame!" Sevim cried. "I completely forgot. How is she? How did the operation go?"

"I don't know."

"Come on, Demir. We need to get going," Suzi said.

"Go where, child? Wherever it is, it can wait until tomorrow. Now come along to the bathroom and let me have a look at that foot."

"I can have it checked at the hospital," Suzi said. "We have to go see Madame. I don't want to wait until tomorrow."

It was only after they said good-bye to Sevim Elliman and were in the stairwell that Demir objected.

"We can't go anywhere right now, Suzi. Let's go to my place."

"We can try, at least. I have to try."

They got only as far as the corner before racing back into the building. If anything, the riot was even worse than before. Suzi took off her sandals and climbed the stairs behind Demir, leaning heavily on the banister and keeping her weight mainly on her toes.

When they got inside his apartment, the curtains were drawn and the shutters closed, just as Demir had left them.

"My mom and dad couldn't have chosen a better time to do something about her rheumatism. And it means you and I have the place to ourselves. I'd better call and tell them I'm okay. I'll try the hospital, too."

While Demir was making his calls, Suzi wandered into his bedroom. She pulled back the curtain and looked out at the distant minarets and the Sea of Marmara. As a child, she'd spent many hours playing in this room. Now, she studied it with new interest. She scanned the books on the shelves, the guitar mounted on the wall, the white cotton coverlet on the bed, the jumble of papers on the desk, and the framed collage of childhood photos. In every single one, there Suzi was, right at Demir's side.

"Like a slave girl devoted to her master," she murmured with a smile.

"*Esclave de l'esclave,*" Demir said as he walked into the room. "I am the 'slave of that slave,' if I can be forgiven for quoting Baudelaire completely out of context. Anyway, your obedient slave and humble servant has just assured his parents that he is well and has learned that Madame's operation has been postponed until she's a bit stronger. They gave her painkillers, and she's sleeping comfortably. You don't have to worry."

"Let's go and visit her first thing tomorrow morning."

"You command. I serve."

"Then help me sit down. My foot hurts."

"The only comfortable place to sit down in this room is the bed," Demir said.

Suzi perched on the end. Demir went to the bathroom and came back with hydrogen peroxide, iodine, tweezers, and some gauze. He sat cross-legged on the floor, her foot in his hand, and removed the last slivers of glass, wiped away the dust and grime with peroxide, and dabbed on disinfectant. When she yelped in pain, he blew on the wounds. Suzi smiled, remembering Demir blowing on her skinned knee when they were little. He once kissed a bee sting on her arm, too.

"Now that you've taken care of me, Madame's house is next," Suzi said. "We need to sweep up the broken glass and replace that window. We can't let her come home to that. Do you have a spare key?"

"No, but I'm sure Raif Efendi does. I'll handle it. There are thousands of broken windows in our neighborhood. It'll take some time, but Madame won't be home for a few days, at least."

"Demir, how am I going to get home?"

"I don't know. If things calm down by the evening, I'll take you. Or you could call your mom and tell her you're staying here."

"She wasn't there when I left. She's probably worried sick."

Suzi hobbled to the entry hall, patiently waited for a line, and dialed.

To the torrent of questions from Elsa, she kept replying, in German, "I'm fine, Mutti. I'm fine." When her mother had calmed down enough to listen, Suzi told her about Madame's fall and how she left home to meet Demir.

"Mutti, I'm at the Atalays' right now," Suzi said. "We came here when we realized we couldn't make it to the hospital. I don't understand why you're still so panicked. I'm perfectly safe. And Dad will be there soon. Imagine how Auntie Sevim feels. She still hasn't heard from Simon or Selin. Please stop worrying."

Elsa made Suzi promise not to leave the building and told her to spend the night at the Ellimans' or the Atalays'. Then she asked to speak to Demir.

"Demir! My mom wants to talk to you."

Demir ran into the hall and took the phone. "Auntie Frau, don't worry. I'll look after her. She's not going anywhere. Yes, I promise. She can stay here tomorrow night, too, if things haven't settled down. Yes, we'll come and get you before we go visit Madame. No, I don't understand why this is happening, either. All I know is what I've heard on the radio."

Demir was four when the Schliemanns moved in. When Elsa was introduced as Frau Schliemann, he'd assumed Frau was her first name and started addressing her in the Turkish style as Auntie Frau. The grown-ups had found it adorable, and the name had stuck.

"Okay, Auntie Frau. Don't worry. Suzi's fine. Yes, you can entrust her to me."

He hung up.

"You call this 'fine'?" Suzi teased. "My hip's still throbbing from when you dropped me on the floor, never mind my poor feet."

Demir picked up his sacred trust, carried her to the bedroom, and set her gently on the bed. When she pulled him down and buried her face in his neck, he said, "I promised your mom I'd take care of you. We'd better behave ourselves."

"Aren't we engaged now?"

"Yes. But I'd hate to take advantage of your mother's trust."

"Fine. We'll be good. Just come and lay down next to me."

They lay together in the narrow bed, heads resting on the same pillow, talking all afternoon. They fell asleep in each other's arms as the sun went down.

A little while later, when Suzi opened her eyes, the streetlight was glowing and the room was dark. Demir was asleep. Suzi listened to his breathing and gazed at the beloved face resting on the pillow, inches away. She softly kissed the corner of his mouth. Then the other corner.

Without opening his eyes, Demir kissed her full on the lips, pulled her close, clasped her tight. Forgetting everything else, they surrendered to the urgency of their love.

Later, when Demir reached over and switched on the bedside lamp, Suzi said, "Don't! Turn it off!"

"There's nothing to be embarrassed about. I've seen you naked before."

"You have not!"

"I remember being in the bathtub with you and Peter when we were still babies. And your mother dunking you in the sea, completely nude, when you were about three or four."

"Demir, I'm staying under these covers until you either leave the room or turn off the light," Suzi said.

"I'll get dressed and wait for you in the sitting room. Be quick about it, though. I'm starving. Let's go down and see if Simon and Selin are back yet."

"What if they ask what we've been doing?"

"We'll say we fell asleep. Why are you looking at me like that? It's true. We fell asleep and had the best dream of our lives."

When they knocked at the Ellimans', Simon answered the door. The rest of the family was sitting around the dinner table, their food untouched, their faces grim. Rafael Elliman was telling them about the moment his shop window was shattered, how he and a few employees had saved what they could and had run to hide in a nearby hotel.

Suzi had been a guest at this table so many times, had shared Passover seder meals, had giggled with Selin and kicked Simon under the table, and had fidgeted as she waited for the Haggadah reading to end. The gathering this evening was more like a funeral, a scene of pain and confusion. The radio was still on, and they listened in silence, hoping for an explanation. But nothing made sense.

After she helped Sevim and Selin clear the table, Suzi called home again and learned her father had arrived safely. Demir had gone home to use his family's phone. He got back a short time later.

"Were you able to get through to your parents?" Rafael Elliman asked.

"I left a message warning them to stay in Yalova until things have settled down. I was able to talk to a friend from the university as well."

"What did he say? Does he know anything?"

"He blames the government. We all expected so much from the Democrat Party, but they have a lot to answer for."

"What do you mean?"

"Some of my friends at the Students Association were involved in planning the demonstrations. They were encouraged to march through the Greek neighborhoods, just to intimidate them, nothing more. But things got out of hand. There have even been attacks on churches and temples and schools. Greek, Armenian—and Jewish. All across the city."

"It's always the minorities who get targeted when nationalism boils over," Rafael Elliman said. "Don't forget, President İnönü imposed the wealth tax, and that was back during one-party rule. But minorities suffered the most then, too. Politicians are all the same, whatever party they belong to."

"It's the system," Demir said. "We've come so far, but there's still a long way to go."

Sevim got up to call Elsa. Suzi and Demir pricked up their ears.

"No, of course it won't be any trouble for her to stay here, Elsa. Suzi can stay in Selin's room. Our girls have shared a bed before. I'll call you again in the morning. Bye for now."

Demir caught Suzi's eye. She shrugged helplessly.

"Come and have breakfast with us tomorrow morning," Sevim said to Demir. "Then we can all visit Madame together."

However, it would be four days before anyone was able to travel to the hospital. Martial law had been declared. Thousands of rioters were in jail. The streets were swept clean of debris. Reparations were being discussed. And tens of thousands of Greek Turks would soon begin fleeing their city and their homeland for a new life in Greece, a country most of them had never seen.

Madame lay in one of the hospital room's three beds. There was an oxygen tube in her nostril and an IV in her right arm. Another tube led to a bottle on the floor. Her face was drained of color, and her eyes were closed.

"Madame? How are you feeling?"

Madame blinked at Suzi and managed a weak smile.

"Demir's here, too. Along with Auntie Sevim, Selin, Simon, and my mother—they're waiting in the corridor. We're all praying for you to get well soon. I'm going to light a candle in church and pray until it burns out."

Suzi gently stroked Madame's hand, which was curled on top of the blanket, its veins visible through tissue-thin skin.

"I wanted to talk to you alone first," Suzi said. "I have some news that will make you happy. Demir and I—made up. Not that we exactly had a falling-out. You know what happened. You always said time was precious, and we should never be afraid to show our feelings, that there's no place for pride in love. Well, you were so right. Demir and I are together now. We love each other."

Madame squeezed Suzi's finger.

"You know how much you've always meant to me," Suzi said. "I wanted you to know how happy I am. After your operation, when you're all better, I want you to come with Atalay's parents to ask my father for my hand. But first, Demir is going to ask you for my hand. You're part of my family. Demir and I spent so much time in your apartment together. Do you remember how he used to find the chocolate eggs and give them to me? I've been in love with him ever since. I haven't even had a chance to tell my mom, but I'm glad you're the first to know. I consider you my grandmother."

A tear was glistening on Madame's cheek. Suzi brushed it away.

"Be happy—don't wait—" Madame whispered.

"Please get well. Come home. I'm begging you."

"My turn," Demir said as he walked into the room.

A nurse asked Suzi to wait in the hall. Only one visitor was allowed at a time. Suzi walked out to the others and burst into tears.

"Is it serious?" Elsa asked Suzi, holding out her arms.

"I don't know, Mutti. This is the first time I've ever visited someone in the hospital. At least Madame doesn't know about what happened. We shouldn't say anything about her window or the riots."

"Of course not!" Sevim Elliman said. "Raif Efendi is having a new window installed today. If she's able to go home, she won't even notice."

"She won't be going home for a while." Demir had walked up behind them.

"Why don't you go in next, Auntie Sevim?" Suzi said. "And Simon and Selin can wait by the door."

In a low voice, Suzi asked Demir if he had told Madame.

"Yes," Demir said.

"Told her what?" Elsa asked.

"Some good news."

"Demir, if you have good news, please share it with me, too," Elsa said.

Demir looked uncertainly at Suzi.

"Mutti, Demir and I got engaged yesterday."

Elsa opened her mouth, shut it again, and swallowed. She didn't want to cause a scene in front of Demir or show how hurt she was. Her daughter had gotten engaged without a word to her or her father. Even worse, she'd told an old neighbor first. What had Elsa done to deserve this? Where had she gone wrong?

"Congratulations," she said through tight lips.

An Unexpected Guest

Elsa, who had opened the door expecting to find the grocer's errand boy, was taken aback to see Hanna and her daughter, Rozi, instead. Rozi was wearing her hair in a ponytail and had grown several inches, at least. That tartan skirt fit her perfectly now. Would Suzi recognize her old clothes?

"Good morning!" Hanna said. "I know I should have called first, but I figured Herr Schliemann would be at work."

"Hanna! You gave me your word!" Elsa said. But she showed them into the sitting room anyway.

"I had to see you. I need to ask a favor. The riots nearly ruined us. You should have seen the shop. What they didn't steal, they destroyed. The floor was ankle-deep in ribbons, yarn, buttons . . ."

"I'm so sorry to hear that, Hanna. Now, I've set aside some things for Rozi, but I'm going to have to ask you again. Will you promise never to come here again without calling first? Believe me, if Gerhard saw you here, it would be unpleasant for everyone."

"Elsa, I wanted to ask if you could—"

The bell rang and Hanna stopped midsentence. Elsa got to her feet, but paused when she saw Suzi running down the hall to the door.

In stepped Eleni the seamstress, carrying a velvet dress wrapped in gauze.

"Is that a dress?" Hanna called.

"It's Suzi's engagement dress," Eleni said. "I designed it myself."

"Suzi! Are you getting engaged?"

"Yeah."

"Go kiss your big sister and congratulate her," Hanna told Rozi.

"Big sister? I'd prefer if she called me Suzi."

"When's the wedding and, more importantly, who's the groom?" Hanna asked.

"You know him," Elsa said. "Suzi's childhood friend, Demir. The dress is for the engagement dinner with the family."

"And I'm not considered family, of course. I left my real family behind to come to Turkey with you. And my husband's family has never accepted me because I'm German. I don't mind for myself, but I do feel sorry for Rozi. She doesn't deserve to be treated like this."

"That's enough, Hanna," Suzi said with a glance at Elsa. "I'm sure Rozi doesn't mind one bit. Children don't worry about things like that."

"I'm not a child," Rozi said.

"You're a child until you turn eighteen!"

"That means I only have to wait three years."

Suzi was helping Eleni carry the package to her bedroom, when Hanna said, "Go help your big sister try on her engagement dress, Rozi."

"Don't call me that! My name is Suzi."

Rozi followed Suzi into the bedroom without a word.

"Hanna, you really shouldn't go on like that. That's why Gerhard and Suzi avoid you," Elsa said.

Hanna was preparing a retort when Rozi tottered back into the sitting room in Suzi's high heels.

"Rozi, take those off at once," Hanna said. "You'll fall and break your neck."

"I won't fall. And they fit me perfectly. Can I have some?"

"I didn't buy Suzi high heels until she was seventeen," Elsa said.

"Girls are growing up faster these days," Hanna said.

Elsa got up and said, "I have a few sweaters and skirts I'd like to give Rozi." As she was leaving the room, she turned and said, "You were going to ask me for a favor. What is it?"

"I wonder if you could spare a little something. School starts next week, and there are so many extra expenses, things I need to get Rozi. If it hadn't been for the riots—"

"I don't have any money at home. But I'll come by the shop next week and leave you what I can."

"The shop? The shop's a wreck. Perhaps you could mention this to Herr Schliemann. I'm sure he'd be willing to help."

"I doubt that. Hanna, I don't know what you did to him, but he doesn't even want to hear your name. Still, I'll do what I can. We must support each other at a time like this."

"Thank you," Hanna said.

When Elsa returned with the clothing, she remained standing. The visit was apparently over.

Hanna stood up and tossed her hair. "The engagement ceremony is one thing, Elsa, but Rozi and I expect to be invited to the wedding."

Elsa bit her lip. In the entry hall, Rozi reluctantly slipped off Suzi's heels and put on her own shoes. When they were gone, Elsa shook her head. "The nerve!"

A moment later, Suzi tripped into the sitting room in a midnight-blue dress with a fitted waist and flared skirt.

"Beautiful!" Elsa gushed, completely forgetting how upset she'd been at the hospital. "I wish you'd dress like this more often."

"You want me to wear velvet every day?"

"No. What I meant is, it's just nice to see you in a dress for a change."

Eleni intervened in time to stop the mother and daughter from squabbling over Suzi's style choices yet again.

"I saved enough velvet for a pair of shoes. I was thinking kitten-heel pumps. Let's order them now so they're ready in time."

"There's no need!" Suzi said.

"You're not thinking of wearing flats with that dress, I hope!"

"Mother, I already have that pair of stilettos. Rozi didn't take them, did she?" Suzi found the shoes in the entry hall and put them on.

"Those won't do," Eleni said. "Shoes and dresses in matching fabrics are all the rage this year. And get the hairdresser to brush your hair under in a soft roll."

"I like my hair straight. I don't care what's fashionable."

"After I worked so hard on that dress, you can't get engaged with stringy hair."

At dinner that night, while Elsa was in the kitchen fetching dessert, Suzi complained to her father. "They're trying to turn me into an old frump. Who matches their shoes to their dress? I wouldn't be surprised if Demir takes one look at me and changes his mind."

"And I wouldn't be surprised if he sent you back after a month," Gerhard teased. "That tongue of yours sent Peter all the way to America. How will our young groom manage?"

"We dodged a bullet today, Dad. Hanna visited and tried to guilt us into inviting her to the engagement dinner. Luckily, Mom wasn't having it."

"Please don't mention that woman at the dinner table. Just her name is enough to give me heartburn," Gerhard said.

Elsa nearly dropped the platter of baklava she was carrying down the hall. She wheeled around and went back into the kitchen. *Oh, Suzi,* she thought, *why couldn't you keep your mouth shut?*

But later that night, when Elsa and Gerhard were alone, he didn't say a word about Hanna. After he gave her a good-night kiss and rolled over in bed, she put down her book and stayed propped up against her pillow for a long while, thinking. Her husband, while as principled as ever, was becoming more forgiving and flexible in his middle age. He fully approved of Demir, a hardworking young man of good character with a promising future as a civil engineer. Still, if Elsa was honest with herself, she wouldn't have chosen a Muslim Turk as a son-in-law. She supposed it was fate that had brought her family to Turkey and fate that had decreed that her daughter would fall in love with the little boy upstairs. She briefly entertained and quickly rejected the notion that all these years of living among Turks had turned her into a fatalist. No. She and Peter would always be German through and through. And she would return to her native land one day.

Elsa had expected Suzi to outgrow her childhood infatuation with Demir. As a young girl, she herself had had eyes for a neighbor boy. But the crush had faded, as they always do. She'd patiently waited for the same thing to happen to Suzi, certain that a new school and a new neighborhood would mean new boys. When Demir had come home from France with a girlfriend, Elsa had thought Suzi would finally move on.

How wrong she had been. It didn't seem right for a girl to get engaged without ever having looked at any other boys. But there was nothing Elsa could do or say now. And it wasn't as though she had anything against Demir. Although it would be nice if the Atalays weren't *quite* so Turkish. If Bedia Atalay knew a little English or German, they could have become friends. And the father, Nazmi, didn't speak a word of German, either. Elsa laughed at herself. The Atalays were probably wondering why her Turkish was still so halting after all these years. She supposed it was because she'd always planned on returning to Germany. In the end, she was a guest here. It was different for Gerhard. She knew that if he returned to Germany, it would be for her sake. She'd asked him recently why he still blamed all Germans for Hitler's madness. He'd said that silence was complicity. Well, perhaps, but those who did dare to speak out ended up dead or in exile. She appreciated Gerhard's point of view—his family had died in a concentration camp, after all. But why had Suzi agreed with her father? If only Peter were here! He'd always understood her best. He would have taken her side.

Elsa switched off the lamp and stretched out in bed, feeling as isolated now as ever before in her life.

Life Changes

On the surface, life returned to normal in the weeks after the infamous riots of September. Right on cue, in late October, came an Indian summer.

The Ellimans and Atalays decided to take advantage of the fine weather with a weekend trip to Büyükada, the largest of the islands off Istanbul's Asian shore. Would Elsa and Suzi care to join them? Elsa was hesitant. They lived a stone's throw from the Bosphorus, so why go anywhere else? Still, she relented for Suzi's sake. She was eager to spend as much time as possible with Demir. Rooms were booked at the Splendid Hotel and an itinerary was agreed upon. First, the young people would take a dip at Nizam Beach. Then the entire group would climb the cobbled path to Aya Yorgi Church to light candles and make wishes, and, last of all, they would take a grand tour in horse-drawn carriages. The following day, they'd feast on fish near the quay before catching a ferry back to the city.

On the way to the island, they were sitting in the first-class section of the ferry, waiting for their tea. It was crowded and noisy, but a strident voice caught Suzi's ear.

"You're in Turkey! Speak Turkish!"

Suzi turned and saw a plump woman in a frilly hat.

"Were you talking to me?" she asked the woman.

"No."

"I've been speaking German with my mother."

"I wasn't talking to you."

"Then who were you talking to?"

"Those Greeks over there. They should speak Turkish."

"And why's that?"

"Because this is Turkey."

"Am I allowed to speak German?"

"Of course you are."

"So German is allowed, but Greek isn't. Is that it?"

"I wasn't talking to you."

"They weren't talking to you, either."

"In Turkey, we speak Turkish!"

"Let's say you were traveling in Germany. Wouldn't you have the right to speak Turkish with your husband?"

"Who do you think you are? I don't have to answer to you."

"Hey!" Demir said, standing up. "You'd better watch how you talk to my fiancée."

The mustachioed man sitting next to the woman said, "That's enough, wife! And sit down, young man. This has nothing to do with you. Why are you causing trouble?"

Two Greek women and a child got up and went down the stairs to a lower deck.

"I'm Turkish, too, but that doesn't give me the right to tell people what language to speak," Demir continued. "See what you've done? They left because of you."

"They live in Turkey. Turks should speak Turkish," the man said.

"But their mother tongue is Greek!"

"They should be more Turkish."

"Maybe you should be more human!" was Suzi's retort. She slung her bag over her shoulder and stood up, sputtering. "Is there no escape from these fascists? First Germany, and now—"

"Fascists? You're the fascists!" the man shouted. "German spawn!"

Demir made a fist, and Elsa seized both his arm and Suzi's. "Come on," she said. "Let's go sit somewhere else."

The Ellimans, Atalays, Elsa, and Suzi started looking around, but there were no free seats in first class. They had to separate into smaller groups and squeeze onto the wooden benches on a lower deck. Bedia Hanım leaned over and whispered in her son's ear, "Are you sure you want to marry that girl? Mark my words; she'll get you both into trouble."

Try as they might to shrug off the disturbing incident on the ferry, some of the pleasure had already gone out of the outing before they'd even reached the island. It was a sign of things to come. The September riots had changed everything. The corruption, greed, and insularity of the Ottoman ruling class had led to the collapse of the empire. Now, the cultural mosaic of Turkey was crumbling due to governance that was inept in a whole new way.

The Greeks were leaving.

Life on the islands and in Beyoğlu was losing some of its shine. Particularly hard hit would be that quintessentially Istanbul institution, the meyhane, where the skilled Greek waiters would guide customers through the treacherous waters of alcohol consumption. In a city with no tradition of bars and barmen, it was the Greek waiter who officiated, commiserated, restrained, and encouraged. The meyhanes of Istanbul would never recover.

Then November arrived, bringing cold rains to the city and bereavement to Grenadier Street.

When the doctors had decided in September that Madame was still too weak for an operation, her neighbors had brought her home and arranged for a live-in nurse. Madame appreciated their love and kindness, but she was ready to die. A bedridden life would be absurd, she decided. Particularly at her age. Morning and night, she prayed to meet her maker. By the end of October, she had summoned her attorney, drawn up her will, and bid farewell to each of her neighbors. She was ready. To Suzi's talk of a wedding the following summer, she turned a deaf ear. She couldn't wait that long.

And as it turned out, Suzi and Demir couldn't either.

It must have been eleven days since Madame had passed, for Demir had already placed eleven chrysanthemums on her bed. Suzi had come up with the idea of placing a flower a day, for forty days, on Madame's rose-colored satin sheets. It was also Suzi's idea to wait until the fortieth day after Madame's death to make the traditional cinnamon-scented semolina. This funeral halvah would be distributed to the bereaved in the Atalay house. Fatma would oversee the frying of the pine nuts and semolina, but everyone who had loved Madame would take their turn at stirring the halvah. In this way, Suzi sought to combine elements of the death rituals of all the Peoples of the Book: Jewish, Christian, and Muslim. After the funeral at Madame's church, Sevim Elliman had invited all the neighbors over and served them hard-boiled eggs and wine. They each drew on their different customs and beliefs in their shared grief for Madame.

"I can understand about the halvah," Demir's mother complained, "but what is the meaning of the forty chrysanthemums?"

"Mother, you know how much Madame loved flowers," Demir said. "Suzi thought it would please her. Don't you dare say anything about it in front of her."

"But it's ridiculous!"

"She's just lost her grandmother. This is how she's coping."

"Grandmother? The woman was her neighbor."

"Suzi loved her. And she barely knew her real grandparents. I'm surprised you're even making me explain this."

On the day of the eleventh chrysanthemum, while Demir was at home grappling with his mother, his fiancée prepared to drop a bombshell on hers. Suzi hadn't been herself at breakfast that morning. When she was pouring tea, the glass overflowed. She burnt the toast. She mistook the sugar for salt.

"You're very absent-minded today, dear," Gerhard said. "Did you sleep okay?"

"My exams are coming up. I've been studying too much is all."

Once Suzi had helped her father into his coat and sent him on his way, she returned to the kitchen and sat down across from her mother.

"Spit it out, Suzi," Elsa said. "Something's bothering you."

"You're right. There's something I need to tell you."

"Don't tell me you don't want to have a reception anymore!" Elsa said. "Your mother-in-law would be crushed. And it was so kind of Hirsch to book the hall at the Moda Club. Peter is coming all the way from America to be here on June 27."

Suzi reached out and gently squeezed her mother's hands.

"I'm pregnant, Mother. The baby will be here well before June 27."

"Suzi! How could you do this to me? I thought I could trust Demir."

"It's not his fault!"

"Shame on both of you, then," Elsa said. "Don't expect me to tell your father for you. You'll have to give him the news yourself!"

Confrontation

The voice on the phone sounded serious and determined. A woman calling herself Hanna was requesting an appointment with Professor Schliemann within the week, at the very latest. When the secretary asked Hanna to leave a number, she responded, "No. Just give me a date and a time and stick to it. I don't have a number where you can reach me."

"Might I ask why you wish to see the professor?"

"That's private."

"I'm afraid I can't arrange an appointment until I've consulted with Professor Schliemann."

"Just give me an appointment. It's not like I'll break the door down if he refuses to see me."

The secretary sighed. "All right then. Come this Wednesday at noon."

When Hanna arrived at the pathology department at the agreed time, she wasn't sure she wouldn't be thrown out. But the secretary immediately said, "Please have a seat. I'll tell Professor Schliemann you're here."

The secretary showed Hanna into an office where Gerhard was sitting behind a desk. He didn't stand to greet her. Hanna walked over and held out her hand. Gerhard still didn't rise, but he took it.

"Sit down, Hanna," he said, motioning to the leather chair on the right. She sat in the one to her left. "I'm listening."

"I hear Suzi moved the wedding forward."

"She did indeed."

"Is she pregnant?"

"That's none of your business."

"Well, if she isn't, what's the rush? I can't think of any other reason to do that. I mean, Demir hasn't even found a job."

"Demir is about to do his military service. He doesn't need a job just yet."

"But what will Suzi do while he's away?"

"She'll be continuing her studies."

"Hmm. Good luck to her."

"What do you want? I don't have much time before my next class."

"I want to take Rozi to Suzi's wedding reception. If I'd been able to arrange it with Elsa, I wouldn't have bothered you."

"There won't be one. The groom's relatives and a few of my close friends and colleagues will be attending the ceremony. If the wedding were taking place in the summer, as originally planned, we would be inviting many more guests. I'm sorry, Hanna."

"I don't want this for myself, I want it for our child. She has a right to get to know my side of the family. I need to know that her big brother and sister would be there for her if anything ever happened to me. Believe me, I'm not trying to cause any trouble."

"Hanna, Rozi is not *our* child. Rozi is your husband's child. Peter and Suzi are not her family. It's time you got over this unhealthy fixation."

"If you try to brush me off like this, I'll have no choice but to tell Elsa."

"A moment ago, you said you weren't trying to cause trouble. It seems to me that you are motivated by malice, Hanna. I can't think of any other explanation. I have tried to have sympathy for your situation,

191

but I can't forgive what you did to me. I'm asking you again to stay away from my house, stay away from my wife, and stay away from my children. If you don't, I'll speak to your husband. You'd end up disgraced and maybe even in jail. This is the second time you've forced me to say this. There won't be a third time."

Gerhard stood up, went over to Hanna, and held out an envelope.

"Elsa told me you were having money trouble and insisted I give this to you. Take it, and tell your husband that the Schliemann family wished to help in some small way." Gerhard closed his eyes for a moment. "*Geh mit Gott.* Go with God, but go."

He dropped the envelope on Hanna's lap and waited until she got up. They walked to the door together. When Gerhard opened it, the secretary sprang to her feet.

"Professor Schliemann, I was about to ask your guest how she takes her coffee."

"She was just leaving. There's no need for coffee," Gerhard said.

Up until the moment she had clicked her way to the end of the corridor, Hanna kept her shoulders squared and her head high.

Gerhard reached for the phone the second he was back in his office. Elsa's bubbly "hello" gave him pause for a moment, but he'd made up his mind.

"Will you be home this afternoon?" he asked.

"Why? Did something happen?"

"Today's class was cancelled. I'm coming home. Unless you've got some urgent business, could you wait for me there?"

"Why don't we meet in Taksim?" Elsa said. "A Lana Turner film is playing at the Yeni Melek."

Gerhard knew this was his last chance to change his mind. "Wait for me at home, Elsa. Perhaps we can go out for dinner tonight."

Picking up his briefcase and his raincoat, he lied to his secretary as he left his office. "Could you ask one of my assistants to cover my lecture today? I'm feeling a little unwell and need to go home."

When Gerhard unlocked his front door, he was greeted by the smell of cinnamon. Elsa was probably baking one of her apple cakes. He hung up his raincoat, set his briefcase down, and, like any Turkish man, took off his shoes. As he padded toward the kitchen, the heavenly smell grew stronger.

Elsa was turning a cake onto a plate. He went up behind her and encircled her waist with his arms.

"Ah! Gerhard, you startled me! I didn't realize you were home. I started making your favorite cake the moment we hung up. Tea is ready, too. It takes the exact same amount of time to bake a cake as it takes for you to get home from the university."

Gerhard had buried his nose in her hair. He was pulling her against his chest. *Something happened,* she realized. *Something terrible.*

"Gerhard, what is it? What's wrong? Was there another problem at work?"

"No. It has nothing to do with work."

Elsa's pulse quickened. First came the riots, then Madame's death, and finally Suzi's pregnancy. What next?

"Elsa," Gerhard said softly, "come and sit down. We need to talk."

"I'll get us each a slice of cake and a cup of tea. It'll just be a minute."

"It's best we talk before Suzi gets home."

"Suzi won't be home until seven. Have your cake, and then we'll talk." Elsa cut two slices of lemon, put them on the tray, and carried everything over to the kitchen table. She sat down across from her despairing husband.

"Elsa, I'd give anything to change what happened. But once a thing is done, it's done. First, I want you to know something. I've always loved you, and I love you now, as much as ever. I'm telling you what happened because I want the lies to end. I respect you enough to risk losing you."

"Gerhard!" The plate of cake Elsa had been handing to her husband retreated along with her hand.

"One night, when you were in Zurich and I was drunk, something happened—something I should never have allowed—"

"Did you sleep with Hanna?" Elsa asked. Her voice was icy.

Gerhard reached over and took her trembling hand. "I didn't sleep with her. She slept with me."

"That's not funny!"

"I was drunk and I'd fallen. She was pulling me up off the floor and—don't get angry, but I was calling out for you. I thought she was you . . . on the floor, in front of the door. But when I woke up, I was in bed and—"

"Shut up! Not another word. I don't want to hear it!" Elsa's left eye was twitching.

What have I done? What have I done? I've destroyed my wife and myself. What have I done? "I sent her away, Elsa, and never looked at her again. That's why—it was to get far away from her and to keep Peter away from her that we moved to Bebek. I swear on our children that I don't even remember sleeping with that woman."

"Why have you waited all this time? You should have told me when I got back from Zurich."

"I didn't want to upset you. No, that's not true. I was afraid of losing you."

"And now you're not afraid of losing me? What's changed? Am I old now, Gerhard? Is that it? Have you found someone younger?"

"Elsa!"

"I want an answer. What's changed?"

"Darling, please hear me out. Hanna said her husband was going to divorce her for being barren. But he was actually sterile, not her. So she hatched a plan. She took advantage of me. If I hadn't come home so drunk, she'd probably have gone after Peter. Less than three weeks after that night, she told me she was pregnant and that she was going to tell her husband the child was his. And he must have accepted it. Obviously, I sent her away at once. And I don't even believe Rozi is my child. She could have seduced any man on the street, then pinned it on me so she could hold it over us. I don't remember that night, not a thing. I was trying to unlock the front door, I fell, and I realized she was on top of me. Then I blacked out, so how could I even have . . . ? If she really did what she says, that's just—it's horrible, Elsa. It's sick."

"Gerhard. You do realize how crazy you sound?" Elsa said wearily.

"I want you to understand, and I want you to forgive me."

"Oh, I understand all right. You got drunk and couldn't help yourself. It probably wasn't the first time, either." Elsa closed her eyes and pressed her fingertips against her eyelids.

"That's not fair. I've only been that drunk three or four times in my entire life. I was waiting for Hirsch, and he never showed up, and—"

"I can't forgive you, Gerhard. I'm going to ask you again. Why did you wait until now to tell me?"

"Because Hanna is using her daughter to worm her way into our lives and the lives of our children. I need your help keeping her away from Peter and Suzi."

Elsa stood up and left the kitchen. Gerhard sat there at the table for nearly an hour, smoking cigarette after cigarette. When he went to the sitting room, Elsa was in the chair by the window. The ashtray on the end table was full, too. Gerhard leaned against the door, unsure of what to say. Elsa spoke first.

"I can't live under the same roof with you. You have to leave."

"I understand. But will you allow me to stay until after Suzi gets married? Let's not ruin her wedding day. I'll go after that."

"Fine, then. But you'll be sleeping in Peter's room."

"What will we tell the children?"

"I'm sure you'll think of something."

"I'm so, so sorry."

"I am, too."

Naming Baby

Demir and Suzi went straight from the doctor's office to İnci Patisserie, where they dug into the famous profiteroles, their faces glowing, their eyes sparkling. And at that moment, neither of them worried about a future in which one would be posted to an army camp while the other nursed their newborn in the home of a mother-in-law furious about their prenuptial indiscretion. They were so young and so in love, and they could overcome anything.

"You know what I was thinking?" Suzi said. "If it's a boy, we should call him Emir. Emir, son of Demir."

"And if it's a girl, we could drop the 'zi' from Suzi. Then she'd be 'Su.' I like that."

"Wait, I've got an even better idea. We'll combine the first two letters of our names: she'll be 'Su-de'!"

"Sude. I love it."

And that's how Sude was named while still in her mother's womb.

Suzi got home that evening in high spirits, but sensed something was amiss when nobody greeted her. Before investigating, she turned her attention to the smell coming from the kitchen and devoured a piece of cake without benefit of a fork or plate.

Her mother was nowhere to be seen, but her father's raincoat was on its hook. She tapped on the door to his study and poked her head in.

"You're home early today! Did the smell of cake reach you all the way out in Beyazit?"

Gerhard just looked at her.

"Shall I get you a piece?"

"No, thank you."

"It's delicious. Mom outdid herself this time."

"I said no, Suzi!"

"Somebody's in a mood. What's wrong?"

"I'm writing something. Now, if you don't mind . . ."

"Well, pardon me." She gently closed the door. *How weird,* she thought. *He never acts like this.* She went to her parents' bedroom. This time, she entered without knocking.

"What is it?" her mother asked, without looking up.

"The cake turned out wonderfully." When there was no response, Suzi added, "Shall I cut a piece and bring it to you?"

"I've had enough. *Merci.*"

"Suit yourself. Mom, we chose a name for our daughter."

"What daughter?"

"Our baby. The one I'm going to have."

"How do you know it'll be a girl?"

"I just do. And if it is a girl—"

"Suzi, have you ever considered doing things in their proper order? You got pregnant before you got married. When the baby comes so soon after the wedding, your father will be too embarrassed to look his colleagues in the eye. 'What's done is done,' I said to myself. 'I'll hold my tongue. Better not to upset her while she's pregnant.' But then I realized you couldn't care less about how this reflects on your family. Especially here in Turkey. Everyone will look down on you. Your in-laws are going to be horrified when they find out—you know that, right? Yet here you are, pleased as punch, when you should be ashamed of yourself."

"Mother, please stop. We moved the wedding up. There won't be a scandal."

"Do you really think people won't guess why you got married in such a hurry?"

Suzi left the room without responding and went to her own bedroom. So that's why her father was so grumpy. Mother and her moralizing. Why, oh why, was her mother so rigid, so German? If only Madame were alive. And she couldn't go see Demir, either. There was an uptight matron in his house, too. The only difference was that one was a tall blonde, and the other a short brunette. She wondered which grandmother Sude would take after. If she was lucky, she'd look like her handsome father.

Suzi paused in front of the door to her father's study. She softly pushed the door open. Gerhard was standing in front of the window, wreathed in smoke. He'd been smoking a lot lately. She softly closed the door and suddenly realized how much she missed Peter. If he were here, she could go to his room and at least pick a good fight.

The Wedding Gift

Elsa didn't recognize the voice on the phone. A what? An attorney? He kept asking for Suzi Şiliman, saying it was a confidential legal matter. What could it be? What new disaster had Suzi brought upon herself? Then the man said something about a bequest.

"A bequest?" she asked. "Do you mean Suzi inherited something?"

A tremor went through Elsa. Her own mother had been in a nursing home since her father's death. Could she have passed?

"Madame Virgine Takuhi Saryan has left a gift."

Oh dear, Elsa thought. *I hope it's not that enormous piano with the two sticking keys. We'll never be able to make room for it, but Suzi won't let us sell a precious memento of Madame, either. Where on earth will we put it?*

"Would you please inform Suzi Hanım that her presence is kindly requested for the official reading of the will. Eleven o'clock in the morning this coming Wednesday."

"I'll tell her," Elsa said.

Shortly after eleven on the appointed day, Suzi gasped as the lawyer read Madame's will.

Earlier that morning, Elsa had begged Suzi not to bring home any dusty, run-down sticks of furniture. There was no space in their apartment for any of it. On the other hand, if Madame had decided to leave Suzi a keepsake in the form of jewelry, then Suzi was to thank Madame's relatives and accept it as a remembrance of the good lady's kindness.

Now, Suzi had returned from the lawyer's office. She was saying, "The bequest is a little dusty and quite run-down, Mutti, but it's very comfortable. Forgive me, Mutti. I couldn't refuse."

Well, Elsa thought, *at least it can't be the piano. Pianos aren't "comfortable."*

"Did she leave you that old burgundy sofa?"

"Yes. Actually, she left us everything."

"What? What are you saying?"

"Once the paperwork has been completed and the taxes paid, the apartment and all of its contents will belong to me and Demir. Madame has given us her home as a wedding present."

Elsa's jaw dropped, and her eyes filled with tears. There were so many things she would have liked to say if only she'd known where to begin.

Suzi and Demir were getting married the following week, just two months before Demir had to report for his military service. For those months, Demir would be living with the Schliemanns most of the time. Elsa suffered heart palpitations every time she thought about it. Suzi didn't want to stay with his family, and Madame's apartment wasn't legally theirs yet, so what could Elsa say? She and Gerhard would have to pretend to be happy together for the sake of the newlyweds. They'd have to pretend their hearts weren't breaking.

A few evenings later, the Schliemanns were gathered around the dinner table at Demir's house. Everyone was watching Bedia Hanım ceremoniously drizzle melted butter over her famous meat dumplings with garlicky yoghurt sauce when Gerhard abruptly spoke.

"I've got some news for you all."

"I've got some news, too," Demir chimed in.

"What's with this sudden inundation of news?" Suzi said. "Let my dad go first."

"I've received an offer from Ankara Numune Training and Research Hospital. After a great deal of thought, I've decided it would be a good career move. I will be teaching in Ankara for the next year, starting in January."

"Whoa. How does Mom feel about living in Ankara?" Suzi said. She glanced over at Elsa, who was staring at the table.

"Your mother's life won't be disrupted in any way. I'll take the train to Istanbul every weekend to visit her."

When Elsa remained silent, Suzi spoke up again. "All right then. Now let's hear from Demir."

"I've decided to give my share of the inheritance to my beloved fiancée, as a wedding gift. I was feeling bad about not having the resources to get Suzi the kind of gift she deserves, and Madame came to the rescue."

"Son, you know our family will be slipping gold bracelets onto the bride's wrists, in keeping with our traditions," Bedia Hanım said. "How can you say we don't have a gift?"

"Mother," Demir said, "the bracelets will be from you and Dad. This is my gift."

"I won't accept it!" Suzi said. "That apartment belongs to both of us."

"I've already signed the forms. Once the paperwork is done, it'll all be yours."

"No, I won't allow it," Suzi said. She took a deep breath. "But if you wait a little while longer, you can give your half to Sude."

"Who on earth is Sude?" Bedia Hanım asked.

"If we have a daughter, we're going to name her Sude," Suzi explained.

"If I were you, I'd consider boys' names for your firstborn," Bedia Hanım said. "You may very well be blessed with a boy."

"No," Suzi said. "Something tells me it's going to be a girl."

"I've never heard of such a thing!" Bedia Hanım said. "Naming your child before you're even married? And without consulting your parents? Well, the child will have a middle name, too, I suppose, and you could always—"

"Demir, what about letting each of our mothers choose a name, too?" Suzi said.

"If we do that, they'll both choose their own mothers' names. Sude would become—Auntie Frau, what's your mother's name?"

"Gertrude."

"Vasfiye Gertrude Sude Atalay. How does that sound?"

"Vasfiye and Gertrude are fine, but where did this 'Sude' business come from?" Bedia Hanım said.

"We combined the first syllables of our own names. I think it's perfect," Demir said.

"These kids are crazy!" Nazmi Bey said. "First you'll get married, then you'll get pregnant, then you'll have the baby and learn its sex—and only then will you name it. I can't believe we're having this conversation."

Gerhard put down his spoon and cleared his throat. The Atalays would find out eventually, and they'd probably resent not having been told earlier.

"Nazmi Bey, it has come to my attention that our children have done things in a different order. For them, pregnancy happens before wedlock. At least it's not a shotgun wedding. They simply loved each other so much that they couldn't wait."

A pained silence fell over the table. Demir and Suzi flushed and joined Elsa in studying their dinner plates.

Nazmi Bey broke the silence by looking directly at Demir and asking in a low voice, "Son, when is it due?"

"In June, Father."

"So that explains the new wedding date," Bedia Hanım said, her voice cracking. "Of course."

Praying that his honesty would not once more tear a family apart, Gerhard fumbled for a new subject.

"Demir, I was wondering if you'd be able to come to the university with me tomorrow. I'd like to find out what your blood type is."

"What? Why?"

"Well, Suzi is AB negative. If you're positive, there might be a compatibility issue."

"Compatibility? I've never heard of such a thing."

"Medical research has increased our understanding of so much, Bedia Hanım. Have you ever wondered why so many infants are born with jaundice? Today, it's possible to assess risks and to take precautions."

"What kind of precautions?" Elsa asked, speaking for the first time that evening.

"Well, for example," Gerhard patiently continued, "we can have compatible donor blood on hand in case a transfusion is necessary."

"God forbid! Blood from a perfect stranger!" Bedia Hanım said.

"Bedia, please let Gerhard finish," Nazmi Bey said, holding a finger to his lips. "You know he is a doctor." He turned to Gerhard. "We already know Demir's blood type. He was tested for his military service. Son, run to your room and get the forms from your physical."

Demir didn't move a muscle. He looked frightened.

"Demir," Gerhard said, "take a look at those forms, like your father said, and you won't have to come with me tomorrow. Go on, child."

Demir slowly rose from the table and went off to his bedroom, head down.

"Dad," Suzi said. "Could you explain, please? Are you saying my blood might be incompatible with my own baby's? How is that even possible?"

"Yes, if a mother's blood is Rh-negative and the baby's is Rh-positive, the mother's blood cells can develop antibodies that attack the newborn's. The risk is highest near or during delivery."

"Why have I never heard of this before?"

"Because we didn't know about it. Research on hemolytic disease in newborns has made great strides since you and Peter were born. I like to think my own work has played some small role in that. Now, don't misunderstand. The risk is tiny, especially for a first-time mother. All I'm saying is that it won't hurt to take precautions. Why not have a blood donor present at the delivery? If Demir is Rh-negative like you are, the baby will be too, so there's no chance of incompatibility."

Demir came into the dining room, form in hand.

"I'm blood type A, Rh-positive. Does that mean everything's okay?"

"Well, that means the baby could go either way. But there's no need for worry," Gerhard said. "It'll be easy enough to find a compatible donor."

"Should all of us donate blood, then?" Bedia Hanım asked. "For the"—here she swallowed hard and stared fearfully at Suzi's belly—"baby?"

"No, no! If you know your blood type, you can just tell me. Otherwise, one drop is enough to find out."

The mood at the table had been ruined, and Gerhard's further attempts to explain hemolytic disease only made matters worse. Coffee in the sitting room was strained, with Demir stealing worried glances at his parents and Suzi keeping her eyes firmly on the ground.

When the Schliemanns got home, Suzi ran straight to her room, and Elsa confronted Gerhard.

"What possessed you to humiliate Suzi like that at the dinner table? I wish you were as frank with your own indiscretions as you are with our daughter's. That was not your truth to tell."

"I didn't mean to—I thought—"

"Shush! And when did you turn into such a pedant? A mother's blood poisoning her baby? If the risk is as minimal as you say, why bring it up? You've caused unnecessary anxiety for an expectant mother—your own daughter, no less."

Elsa sailed into the kitchen with Gerhard trailing in her wake.

"It is my responsibility as a scientist—"

"What about your responsibilities as a father and as a husband? Was it right to inform me at the Atalays' dinner table, in front of everyone, that you'd accepted a position in Ankara? Until we're officially divorced, the decisions that affect us both should be made together, but you're obviously so eager to be free of me you couldn't wait another minute."

"Elsa, the offer was finalized only today. And what's more, I accepted it for your sake. My very presence has become intolerable to you. You don't want me at home, so I thought you'd be pleased if I left."

"You chose the wrong place and the wrong time to tell me."

"Well, if it makes you feel better, I'll be spending the winter in Ankara as punishment."

"That's a punishment of your own choosing. It didn't come from me. It must have come from your conscience."

Gerhard retreated to Peter's bedroom and put on his pajamas. He'd just collapsed on the bed when Suzi burst in.

"Dad! What are you doing in here?"

"Sleeping. What are you doing?"

"I was looking for a book. Why are you sleeping in here?"

"I don't want to disturb your mother with my snoring."

"That's ridiculous! After all these years? Why's she making a fuss about it now?"

"It's not her fault. I might want to wake up in the middle of the night and read a book."

"Dad, tell me the truth. What are the chances my baby might die because of my blood?"

Gerhard took Suzi's hand. "Zero," he said.

"Well, then, what were you talking about at dinner?"

"Suzi, I regret having brought it up. I'm just being overly cautious. I didn't mean to alarm you. Please don't worry."

"Okay, Dad."

Suzi took a book off the shelf and gave Gerhard a kiss before returning to her room. She hadn't realized her parents were sleeping separately, and it worried her. She swore to herself that she'd never sleep apart from Demir, even if he snored like an orangutan.

Flesh and Blood

On a winter afternoon in 1955, under the watchful eye of a registrar general in red robes, Demir and Suzi affixed their signatures to a marriage license. In the eyes of the Turkish state, they were now man and wife. That evening, the Atalays held a small reception at the Pera Palace Hotel for a few select guests who included the Ellimans; Hirsch, who had traveled from Ankara for the occasion; his wife, Holde; their son, Enver Tandoğan, now ten; a few of the Atalays' relatives; and close school friends of the bride and groom. Suzi, who was not yet showing, wore a white gown with a flounced skirt and her mother's ruby brooch.

In keeping with German tradition, Gerhard delivered a speech. He was followed by Hirsch, who concluded by addressing Suzi as Mrs. Atalay and inviting those assembled to raise their glasses to the newly married couple. Suzi then stood up and gave a brief but emotional toast of her own.

"I would like to thank all of you for coming today to share our happiness. I so wish that Madame could have been here as well," she said, brushing away a tear. "My dear brother, Peter, has also been unable to attend. I am confident that they are both here in spirit."

All eyes turned to Elsa, who had gotten to her feet and lifted her glass. "And I wish my father and mother could be here. My father has passed, and my mother was not strong enough to make the long journey to Istanbul."

"Demir and I will visit Grandmother at the first opportunity," Suzi said. "I'm so happy she was able to visit us in Turkey and meet Demir, even if he was still a child. And when she does see him again, I'm certain she'll agree that he has grown into the handsomest groom ever."

When the dinner was over and the last of the guests had been seen off, the bride and groom took the elevator to their hotel room. The couple's parents left the hotel and walked to the corner together. It was drizzling.

"Rain brings fruitfulness," Bedia Hanım said. "It's an auspicious sign."

Gerhard and Elsa said their good-byes to the Atalays and were walking toward Taksim when Elsa seemed to read Gerhard's thoughts.

"Pleased that Hanna didn't swoop down on the reception?"

Gerhard closed his eyes. "Has she been bothering you again?"

"Threatening me is more like it. She dropped in unannounced last week and demanded again that she and Rozi be invited. I told her that our list of guests was limited, and we had been unable to include her."

"Thank you."

"I'm not finished, Gerhard! Do you know what she said? She asked me to give you a message. I asked her what it was. 'Just tell him I have a message,' she said. 'He'll know what I mean.' And that's when I told her that I knew all there was to know and that if any messages were going to be delivered, it would be one from me to her husband."

Gerhard flushed red.

"What I mean to say, Gerhard Bey, is if that woman didn't suddenly show up today, you have me to thank for it."

"Why didn't you tell me sooner, Elsa?"

"Look who's talking."

Over the following weeks, the newlyweds diplomatically shuttled between their in-laws' two houses in a bid to please everyone. The paperwork for Madame's apartment was going nowhere. Like characters in a nineteenth-century Russian novel, they faced bureaucratic hurdle after hurdle: a new tax, another fee, additional paperwork, an incomplete form, an absent manager, a sour-faced clerk, a barked instruction to "go away and come back tomorrow!" The plan had been to rent out the apartment until Demir completed his military service, which would give them a little nest egg for baby expenses. Other than Madame's portrait in oil, which they kept for themselves, they had auctioned off all of their benefactress' furniture, using the proceeds for fresh paint and repairs. However, without an official deed, they couldn't draw up a rental contract.

In the meantime, Elsa and Bedia Hanım were collecting things for the baby: a cradle, sleepers, booties, cloth diapers, blankets . . . As much as they enjoyed the process, neither woman had forgotten that bewildering warning about blood incompatibility. It was a nagging worry they pushed to the backs of their minds and never mentioned to each other.

Gerhard determined the blood types of all the close relatives and tried to identify possible donors. The baby's blood type would be A, B, or AB, but what if the baby was AB positive? It was unlikely, but it would be nice if an AB positive donor were available in case of emergency.

Elsa seldom spoke to her husband those days, but she frequently asked, "Have you found the blood you're looking for?"

He always replied, "I've found donors for all types but AB positive. Don't worry, Elsa. It'll be okay."

After too many days of this response, Elsa put on a new dress, applied lipstick and blush, and set out for Taksim with her handbag on her arm. She strode down the main shopping avenue without so much as a glance at the window displays and turned into a certain shopping arcade.

Was she making a mistake? What if Gerhard found out? Damn Gerhard! In she went. There was no sign of Hanna. A young lady with brassy blond hair sat behind the counter.

"I was looking for Madame Benhayim . . ."

"The grande dame or the daughter-in-law?"

"Hanna."

"She comes in around noon."

Elsa scurried out of the arcade and to the post office on the main avenue, where she bought a phone token and dialed Hanna's number.

Hanna gave a little gasp of surprise when she heard Elsa's voice.

"Hanna, I was in the area and wondered if you cared to meet at Markiz? We could have some nice pastries and a chat. I've been thinking about what you said about Rozi. Perhaps you're right. Our children have never had the opportunity to get to know one another."

Hanna seized the moment. "I'll be there in half an hour."

Less than ten minutes later, Elsa was sitting at a table in the back of the café. She ordered a tea and waited. When Hanna arrived in her best outfit and didn't see Elsa at any of the tables in front, her face fell. Elsa had to vigorously wave from the back.

"Why are you hiding way back there?"

"I didn't want anyone to overhear us."

"But we're speaking German," Hanna said.

"In this city, everyone knows a word or two of every language. What would you like to drink?"

"Hot *chocolat*, please. And a mille-feuille."

Glutton, Elsa thought, then shook the ungenerous thought from her head. Once the waiter was out of earshot, she got straight to the point.

"Hanna, life is full of twists and turns. If what you say is true—that is, if Gerhard really is Rozi's father—we'll protect your honor by keeping it a secret to our dying day. But in return, we might need your help." Elsa proceeded to explain that a blood transfusion might be needed for Suzi's baby and that Rozi could be a suitable donor if Hanna would agree.

"Yes, Frau Schliemann, absolutely. Even if they don't know they're related, our children should be encouraged to become friends, at least. They could be so much help to each other."

"Hanna, call me Elsa. If our children are in fact siblings, well, I agree."

"They are! How can I prove it to you?"

"With a blood test. If I knew Rozi's blood type, I might be able to do something. We'll have to get her tested."

"I already know her blood type. They told me at the hospital when she was born."

"What is it?" Elsa asked, holding her breath and clasping her hand to her bosom. "Is it AB positive?"

"That's it! How did you know?"

"Oh, Hanna, if there's a problem and Rozi needs to give blood, I promise to do everything I can to make Rozi feel more welcome in our family. The children can help each other throughout life even if they never know the truth."

"That's exactly what I've been trying to tell you."

"Would you like another hot chocolate?" Elsa asked with a smile.

"Sure!"

Elsa patiently waited until the second cup of hot chocolate was finally gone, nodding vacantly as Hanna chattered away about that year's fashions and the shapeless shift known as the "sack dress." Then she asked for the check.

As soon as she was free of Hanna, Elsa went back to the post office and called home.

"I found the blood you were looking for," she told Gerhard.

"What? Who is it?"

"You'll find out when the time comes."

"I need to know in advance. I must screen for certain diseases."

"She's healthy—it's Suzi's sister."

There was a moment of silence on the other end of the line.

"Are you out of your mind, Elsa?"

"If you're too proud to accept help for the sake of your grand-child's health, you're the one who's out of your mind!" Elsa hissed before hanging up.

To a dead line, Gerhard said, "Don't make me depend on the child Hanna's trying to pass off as my daughter."

The Unraveling

Elsa focused all her attention on the preparations for their grandchild. She and Gerhard were still sleeping in separate rooms and speaking to each other only when necessary. Thanks to Suzi and Demir staying over so many nights and frequent dinners with the in-laws, at least they didn't have to spend much time together on their own.

Gerhard tried not to let on how stressed he was by the prospect of moving to Ankara, adjusting to a strange city and new colleagues. He had decided to stay in university housing until the summer rather than rent a place off campus. How he rued that drunken night so many years ago! It had changed the course of his life, depriving him of what should have been a joyful period anticipating and then enjoying his first grandchild. His one consolation was that his old friend, Hirsch, would also be living in Ankara. It was Hirsch, in fact, who had been instrumental in getting him a position there.

One uneasy day was much like the last until the news came that Demir would be stationed in Ankara. Suzi and Demir were thrilled. He would be a mere overnight train ride away, and she could stay with her father when she visited. What they didn't realize was that Gerhard would be living in a single room as small as any student's.

The Schliemanns marked the arrival of the new year at home with some close friends. Elsa grudgingly roasted a turkey and asked Fatma to help make a rice pilaf with onions, nuts, diced liver, and currants. Suzi decided to celebrate with her husband and friends rather than her family, but feeling guilty, she'd stopped by during the day with a box of profiteroles.

The little dinner party was more of a success than Elsa had expected. At least she and Gerhard managed to hide the strain on their marriage, though Hirsch and Holde did a poor job of hiding theirs. At one point, Hirsch drew Elsa aside to whisper his apologies: "Elsa, I'm sorry if we've ruined the evening. I promise it will never happen again. Holde now agrees that a legal separation would be best."

"Don't worry about it," Elsa said. "We've all had a bit too much to drink. What's more, there isn't a family in the world that doesn't have its problems. So much happens behind closed doors. Believe me."

The couples bid each other a joyless good-bye at the end of the night.

The following morning, the Schliemanns' front door was the scene of another unhappy parting. His bag packed and waiting at his feet, Gerhard embraced his wife and said good-bye. Elsa didn't push him away or resist, but she was unresponsive and unyielding in his arms. "Have a safe journey" were her last words, and she didn't accompany Demir and Suzi to the train station to see Gerhard off.

A few days later, Suzi said to her mother, "I'm surprised by how much I already miss Dad. He always left early in the morning and never came home before seven, but the house just doesn't feel the same without him. It's funny, isn't it?"

"I felt the same way when Peter left. I even missed your squabbles. It'll pass. You'll get used to it."

Suzi wondered why her mother was moping around instead of embracing the opportunity to spend time in Ankara and get out of the rut of her daily life. *Maybe it's true,* she thought, *what they say about women making a big deal out of nothing.* She herself would never do that and would certainly not let her husband go and live in another city.

Suzi was still adjusting to her father's absence when Demir received his marching orders. Unlike Gerhard's muted departure, Demir's was attended by his aunts, uncles, cousins, nieces, nephews, friends, parents, mother-in-law, and wife, all of whom flocked to Haydarpaşa train station.

Elsa watched in amazement as a tearful Nazmi Bey hugged and kissed Demir. *Turks can be so emotional,* Elsa thought. *They send their sons off to military service as if they're going off to war.*

Having lost their husbands to Ankara for very different reasons, Suzi and Elsa were now alone at home together for the first time, and they grew as close as they'd ever been. Not that they didn't find plenty to disagree about. For example, Suzi couldn't understand why her mother was still friends with Hanna. When she complained about Elsa having bought all the wool and thread for the baby clothes from Hanna's shop, Bedia Hanım said, "It's only natural that Elsa Hanım would want to spend time with someone who speaks her mother tongue. Try to be a little more understanding."

"As if she can't speak German with me," Suzi wanted to say. But she held her tongue and tried to be accommodating to both her mother and her mother-in-law.

A Baby Already on Guard

Sude was born on a day in June with the roses in full bloom. Demir had been unable to get leave and would not see her until the weekend, but Gerhard, who was in Istanbul for the birth, had taken Suzi to the hospital when her contractions started. Elsa had hurried to Hanna's for Rozi. Hanna had been calling several times a day to ask after Suzi's health, in a show of solicitousness that seemed excessive and odd. Elsa couldn't stop wondering: If Hanna decided not to let Rozi donate blood, would they be able to find someone else? What if there was an emergency? As Elsa fretted and fielded Hanna's calls, Gerhard and Suzi were oblivious to her distress.

Thankfully, on the morning of the birth, Hanna was friendly and compliant, and even agreed not to come.

When Elsa first arrived at the hospital, she left Rozi in the garden and went up to her daughter's room. She asked Gerhard to go down and explain to the donor what would be required of her.

"Who is this donor?" asked Suzi.

"It's Rozi. She's the only person we could find who shares your blood type," Elsa said.

Suzi made a face—either from labor pains or in reaction to the news.

"Suzi, please be nice to Rozi. She didn't have to agree to give blood. Thank her when you see her."

Elsa walked over to the window and looked down at the garden. Gerhard and Rozi were standing under a tree, talking. Not for the first time, Elsa observed that there was absolutely no resemblance between them. She opened the window and called out, "Come upstairs. Suzi wants to see both of you."

By the time Gerhard and Rozi got upstairs, two nurses were preparing to wheel Suzi to the delivery room.

"Listen, Dad," Suzi said. "I don't want you in the delivery room. If you follow us in, I swear this baby's not coming out."

"Okay then. But I won't go far. I want to test the baby's blood as soon it's born."

"I know, Dad. We already talked to the doctor. And thank you, Rozi. Truly."

Rozi blushed and hung her head. Elsa was relieved that both girls were acting so angelic. Not that she expected it to last.

"Would you like me to be there?" Elsa asked.

"No, Mom," Suzi said. "And if Demir were here, I'd say the same to him."

As the nurses pushed the wheeled bed down the corridor, Gerhard said, "Come along, Rozi. Let's head down to the laboratory for a quick test."

Alone in Suzi's room, Elsa sat down in a chair by the window. If Rozi's blood ended up saving the baby, perhaps Gerhard's indiscretion all those years ago was a blessing in disguise. Hanna had turned up just as Elsa was leaving for Zurich. Then her return to Istanbul had been unexpectedly delayed. And Gerhard had chosen that moment to get drunk, which, to be fair, he did rarely. It was almost as though Rozi had been specially created to save Suzi's child one day.

Should she forgive Gerhard?

Elsa's thoughts were interrupted by Demir's parents.

"Elsa Hanım, why didn't you call sooner?"

"I'm sorry, Bedia Hanım," Elsa said. "Things happened quickly. But don't worry, Suzi was just taken to the delivery room. Nothing's happened yet."

"Is Gerhard Bey there with her?"

"Dr. Erez will be delivering the baby. Gerhard is around here somewhere."

Ten minutes later, Elsa went out into the corridor and started looking for Gerhard. Perhaps he'd decided to wait outside the delivery room? She went over to the desk and asked the nurse on duty if he'd seen her husband.

"He went down to the laboratory with a young woman," the nurse said. "He said something about getting a blood sample."

"Where's the laboratory?"

Following the nurse's directions, Elsa found the laboratory two floors below at the end of a long corridor. She pushed open a glass door. The nurse inside was attaching a label to a small test tube. Spying her husband and Rozi, Elsa went up to them.

"Bedia Hanım and Nazmi Bey have arrived," she said.

"We were just about to join you. Our work here is done," Gerhard said.

"You already took blood from Rozi?"

"No, no. Just a drop from her finger. It didn't hurt at all, did it, Rozi? We'll wait until the birth to find out if the baby needs a transfusion. I'm sure it won't."

Elsa leaned close to Gerhard and whispered, "What's going on? Did she change her mind?"

"I'll explain everything later, Elsa," Gerhard said. "Let's wait until after we see our grandchild."

Gerhard and Elsa went upstairs and began waiting with the Atalays. A few hours later, the news came that Suzi's cervix was already fully dilated. The birth was imminent, and the mother was doing well.

"I'm going to go to the delivery room and wait by the door," Gerhard said. "Just in case."

"Take Rozi with you," Elsa said.

"She can stay here for now. I'll let you know if we need her."

A little while later, Rozi said she needed to go to the bathroom. When she didn't come back, Elsa assumed she was with Gerhard.

Gerhard ran into Dr. Erez on his way to the delivery room.

"Congratulations," Erez said. "You have a healthy granddaughter. It was an easy delivery."

Gerhard heard the baby before he saw her. His face broke into a grin.

"It's a girl!" a nurse said. "Would you like to watch me bathe her, Professor?"

"And the blood type?"

"The same as her mother."

Gerhard kissed Suzi on the cheek and walked over to the baby, uttering a silent prayer of thanks in every language he knew.

The sound of wheels rolling down the corridor alerted Elsa and the Atalays. Suzi looked tired but happy. Not long after, Gerhard came in, pushing a wheeled crib.

"Introducing Sude Hanım," he said.

Elsa, Bedia Hanım, and Nazmi Bey gathered around. The baby's eyes were squeezed shut, two thin lines in a little red face. Her curly, damp hair was chestnut brown, and her tiny fists, wrapped in white mittens, were held up on either side of her face, like a boxer already on guard against the blows of life.

"Welcome, Sude," Suzi said when the baby was brought over to her. "Look! She's smiling!"

"Newborns can't smile," Bedia Hanım said.

While the Atalays and Suzi fussed over the baby, Gerhard gently guided Elsa out to the corridor.

"There's something I want to tell you," he said. "I was going to wait until a more suitable time, but I thought you'd want to know. Rozi doesn't have the same blood type as Suzi. And what's more, she couldn't be my daughter."

"Oh my God! Hanna lied? But how could she have known Suzi's blood type? Unless—I must have said it. I told her we needed to find an AB positive donor. But—oh my God—what if we really had needed a transfusion for the baby?"

"Hanna must have decided to take a gamble. As I told you, the risk was very low. But if Rozi had given blood, it would have—where is Rozi, anyway?"

"She said she was going to the bathroom. I haven't seen her since. Gerhard! That woman is pure evil! Either that, or she's crazy."

"I think she really might be mentally unbalanced."

"Well, even if she is, how could her daughter have gone along with this?"

"The girl's innocent, Elsa. She was just obeying her mother. If Rozi had known, she wouldn't have agreed to give me a blood sample."

"I need to sit down."

Gerhard helped Elsa to a chair at the end of the corridor.

I can't faint now, not when my daughter needs me. She'd planned to spend the night at the hospital with Suzi. She'd have to pull herself together and think about the implications of Hanna's lies later.

"I'll join you in a minute," she told Gerhard. "Go back to the others."

By the time Elsa got to her feet, she had made up her mind to visit Hanna in a few days and confront her about Rozi's blood type. It would, she decided, be the last time she ever saw Hanna's deceitful face.

When Elsa got back to the hospital room, the Ellimans were there, as well as Dr. Erez, who had a chart showing the baby's height and weight. The doctor said that Sude would be given a little sugar water, but that she could start nursing the following morning. On his way out, he turned to Gerhard.

"Relax and enjoy your beautiful granddaughter, Gerhard. Everything turned out as well as I expected. While I understand taking precautions, you were getting a little overanxious." The doctor turned to Elsa. "And please tell your sister everything is fine. She was so worried."

"My sister?"

"She came to talk to me about blood incompatibility. I assured her there was almost no chance that a transfusion would be necessary, but she seemed even more anxious than your husband."

"Hanna came to see you?"

"I don't remember her name. A tall, blond woman."

"I see. I'll tell her for you," Elsa said, moving aside so the doctor could leave.

Elsa spent that night at the hospital, as planned. The next morning, Gerhard came and took his newly enlarged family home in a cab. He would be leaving that evening on the overnight train to Ankara and asked Elsa to join him for an early dinner out.

"I can't leave Suzi on her own," Elsa said.

"Mother, please! I'm not a baby. In fact, I have a baby of my own now," Suzi said. "Besides, Demir will be here in an hour, and I'm sure his mother will be with him."

"We'll just have a quick dinner at the station," Gerhard insisted. "You'll be back home in no time. There are some things we need to talk about."

"Are you two keeping secrets from me?" Suzi asked.

"Can't a husband and wife talk in private?"

"I suppose so. On the condition that you tell me everything later," Suzi said with a laugh.

When Elsa had gone to change, Suzi teased Gerhard. "Dad, are you two dating all over again? I've seen the looks you give each other. And now you're having dinner and a secret talk."

"So what if we are?" Gerhard said. "We may be grandparents now, but we're not quite ready to be tossed onto the scrap heap."

Sitting across from each other at a small table in the Haydarpaşa station restaurant, Gerhard and Elsa each ordered a bowl of stew. When the waiter was gone, Gerhard leaned forward.

"Elsa," he said, looking into his wife's eyes, "I hope you understand now what Hanna is really like. I'll be staying in Ankara until the end of the term, but after that, I'd like to come home, if you'll have me."

"I still don't understand why that woman would wish us harm."

"Obviously, she's not well. How much did you know about her before you agreed to bring her to Istanbul? Can we believe anything she's said? She might even have made up that story about her husband being sterile."

"Be that as it may, it doesn't excuse your behavior. You got drunk and then—then it happened. The thing you claim not to remember."

"You know what the Turks say. From every evil comes some good. Ever since that night, I haven't allowed myself more than two drinks at a sitting. Elsa, please. Can't we agree never to talk about Hanna and Rozi again?"

The waiter arrived with two steaming bowls of stew and a basket of bread. Gerhard and Elsa talked only about their granddaughter and children for the rest of the meal. She then accompanied her husband as far as the train carriage.

"I need to think over what you said. There's plenty of time until the end of the term."

When Gerhard hugged Elsa good-bye, she was as stiff as before and, as the train pulled out of the station, she didn't wave back. What he didn't know was that she stood on the platform for a long time after the train had disappeared.

Two days later, Elsa called Hanna and invited her to Markiz again, asking that she come alone. Hanna arrived with a gift-wrapped package and found Elsa at the same back table as before. This time, though, Elsa didn't ask Hanna what she'd like.

"Congratulations! I was so happy to hear that the baby was healthy. Still, it's nice to know that Rozi could be a donor in the future."

"If the baby had been given a transfusion of Rozi's blood, it would have died. And you knew it. Your lie would have killed my granddaughter, Hanna! I won't be filing an official complaint. My husband and I have decided that you need mental help, and I hope that you get it, for Rozi's sake. Now listen to me very carefully. If you ever bother me or any members of my family, if you so much as call us on the phone, I will go straight to the police. When they've learned what you've done, your husband will divorce you, and you'll go either to prison or a mental hospital."

"But I knew there would be no need for Rozi's blood. Otherwise, I'd never—"

"Stop! Don't say another word!" Elsa pulled an envelope out of her handbag, threw it on the table, and pointed at Hanna. "Now you have a copy of the blood test. We have the original. Stay away from us!"

Elsa was walking to the door when Hanna called out after her. "Elsa, you forgot my gift for the baby."

Elsa spun around. "Go see a doctor, Hanna, before it's too late. Do it for Rozi."

Scenes from Sude's Life

There was nothing special about 1956, the year of Sude's birth, or so she decided when she was still a little girl. At school, she learned about all the amazing things that had happened in 1932, when her mother was born: the National Wrestling Team won the Balkan Athletics Championships, Miss Turkey was crowned Miss Universe, Turkey joined the League of Nations, the Turkish Language Society was convened, the first official Turkish yacht race was held, and Müfide Kazım became the first female government physician. In the year Sude was born, an earthquake struck Eskişehir. That was about it. No special Turkish achievements to be proud of.

Her mother and Grandpa Gerhard knew all kinds of other things about 1932, things that Sude hadn't learned in school. For example, it was the year that radio waves from space were first detected, that vitamin B3 was extracted from a lemon, and that a Swiss professor named Malche came to Turkey to reform the universities. Grandpa Gerhard could talk for hours about Malche and his reforms. Sude's father would joke that Grandpa and Sude's mother were like walking, talking ency-clopedias when it came to the early days of the republic.

If there was one thing that kept Sude from feeling like a boring girl born in boring times, it was her father's devotion. He hadn't been able to see Sude until she was three days old, he told her. Still wearing his uniform, he had cradled her in his arms and said, "Everything is about you now. I'm going to work hard and become a success just for you." Even a newborn knows when she is truly loved.

Naturally, Sude's early life and outlook were formed in large part by the era in which she lived, and by her parents. Living on a university campus, Sude was sheltered from the wider world but simultaneously exposed to bewildering ideas and student activism. Between the ages of four and fifty-six, she would live through three failed coups, two suc-cessful ones, and several "memoranda." That was what they called a po-lite coup, one in which the military toppled the government through a tersely worded communique and didn't even have to get into their tanks. It was a dizzying, restless, and exciting time to be alive, even if Sude didn't always realize it.

Sude's first coup was on May 27, 1960. She had been living in Ankara with her family for eight months and was about to turn four. Those were the days when the Menderes government was regularly broadcasting the names of everyone they claimed was joining their grand "National Front" of supporters. Sude's father, who supported the main opposition party, would curse and switch off the radio every time the propaganda started. But on May 27, he turned up the volume and listened all day long.

At that time, Demir Atalay was one of the engineers employed on a construction project for the newly founded Middle Eastern Technical University (METU). He and his family lived in a two-bedroom state housing unit right on campus. Suzi Atalay was looking after Sude and giving private English lessons to prep school students. A year later, she would join the faculty at METU, first as an English teacher and then as a professor of English literature.

A year and a half after her first coup, Sude was in primary school and was already taking private violin lessons from Mr. Zuckmayer when former prime minister Menderes, his foreign minister, and his economy minister were taken from their prison cells and hanged. Even her dad, who had never liked Menderes, was horrified. The image of Menderes dangling from a rope haunted Sude's dreams for weeks.

Two years later, in 1963, her father came home one day, shouting, "A coup! There's been another one!" Her mother was sitting at the kitchen table, grading papers.

"Again?" Suzi asked. "Who did it this time?"

"Who do you think?"

"The military."

"Ding ding ding! Sude, your mother got the answer to today's pop quiz."

"Demir, that's quite enough out of you. Be quiet while I turn on the radio and find out what happened."

"Please don't, Suzi! I've already heard more than I can bear. Colonel Talat Aydemir was behind it, but Prime Minister İnönü was too quick for him."

"Meaning?"

"Meaning the colonel and his friends are about to enjoy an early retirement."

"Perhaps we should lead a coup," Suzi said. "I'm fed up with grading papers."

"Don't worry. You'll only be doing it for another thirty years or so."

"And they wonder why there are so many demonstrations against capitalist exploitation."

"We need to cheer your mom up," Demir said, leaning across the table and kissing Suzi on the lips. "Sude, go get your violin and play us something nice."

Sude remembered another night when her father had kissed her mother on the lips right at the kitchen table. It was a couple of years ago, her first day of kindergarten.

That evening, her father had come home carrying a bottle of rakı.

"Finally!" he said. "Parliament just agreed to debate the land reform bill. Large land holdings are going to be nationalized and redistributed. Peasants will finally own their family farms."

"Daddy, are we peasants?" Sude asked.

"No, sweetie, but we are leftists. We believe in social justice and the fair distribution of wealth, and we think people shouldn't be greedy."

"Your father's a dreamer," Suzi said, but she was smiling.

As it turned out, the land reforms would never be carried out, and Demir's dream of equality would remain just that.

A year later, in May, not long before Sude got her report card, retired colonel Aydemir and his supporters attempted to stage another coup, even occupying the state radio building and the military academy in Ankara. This time, Prime Minister İnönü had the ringleaders hanged.

Sude's parents spent that whole summer arguing about the European Economic Community. It was one of their rare disagreements. Demir opposed Turkey joining the EEC, but Suzi insisted that a prosperous, democratic future could only be achieved through closer integration with Europe. When the Ankara Agreement was signed in 1963, Sude didn't know whether to celebrate with her mother or comfort her father.

Coca-Cola entered the Turkish market shortly afterward. Local *gazoz* producers across Anatolia sent delegations to Ankara to lobby for their sweet, fizzy beverages, and Demir joined the calls for a nationwide boycott by banning Coke from his house. But there was no turning back the onslaught of American culture and products, which brought with them the first anti-American demonstrations. Refrigerators across the land would be ruled by Coca-Cola from then on.

Sude was nine years old when the right-wing Justice Party won 52 percent of the national vote on a platform of fighting communism. The election results were met with dismay by her parents, who believed that the real threat to Turkey's future was the stealthy but steady effort to roll back Atatürk's secular, modernizing reforms.

Political differences were temporarily put aside when an earthquake killed 3,162 people in Varto in August of 1966. Sude threw herself into the relief fund campaign and was a little resentful when her father couldn't make a big enough donation to win her the title of "top fund-raiser."

The rest of the 1960s were marked by protests and violence. Young revolutionaries demonstrated against the visits of the US Sixth Fleet in Istanbul and İzmir, labor strikes were never-ending, and nationalists firebombed cinemas, teahouses, and restaurants popular with leftists.

The nation was restless. Its people were poor. Its people were angry.

Sude was dealing with her own issues, chief among them the eruption of pimples, the attentions of boys with cracking voices, and the extent of her popularity with a gaggle of giggling girls.

She was twelve when her mother scolded her for coming home late from a New Year's party. Sude cried, slammed her bedroom door, and refused to talk to her parents or even Meral the cleaning lady when she got up the next morning. With the logic of a twelve-year-old, she believed that a good, long silent treatment would force her mother to relent and allow her to attend a birthday party that coming weekend. If she couldn't go to that party, her life would be over!

She was on her way home that week when she noticed a police car at the campus gate, then barricades—the roads were cut off! Apparently, when American ambassador Komer had visited the campus earlier that day, students had overturned his car and set it on fire.

When Sude was finally allowed to go home, she found a bunch of men, some of them in uniform and some in suits, ransacking her house. Books had been swept off the shelves; drawers had been emptied. They were putting some of her family's things in a big bag. Meral was trying desperately to clean up.

One of the men picked up her violin, turned it upside down, and held it up to his ear, shaking it to see if anything was hidden inside.

Sude rushed up to him. "Leave my violin alone, please. It's a very delicate instrument!"

"Who plays this? You?"

"Yes."

"Don't you have anything better to do?"

"Like what?"

"I don't know. Learn to sew. Learn to cook."

"I know how to make spaghetti," Sude said.

When the men were gone, Sude went to the window and watched for her parents. It got late, and still they didn't come. Meral finished cleaning up, then brought Sude some tea and cake.

"Listen, child, it's already late, and they'll be wondering about me at home," Meral said. "Maybe you should come with me?"

"You can go home," Sude said, "but I'm waiting here for my mom and dad."

Meral left. Sude stayed by the window, regretting how she'd treated her mother and father. About an hour later, her father's assistant came to the house with a note in her mother's handwriting.

> Sude,
> Don't worry. Your father and I are fine. We're helping with an investigation and will be home soon. Spend tonight at Hülya's and call your grandparents as soon as you get this note. Ask your grandma Bedia to come and stay with you until we can return home. See you soon. Your father sends his love, too.
> Mom

Sude raced to the phone. She'd have preferred to call Grandma Elsa, but she and Grandpa Gerhard were in Frankfurt for the winter, and even when they did come to Turkey, they spent most of their time at their summer house in Side. Praying that Grandpa Nazmi would answer the phone, not Grandma Bedia, Sude gave the operator their long-distance number in Istanbul. Then she called her classmate and neighbor, Hülya, and told her what had happened. The operator still hadn't called back with a connection to Istanbul when Hülya's mother arrived. Vicdan Hanım reluctantly agreed to wait.

Once she'd finished a slice of cake, though, Hülya's mom said, "Come on, Sude. This is taking forever. Go and get your toothbrush, your nightgown, and your stuff for school tomorrow."

"But if the operator does put the call through and I'm not here to answer, Grandma will be so worried."

"You can call again from our house."

Sude packed her things, but just as they were leaving, the phone rang. Sude was helpless to answer the flood of questions from Grandma Bedia. All she knew was what was written in the note. Yes, she said, the ambassador's car was set on fire, the campus was crawling with police, and her parents were supposed to come home soon.

Her grandfather must have snatched the phone. "We're leaving tonight, and we'll be there tomorrow. You can tell us everything then," he said.

By the time Sude finished school the next day, her grandparents had arrived in Ankara. Her grandmother talked nonstop, grumbling about how many times she'd warned Demir and Suzi to stay out of politics. But Grandma Bedia's food tasted better than anything Sude's mother or Meral ever made. Sude gobbled down plate after plate of stuffed grape leaves, baked pastries, and stuffed zucchini. Meral scowled and dusted, upset at having been ejected from the kitchen.

Three days later, Sude's mother and father got home just as everyone was sitting down to dinner. Bedia Hanım kept asking why it had taken four days for the police to question them, but all they would say was that they'd had to wait their turn. The students had all been interrogated first.

From then on, Sude lived with the anxiety that her parents wouldn't come home one day. She followed current events, not because she was interested in politics, but because she worried they would get swept up in another disturbance. The "Bloody Sunday" attack by right-wing militants on left-wingers demonstrating against "imperialism and exploitation" left two dead and hundreds injured. It happened in Istanbul, but it could just as easily have been Ankara. And Sude knew that hers wasn't any ordinary family. Her parents were left-wing intellectuals at a time when leftists were being interrogated, arrested, and shot.

In a drastic measure aimed at putting an end to the widespread boycotts and sit-ins, Middle East Technical University was closed indefinitely in 1971.

That was when Suzi and Demir decided that their daughter was no longer safe in their home. Even though it meant repeating a year of school, Sude was sent to Istanbul. She started boarding at Robert College, which had just merged with the American College for Girls.

Sude missed her parents, of course, but she didn't miss the drawn-out political discussions around the dinner table. So removed was she from current events that the "coup by memorandum" on March 12, 1971, completely passed her by. Eager perhaps not to become the second executed prime minister in Turkish history, Demirel obligingly resigned and was replaced by a nonpartisan interim government headed by a member of the main opposition party.

On a day in early May, her mother answered the phone in tears when Sude called.

"Mom, what's wrong?"

"It's Deniz Gezmiş. They hanged him this morning. Along with Yusuf and Hüseyin. How could they? They were still so young."

"Were they your students or something?"

"Does it matter? What kind of question is that?"

"You're acting like you knew them. That's all I meant."

"Sude! They were fighting for justice. Perhaps they made some mistakes, but they didn't deserve to die!"

After she hung up, Suzi turned to Demir and said, "How can Sude be so insensitive? Where did we go wrong?"

"My father was a cloth merchant who wasn't interested in anything but the bottom line. In the same way I reacted to him, Sude might be reacting to us. You know she hates politics."

"Oh, Demir, do you think she could become right-wing just to spite us?"

"No, never. She'll probably just be apolitical, at least until she comes into her own."

Sude had no interest in either CHP leader Ecevit's famous slogan, "Soil belongs to whoever tills it, and water belongs to whoever uses it," or the founding of Erbakan's ultraconservative National Salvation Party. Those were the boring things her parents always discussed at the dinner table. She was so removed from the political pulse of her country that she didn't even realize how religious extremism for political gain was sowing the seeds of anti-Semitism.

The one political event about which Sude expressed any opinion was the reception given to *Beautiful Istanbul*, one of the sculptures erected in Istanbul to mark the fiftieth anniversary of the Turkish republic. The conservative partner in the coalition government condemned the stone figure of a reclining nude as a disgraceful attack on Turkish motherhood. It was soon removed from the square in Karaköy. Sude snickered and said, "They're such silly prudes."

That same year, again in the name of public morality, the conservatives managed to block three major tourism projects.

Unlike her daughter, Suzi sensed that something was changing in Turkey. This wasn't the classic tug-of-war between left and right. This was something new and insidious.

Sude spent her free time making décor in the theater club, listening to the recitals of the jazz club, playing violin in the classical music club, and falling in love in the debate club. The young man who had caught her eye was a year ahead of her and a great debater. There was so much to love about life at Robert College.

When the entire family gathered at Grandpa Gerhard and Grandma Elsa's summer house that year, everyone commented on how sweet and happy Sude had become.

The house in Side was on a small promontory jutting into the Mediterranean Sea. Several other retired German professors had also bought houses there. The site of an ancient port, Side was a paradise of blue seas, sandy beaches, and Greco-Roman ruins. Some of the Germans chose to live there year-round, but Gerhard and Elsa would arrive at the beginning of June and leave at the end of October. The house had plenty of room for children and grandchildren, and a spacious garden with a long wooden table. There, in the shade of pomegranate and fig trees, the family would have leisurely meals, watch the sunset, and enjoy impromptu concerts organized by Hirsch. Hirsch and his fellow musicians were known simply as "The Players." Occasionally, some locals would drift in to listen, and The Players would intersperse their Schubert and Mozart with lively village tunes.

In July of 1972, The Players were awaiting the arrival of their venerable violin player, Professor Zuckmayer, when the news came that he had passed away. Sude burst into tears when she learned that her teacher had died. When Gerhard and Hirsch decided to set out that night for Ankara so they could attend the funeral, Sude insisted on going with them.

As Hirsch was pulling out of the driveway in his pale-green Murat, with Gerhard in the passenger seat and Sude in back, Suzi ran after them with a pillow in one hand and a bowl of water in the other. She handed the pillow to Sude and urged her to get some sleep on the way. She poured the water onto the ground as they drove away.

"Mom always does that," Sude said.

"It's a wonderful Turkish custom," Hirsch said. "It means 'Go like water and return like water. May your journey be as smooth as flowing water.'"

"I know what it means, Uncle Hirsch. But what good does it do?"

"We'll talk about that when we get home safely."

"Sude's a teenager," Gerhard said. "She has the right to object to everything."

"I'm a young woman," Sude snapped. She crossed her arms and stared out the window.

Assuming she'd fallen asleep, Gerhard and Hirsch were soon deep in conversation.

"Zuckmayer had a much harder time than we did," Gerhard said. "Did you know that he wasn't granted Turkish citizenship, even though he applied? He spent eighteen months interned in Kırşehir back in 1944."

"Yes, but did he ever tell you what he did there? He formed a choral society. The internees sang and played instruments. They started giving concerts every weekend for the locals."

"Did you know that the Red Crescent gave all the internees monthly aid of twenty lira?"

"Really?" Gerhard said. "I didn't realize."

"Not that there's much to spend money on in Kırşehir. Even the most beautiful *Dirne* out there couldn't have charged more than five lira."

"Assuming Zuckmayer could ever look up from his violin long enough to notice her."

Both men burst out laughing.

"Shh," Gerhard said. "Sude will wake up."

"I've been wide awake the whole time."

"You mean you were listening to us?" Hirsch said.

"No, she wasn't," Gerhard said. "You were sleeping, weren't you, Sude?"

"Grandpa, what's a 'dirne'?"

"I'm glad you're awake. There's a lot you can learn from Hirsch. Did you know the pivotal role Zuckmayer played in popularizing classical music in Turkey? He arrived in Ankara a few years after we came to Turkey and founded the music department of the Gazi Teacher Training Institute. You're a very lucky girl to have had him as your teacher."

"Grandpa, what's a 'dirne'?"

Hirsch intervened. "Sude, when Zuckmayer was finally allowed to leave Kırşehir, a huge crowd assembled to see him off. They showered him with gifts. And even in spite of being interned, he still loved Turkey so much that when his wife and daughter moved back to Germany, he stayed at the institute, living in a single dorm room. Did you ever go there for your lessons? If so, you must have seen all the keepsakes from his days in Kırşehir."

There was no response from the backseat. Gerhard turned and looked.

"Thanks, Hirsch. Your lecture must have put her to sleep. Hopefully, she won't ask again about 'dirne' when she wakes up."

"I think you might have to tell her. Kids remember the craziest things."

When they reached their hotel in Ankara, Sude was still sound asleep. She staggered to the hotel room, rubbing her eyes. She slipped into her nightgown, and was soon oblivious to the world, on the bed by the window.

Gerhard was surprised at how difficult it was to wake Sude the next morning. Because of her, they were nearly late for the ceremony at the institute. It wasn't until they ran into young Kurt Lütfü Heilbronn, the son of a German botanist and his Turkish assistant, that Sude seemed to fully wake up. Kurt's eyes widened in amazement when he realized that the beautiful young woman shaking his hand was none other than Sude Atalay, whom he remembered as a shy little girl with stringy hair who kept her nose in a book.

It didn't escape Hirsch's notice when Kurt and Sude sat next to each other at the ceremony. He nudged Gerhard. "Looks like Sude made a friend."

But Gerhard was too preoccupied with old friends to take much notice. He gazed around the room at the men and women who had shared his fate all those years ago. Some had gone bald and grown a bit stooped; others looked like wrinkled versions of their younger selves. He spotted the mathematician, Prager, and the professor of dentistry, Kantorowicz. He'd heard that the latter had returned to Germany and settled in Bonn. Perhaps he spent part of the year in Turkey as well? It was Kantorowicz who had fitted orthodontic braces for Peter and Suzi, without which they would both be slightly buck-toothed today. It was also Kantorowicz who had been urgently summoned to Dolmabahçe Palace in 1934. Apparently, the shah of Iran had so admired Atatürk's teeth during a state visit that he'd asked to meet the Turkish president's dentist.

Gerhard smiled at the memory: a German refugee crafting false teeth for an Iranian shah in the middle of the night in a former Ottoman palace. Then he thought back to that evening when he and Hirsch had looked out at the Bosphorus from a window in that same palace. He had so much to be grateful for. He'd survived and thrived, had children, and lived to see his grandchildren. So many hadn't . . .

"Are you thinking about Zuckmayer?" Hirsch asked. "You don't seem at all interested in your granddaughter's little flirtation."

Gerhard looked over to where Hirsch was pointing. But then he felt a tap on his shoulder and turned around—Kosswig! Gerhard hadn't seen Kosswig since he and Elsa moved to Frankfurt. They kissed each other on both cheeks.

"That's how you know we've spent so many years in Turkey," Kosswig said. "Otherwise, we'd have settled for a stiff handshake."

"It's wonderful to see you. And you're looking so well. How are your bald ibises?"

"My birds are fine, but Leonore's ailing. She wasn't feeling well enough to come today. I'd love to have a chance to sit down and talk with you, Gerhard," Kosswig said.

"Let's go somewhere after the burial. Hirsch and I drove up from Side. We don't have a bus to catch."

"How are Elsa and your kids doing?"

"Everyone's well. The kids are all grown up! In fact, do you see that young lady sitting over there next to Kurt? That's my granddaughter, Sude."

Kosswig craned his neck. "I don't believe it! She's the spitting image of Elsa in her youth. The only difference is that Sude's hair is darker."

Gerhard regretted having asked about Kosswig's birds instead of his wife and wondered if he should offer to examine Leonore. Maybe he should stay in Ankara a while. If Hirsch and Sude were eager to get back, they could take the car, and he'd catch a bus later.

To be fair, Curt Kosswig was famous for his birds. A student's description of a bird with black plumage, a bald head, and a curved, red beak had sent the professor in pursuit of the northern bald ibis, an ancient species that would probably have gone extinct in Turkey if not for his tireless conservation efforts. It was also Kosswig who documented the flora and fauna in the Bird Paradise in Manyas, a wetland designated a national sanctuary in 1959.

The ceremony was about to start. Everyone took their seats. The mood in the hall was somber. The youngest of that group of men and women who had arrived in Turkey in the 1930s was at least seventy. Whose funeral would they attend next?

About ten days after Gerhard's return from Ankara, Peter arrived in Side with his wife and children. The sun was out, as always, and everyone was either stretched out on the white sand or splashing in the surf.

Elsa peered out at her grandchildren from under the brim of her straw hat. "Look at them, Gerhard. Here we are, a German Jewish couple on a Turkish beach. Our son is American, and our daughter is Turkish. Our grandchildren are all Christian or Muslim. Was this our destiny?"

"I don't have any complaints, Elsa. And anyway, don't blame destiny. Blame Hitler!"

Sude returned to school at the end of the summer, relaxed and tanned. She continued to do well in her classes, with perfect grades in German boosting her grade point average even higher. Most weekends were spent with her grandma Bedia, and every Sunday morning, she would play the violin with Hirsch, who had moved to Istanbul. She spoke to her parents at least once a week and visited them during semester breaks and holidays.

Sude finally got to know the handsome boy from debate club. They were in the same circle of friends, and started going to the same parties, plays, and movies. His name was Enver. During one of their weekly phone calls, Sude told her mother she'd met a boy who was smart and kind. Suzi asked if Enver was as handsome as Hirsch's son with the same name. Maybe not, Sude admitted.

"But he's so nice and he's got a great smile. And he makes me feel special."

"Are you head over heels?"

"I mean, it's not like how you feel about Dad. But I like him a lot."

"What do you mean, not like how I feel about your father?"

"It's like you two were made for each other. Like you could never love anyone else. The way I feel about is Enver is more—reasonable."

"Good luck with that, sweetie! When will I get to meet this 'reasonable' boyfriend of yours?"

"I'll introduce you at the graduation ceremony."

In bed that night, Suzi turned to her husband and said, "I think our little girl's fallen in love."

"Good for her," Demir said. "You worried she was unfeeling. See! Sude has a heart after all."

Grandma Bedia had far more questions about young Enver than Suzi did. She ticked them off: What did his father do? Were they well-off? Where was his family from? Did he have any brothers or sisters? Enver Semercioğlu, she learned, was the son of a processed food industrialist with his own factory on the outskirts of Istanbul. The family was originally from the provinces, but had grown wealthy. Since graduating from Robert College, Enver was studying at a local university. He had two sisters. Bedia Hanım thought it was safe to assume that the father's factory would be passed on to his only son. While her own son hadn't turned out quite as she'd hoped, it would be wonderful if his daughter enjoyed a comfortable life with the kind of enterprising young man Demir had never become.

A Door on Life

Sude wore a sleeveless white mini-dress with beige polka dots to her commencement. Suzi and Demir marveled at their daughter's beauty. Her thick chestnut hair hung down to her shoulders. She had her mother's complexion, nose, and mouth, and was nearly as tall as her father.

Bedia Hanım had already produced a handkerchief and a few tears to go with it. When Sude saw that her family was comfortably seated, she dashed off to get into her gown and cap.

Suzi ran after her and asked, "Is Enver coming?"

"Mom, don't look now, but he's talking to his friends right over there. The tall one in the red tie and white shirt. Whatever you do, don't point him out to Grandma!"

Suzi snuck a glance. He looked like a nice enough boy for a first crush.

Ten minutes later, the students filed into the auditorium to the strains of *Pomp and Circumstance* and took their seats behind the faculty members. An illustrious alumnus walked to the microphone and began delivering the commencement speech: "A high school diploma opens a new door on life, but you will be faced with many different paths once you have passed through that door . . ."

Sude started fidgeting almost immediately. She glanced over at Enver, who was sitting in the fifth row, and blushed when their eyes met.

When the ceremony was over, Sude introduced Enver to her family. They stood and chatted for a moment. Enver, who had graduated from Robert College the year before, explained that he was studying at Bosphorus University, but planned to transfer to a school in America. Sude was trying to hide her dismay at hearing this when Enver surprised her once again.

"The graduation party is tonight, at the Hilton rooftop," Enver said to Demir. "With your permission, I'd like to take Sude to the party. I'll drop her off at her grandparents' house afterward."

"I'll agree on one condition. I don't want her staying out too late," Demir said.

"Demir, it's such a special occasion," Bedia Hanım chimed in. "You could be a little lenient, just this once."

"All right, but make sure she's home by one o'clock."

"Come on, Dad. Please make it two," Sude said, looking at her grandmother for support.

Enver took Sude's hand and led her from the rooftop dance floor to the elevator. A few moments later, they were walking along a winding path through the grounds of the hotel. They reached the swimming pool and sat down side by side on a lounge chair.

"Sude, I'm sorry for surprising you earlier. I—I've been accepted at a university in New York, starting in September."

"Why are you transferring? What's wrong with the university here?"

"In America, you're allowed to take extra credit hours and graduate in three years. My father's eager for me to start at the family company. I'm doing it so I can finish my studies and get started in life."

Sude studied Enver's face for a moment. "What do you expect me to say?"

"Come with me."

"I was planning to study in Germany. My parents would never let me go all the way to America."

"My parents would let you."

"What do you mean?"

"Let's get engaged, Sude. Then we can go to America together."

"My parents would never allow it, not in a million years. I'd be disowned."

"But if we got married . . ."

Sude's heart started beating faster. Was this a marriage proposal?

"You don't know my parents."

"I don't want you to study in Germany all alone."

"I won't be alone, Enver. I'll live with my grandparents in Frankfurt."

"Think it over. Why not talk to your parents and see what they say?"

"Okay, I will," Sude said.

Nobody else was sitting at the pool, so they kissed for a while. Then, still holding hands, they returned to the rooftop and joined the other couples dancing cheek-to-cheek. Several drinks later, the DJ switched to Turkish pop and everyone started singing along to Ajda Pekkan. Finally, when it was nearly two, Enver dutifully drove Sude home in his new car.

The steady decline of Beyoğlu had caused Nazmi Bey and Bedia Hanım to move to Şişli, several miles away. Most of the apartment buildings vacated by the Greeks were now occupied by the poor migrants flooding into Istanbul from the countryside in search of jobs.

Demir and Suzi continued to rent out the place they'd inherited on Grenadier Street in what was an increasingly undesirable neighborhood. They stayed with his parents whenever they were in Istanbul.

After their good-night kiss in front of the door, Enver said, "Talk to them."

"Don't you think we're rushing things a bit, Enver? I graduated from high school today. Why don't we wait until the end of the summer?"

"I need to know before you go to Side. Talk to your mom tomorrow morning. She'll help you persuade your dad."

"Okay, I'll talk to her."

A bouquet of white roses was delivered to the Atalays' apartment the next morning while the family was having breakfast. The card said: "Let's step through the door to life together."

Sude felt cornered, and as though she had to tell not only her mother, but also everyone. Bedia Hanım congratulated her granddaughter on making a good match, but Demir immediately put his foot down.

"She's far too young to get engaged."

"Sude, what do you think?" Nazmi Bey said.

"I need to think it over."

"That's good. But you'd better decide before his family comes and asks for your hand. It would be shameful if they came here with flowers and chocolates only to be refused," Nazmi Bey said. "You know that an official engagement is nearly as meaningful as a wedding for us Turks."

After Sude fled to a friend's house, her parents and grandparents debated the matter for the rest of the day. It was finally agreed that Suzi would meet with Enver and Sude for a cup of tea, learn all she could about him and his family, and provide a frank assessment to the others. They weren't trying to stop Sude from getting engaged, but they thought it wise to delay things for as long as possible.

Enver responded to the invitation to tea with a counterproposal for dinner. Suzi agreed and a date was set in late June, just before the family was to set off for Side.

Enver picked up Suzi and Sude and drove them to Abdullah Efendi Restaurant in Emirgan, where he'd reserved a table by the window.

Once they were seated, he said, "I wanted to bring my mother as well. But Sude wouldn't let me."

"I do hope to meet her one day," Suzi said.

A bottle of fine wine was opened, and Enver urged Suzi and Sude to order the most expensive items on the menu. Barely pausing to draw breath, he earnestly explained in minute detail the courses he intended to take, the number of credits he would earn each semester, and the responsibilities and salary of the position awaiting him at the family company when he returned to Turkey.

Rather than peppering Enver with questions, Suzi kept trying to guide him into more general conversation, both to help him relax and to give her a better sense of who he was.

"Do you know what your name means?" Suzi asked with a smile when she found an opening.

"It was my grandfather's name. My father's father."

"But do you know what it means?"

"No. I never thought about it."

"It's a lovely name. It's Ottoman for 'an enlightened person.' It's derived from the word *münevver*."

"I should have brushed up on my etymology before having dinner with a professor."

They both laughed.

"The only reason I know is that a close family friend of ours chose to name his son Enver Tandoğan. Perhaps you've heard of Ernst Hirsch? He's one of the architects of the Turkish legal system."

"But Enver is a Turkish name."

"They became Turkish. Just like my family."

"Do you mean you aren't Turkish?"

"I'm Turkish, but my mother's parents are German," Sude interjected. "I mean, they're Turkish citizens of German descent. My grandfather's Turkish is better than mine, but Grandma still has an accent."

"I don't understand," Enver said. "Are you German?"

"My father was born Turkish," Sude said. "And my mother's heart beats for my father and for Turkey. I guess that makes her a Turk. Let's say she's a Turk transplanted from Germany."

"Oh. How did that happen?"

Suzi said, "In 1933, my father was one of the first foreign professors invited to teach at Istanbul University. It was a personal invitation from Atatürk, no less. We ended up staying in Turkey. That's the short answer."

"So Sude is half German, then?"

"That depends on how you look at it, Enver," Suzi said. "She's Turkish on her father's side. I'd say she's pretty much Turkish on my side, too. I'll tell you what, let's say she's 80 percent Turkish. It's only fair for my parents to contribute a little bit of Germanness!"

Enver threw his head back and laughed. "My father will be thrilled when I tell him. He loves Germans. He's always going on about how disciplined and hardworking the Germans are. He even admires Hitler."

Suzi set down her glass and looked at Sude, who had gone white. Enver immediately realized he'd put his foot in his mouth. Sude's parents were lefties! Why had he been so stupid?

"Was Hirsch's wife Turkish?" he asked, desperate to change the subject.

"Both of Enver's parents are German. They chose to become Turkish." Suzi had put her hands in her lap, but she couldn't hide the quaver in her voice.

"Why did they do that?"

"The German professors who came to Turkey in 1933 were all fleeing Hitler's oppression. There were hundreds of them. Some became

Turkish citizens, like us, and others eventually went back to Germany after the war. Many of them are buried in cemeteries here in Istanbul and in Ankara."

A cloud passed over Enver's face.

"Does this mean you're Christian?" he asked.

"No. We're not."

After a moment of uncomfortable silence, Suzi decided to explain. "I'm Jewish. And I grew up respecting people of all faiths."

"You said you were Turkish!" Enver protested. "If you're Turkish, you have to be Muslim."

"You're confusing two very different things, nationality and religion. I know a lot of native-born Turks who aren't Muslim." When Sude kicked Suzi under the table, she turned to her daughter and continued. "Hey! You know Simon and Selin, and our friend Madame was—"

"That's enough, Mother," Sude said in German. "You made your point!"

The wine had gone warm and the food had gone cold. Feeble attempts at further conversation faltered and died. Nobody felt like having dessert.

As they waited for the coffee, Suzi said, "Thank you for inviting us, Enver. I still feel as if there's so much I don't know about you, though. You haven't told us a thing about your family."

"We're from central Anatolia. But I grew up in Istanbul."

Suzi finished her coffee, and Enver asked for the check. Sude didn't say a word.

On the way home, they all agreed that it was a warm summer evening and that rain was unlikely for the rest of the week.

Enver didn't walk Suzi and Sude to the front door, but he did wait in his car until they were in the building. In the elevator, Suzi put her hand on Sude's shoulder and said, "I'd suggest you tell your grandmother as little as possible about this evening."

Sude nodded.

Bedia Hanım pounced as soon as they stepped into the entry hall.

"So, tell me all about it. Suzi, what did you think of the bridegroom?"

"To be honest, I didn't think much of him. You know what the children of the newly rich are like. He's a bit of an empty suit, I'm afraid."

"Sude, don't listen to your crazy mother," Bedia Hanım said. "Where did you go? What did you have for dinner?"

"Grandma, I've got a headache from the wine. I need to go to bed. I'll tell you about it tomorrow."

A less extravagant bouquet arrived the following morning. This time, it came with a sealed envelope. Sude took the envelope to her bedroom, opened it, and read the note on the pale-blue paper.

Dear Sude,
You were right. There's no need to rush things. I need
some time to persuade my father. Have a great time in
Side. Look forward to seeing you when you get back.
Enver

Sude put the letter in the envelope and the envelope in the book she was reading. Then she got out her diary, recorded the date, and wrote:

I'm stepping through the door to life alone. And if I keep
living in this country, I'll probably be alone forever. I
have Jewish blood.

New Horizons

Sude spent the first month of that summer in Side nursing a broken heart. It didn't matter how often her mother and father consoled her with the obvious truth that Enver was a complete idiot. She'd been rejected, and it was because of what she was, not who she was. Grandpa Gerhard, Grandma Elsa, and her mother were Jewish. But what did that mean, exactly? How should she feel about it? She'd always imagined that because such things made no difference to her, they wouldn't matter to anyone else, either.

Enver hadn't minded that she was German. He'd dumped her because she was Jewish. His father admired Hitler! Was that possible? How could anyone admire Hitler? Was it because he hated Jews? Of all the boys at school, why, oh why, had she gone and fallen for Enver? Or were the other boys' fathers just like Enver's, fathers whom Sude's parents would have called fascists. It seemed so unfair. She'd been to a few Bar Mitzvahs, a couple of Jewish weddings, and one funeral. Those were the only times she'd ever even been in a synagogue. As far as she knew, her mother went only very occasionally, and she'd never pushed Sude or given her any religious instruction. Besides, what if she did go to the synagogue every single day of the week? What business was that of Enver's and his stupid father? If being Jewish was so bad, why had Grandpa Nazmi let his only son marry her mother?

After several sleepless nights, she was ready to speak frankly to her grandfather.

"Your mother grew up with us," Grandpa Nazmi said. "When your grandparents moved to our building, she was about a year old. We adored her. We've always considered her to be one of us."

"Would you have let your son marry a Jewish girl you didn't know?"

"Yes. As long as our grandchildren would be brought up as Muslims."

"Grandpa, am I a Muslim?"

"Of course."

"But I never pray or fast. And for that matter, neither do you or Grandma."

Nazmi Bey didn't say anything for a moment. Then he looked his granddaughter in the eye and said, "Look inside your heart, Sude. You're whatever it is you see there."

Sude's heart was broken. And empty. She didn't feel as though she belonged to any religion, and she was certain she would never love again. All she wanted was to be left alone.

Her grandma Bedia kept saying, "They'll be lining up for you, my dear. You're a beautiful girl. Now stop moping!"

Her grandma Elsa said, "Life isn't always easy, Sude. Be ready for anything and learn to pick yourself up when you fall. Above all, don't let a silly boy make you so unhappy!"

Her mother told her, "When you start university in Frankfurt, the world will seem like a completely different place. Who knows how many boys you'll fall in love with? Just be yourself. Don't let anyone tell you what to do. What could be more precious in life than the freedom to make your own choices and your own mistakes?"

"I don't know what's precious in life, Mom! Nothing makes sense."

Then, six weeks before the end of summer break, along came Korhan.

It was evening. Sude was sitting on the stone steps in the ruins of Side's ancient amphitheater, watching the sea. She heard a click, but took no notice. Then it happened again. Click. Click. Click. She turned and looked. A shaggy guy in shorts was coming toward her, springing up the steps two and three at a time.

"I took your picture," he said.

"Why?"

"I'm going to hold an exhibition. On solitude. I didn't want to use your photo without your permission. Nobody will know it's you. I took them all from behind."

"What's a picture of someone's back got to do with solitude?"

"You should see the way you hold your shoulders. It's a study in loneliness."

"Are you sure you're not crazy?"

"No, I'm not crazy. But I know what it is to be alone. And I recognized something in your shoulders, something I can see in your eyes, too."

Sude reflexively covered her eyes with her hand as she stood up.

"I could keep you company, if you'd like," the shaggy man said.

"No! I'm leaving."

"I knew it."

"Knew what?"

"That you were about to leave. You always get up and go when the sun disappears behind that column over there."

"Have you been spying on me?"

"It's not spying if you happen to sit right where I'm looking. Do you see that house over there?" he asked, pointing to a stone building with a red tile roof. "I live there. And I've seen you sitting up here alone for weeks now."

"Don't you have to go to work?"

"I don't work. I paint, I cook, I take pictures, I play the flute. Sometimes I read books, and sometimes I write them."

"You're either a dreamer or a loafer. Or maybe both."

"Both!"

"It's a wonder you don't starve to death."

"Oh, I'd never starve. I'm a great cook. I make my own pickles and bread. I've got some homemade cherry liqueur if you're interested."

Sude looked the shaggy man up and down. His skin was the color of copper, and his wild brown hair was sun-bleached. His eyes were a strange color somewhere between green and light-brown. He was taller than she was, which made him tall, even for a man. For some reason, she felt like she could trust him.

"I'm Korhan."

"Sude."

An hour later, Sude was sitting in Korhan's stone house. She was sipping sour cherry–infused vodka and studying the paintings on the wall—watercolors of the sea, mostly—while he developed his latest roll of film in a makeshift darkroom.

The furnishings were spare. Plank floors and handwoven carpets. Stained wood and bright cotton curtains. It was everyone's fantasy of what a village house should be. Perhaps Korhan had designed it himself? Sude decided not to ask any questions. And she wouldn't tell him anything about herself, either.

By the end of the second hour in Korhan's stone house, Sude was kneeling on a cushion in front of the photographs he'd laid on the floor.

In the first photo, the rays of the evening sun created a halo effect around her head. Her shoulders—he was right, her shoulders were crying, if shoulders can cry. She looked at the next one. It was taken from behind, too, but his camera saw right through her. Was he some kind of wizard?

Korhan came over and knelt next to her. "Why are you so sad, pretty girl?"

Sude found she'd rested her head on his shoulder. He smelled like the sea.

"I'm not sad," she said. "I'm just lonely."

Three hours later, they'd reached the bottom of the bottle, and Korhan had learned that Sude was going to Ankara in September and from there to Frankfurt. He gently pushed her hair back from her face. He kissed her.

They sat like that for a while longer, their shoulders touching.

Sude got up and said, "I've got to go home."

"Don't go."

"They'll get worried."

"I mean, go to your summer house now. But come back and stay with me. Don't go to Ankara or Germany."

"What will we do if I stay with you?"

"We'll cook, we'll paint, we'll take pictures, we'll read, we'll swim, we'll go on walks, we'll explore . . . and, if you like, we'll make love."

"I'm half Jewish, you know."

"So what?" Korhan said.

"You don't mind?"

"Why would I?"

"It doesn't bother you?"

"Should it?"

"Okay. Then I'll see you tomorrow, at sunset," Sude said. She ran all the way home and went straight up to Suzi, who was doing the dishes.

"I think I found the man of my life, Mom."

"Well, that was quick. Weren't you saying something about your heart being empty just this morning?"

"Korhan, the guy I met, doesn't care at all that I'm Jewish."

"Number one, if you're not going to be home for dinner, let us know. Number two, that doesn't make him the man of your life."

"Mom, why won't you let me be happy?"

Sude started spending mornings with her family on the beach and evenings with Korhan. A couple of times a week, she'd make a point of having dinner with her family, but always sprang up and ran off when the meal was over. When Korhan wasn't at home, she would find him playing the guitar in front of a bonfire on the beach with the tourists he sometimes guided through the ruins. After everyone went back to their hotels, she and Korhan would walk to his house together. Sometimes they made love, and sometimes they sat there together without a word.

"What are you thinking about when you get that faraway look?" Sude asked him on one of those silent days when they were sitting in the courtyard.

"I'm listening to my inner voice."

"And what's it telling you?"

"That I should savor every second."

"But all you do is waste time, Korhan! You don't have a family or a proper job."

"I've got peace of mind! Nothing's more precious than that."

"Love is precious, too."

"Come on, then. Let's go and make some." Korhan gathered Sude up in his arms and carried her into the house.

And so the days of August passed, mellow and easy.

In mid-September, Sude said to her mother, "I'm not going to Ankara with you and Dad at the end of the month. And I'm not going to Frankfurt, either."

"Sude! You're already registered for classes. And we've paid the fees. What are you talking about?"

"You told me there was nothing more precious than having the freedom to make my own decisions. I've decided to stay here."

"Once the season's over, everything will be closed. You'll be bored to death. What do you plan on doing all winter long, in Side of all places?"

"I'm going to listen to my inner voice and find myself, Mother. I'll never find myself until I get away from you and Dad and my grandparents."

Suzi stared at her daughter. Inner voice? Sude must have picked that up from her new boyfriend.

In tears that night, Suzi told her husband what had happened. "Please talk to her, Demir. She's making the worst mistake of her life!"

"She's got the law on her side, dear. If she were under eighteen, I'd sling her over my shoulder and carry her home."

"What are we going to do?"

"We'll let her live her life. It won't hurt for her to have a year to herself. She'll be eager to go to university next year."

"You realize why she's doing this, don't you? She's had a complex about her Jewish heritage ever since that imbecile, Enver."

"I suspect it's more than that. But if she has developed a complex of some kind, this might be just the opportunity she needs to get over it."

Now it was Suzi's turn to suffer sleepless nights. Careful not to disturb her parents, she'd end up tiptoeing around the house until dawn. Was it right to leave Sude behind with a perfect stranger? Technically, she was an adult, but she still seemed like a child. Were Suzi to confide in her own mother, she knew she'd get an earful. They'd end up talking about how Suzi got pregnant before she was married. But it wasn't the same thing. She and Demir had been madly in love, and they'd known they would spend the rest of their lives together. What's more, they'd grown up together, where everyone knew them. This was different. They were about to leave their daughter, who was barely out of high school, in a little seaside town with a strange man who was nearly thirty! And Demir refused to do anything about it.

Early one morning, Suzi slowly opened the door and slipped out into the garden, barefoot. As she stretched out on a garden chair, heedless of the dew, she started. It felt like a cold hand had touched her shoulder. She turned and looked, but nobody was there. The sky paled and a hint of pink appeared on the horizon. It reminded Suzi of a moment years ago, back before she'd married Demir.

She had attended a wedding reception at the Pera Palace Hotel and was spending the night at Madame's afterward. Wide awake, she'd sat in front of the window, waiting for the sun to come up, just like this. Except, that night, she was up thinking about Demir. Madame had come in and covered her shoulders with a shawl.

"Suzi," Madame had said, "never let your pride get the better of you. Life isn't nearly as long as you think. It gallops by. Blink, and you miss it. If you love someone, never hide it. Open your heart."

She'd rested her head on Madame's shoulder and fallen asleep right there on the sofa in front of the window. She'd always told Madame everything, all the secrets she kept from her mother. Perhaps that's why she was being punished now? Sude never told her anything.

She felt it again! A touch on her back . . . but this time she didn't need to turn around and see what it was. Demir was draping a robe over her shoulders. She smiled.

"You'll catch a chill out here. Come inside. You can think in bed, too, you know. Or better yet, stop thinking! Sude's ready to fly out of the nest. Let her go."

"But she's so alone."

"So be it! She'll feel lonely until she meets the right person. If we try to restrict her freedom, she'll just get miserable and blame us."

Suzi got up a bit stiffly and groaned. Demir put his arm around her waist, and they walked into the house together.

"All I want is for her to be as happy as I am. Am I asking too much?" Suzi said.

"She'll have to find her own path and her own happiness. Just don't expect her to be like you. That would be asking for far too much."

Suzi got into bed and nestled against her husband. Demir pulled the blanket all the way up over her head so the early morning light wouldn't get in her eyes. Her last thought before she fell asleep was, *Perhaps Korhan will show this same tenderness to Sude.*

At the end of September, the Şilimans returned to Frankfurt, the Atalays returned to Ankara, and Sude stayed in Side with Korhan.

Their first winter together wouldn't be their last. In their early days, they did all the things Korhan had promised. They painted and cooked and made pickles. Sude had her violin sent from Ankara, and Korhan would accompany her on the flute. Sometimes they'd give impromptu concerts in the Roman amphitheater for tourists and locals. They'd get into Korhan's beat-up old car, drive to nearby villages, and talk, talk, talk. Sude would tell Korhan things about herself she'd never put into words. It was during those long talks that she realized she'd never been in love with Enver and that she was absolutely devoted to her mother.

And they made love.

It didn't take long for Sude to realize she wasn't in love with Korhan. She liked him a lot and thought he was interesting, smart, and good with his hands. She and Korhan could talk about everything but politics. No, there was one other thing: the forbidden zones were Turkish politics and Korhan's earlier life. He was an easy companion and a good listener. He had interesting ideas and helped her learn about herself. But Korhan preferred listening to talking, for some reason. The more Sude opened up to him, the more he seemed to retreat inside himself. By reading between the lines, she learned that her lover's family was originally from the Balkans and that he'd studied archaeology. His house was full of books on art history and ancient civilizations, so that was no surprise.

One piece of information that did astonish her was Korhan's friendship with Suat Şakir, the brother of the novelist and travel writer Cevat Şakir. Korhan told her many stories about all the things he had learned as a kind of apprentice at Suat's famous dinner table.

He never told her about the woman he had loved and lost, but he didn't need to.

Two years passed, and if Sude ever worried that she was looking for herself in all the wrong places, she didn't let on. Her family sighed and told themselves she seemed happy. At least she was living near the summer house, and they could see her for several months a year. And her friend seemed nice. A self-made, soft-spoken intellectual. By refusing to criticize their daughter's relationship, Demir and Suzi prevented others—chiefly, Nazmi Bey and Bedia Hanım—from daring to make a fuss.

After two years of wandering, music, relaxation, and chess, Korhan and Sude opened a little restaurant in the courtyard of the stone house, just in time for their third summer together. Korhan was the cook. He specialized in the local seafood, invented elaborate salads, and made liqueur out of mandarin oranges. Following her grandma Elsa's recipes, Sude baked cakes with walnuts, cinnamon, and raisins, and sold them to the coffeehouse in the town square. That summer, their house was fragrant with vanilla and clove.

The money they made was spent on winter trips to Egypt and India, where they met a roaming band of kindred spirits, the flower children out making love, not war.

Suzi and Demir kept track of their daughter's whereabouts through the postcards they received. Whenever they started to worry after not hearing from her for too long, they'd get a call from Side saying Sude and Korhan were back home.

When Sude and Korhan weren't traveling during the winter, they'd go into a form of hibernation. Korhan never read the paper or switched on the radio. He didn't own a television, either. Winter was for reading, music, and resting.

In 1976, Sude learned about the student occupations of the universities, the paramilitary attacks, the protests, the long lines for gas, and the Van earthquake from the television set at Grandpa Gerhard's summer house. In 1977, she was watching the news in the town coffeehouse when she found out that at least thirty-four people had been killed by mysterious rooftop snipers during the May Day celebrations in Taksim Square. She didn't know that the sermons delivered in some of the mosques were now calling on the pious to attack leftist demonstrators. Religious passions were being openly inflamed to serve a political agenda. Governments fell and were formed, power outages lasted for over five hours, and inflation was rampant.

In 1978, terrorism got even bloodier. Homes and shops were firebombed in Kahramanmaraş. Clashes between the police and the activists trying to occupy a government building killed seventy-eight people.

When Sude tried to bring up politics or current events with Korhan, he would cover his ears. "I don't want to know," he'd say. "There's nothing I can do." All Sude wanted was some words of comfort and the chance to share her worries with her lover. But it had become painfully obvious that Korhan wasn't capable of that.

Another winter passed and another summer came. New restaurants opened in Side, poaching many of Sude and Korhan's customers. They couldn't compete. The new restaurants didn't bother to catch their own fish, hunt their own octopus, and gather their own mussels. That winter, they hadn't made enough to go anywhere. Sude started spending more time at the town coffeehouse. All anyone could talk about was the new Kurdish terrorist organization led by Apo and the latest round of assassinations, this time of journalist Abdi İpekçi and of two outspoken professors—but at least they were talking. Sude couldn't take any more quiet.

By 1980, even Korhan was growing alarmed. With March came a memorandum, more bloodshed, eight devaluations over six months, another ultimatum from the army, and then, finally, on September 12, another coup.

The street violence stopped, but tens of thousands had been rounded up and thrown into prison. Revenge for Apo was wreaked on the Kurdish population at large. It was a dark time, both in Turkey and in the stone house. They stopped playing music and chess. Sude started going over to her grandparents' house more often, not just to water the plants but as an excuse to run into a few neighbors or a tradesman. Sometimes, she would sit in the summer house and watch TV for hours. News, entertainment, soap operas . . . it didn't matter as long as she heard new voices.

On one of those days, she switched on the TV to find a blond woman in a floor-length gown singing in a mournful alto in front of an orchestra: "I am swept away by the winds of destiny, to the horizons I say, tomorrow I'll be on my way."

Those lines were stuck in Sude's head for the rest of the day.

The following morning, Sude got up, made some tea, carried it out into the courtyard, and looked up at the spot where Korhan had first seen her. In her mind's eye, she could see the outline of a young woman with slumped shoulders. The very picture of misery.

She didn't like what she saw.

She went to the bedroom and got dressed, tied her hair in a pony-tail, packed a few items in a large leather saddlebag, and put her violin in its case. Then she went to the kitchen.

Korhan was leaning against the doorway, smoking a cigarette.

"I'm going, Korhan."

"To the market?"

"To Frankfurt to live with my grandparents."

"Really?" He took a deep drag on his cigarette. "Did something happen?"

"Yes. I've decided to get a degree."

"Oh! I thought something bad had happened."

"No, God forbid. Grandpa's eighty-six, but he'll easily live to a hundred."

"What are you going to study?"

"Art history."

Korhan tossed the cigarette on the ground and stepped on it. He glanced over at the amphitheater. Then he looked at the sky. "I knew you'd leave one day," he said. "I've been expecting it. But why now?"

"I received a sign that it was time to go."

"Do you believe in signs?"

"Yes."

"Well, then I wish you all the best."

Sude went over to her lover of the past six years and gave him a peck on the cheek. He put his arms around her, sniffed her hair, kissed her on the forehead, and held her for a few minutes.

"Do you want me to drop you off at the bus station?" he asked.

"That's okay. I'll walk."

"I'll miss you," Korhan said. "When you get your diploma, come back and celebrate with me."

"Okay. I'll leave my violin here, then. We'll play something by Mozart again."

"Come back to me," Korhan said. "Travel, enjoy, learn, chill, and then come back to me."

Sude walked through the kitchen door and into the garden. She reached the garden gate without looking back.

She kept walking. She considered saying good-bye to a couple of friends, but she didn't want to have to explain why she was leaving.

Taking deep breaths of the morning air, she went straight to the station. At the ticket office, they told her there weren't any window seats left on the bus to Istanbul and warned that the only aisle seat was next to a man. For years now, conservative agitators had been trying to segregate unrelated women and men on bus rides. But this was Western Turkey, and people here were still resisting.

After she'd sat down next to an elderly man, Sude closed her eyes and started thinking.

Had she and Korhan just spent six wonderful years together, or had she let six years slip through her fingers? She couldn't decide. She'd learned to play the flute, make cherry liqueur, take good photographs, run a small restaurant, and appreciate archaeological ruins. She'd also learned how to share her life with someone. But she was still very much on her own, sitting on the stone steps, with no idea of what was most important in life.

She would go and find out.

When the bus pulled out onto the highway, the old man turned and smiled at her.

"Enjoy the journey, my girl," he said.

Part Three

Time to Go

April Fools

The locals in Side thought I was a "love child." But my mother insists I was conceived not in love, but in logic. If I'm a logical person today, however, it's not thanks to either of my parents. I credit my great-grandfather Gerhard, a Jewish German doctor. Grandma Suzi agrees that I take after him. Otherwise, how could I, the offspring of a philosopher bum of a father and an aimless free spirit of a mother, have managed to get through medical school?

I should give my mother her due. Her time with my father transformed her from a middle-class girl in search of comfort to an independent woman in search of freedom at all costs. And she's not unintelligent. But what defines her in my mind is her status within our family as the only baby who was *truly* conceived in love. That, and the fact that she is unapologetically self-centered, just like my father.

My parents have always thought only of themselves and have lived only for their own pleasure. They couldn't care less about stepping on toes, about hurting feelings, about breaking hearts. When my mother chose to shack up with her lover in a small seaside town, she didn't stop to think about what the consequences might be for her family. Nor did she spare a thought for my father the day she suddenly walked out on him.

I asked her once why she'd done it. I must have been about fourteen.

"Turkey had become unlivable," she told me. "The power was always out, there were long lines for everything, and there wasn't any coffee. And then, on top of that, there was a military coup! Communists, Kurds, and homosexuals were being persecuted, arrested, tortured . . . I couldn't bear it, so I left." But I already knew that those things had happened in the big cities, not in Side. Plus, at the time she left, nobody knew about the widespread torture. In short, she was making things up. The reality is that one morning she realized she was fed up with the man she had been living with for six years. So she left him.

My mother went to Germany to live with her grandparents.

She left my father's home in the midst of spectacular ruins and, finding that contemporary art was all the rage in her new circle, decided she was just crazy about it, too. First, she got an undergraduate degree in art history; then she went to a doctoral program in England and traveled the world, doing research and writing her dissertation. It was called "The Social Impact of the Arts." After that, still feeling restless, off she went to New York, where she became a guest lecturer at Parson's. Along the way, she found time to fall in love. She followed a colleague and lover to South America, where they lived together for a time.

As my mother flitted from adventure to adventure, the country she'd left behind was being transformed. The new prime minister, Turgut Özal, opened his insular but self-sufficient country to the world. The monetary policy was recalibrated. The invisible hand of the market was given free rein. The children selling black-market Marlboros on street corners and the men making home deliveries of bootleg whiskey found themselves out of a job. Even the dustiest corner grocer started carrying international brands. Turks became enamored with sliced pineapple and Chiquita bananas, a giant, flavorless version of the sweet fingerlings grown along the coast near places like Side. The orchards near the coast between Antalya and Mersin were uprooted, and five-star, all-inclusive resorts were erected. On the bright side, the local women, whose share of the family inheritance had always been the salt marshes and rocky plots least suited for farming, discovered that they were sitting on gold mines.

In the meantime, the Islamist movement bided its time. Even back then, there were those who suspected that the invisible hand pulling those particular strings belonged to Uncle Sam.

I learned about some of my history from Rozi, who, even though she wasn't a real relative, was treated like a member of our family after her mother died in the Lape Mental Hospital.

My mother never visited Turkey in those years. She learned about the country she'd left behind from the occasional letter and during rare meet-ups overseas with family and friends.

She wasn't at all pleased with what they told her.

Side wasn't protected from the new Turkey. Investors had stepped in and concrete monstrosities were built. It started attracting a different kind of tourist, too: people who didn't care for the local food, culture, or even the folk music.

The one constant in Side was Korhan. A Robinson Crusoe marooned in a rising sea of change, he stayed in his stone house and painted, cooked, and read. I picture him in those days as a kind of lean tomcat stretched out in the sun, oblivious to the world. That would all change, of course, the day Mother came back into his life.

How did that happen, you might wonder?

Like this: My mother had decided she was weary of travel and was "totally into" Eastern philosophy. She was literally sitting in the lotus position on a mountaintop in Nepal, pondering the meaning of life, when it hit her.

She knew she wasn't interested in money, or becoming a famous professor, like her grandfather, or becoming a nature lover in permanent hibernation, like her ex. There was a hole in her soul, a void that only the most precious gift of all could fill.

Unconditional love.

And there was only one way to get it. A child!

That is, me.

The seed for this child should come not from just any old lover or a sperm donor, but from the man who had first taught her the importance of being herself.

She was in her midthirties. She was running out of time. She returned to Side.

I've heard the story a million times. She retells it every time I see her.

My mother supposedly went straight to Korhan's house. The gate was closed and locked. She climbed over it and landed on her feet in the garden. The kitchen door, which they'd always left open, was locked, too. She went to the coffeehouse in the square, but it had turned into a pizzeria. It was the off-season, and the seedy souvenir shops now cluttering the area around the ruins were mostly shuttered. She didn't recognize Side anymore. Everything had changed. In one of the narrow alleys, she found Şükrü's barber shop. He was sitting on a stool out front, smoking a cigarette. Immediately recognizing my mother, he jumped up and told her she'd gotten even more beautiful. She accepted his offer of tea and sat down in one of the empty chairs. After a few sips, she asked about Korhan. Apparently, he'd left on a trip to Vietnam two months earlier.

"He'll be back soon," Şükrü told her.

When she asked if there was anyone in Korhan's life, Şükrü laughed. "They stay with him for a night or two," he said. "But there hasn't been anyone serious since you left."

My mother dug a little deeper, not about what Korhan was doing now, but about the man he was before she met him.

"A lot of people have come in and out of this shop over the years," Şükrü began, twirling his mustache. "I've heard things. Something about a motorcycle accident. Something about a wife. They say she was pregnant at the time. Korhan survived, but he was badly hurt. A friend of his told me he was driving the motorcycle when it happened."

So that explained the scar on his chest and the one on his cheek half-hidden by his beard. He blamed himself. That explained a lot.

My mother let herself into my great-grandparents' summer house and waited. Every evening, she'd go to the Roman amphitheater, sit on the stone steps, and watch as the sky blushed pink.

Near the end of the third week, the sun was sinking into the sea, dragging my mother's plans with it, when a sound came from behind a column: Click, click, click.

There he was, shaggy as ever, his skin still the color of copper, wearing a ragged T-shirt, a pair of cargo shorts, and a huge smile. But his hair was no longer a light brown with streaks of blond. It was a faded mop of brown and gray. And the smile accentuated the lines around his mouth and his eyes.

"Welcome," he said.

My mother got up and said, "Have you got any of that cherry liqueur?"

"I sure do. I always have a bottle set aside just in case you show up," Korhan said.

He threw his arms around her. He still smelled like the sun and the sea. Arms linked, they walked to the house. When my mother tripped on a bag resting near the doorway, Korhan caught her by the waist, and they kissed.

He didn't ask my mother if there was anyone in her life or how long she planned to stay. It was as though she'd been gone for a day, not a decade or so. He got out a chilled bottle of liqueur and a couple of glasses. Later, he brought his flute and her violin. Like always, they went out into the courtyard and started a flute concerto by Mozart—no need for sheet music, no need for words.

When the piece was done, my mother looked at Korhan and said, "When did you tune my violin?"

"This morning. Life's full of surprises. It pays to be prepared."

They stretched out in bed with the bottle of cherry liqueur. My father opened the curtains all the way to let in the sea air. And then they made me.

"I suppose that's why you can be a little sour sometimes," my mother always says at this point in the story. "It's those sour cherries that steeped in the vodka."

"You don't think maybe I'm sour because my father never wanted me?"

"What makes you say that?"

"If he'd wanted me, I'd have grown up in his house, not Grandmother's."

"It's not that he didn't want you. He didn't want a child," my mother said. "He always said that the world was no place for a child."

Mother wanted to have me to herself. She thought I'd be happy to hear that. Well, I suppose it's better than being conceived just to complete a family tableaux: husband, wife, dog, baby.

"I want a baby," my mother had told Korhan.

"Don't let me get in the way," he'd said.

In short, my father is as self-centered as my mother.

I had the double misfortune of being the product of this selfish couple and of coming into this world during what are euphemistically known as "interesting times." A ceasefire with the PKK was in effect the day I was born, but fell apart not long afterward. I was only sixteen days old when Turkey was plunged into mourning over the untimely death of President Özal. About two weeks after that, a garbage dump exploded in Istanbul, killing thirty. I was still in the womb when a car bomb killed investigative journalist Uğur Mumcu. Even years later, Grandma Suzi and Grandpa Demir would get tears in their eyes when they talked about him. When I was old enough to understand, my grandparents told me that good things had also happened in 1993.

"It was an important year for women," Grandma Suzi said. "The president presented Matild Manukyan with a plaque for being that year's top taxpayer. Now, it's true that part of her fortune came from brothels, but she was a real estate investor, too. And I'll always remember 1993—or was it 1992?—as the year that Parliament rejected legislation that would have required women to get their husband's permission to work. I spent a lot of time protesting against that bill."

"Is that when Tansu Çiller became Turkey's first woman prime minister?" I asked.

"That was definitely in 1993. She could barely speak Turkish. Her stint as prime minister was never something I could celebrate, woman or not."

"We're forgetting a major milestone that happened not long before you were born," Grandpa Demir said. "Sephardic Jews first arrived in Istanbul in 1492. In 1992, they held a ceremony to mark the community's having been in Turkey for five hundred years."

"Is that so important?" I asked.

"Of course it is. Where else in the world have Jews been able to live in peace for that long? And they've been able to preserve their language and their traditions. It's funny. You're just like your mother at your age. She was always asking questions about the year she was born. And when she got a little older, she decided it was a terrible time to be alive and that she'd rather hide from it."

Until I was eight years old, I would see my grandparents and great-grandparents only when they came to Side in the summers. My mother was always busy teaching summer school or guiding tourists, so they looked after me. When the season ended, everyone would leave, and I would be alone with Mother again. She's the one who showed me how to paint and crochet and who taught me the alphabet before I'd even started kindergarten. My father taught me how to catch fish, play the shepherd's pipe and flute, and polish shoes.

Father never lived with me and Mother. He had his own house, where I was allowed to stay only if Mother was away.

I was eight when Mother went to Thailand for a months-long yoga retreat. I was thrilled to finally spend time living with my father. Unfortunately, I came down with measles. Grandma Suzi came to Side and nursed me in my great-grandfather's house. When I got better, she took me to their old apartment in Istanbul. They'd moved back there after many years in Ankara. Father didn't even try to stop Grandma from taking me away. He just smiled and said they could discuss it with my mother when she got home.

I still don't know quite what happened, but from then on, I went to Side only for the summer holidays.

When Mother finally got back from Thailand, I remember how she tried to explain to me that, of all the men she'd met in her life, my father was the most decent one, with the best genes. That's why she'd chosen him, even if he didn't want to be much involved with raising a child. Anyway, she said, a clever girl like me should stay in Istanbul and get the benefit of the good schools.

I had no idea what she was talking about. All I knew was that I'd been forced to leave everything behind.

My mother had been desperate for a baby before having me. But I suppose that by then, she was desperate to throw off the shackles of motherhood.

That must be why I was brought up by my grandparents. To me, Grandpa Demir and Grandma Suzi were the dearest people in the world. I sometimes called them Demdem and Su.

And as for my mother, I saw her every summer. She'd arrive at the family vacation house at the beginning of June with a suitcase full of presents and a fascinating new friend or two. If Su and Demdem liked them, the friends would stay in the big house with us. But if they didn't, off the visitors went to Father's little stone house.

One summer, there was a man and a woman covered in tattoos. They were instantly dispatched to the stone house, but they painted a peacock on my arm in watercolors, and Su didn't even make me wash it off. Another time, Mother came to Side with a blond woman even taller than her. She had huge feet and a voice like Demdem's. She was banished to the stone house. The giant lady taught me how to belly dance, and I can still undulate like a snake if the music is right. The Australian couple with the little baby, and the German archaeologist, were allowed to stay in the big house. And so was the African woman with skin as dark as her hair.

Another thing I loved about the summers was seeing my great-grandparents, who came from Frankfurt, and my other great-grandparents, who came from Istanbul, along with uncles and cousins and all sorts of relatives from America. Great-Grandma Elsa and Great-Grandpa Gerhard would stay all summer, but the others only ever stayed for a week or two.

Demdem and Su's apartment in Istanbul was busy, too. Their old students visited sometimes, and they were always involved with NGOs and charities and environmental groups, especially after they retired. Unlike my mother and father, Demdem and Su believed they could make a difference, whether by planting a tree or leaving a bowl of water in the street for the stray cats. They were so full of love and a sense of purpose. Grandma Su retreated from the world a bit after she lost Grandpa Demir, but she's still always there for me.

   She was the reason I decided to become a doctor. In a sense, I felt I owed it to her and to my great-grandfather Gerhard. I want to repay the world for the generosity and love those two have always shown me.

A Broken-Winged Bird

It was a Saturday, my favorite day of the week. I'd started at the Austrian school in Istanbul. But on Saturday, there were no classes, no German grammar, no tests, and no uniform. I could even leave my homework for Sunday. How nice to sleep in, to have time for the movies, TV, and friends.

Demdem and I were playing backgammon in the kitchen. Su brought us glasses of fresh-squeezed orange juice and a plate of peeled, sliced apples. We'd just finished breakfast.

"Don't complain if we're not hungry for lunch," Demdem said.

"Oh, you'll be hungry," Su called out from the living room. "I'm making dumplings."

"Yeah!" I shouted. "Did you hear that, Demdem? Dumplings!"

Su must have switched on the television.

"Shh! Be quiet in there. Something terrible has—"

There was a deafening bang, and the whole building shook. The mirror fell off the wall and shattered. The panes of glass enclosing the balcony cracked. There were books all over the floor. Demdem and I

Ayşe Kulin

ran to the window. Sheets of paper and strips of fabric were floating through the air. We could hear sirens, screams, cries, moans.

"Get away from the window!" Su screamed. "It could be an earthquake."

"It's not an earthquake. It's a bomb," Demdem said.

"It might be a plane crash," Su said. "Like in Ankara that one time. Don't open the window!"

A brown cloud had settled over the street.

We all went to the television. While we'd been playing backgammon, a bomb had exploded at the Bet Israel Synagogue in Şişli. Now, they were reporting, another bomb had just exploded at the Neve Shalom Synagogue on our street. Two synagogues, minutes apart. We stared at each other with our mouths open. Su grabbed her jacket from the hook in the hall.

"Stop! Where are you going? Wait for me!" Demdem said. He ran down the stairs after her. A second later, he came back and said, "Don't leave the apartment! Lock the door and stay inside until I come back."

Still in my nightgown, I sat down on the sofa in front of the TV and cried as the death toll rose.

The phone rang. My father was calling from Side. He sounded so shaken. He kept asking if I was okay and told me not to be scared. He wanted to know where my grandparents were. He asked if I wanted him to come to Istanbul and get me. Maybe we should all stay in Side for a while. He kept talking and talking.

"You should all move here," he said. "There are schools. They might not be as good as the ones in Istanbul, but you'll be safe."

For the first time in my life, my father was treating me like his daughter. I wanted him to keep talking. But it had to end. A moment after I hung up, my mother called from overseas. I think she must have had an English boyfriend. She'd been living in England ever since she sent me off to my grandparents. (Su always got angry when I said Mother sent me away. She claims my mother didn't want to let me go.) My mother was crying too hard to talk. Between hiccups, she asked me the same questions

276

my father had, and asked if her parents were okay, too. She insisted we all move to England. She'd find a school for me. We'd rent an apartment and live together, the four of us. Turkey wasn't safe anymore, she said. When I hung up the phone, I felt like a girl whose parents loved her a lot.

It was a nice feeling.

The phone rang again and again. There were calls from Ankara, from Germany, from Side. I repeated the same things to all my relatives and friends. When I was finally able to return to the TV, I learned that over three hundred people had been wounded and at least twenty had been killed.

My grandparents came home a little while later. I'd never seen them so defeated and helpless. They'd aged fifteen years. They tried not to cry, but I wasn't fooled.

"My father called," I told Su. "He wants us to come to Side right away."

"Oh, well, that's nice of him!" she said.

"Suzi! Not now," Demdem said.

"And my mom called, too. She wants us all to go to England."

"There's no reason to panic," Demdem said. "When was it, Suzi, 1986? Gunmen opened fire during a Shabbat service at Neve Shalom. They killed about twenty worshippers. It was early September and a lot of families were still on holiday. It could have been much worse. And then what happened? Life went on. We can't let them terrorize us."

"This was two synagogues. Two simultaneous bombs. How can we go on as though nothing has happened?" Su said.

"Your grandmother's just upset right now," Demdem said, looking over at me. He hugged her. "Come on, darling. Let's go to the bathroom and splash some water on your face."

Five days later, I was in math class waiting for the bell to ring when something exploded. "Get under your desks!" the teacher shouted. We could hear sirens and screams for a long time. When it got quieter outside, we were allowed to get up. Everyone was talking at once. This time, we knew it was a bomb. Parents came rushing into the building.

"Was it the synagogue again?" I asked Su.

"No. This time it was the British consulate. A truck bomb," she said.

It wasn't until we got home that we learned about the second truck bomb, the one that had exploded at the HSBC headquarters just minutes before the attack on the consulate. At least thirty people were dead, including the theater actor Kerem Yılmazer, a friend of my grandparents.

After that day, my grandmother started hovering over me all the time. She wouldn't let me walk to school alone, even though it was just around the corner.

"Why are you so worried?" I asked her. "Whoever's doing the bombing doesn't like English people and Jewish people. I'm neither, so I'll be fine."

Su and Demdem exchanged glances. "Everyone needs to be careful these days" was all she said.

Phone calls came from around the world again, if in a slightly different order. The first ones were from my great-uncle Peter and some relatives in Germany. When my parents got through, they each insisted again that we move to Side or England.

"What's the point in going somewhere else?" I heard Su say. "A bird with a broken wing can't ever relax. We fled here from Germany, didn't we? We'll be outsiders no matter where we go."

Like always, Su came into my room that night with a cup of linden tea and honey. She stood there, waiting for me to finish it.

"Were you scared?" she asked.

"No. It was scarier the first time."

She stroked my hair.

"Grandma, what did you mean by 'a bird with a broken wing'?"

"Don't mind me, sweetie. I'm getting old and starting to say silly things."

"You never say silly things. What did you mean?"

"It's late. Let's talk about it tomorrow."

She looked so tired, I didn't want to pester her. I got under the covers. I was tired, too. She didn't say anything the next day about birds with broken wings, and I didn't ask her.

About a month later, I was sitting at the table wrestling with my German homework. *Der, die,* and *das.* And all those different endings for different genders. In Turkish, a chair is a chair and a table is a table. Su was sitting at our plain old Turkish table with her glasses on, looking at her computer screen. Demdem was watching football.

"Oh!" Su said in a funny, high voice. "Uncle Arthur passed away. Peter just sent me an e-mail."

"Who?" Demdem asked.

"Uncle Arthur. I'm sure I've mentioned him before. He and his wife lived in Bebek when we were little. He even came and stayed with us in Side one summer. Don't you remember him? He wasn't my real uncle, of course."

"Was he a friend of your father's? He must have had a long life."

"Peter says he was 105! Our dear old Arthur von Hippel."

"Wait, von Hippel?"

"Do you remember him now?"

"He was a famous scientist! I've read about him. They named an award after him. He had something to do with radar."

"Hang on a second while I search. Here's an obituary. He died in Massachusetts. It says here that he was a codeveloper of radar during World War II. And there *is* something called the Von Hippel Award. It says his wife, Dagmar, died way back in 1975."

Grandma wiped away a tear.

"Suzi, the man lived to be 105, he has an award named after him, and he'll never be forgotten. Why are you crying? We've all got to go sometime," Demdem said.

"I'm crying for us, for Turkey. I remember my parents talking about how badly von Hippel was treated at the university. I was a little girl, but I could tell how upset they were. Thinking now about what could have been, about where we're going as a country—" Grandma Su looked at me. "Don't pay any attention to me. I'm just emotional."

But I couldn't help worrying about her. She seemed mixed up.

Turkey was also mixed up in those days, undergoing the growth pains of rapid development. Economic indicators pointed to a prosperous future, but the series of unsolved, high-profile murders told another story. Apo's PKK was going on killing sprees in the spring and hiding out in the mountains in the winter. People had grown battle-hardened by then, inured to death and not easily shocked. What I and so many others failed to realize was that something had settled over our country, something hazy and black, and it was muffling our speech and stopping us from seeing the world clearly.

I was still in middle school and must have been nearly fourteen. I was old enough to know better.

One day, I noticed that two of my classmates were pointing at me and whispering as I sat down at my desk. I stared right back at them. Then I looked at my blouse and hands, but I couldn't find anything wrong. I even tried to check the back of my skirt. After class, I ran to the bathroom and saw nothing out of the ordinary. Why had they been looking at me like that?

When I sat back down for my next class, I found that someone had left a piece of paper on my desk with a large *Y* on it. What did it mean? I had a classmate named Yakut and another one named Yusuf. But when I asked them about it, their faces went blank.

I was leaving school when a couple of boys ran past me and yelled, "Yahudi!" They circled and came running back. This time, I stuck out my foot, and one of them fell on his nose. The other one ran away. I knelt on the boy on the ground, grabbed his hair, and said, "I don't know why you're calling me that, but I'm not a Jew. You're the Jew, a scaredy-cat Jew!"

When I got home, I told Demdem what had happened.

"How could you?" he said. "What's that supposed to mean? 'Scaredy-cat Jew.' Where did you hear that?"

"Somebody said it at school."

"Never say it again. Never say anything like that. We don't make fun of people for their religion or nationality. Ever!"

"What was I supposed to do?"

"You could have ignored him. Or given him a bloody nose. Or called him a fascist."

"A fascist? Like Hitler?"

"Yes, Hitler was a fascist. If we were living in Germany, that boy would have been taken in to see the principal, and his family would have been notified. It's hate speech."

As sheltered as I'd been growing up in Turkey, I knew, of course, that fascists were terrible and that Hitler was even worse. At school on Monday, I made sure to call that boy a fascist. I thought that was the end of it, but my grandparents had other ideas.

I sprawled out on the sofa that evening to watch my favorite show. When the commercials came on, I decided to go to the bathroom. On the way, I overheard Su talking in the kitchen.

"A discussion program on a major channel. And he was waving a list of the names of supposed Crypto Jews and secret followers of Rabbi Sabbatai. He claimed that certain Turkish surnames are 'suspect.' I was horrified! Doesn't he realize people will be targeted because of his so-called research? He's a historian and a professor, for God's sake!"

I burst into the kitchen.

"Who is? And who's Rabbi Sabbatai?"

"Were you eavesdropping on us?"

"No! I had to go to the bathroom. But then I heard you say 'Jew.' Did Demdem tell you what happened?"

Ayşe Kulin

"I didn't want to worry your grandma because of two little brats and their dumb prank," Grandpa said.

"Then what were you talking about?"

"There was a news program, and one of the guests was talking about the German scientists who came to Turkey to get away from Hitler."

"Okay," I said. "Why are you so upset about it?"

"There's something you should know," she said. She had a terrible look on her face.

"What?"

"It's nothing bad. It's just that I think the time's come for you to learn a little more about our family. My parents are Jewish. Your great-uncle Peter and I were the first ones in our family to marry someone who wasn't Jewish."

"But my great-grandparents are German. Aren't Germans Christians? And aren't we Muslims?"

"You can be Jewish and German, and you can be Jewish and Turkish. My parents are German Jews. I fell in love with someone who was Muslim and became a Muslim, but my heritage is still Jewish. We respect all faiths, Esra. And people who aren't at all religious, too. You can think of faith simply as a kind of path from your heart to God."

"Then why are there are so many different religions?"

"Rituals and community can help people find their path. Most people adopt their parents' religions without ever thinking about why. Here in Turkey, most people are Muslim. You're Muslim, too."

"But they called me a Jew in school today!"

"That must be because of me. My family is Jewish. We came here from Germany because Hitler was killing all the Jews. It's important to know your family history and your background, even if you were brought up Muslim."

"Is that why you were so upset when they bombed the synagogue?"

"Esra! How can you even think that? People died! Some of them were Jewish, but many of them were local shopkeepers, Muslims."

Grandma put her arms around me, and we stayed like that for a long time.

That night in bed, I thought about religion for hours. What was I, really? My heart wasn't telling me anything. All I knew for certain was that one branch of my family tree was Jewish and the other was Muslim. But I was Turkish. And most Turks were Muslim. *Enough,* I thought as I drifted off to sleep. I was Muslim and that was that.

Like most teenagers, I teetered between the joys and disappointments of my own little world, which rotated around schoolwork, socializing, and sports. The protective wall my doting grandparents had erected between me and the real world kept out some of the ugliness, but not all of it.

Inexplicable things were happening in my country. A number of engineers working on software for the defense industry, scientists and bureaucrats, died in mysterious car crashes. A helicopter carrying the leader of a political party crashed on a snowy mountainside, and some said it was no accident. A sixteen-year-old boy shot and killed a Catholic priest in Trabzon.

Then, on a winter's day in 2007, Hrant Dink was killed.

This time, too, the gunman was just a boy.

This time, the public decided that enough was enough. Hundreds of people got red carnations and laid them on the spot in front of the Armenian newspaper's offices where Hrant Dink had fallen. Tens of thousands started gathering in a spontaneous outpouring of grief and rage. The crowd of men and women, young and old, grew and grew, spreading to Taksim Square and then Şişli. The funeral procession stretched from Taksim to Mecidiyeköy.

Su asked me to attend the funeral, for Madame. I didn't see the connection, but I knew that certain things were sacred to my grandmother, and the memory of Madame was one of them. There was no way I could get out of it. We took the tram from Tünel to Taksim and marched from there. I had never seen anything like it, and that day would stay with me forever.

Hrant Dink wasn't a religious figure, a celebrity, or a politician. He was a writer, and only a handful of intellectuals knew him from his articles and books. An Armenian Turk born and raised in Istanbul, he was also editor-in-chief of *Agos*, the newspaper.

"It's bubbling over," Demdem said, gesturing at the crowd. "We've all had it up to here! This is a show of love for Hrant, but we're also saying, 'Enough hate!'"

I asked Su what he meant. She tried to explain, but even on that day and at my age, she couldn't quite bring herself to tell me the whole truth.

But it was too late. My eyes were finally beginning to open.

About four months later, three Christians, one of them German, two of them Turkish, had their throats cut at Zirve Publishing House, in Malatya.

I was home sick with a fever that day. Grandma was insisting, like she always did, that I have some linden tea with honey.

"Su," I said, "what's going on? Why do these people have such a problem with Christians and Jews?"

"They hate anyone who isn't like them."

"But—who are they?"

"People who don't know how to use their brains."

I couldn't think of a single person who fit my grandmother's description. From the janitor to the delivery boy at the corner grocery, from our neighbors upstairs to the colorful characters my crazy mother brought to Side: they were all different, but they all had brains and knew how to use them. They had hearts, too, and tried to be kind, not just to me, but to everyone around them. Rozi and her children were Jewish. So were my grandparents' old neighbors, Selin and Simon, along with their spouses, children, and grandchildren. My grandparents had Christian friends, too. Wasn't that normal?

The people planting bombs, the ones who hated anyone who wasn't like them . . . didn't they know anyone who wasn't like them?

It's absurd now to think how naïve I was. I assumed people were good and the world was a mostly kind place. For that, you can blame my grandparents, the nicest people in the world.

In 2010, when I was eighteen, I finally saw just how cruel and unjust the world can be. And it was like a slap in the face.

The *Mavi Marmara* was part of a flotilla of ships carrying aid for Palestinians. It sailed out of Istanbul on its way to the Gaza Strip. We all followed its progress. Then, in the dark of night, Israeli army commandoes opened fire before the ship reached shore, killing nine and injuring up to fifty. Demdem and Su watched as the disaster was broadcast live on TV. At our house, and in houses across Turkey, the reaction was one of indignation, rage, and sorrow.

And then something inexplicable happened. In the street, at school, and on social media, anger started building toward Jews everywhere, including in Turkey. A popular singer tweeted, "God bless Hitler!" Even Su and Demdem couldn't shield me from this.

And when I joined one of the marches to protest what happened, I was horrified to find many of the demonstrators pouring out their hatred for Jews in general.

"Why can't they tell the difference between being Jewish and what the Israeli government did?" I asked Su.

"Some people don't think clearly when they're angry," she said. "Political leaders take advantage of it. And Jews end up being the target. It's why my parents lost their home, their country, everything. It's why my dad's mother and sister were murdered by the Nazis. It seems like it's part of being Jewish, even if you're not religious."

Just then, feeling the unfairness of a target on my own back, I didn't know whether to resent my great-grandparents or cry for them.

Love in the Days of Resistance

It was 2013, near the end of May. Having transferred from the Austrian school to the Italian school near our house, mastered another language, and graduated, I was now enrolled in med school.

The classes were hard, so I was determined to keep my head down and focus on my work. Love and everything else could wait. But that summer, I got swept up in something bigger than my academic plans. I became a protestor.

Three days earlier, five trees had been uprooted when a wall in Gezi Park was torn down. Members of a group calling itself Taksim Solidarity had set up a camp in the park and were staging a sit-in against the desecration of one of the last green spaces in central Istanbul.

The next morning, more people joined the protest. With the support of a few opposition leaders, the demonstrators blocked the developers' backhoes. It was a peaceful gathering with chants, songs, and lighthearted, poetic signs. They cared about the trees, of course, but young people were also tired of our prime minister, who had been chastising us on every aspect of our lives, right down to the length of our skirts. The protest was a rebellion of sorts.

Those first days of the "resistance" were festive, with impromptu jam sessions, street theater, and dance performances. A concert and film screening were scheduled for the following day. But in the early dawn, the police set fire to the tents where the protestors were sleeping, and a lot of people got hurt. The next day, the families of the kids nearly burnt alive took to the streets.

And I went from tweeting about the protestors to joining them.

The day I joined the resistance, the police clamped down harder. Water cannons knocked people to the ground, but they got back up. The police fired pepper spray and tear gas, but the protestors held their ground. Barricades were set up around the park, so the protestors moved into the adjacent streets and into Taksim Square. The prime minister issued inflammatory statements. But the protestors refused to back down. And tens of thousands of us joined them.

I got home late that night, my clothes wet, my eyes burning. Demdem rushed at me the moment I stepped through the front door.

"Where have you been?" he said. "It was all I could do to keep your grandmother here. She was going to go to Taksim and look for you. If she didn't have asthma, I might have let her. You know what she's like! Why didn't you call?"

"I'm sorry, Demdem. My phone died."

"Then you should have used someone else's. Are you trying to kill your grandmother?"

"You're right," I said. "I'm sorry. I need to lie down."

I escaped to my room, but I was too tired to sleep. My back and legs still ached the next morning.

I'd intended to stay home the following day, but when I learned that the Turkish Medical Association was setting up a free clinic in Taksim to treat protestors, I decided to volunteer.

"Whatever you do, don't let your grandma hear about this," Demdem whispered to me in the kitchen.

I sneaked out of the house. The main boulevard had been blocked off by the police, but I followed the back streets to Taksim and found the clinic.

There were no formalities. When I told the young woman in a white coat who opened the door that I'd started studying medicine, she cut me off and said, "Follow me." We rushed to a room at the end of a long corridor. There were several people inside. Someone was giving a man on the floor CPR. Another patient was wearing an oxygen mask. A third was leaning against the wall with his arm above his head. Blood was dripping onto the floor, and his shirtsleeve was soaked.

"Take care of him," the woman in the coat said. And then she was gone.

I went over and looked at the man's hand. A rubber bullet had pierced his finger, just under the nail. The laceration on his arm was bleeding heavily. I found a medical kit and pulled out a bandage, a tourniquet, and a needle and thread. Once I'd stitched up the wound, I pulled the scarf off my neck to make a sling.

"What's your name?" he asked.

"I'm Esra."

"I'm Tarık. Thank you, Dr. Esra."

"No, I'm just a med student. But I hope to be a doctor one day."

"You'll make an excellent doctor."

"Thanks. Tarık, you've lost a lot of blood. Try to find a place on the floor to rest for a while. I'll be back in a minute with something for you to drink."

"Actually, I'd like to buy you a drink."

"I'm a little busy."

"I meant when you're free. What about this evening? Please. Let me thank you with a cup of coffee or a glass of wine. Whichever you prefer."

"Rest for a while. We can talk later," I said.

I knew I should have refused him outright, but something stopped me. Was it that he reminded me of my father, of all people? We'd barely met, but I felt at home with him. He was good-looking, with an easy charm.

I went to the large room at the other end of the corridor. At least a dozen more patients had come in. A middle-aged woman was crying as she scanned the crowd for her daughter. I went to the nurse sitting by the front door, told her I'd stitched and bandaged the man with the rubber bullet wound and gash on his arm, and asked if we had any painkillers and antibiotics.

"You're in luck," she said. "A pharmacy just made a donation. See that box on the floor? If we have anything, it's in there."

"Do you know anything about that patient?"

"You didn't recognize him? He's a war correspondent. I know him from a weekly news show called *The Front Line*. Tarık Azak."

"I don't watch much TV these days."

The nurse had moved on to the next patient and wasn't listening to me. I rummaged through the box, found what I needed, got a glass of water and a glass of tea from an adjacent kitchen, and went back to the small room.

"Drink this tea, and then you can take these pills," I said. "You should stop by a pharmacy when you leave here. You'll need to take antibiotics for at least three days."

"Where do you live, Dr. Esra?"

"Tünel."

"Great. There's a rooftop bar at a hotel there with an amazing view. Shall we say seven?"

"I don't drink."

"I won't be drinking either, not while I'm on antibiotics. But we can always have sparkling water. Please come. I'd like to thank you."

"There's no need. I was just helping."

"I'll be waiting there at seven. I hope you can come. But if you don't, thanks again."

I left the room without another word. Every time I thought about leaving the clinic, another wave of patients arrived. I finally got home a little after five.

I couldn't decide whether or not to meet Tarık. I was just thinking that this was one of those times when I wished I was more like my mother when the door opened and my grandma poked her head in.

"What's going on?" she asked.

I blushed. "What? Nothing. What do you mean?"

"You can't fool me. Come on, spill the beans."

"It's nothing—I was just wondering what to wear. I'm going somewhere this evening."

"Going where? And with whom? Don't look at me like that. I can't help you pick an outfit unless you tell where you're going."

I told her everything, every detail of my work at the clinic and my encounter with Tarık.

"This young man sounds a little like Korhan."

"He's nothing like my dad!"

"Mm, maybe a little. A younger version, but with combed hair. And more ambitious, too."

"Su! Please."

"Wear your red dress tonight. He sounds like the kind of man who likes bold women. And the image of that girl in the red dress has been all over the front pages. You know the one. That photo of the girl being teargassed by a cop. Wash your hair, and I'll help you blow it out. Get going; it's after six!"

Su sent me off that evening with a kiss on the cheek and a knowing wink.

I got to the hotel at exactly seven and went straight to the ladies' room on the ground floor to touch up my makeup and stall a few minutes so I wouldn't seem too eager. When I finally took the elevator to the rooftop bar, it was a quarter past. He wasn't there. I was wondering whether to hide out in the ladies' room again or go home.

"If you're looking for Tarık Bey, he's expecting you on the upper terrace," a waiter said.

I followed him up a staircase, both in awe of the view and annoyed with myself for not knowing about it.

Then I saw him. Tarık. He was still wearing my scarf as a sling. As I approached him, he reached out his good hand and squeezed mine. I sat down on the white cushion next to him. We both ordered sparkling water with a slice of lemon.

"Does it hurt?" I asked him, looking at his hand.

"No. I took an extra painkiller before I came here. Since we can't drink, I thought we might as well have a quick dinner. I've reserved a table downstairs for eight o'clock. Your family will worry if you stay out too late."

"What if I told you I lived alone?"

"Oh, come on. It's obvious you don't."

"Oh no! Does that mean I put on my bold red dress for nothing?"

"You're sharp-witted, too."

"It's my wits that got me into medical school."

"And confident."

"Not really. I'm just quick on the uptake."

Sitting on the terrace of Mikla Restaurant with a bunch of stranded tourists, we flirted and traded questions for a long time, trying to get a sense of one another. And we both liked what we learned.

When I heard the next day that over a thousand people had been injured in Istanbul and Ankara that night, I felt terrible. There we'd been, admiring the view, oblivious to the clouds of teargas and the chanting crowds seventeen floors below. I hadn't imagined the violence could get even worse.

Meanwhile, I'd plunged unprepared into not only love but also my vocation. My days at the clinic were teaching me how to set casts, do artificial respiration, stanch bleeding, and do much with little. I was learning the practical skills normally required of an intern, not a med student.

I also learned what it was to have an aching heart.

Tarık and his production crew left for the Far East five months after we met and four and a half months after we became lovers.

I told myself there was a silver lining. No more would I neglect my studies or stumble home late after hours of love and drink. There had been some nights when I didn't come home at all. I always told my grandparents I was staying at my friend Güzin's. I'm grateful they never called her to find out.

When I started the next school year, it was without Tarık in my life. It wasn't easy, but I returned to my diligent ways and learned to live without him. I was alone, but at peace. And anyway, how could a medical student and a war correspondent ever hope to make it work?

In the beginning, we talked on Skype virtually every day. I'd expected him to return to Istanbul within a couple of months, but he kept getting new assignments in different countries torn apart by civil war and unrest. There was never a shortage of trouble in the world.

We started Skyping less. The time difference had always been a problem, but we went from two or three chats a week to one, and finally to none.

We remained friends, but our relationship had to go on the shelf.

Eight months after Tarık left, I started dating Burak. He didn't last very long.

In my fourth and final year of medical school, all I did was study. My dreams were filled with skeletal, muscular, and nervous systems. The people around me turned into walking and talking anatomy lessons.

It was during that final year of school that we lost Demdem. His funeral brought together the members of our far-flung family. Mother arrived from England, and Father came up from Side. Great-Uncle Peter's son, Kurt, flew in from America. Kurt had gone completely bald. My father had tied his gray hair into a ponytail, and when I first saw him standing at our door in a suit, I wondered who the old man was. But his voice was the same. I would have recognized it anywhere. And his anxieties were the same. He looked pretty nervous when I gave him a big hug and told him he was now more important to me than ever.

The only person untouched by the years was my mother. I don't know if it was the yoga, the vegan diet, or the meditation, but she looked closer to forty than sixty, even without makeup. She was wearing a long, bright skirt fashioned out of handwoven silk; lace-up flat sandals; and a fluttering, Indian-design shawl. I caught my father eying her. In fact, I even found myself hoping that they might get back together. How conventional of me. What is it with people wanting what they can't have?

We left the house on Grenadier Street and headed to the mosque courtyard for Demdem's final rites. I motioned for my grandmother to get into the car following the hearse.

"I'm going with my husband," Su said.

"I will, too," I said, but the hearse had only one row of seats, and that's where the imam always sits. I had no choice but to squeeze into an Uber with my parents, Kurt, and Rozi.

I watched as the hearse carrying my beloved Demdem wove through the streets, crying on the shoulder of the man who'd never really been my father while I mourned the loss of the man who'd been grandfather and father both. I realized how alone I was in the world, and it made me shiver uncontrollably. Korhan took off his suit jacket and wrapped it around me. I was grateful.

That night, my father left without even attending the evening prayer service. Kurt stayed another two days. My mother stayed for a week. On the third day, she joined me and Su in the ritual planting of flowers on Demdem's grave.

Then Mother was gone, and Su and I were alone.

Home had become a sad, dark place. Grandma Su would never be the same, but she still looked after me, making my favorite meatballs or zucchini croquettes and trying to find TV shows she thought I'd enjoy.

One day I said, "You're wearing yourself out, Grandma. Take care of yourself even if it's only for my sake. Without you, I won't have a single person left in the world who truly loves me."

"Your mother loves you and so does your father, in his way," she said. "And your great-uncle's family would always welcome you with open arms. You're not alone."

"My great-uncle's family lives in America. My father . . . doesn't count. And my mother has no time for anyone but herself."

"Don't be so unfair to your mother! She seems self-centered, but she's got a huge heart and makes room in it for everyone."

"Are you sure you don't mean she makes room in her bed?"

"Don't make me wash your mouth out with soap! I blame myself and Demir for not helping you appreciate your mother. You have no idea how tenderhearted she is."

"I'm not buying it."

"No? Do you remember Renate?"

"Of course I do. She had the biggest feet I ever saw on a woman. And she taught me to belly dance."

"Do you know what Renate's real name was?"

"It wasn't Renate?"

"No. It was Ratip."

"But that's a Turkish name. And a man's name—"

"Ratip was tortured after the September 12 coup for being a transsexual. You do know what that is?"

"Grandma, of course I know. And, we say 'transwoman' now, not transsexual. How did Mother meet her?"

"When my mom, your great-grandmother Elsa, was hospitalized, Sude went to Frankfurt and stayed there for quite a long time, taking care of her. One day, Renate heard your mother speaking Turkish to one of the Turkish doctors in the hall, and she came over and introduced herself. That's how they met. Renate was undergoing some kind of psychological evaluation. She and your mother got to talking. Sude was horrified when she found out what Renate had been through."

"What happened?"

"We all knew what they did to the leftists, the Communists, and the Kurds after the coup . . . but it was just as bad for homosexuals and trans—men and women, as you said. They were held in the Sansaryan building for days, harassed, beaten, raped . . . Then, their heads shaved, they were crammed onto trains at Haydarpaşa station and taken to different cities in the middle of Anatolia. Renate said some of them were even thrown out of a moving train as it passed through the outskirts of Istanbul. She said she witnessed it herself."

"That sounds like a horror movie!"

"But it was a real-life horror. Later, some of them managed to get away from the police. The lucky ones fled Turkey. Most were never heard of again. There was no social media in those days, and the newspapers never breathed a word about it. Renate was one of those lucky ones. She made it to Europe and found work in bars. But she struggled with posttraumatic stress, as you can imagine. Your mother invited her to visit us in Side."

"But you had her stay in my dad's house."

"We did—for your sake."

"Oh please, Su! Don't hide behind me."

"Hey. You were still so little. And we didn't know much about those things or whether it would be rude to her if we tried to explain it to you. What if you'd burst in on Renate while she was changing? Anyway, the point I'm trying to make is that your mother took care of

Renate that entire summer. She introduced her to people, bought her medication, found her a job in a café. Does that sound like the kind of thing a selfish woman does? And Renate's just one of the many people your mother's taken under her wing. You misjudge her."

"Well, how was I supposed to know any of this? I was only eight when I came to live with you. I thought Renate was my dad's girlfriend. Why didn't you tell me about my mom before?"

"Esra, don't forget: Sude's my daughter. I never felt as though I needed to tell my granddaughter about her mother. And you never asked. You're old enough now to understand that things aren't always what they seem. People are complicated. I hope you're able to get to know your mother one day. It's time you forgave her. You've never understood how difficult it was for her to let you come and live in Istanbul. It was our idea, not hers."

I didn't say anything. But that voice inside was still there, the one saying, "My mother abandoned me."

It's not like I could claim I'd had an unhappy childhood. Su and Demdem loved me and taught me I could do anything. All they asked was that I did my best. It was because of them that I'd had the grades and the confidence to become a med student.

I graduated with honors from the School of Medicine at Istanbul University and prepared to move to İzmir for an internship at Ninth of September University. I wanted Su to come with me to İzmir, a sunny, modern city with a laid-back lifestyle. We could promenade along the sea, I told her. We could have a glass of beer or wine and watch the sun set. She could even teach literature at a private school, if she wanted.

But Su was having none of it. She was determined to spend the last years of her life in the building where she'd met Demir, and the last moments of her life in the bed they'd shared.

I understood. I didn't insist.

Mother was somewhere overseas, as always.

Korhan was in Side, as always.

I arrived in İzmir alone.

As it turned out, between my internship and my exams, I had no time to enjoy İzmir. The rare opportunity to relax came during national holidays, when I'd fly to Istanbul for long weekends with my grandmother.

It was hard, but I knew this period in my life would soon come to an end.

Once I became a specialist, I would move to Istanbul. That was the plan, anyway.

But Su had other ideas.

Ups and Downs

I wasn't used to seeing my grandmother lying in bed. She'd always been busy making breakfast by the time everyone else got up. She could set and clear the table and still be the first one ready to go to the beach in Side or out shopping in Istanbul. She always held herself so straight. Her hair was always neatly tied in a ponytail. Or at least it used to be. Then, when she reached her sixties, she started pinning her hair into a bun and claiming that she preferred pants now because she was tired of getting runs in her stockings.

It pained me to see her long white hair spilling over her pillow and her body so tiny in a white gown. I hadn't realized how much she'd aged, how hunched she was, how thin her arms had become.

When she saw me standing in the doorway, her face lit up, but she said, "Why did you come? I told them not to worry you. There's no need to be alarmed. I'm not the only person who gets a little dizzy sometimes."

"I was already planning to come to Istanbul," I lied. "I'm attending a seminar."

"How long are you staying?"

"Until you're discharged."

"I won't let you. You must have patients scheduled for Monday. I'm a doctor's daughter. I know how it is."

"I'm on leave, Su. First, I'll help you get settled at home. Then, when you're stronger, you'll come and live with me in İzmir. The warm air will do you good. If you like it, we can rent out your apartment here."

"Esra, there's only one way I'll agree. Do what I asked. I sent you an e-mail. I told you on the phone, too."

"Grandma, I can't. I'd never thrive in a strange country, career-wise or in general. Do you think it's easy for a Turk to live overseas?"

"You'll never thrive here, either. Not with the way things are going in this country. They're inventing common enemies to try and unite the religious factions. Anti-Semitism has come out of the shadows. They're not even trying to hide it anymore."

I smiled and looked her in the eye. "Grandma, for the millionth time, I'm Turkish. I'm a third-generation Muslim Turk!"

"Oh, Esra. I know. I'm Turkish too, even though I was born in Germany. I looked up to Atatürk as a father. I grew up chanting, 'Happy is he who can say, "I am a Turk."' The tenth anniversary march always brought tears to my eyes."

Grandma was tearing up now, and her nose was running. I tried to wipe it with a tissue, but she pushed my hand away.

"Don't interrupt me. I was so Turkish, Esra, that I got furious when other Eurovision countries gave us low scores due to politics. It was the same every year. I'd pray Turkey came first and Germany second. The Peace Operation on Cyprus kept me up nights. I was always afraid European countries would blame us when there was a coup or when a synagogue got bombed—"

She started coughing.

"Grandma, I know all of this. You don't need to tell me again. You should rest."

"I'm not finished! I was the proud daughter of a nation with a shining future. My father devoted his life to the advancement of science and medicine in this country. If we enjoyed a mini Renaissance, we owe a debt of gratitude to him and to the other scientists and academics, mostly Jewish German, who came here. They educated a golden generation of high achievers."

I'd already heard all about her golden generation, but noticed that she was now saying "Jewish German" scientists, instead of simply "German" scientists.

After another fit of coughing, I plumped Grandma's pillows and helped her sit up against them.

"Su, we can talk about this later. You're tiring yourself out."

"We have to talk. It's our last chance."

"No, it's not! Weren't you listening to anything I said? I'm going to take you to İzmir and—"

"I had it all planned out. If I hadn't gotten sick, everything would be ready. The nephew of an old friend is an administrator at Guy's Hospital, in London. I wrote to him. A lot of wealthy Turks go there. It's on the—what's the name again?—the Thames."

"Guy's Hospital is going to hire a female Turkish doctor? Don't make me laugh."

"You speak four languages," Grandma said before another coughing fit hit.

"It's not a language school. It's a hospital."

"This is serious, Esra! Enough of your jokes. The nephew even wrote back to me."

"Grandma Su! How could you do that without asking me?"

"I haven't done a thing. You just have to finish what I've started. Apply to that hospital. If you want my blessing, if you want me to go to İzmir, do it."

Now a little out of breath, Grandma fell silent.

"We'll talk about this again in İzmir. I promise," I said, squeezing her hand.

"No. We're getting this squared away right now."

"All right," I said, bowing my head.

"Bring over a chair."

"Okay. I'm listening, Su."

"First, I want you to make peace with your mother."

"We're not fighting!"

"You resent her. If you need to resent someone, take it out on me, not her. I'm the one who took you away from your mother. She's been mad at me ever since."

"I didn't know that."

"There's a lot you don't know, so listen while I can still tell you a little. My mother, your great-grandmother Elsa, resented my relationship with Madame. I resented how she favored Peter. We argued all the time. Then, one day, I found out that she stayed with my father for me." A tear rolled down Su's cheek. "Peter left home at a young age, but I was still living with my parents when I graduated from college. For my sake, my mother"—Su's voice was barely audible now—"put up with certain things from my father."

"What are you saying? Not my great-grandpa Gerhard!"

"Yes. Even him. Ah, my girl. Life is full of ups and downs. Sometimes we get caught in a snare, and sometimes we're too weak to resist. Our mistakes can carry a heavy price. They thought I was too young to understand. Esra, I don't have much time. There are two things I ask of you. One is to learn to forgive those you love. Be prepared. You will be called on one day to forgive."

"I'd never forgive anyone for cheating on me."

"You might be the one doing the cheating. How do you know? You're only human. Everyone has their weaknesses."

"Are you trying to tell me something? Su, I swear I'll kill you if you ever did anything behind Demdem's back." I began tickling her. "And this is how. I'll tickle you to death."

Su seized my hand and tried to pull me closer. "Forgive her. Promise me. She doesn't have anyone but you."

"Okay, Grandma," I said, stunned to find that I was crying, too, now. "I promise."

"And now for the second thing. Listen carefully. Don't interrupt. Come closer . . . closer." I stood up and leaned over her. She shut her eyes and fell asleep.

I ran out into the hall and up to the first doctor I saw.

"My grandmother, Suzi Hanım, she suddenly fell asleep. "Can you come?"

"She's eighty-four. Old people sleep a lot," the doctor said. "She'll be discharged in a few days."

"But could it be dangerous?"

"She'll be fine. The monitors would tell us if her pulse dropped or anything."

He rushed off to his next patient. Just at that moment, a child with a completely bald head and a mask was wheeled past me.

I went out to the garden. It was one of those moments I wished I were a smoker. But I was a doctor. Not that that had stopped my great-grandfather. I remembered him puffing away, even in his nineties. Su said it made him feel like he was communing with all the friends he'd lost. Why wasn't I born back then? Modern times were cruel and confusing. The world wouldn't let you smoke, and my country was even trying to stop me from having a drink!

My phone beeped. A text message.

Where are you, Esra? If in Istanbul, same time, same place?

Tarık!
And to think, if it weren't for Su, I'd have been in İzmir.

I left the hospital and walked to the metro. Fifteen minutes later, I was in the old family apartment on Grenadier Street. I washed and blow-dried my hair. The chest from Great-Grandma Bedia was still in my old bedroom, and it was still full of my cast-off, cedar-scented clothes. I pulled out the red dress Su and I had picked out for that first date. After it aired on the balcony for a bit, I ironed it and put it on. I arrived at the hotel at seven on the dot. This time, I didn't hide out in the ladies' room. As I walked over to the bar, I saw him. He was in front of the door leading to the terrace, looking at the view. Involuntarily, I clapped my hand over my heart. Then I walked up to him. He put his arm around my shoulder and, together, we watched the shifting city lights and the minarets.

How could I ever leave this city?

"I don't have much time," he said. "I've got meetings all day tomorrow and an early morning flight the next day. I got us a room here so we won't have to waste a moment. What do you say?"

"That sounds great."

We finished our glasses of champagne and went down to our room. For a long time, all we did was sit on the edge of the bed together and gaze out through the picture window at the horizon. After we made love, we ordered room service. I asked him where he'd been, hoping he'd say he was ready to settle down. But he just sighed and said he'd been so many places, and he was going to Syria next. We made love again. As I was falling asleep, I had the strangest sense of déjà vu. Mother had told me how she and Korhan conceived me when they got back together . . . Actually, Mother had conceived me on her own, or at least with minimal assistance from my father. When she had told Korhan she was pregnant, he'd said, "The baby will be yours, not mine."

I was a doctor. I knew better than to get pregnant by mistake. But what if I wanted to have a baby one day? Would Tarık react the same way my father had?

Of course, my mother hadn't wanted my father. She'd wanted a baby. Whereas all I wanted was Tarık.

We were reluctant to disentangle ourselves the following morning. Tarık was just about to leave when I casually asked, "When are you coming back to Istanbul?"

"I can't give you an exact date. Nobody knows what's going to happen in Syria. All I can tell you is that I'll call the second I'm back."

"I'll be either in Istanbul or at the hospital in İzmir. You know where to find me."

"Oh, I'll find you. And this time I'll be back for a long while."

"Really? But what about your work?"

"I've been traveling for years, Esra. I need to rest for a while. I'm thinking of publishing a book of my photographs. I want to relax, write, be happy. And I can't think of a happier spot in the whole world than in your arms."

"Do you mean that?"

"I do."

I flushed and shifted nervously, trying to take in this confession. "I'd love to see a book of your photos. Each of them must be more beautiful than the last."

"I wouldn't say that. My photography documents war and the aftermath of war. Call me an idealist, but I still believe that if more people understood what war was, there'd be less of it."

"I hope you're right."

He hugged me again at the door.

"Promise you'll come back to me in one piece," I whispered. I loved him. But I still doubted I'd follow Su's advice if he ever cheated on me.

A moment later, Tarık was gone. As I took one last look at our room, I felt confident, this time, that he would come back.

When I got to the hospital, Grandma was sitting up in bed, alert as ever.

"The red dress!" she said. "Your phantom boyfriend must be back in town."

I just shook my head and laughed. We chatted for a bit about my night with Tarık, but she was anxious to continue from where we'd left off the previous day. She patiently explained to me that the Jewish community in Turkey would be blamed for anything Israel did and even for anything anyone who was Jewish did, no matter where in the world it happened. That's why she wanted me to leave.

"Grandma Su, don't you think you're being a little paranoid? Where are all these anti-Semites you're so worried about?"

"Don't you ever use social media? They're everywhere!"

"Just about everything I read is work-related, Grandma. But I do know that there are a lot of trolls on the Internet."

"Don't you expect me to believe you haven't noticed. If they're sending me hate messages, you're getting them too. Esra, pass your medical specialty test and then apply to the hospital in London. There's no future for a Şiliman in this country!"

Except I wasn't a Şiliman. My name was Elsa Esra Atalay Solmaz. Taking Korhan's surname was another one of the decisions Su had made for me. "Korhan's family owns land in the Edirne area," she told me. "Take your father's name so you won't have to fight with the courts later." When I told her I was going to become a doctor and didn't expect or need any inheritance from my father, she told me I could use the money to help people, just like my mother had. Once again, Grandma won. I did what she said.

This time, though, I was going to resist.

"I'm a doctor," I told her. "I have responsibilities."

"You can treat patients anywhere."

"I have a special obligation to Turks."

"As a doctor, you can't discriminate like that."

We spent the next three days arguing. On the fourth day, Grandma was ready to be discharged. I asked Rozi's Moldavian nanny, Nadya, to help me look after her for a little while.

On the third day after we got home from the hospital, the coup happened. It was July 15, 2016.

But the sonic booms of F16s circling over Istanbul and the sound of gunfire didn't disturb my coup-hardened grandmother in the slightest.

"Is it another coup?" she shouted from her bedroom. "I thought they'd neutered the army! The top brass got tossed in jail!"

"It's been years since those officers were acquitted and released. This is something else. We're not going to find out what's really going on until tomorrow."

She insisted that Nadya and I help her into the living room and sit her down in front of the TV. A moment later, she called out again. "Take me back to my bed. This isn't a coup; it's an embarrassment!"

"Since when are you an expert on coups?"

"I've lived a long life in this country. And I can tell you that coups happen while people are in bed, asleep. Coups aren't televised!"

As Nadya and I were walking Grandma back to her room, I muttered under my breath that they should consult her the next time they staged a coup. At that very moment, the president appeared on TV and called on the people to fill the city squares.

"Doesn't the state have its own forces?" Grandma asked. "How are ordinary people supposed to stop the tanks?"

"The people need to fight back, too. I learned that from you, Su."

"Well, you're not going anywhere! Sit down! You'll end up shot, and we'll never even know which side did it."

"I'll just go up to the corner."

"No! They'll follow you back here, and we'll all end up dead."

An F16 passed directly overhead, and there was the crash of broken glass. Fortunately, the three of us were still in the hall. I instinctively huddled over Grandma.

"Get off me," she said. "And go and get some quilts. We can wait this out in the bathroom."

Nadya and I ran to the living room. The curtains were fluttering. Leaves and scraps of debris were floating through the air. Every single window had been shattered. On TV, the president was still exhorting the people to take to the streets.

"Get out of the living room. Come to the bathroom," Su shouted.

"We'd better listen to her," I said to Nadya. "Otherwise, we'll never hear the end of it."

Together, we gathered all the pillows we could find and got a stack of quilts from the linen closet. Once I had Grandma seated on the floor with a couple of pillows behind her back, I got into the bathtub. Nadya squeezed in next to my grandmother.

"We're not leaving here until it's over," Grandma announced. "We'll be safe in the bathroom. Madame always put me and Peter in here whenever there was an earthquake."

"An earthquake? In Istanbul?"

"Of course! You're too young to know anything. In the early sixties, Istanbul was rocking like a cradle. A lot of people ran away to the islands."

Nadya asked Grandma who Madame was.

"She was our family's guardian angel."

Nadya looked puzzled, but she patted the old woman's hand and smiled.

An hour or so later, when Grandma dozed off, Nadya and I crept out of the bathroom, got our slippers, and crunched across broken glass to the living room window. We didn't see anything unusual on our street, but shouting was still coming from the main boulevard, and we could hear the announcements coming from the loudspeakers on the minarets, telling the people to take to the streets.

We swept the glass off the sofa and draped a blanket over it. Then we sat down, surfed the channels, and tried to make sense of it all. We both fell asleep there. Toward dawn, Su's cries woke us up. She needed to use the toilet, but couldn't get up off the floor.

"So how did it end?" she asked.

"The government won; the coup lost."

"Good!"

"You've got to let me go outside now," I said. "The people rose up. It's all over."

"It's still too early to be sure, my dear," she said, but I could see her relief.

I checked my cell phone. The battery was nearly dead, and I had dozens of texts and missed calls. Tarık had called, then Korhan, Tarık again, my mother calling from England, Tarık again. There were calls from friends, then again from my mother, three more from my father, and then Tarık, yet again.

I read his text messages first.

Are you okay? How are you? Where are you? Call me. Call me! Please call!

I sent everyone a message saying I was fine.

Nadya and I spent the day sweeping up glass and dusting. New windows were installed by evening.

The squares were still full of people holding democracy vigils. They stayed there for weeks. The TV showed nonstop footage of the night of the coup and live broadcasts of ordinary citizens waving flags for the cameras. The ruling party transported its supporters to the city squares, and Istanbul's metro, buses, and ferries were free for the next two weeks.

"Why are all those people still out in the streets?" Grandma asked. "What on earth are they celebrating?"

"They're not celebrating. They're holding vigils to prevent another coup attempt," I told her.

"Who was behind this coup? I know you told me, but I can't remember."

"An imam."

"An imam? Imams don't stage coups."

"Well, an imam staged this one," Nadya said. "I heard it on TV."

"Don't be ridiculous! Soldiers stage coups. Imams lead prayers."

"These are strange times, Su."

"Esra, I know my memory's going," Grandma said, "but I'm not senile yet. I don't care what Nadya heard on TV. Who was really behind the coup? A group of young officers, probably? They must have gotten restless."

"Grandma, we're telling you, the military wasn't behind it this time. It was FETÖ."

"What's a FETÖ?"

"You remember Fethullah Gülen? The cleric? FETÖ is what they're calling the Fethullah Terror Organization. It's some kind of shadowy network that's infiltrated the security forces and the state. You always said Fethullah was up to something. Well, you were right."

"If we've really reached the point where a weepy imam can attempt a coup, there's no point in my remaining on this earth."

"You have to stay here and take care of me!"

"I'm only a stand-in. When I quit, your real mother will take over."

"Su, I'll never accept your letter of resignation," I said, giving her a kiss.

"It's not your call to make," Grandma said. "The All Powerful makes those decisions."

But the All Powerful was not yet ready to claim my grandmother. She grew stronger each day. Rozi agreed to let Nadya stay with Su, so I reluctantly returned to İzmir.

I still hadn't heard back from Tarık. Every time I tried to call, his phone was off, and he never answered my text messages. He's like one of those fishing birds, I decided. He surfaces, makes a big splash, and then, in a flash, he's gone. Somehow, I'd fallen for his little speech about finding happiness in my arms. I was furious at myself for remembering every word he'd said, for daydreaming about a life together, for having believed that things would be different this time.

Tarık was gone. Again.

He'd probably text me again one day, months or years later. Same time, same place? But next time, the answer would be no.

I stopped trying to reach him.

I passed my exams, but my heart wouldn't seem to heal. Istanbul was Tarık now. Everything reminded me of him. Perhaps Su's idea about London wasn't so bad after all.

I found the application form and filled it out. Late at night, after half a bottle of white wine, I signed it. Three days later, I sent it to the hospital in London.

When I called Grandma to tell her what I'd done, she said, "Come see me this weekend. Let's celebrate. The return ticket is on me."

Time to Leave

Su had prepared a feast with all my favorite dishes: meatballs, zucchini croquettes, fried eggplant and potato, chilled green beans with olive oil, tomato rice pilaf, and blancmange with ice cream.

"What are you trying to do, Grandma?" I said. "Do you want me to get so fat nobody will want me?"

"On the contrary. I want you to go to London and find a husband. Men look at skinny blondes, but they marry nice, plump brunettes."

"Are you speaking from experience?"

"Don't get smart with me, young lady! I can give you plenty of examples from art and literature. Is that what you want?"

"No, please don't. Let's just enjoy dinner."

"And let's be serious for a moment. When are you leaving?"

"I told them I could be available starting at the end of October. I'm waiting for a response."

Nadya brought in a platter of fried meatballs.

"Thank you, Nadya," I said. "Those smell amazing."

That's when my phone beeped. An unknown number. I ignored it. Doctors need time off, too.

"What about Tarık?" Grandma asked. "Where is he?"

"I don't know."

"So what about your red dress?"

"I'll never wear it again. I'm doing what you wanted. I'm going to London."

"Didn't you say he was going to work on a book? He can do that in London."

"I'll work and he'll sort photos? No, thanks."

"Sweetheart, you work so he can finish his book. Then you celebrate together when he's done. That's what people in love do. Demir and I always supported each other."

"That was in the old days, Grandma. Love, happiness, a baby."

"Our president wants you to have five babies." She laughed. "One's not enough. He's trying to turn our women into brood hens. Have some more pilaf, dear."

My phone beeped again. I glanced at it out of the corner of my eye.

"Go on, read it," Su said. "I don't want you thinking about unread messages while I'm trying to talk to you."

I reached over and picked up my phone. Nadya was putting more meatballs and pilaf on my plate.

"No, thanks. I want to leave room for dessert," I said.

Then I read the message. Three times.

"Esra? What happened?" Su said. "You've gone pale. Esra?"

Someone took the phone out of my hand. Someone held a glass of water to my lips. Or were they splashing it on my face? I could hear Nadya: "You made me cook enough food for ten. The poor thing's stuffed. It's no wonder she fainted."

My stomach was churning.

"Bring a bucket! Quick!"

I threw up.

"That's it, dear," Grandma was saying. "You'll feel better now. Lie down on the sofa. Come on, dear."

The ringing in my ears began to subside. I looked for my phone. I'd dropped it on the floor. I read the message again.

"Su, call a cab," I said. "I've got to go."

"But you just got here!"

"It's Tarık. He's at a hospital in Mardin."

"What!"

"I tried to call him—but I thought . . . He was injured. In Syria. They just brought him to Turkey. A bomb attack."

Su snatched the phone from my hand and read the message.

I was crying now. My hands were shaking. I think I was rocking back and forth. A hand slapped me. Hard. I blinked at Grandma. It was the first time anyone had ever hit me.

"Pull yourself together, Esra! First, we'll call the airport. Let's find out if there are any flights to Mardin."

"And if there aren't?"

"We'll call your father. You can always find a flight to Antalya. He can drive you the rest of the way."

"My father?"

"Yes, Korhan, your father! You have a father. That's what fathers do."

"Su, you hit me."

"Of course I did. I'm a doctor's daughter. Even babies are slapped for their own good. You don't have to go to medical school to learn that," Grandma said. "Nadya, get me my phone book—and my glasses." She turned to me. "Go and wash your face. Your mascara's running. You look a fright."

When I stood up, she was rereading the text message.

I spent a long time in the bathroom, staring at myself in the mirror. I smelled of vomit and my stomach ached.

"Are you okay?" Nadya called through the door.

"I'm fine," I said. "Don't worry about me."

When I came out of the bathroom, I changed my clothes. I felt calmer now, no more tears. I knew that Su would help me figure everything out.

When I finally made it back to the table, she said, "There's a flight to Mardin. If you can't catch it, you can switch your ticket to the nearest airport and let Korhan know where you're landing. He'll jump in the car and try to get there before you do."

"Su, I'm scared. Maybe we should pray for Tarık."

"Tarık is fine. I called the hospital where they put him. He's got some broken bones, but he's conscious. He was well enough to send you a text message, right? He wouldn't have asked you to come unless he was fine. Men are worse than women. If he were helpless or disfigured, he wouldn't want you to see him. Nadya, where's Esra's tea?"

"Tea?"

"Have some weak tea and some bread with cheese. You threw up your dinner. You can't travel on an empty stomach."

"I'm so sorry I ruined our dinner."

"Never mind that now."

"I still can't believe you slapped me, Grandma!"

She looked a little guilty. I got up and put my arms around her. She smelled so good. The home phone was ringing.

Nadya brought the phone over and said, "It's your mother."

My mother?

"Hello?"

My father had called her. Did I want her to come? Or did I want to come stay with her in Holland?

No, I told her. Tarık needs me. First, I would wait for him to recover. Only then would I decide what to do and where to live. I promised I'd call her soon.

"Mom?" I said before hanging up. "Thank you for calling. I love you."

Now I felt strangely buoyant. My mother was ready to drop everything. My father would drive as far as I needed. Su was still strong and still taking care of me. Tarık wanted me at his side.

I got down half a slice of toast, a bit of cheese, and a few swallows of tea. The cab was on its way. Nadya had packed a small suitcase. First, I hugged her and thanked her. Then I held my grandmother in my arms for a long while.

"Wait for me, Su. Don't go anywhere until I get back," I said.

"That's all I do these days. Wait for you," she said. "What about that hospital in London? Should I call and arrange a later date?"

"Let me see Tarık first. Whatever we decide, we'll do it together."

"You can go to London together."

"Or we can stay in Turkey together. It's what you and Demdem did. You chose to stay here, despite the arrests and the torture."

"But we always felt like we belonged here. Now, I feel like a foreigner in my own country."

"We'll talk about this later. I'll call you."

"Okay, dear. You're not alone. Do whatever you two decide is best," she said.

I kissed her cheeks, her white hair, her hands . . . I was so afraid of never seeing her again that I even kissed the back of her neck.

"Enough! I'm not going anywhere. You know how stubborn I am. It's time to think only about yourself and your lover. I'll air out your red dress while you're gone."

She turned around so I wouldn't see her tears and walked away on Nadya's arm. I was getting into the cab when Nadya came running out with a bowl of water. She threw the water at the back of the cab.

"Go like water and return like water," she shouted, just like Su must have told her to.

I looked back as the cab pulled away. I could see my grandmother, huddled in the window like a bird with a broken wing. My home, my street, my whole life . . . they were all receding.

I, Dr. Elsa Esra Atalay Solmaz, the descendant of German Jews who had to flee their homeland and of Muslim Turks who devoted their lives to theirs, might have to leave the country where I was born. I am on my way to my lover, and perhaps, one day, I'll be able to live in a country that I can call home.

About the Author

One of Turkey's most beloved authors, with more than ten million copies of her books sold, Ayşe Kulin is known for captivating stories about human endurance. In addition to penning internationally best-selling novels, she has also worked as a producer, cinematographer, and screenwriter for numerous television shows and films. Her novel *Last Train to Istanbul* won the European Council Jewish Community Best Novel Award and has been translated into twenty-three languages.

About the Translator

Born in Salt Lake City, Utah, in 1964, Kenneth Dakan lives in Istanbul, where his focus is on literary translation from Turkish to English. Among the works of fiction and nonfiction he has translated are Perihan Mağden's *Escape*, Ayşe Kulin's *Farewell: A Mansion in Occupied Istanbul* and *Love in Exile*, Ece Temelkuran's *The Time of Mute Swans* and *Deep Mountain: Across the Turkish-Armenian Divide*, Birgül Oğuz's *HAH* (co-translation), Murat Somer's Hop-Çiki-Yaya murder mystery series, and Buket Uzuner's *Istanbulians*.